Bad Cop

To Jay ♡ —
The Baldecchi
Bad Cop
You'll always be my hero!
Love you —
Liz Kelly

LIZ KELLY
www.LizKellyBooks.com

BAD **COP**

HEROES OF HENDERSON: BOOK 2

Liz Kelly

Published by Kelly Girl Productions
©Copyright 2013 Liz Kelly
Cover design by Tammy Kearly

ISBN: 978-0-9889838-4-7

This book is a work of fiction. The characters, events and places portrayed in this book are products of the author's imagination and are either fictitious or are used fictitiously. Any similarity to real persons, living or dead, is purely coincidental and not intended by the author.

For more information on the author and her works, please see www.LizKellyBooks.com

To

Pam, Danny, Jay, Chuck
and
Mr. & Mrs. B.

My heroes of Henderson

CHAPTER ONE

Early Morning, Monday July 5

When Vance Evans rolled over in his bed, he found his mouth nestled up against warm feminine flesh, right in that intriguing place between two soft curves. Smooth and taut, her skin reeled him in with its sultry scent. Feeling his body tighten, he groaned.

It had been too long since he'd had a woman in his bed. Too. Damn. Long.

Adrenaline kicked in, shaking off the lethargy that gripped his extremities. Torn between moving up to suck on that berry-ripe mouth or sinking himself deep between long, firm legs, Vance slid his hands from her hips to waist and then up over small mounded breasts, where his fingers clutched and splayed. His lips toyed with one extended nipple and then sucked deeply. He moaned with the pleasure of finally having his mouth on the one he wanted.

That's when he remembered her tight little ass. The pert little bottom that had been flirting with him for weeks. In running shorts. Whenever she bent over in her tennis dress. In that fucking spandex golf skirt. The drive to get his hands on her naked backside was overwhelming. He needed to do it now.

Flipping her over was easy. So easy he didn't remember doing it. Then he kissed his way down her spine, his hands caressing their way along her sleek, firm back, down to that solid, round—

"Holy backstabbing son-of-a-bitch," he shouted, leaping from the bed and throwing an arm out, knocking over a lamp from the bedside table as he fought for balance. He stumbled about looking for…for what?

His vision faded to black and he felt for the bed blindly. *Fucking head rush.* Bracing one hand on the mattress he reached out and felt around the sheets while his head started to clear and his vision began to return.

Moaning when he realized the bed was empty he moved himself down toward its end looking for evidence of red high-top sneakers or a white halter tennis dress. When he was able to hold himself erect, he looked around the darkened room and noticed the pale sliver of light underneath the bathroom door. For one agonizing second he didn't know what to hope for.

Sliding a hand down his face, Vance walked slowly toward the bathroom. He knew it then. Knew he'd had a momentary psychotic break in the form of a sex dream and had landed right back into his own empty existence. He pushed the bathroom door open and found…nothing.

Lolly wasn't there.

She wasn't there because she was right where she was supposed to be. With his best friend, Brooks.

After staring into the void of his bathroom for a good ninety seconds and letting all that fantasy separate itself from all the actual ball-and-chain reality, Vance returned to his bedroom and sat down on the side of his bed.

Lolly DuVal is going to be the death of me.

Sucking in a deep breath, Vance collapsed onto his back. That woman had certainly done what she'd set out to do. What he'd *asked* her to do. Eight weeks ago, after waking up next to a woman and having no recollection of her name for the third time in as many weeks, Vance had taken a good hard look at himself and decided to make a change. A big change. Because it had become abundantly clear that he did not like women.

Oh, he liked their bodies well enough. As long as it was after midnight and he was heading to bed anyway. And he sure enjoyed the aggression of the sex act, and the release it provided him—for about seven fucking minutes after it was over. But having to deal with all the fallout the next morning? No. And having to act interested in all that high-pitched jibber-jabber over the breakfast table? Definitely not.

His buddy Brooks had finally spread all the evidence out before him. Vance did not like women. Which was a problem because now that he was turning thirty, time was starting to fly by. And with all Vance planned to accomplish in his life, he knew he first needed to address the continuous practice of abusing himself and the women who fell for his bullshit.

So he had turned to Lolly.

He'd met Lolly two months ago when she'd come home for the summer. Brooks had already snapped her up before Vance even knew her last name. Damn Good Cop. Although, Vance conceded, Brooks had certainly been a champ about it all. Because while Brooks wined and dined Miss DuVal—trying to flesh out something between those two that had apparently started a good number of years ago—he was willing to stand on the sidelines while Lolly voluntarily schooled Vance on appreciating women outside of the bedroom. And being that Lolly was as competitive as Vance himself, she worked her magic on him all over the golf course, the tennis courts and, for a short time, on his morning runs.

Which was exactly what he needed right now he thought as he rolled off the bed and into a pair of running shorts and a T-shirt. Having a sex dream about your best friend's girl was so not cool. He laced up his Nikes, hit the door of the pool house, stepped onto the stone patio of his father's estate, and tried desperately not to think about Brooks and Lolly and the extreme likelihood that she was waking up in Brooks' bed for the very first time.

Fucking asshole.

"Jesus," Vance said out loud as he stretched, eager to get the run started to move all this suffocating anger out of his body, hoping to leave it on the railroad trail at least for the day.

He didn't begrudge Brooks, he thought as he moved off the patio and began a slow jog down the grassy hill. He passed his father's fleet of sports cars sheltered inside what resembled the horse stables at Churchill Downs. No, he didn't begrudge Brooks at all. And if he could somehow clear out the darkness he felt all bottled up inside, Vance was certain he'd be downright happy for the guy.

After all, Brooks Bennett did not have a selfish bone in his body. After pitching their team to the State Championship back in high school, he bore the responsibility of being this town's favorite son with honor and integrity, rescuing dogs and old people, remembering first names and relations. He was the Golden Boy of Henderson, and Vance was proud to be his friend.

But more than all that, Vance knew that for some squirrelly reason Brooks had loved Lolly DuVal since she was a girl—so no, he didn't begrudge Brooks for finally landing the love of his life. He only wished Lolly had been cloned.

Because Lolly was perfect from the top of her dark brown ponytail to the tips of her high-top sneakers. And throughout the last eight weeks, she had managed to find a way to like Vance for who he was, including all his bullshit history and womanizing nonsense. She cared about him like no other woman ever had. And the good Lord knew he loved her for it—loved her hard—and it wasn't going to be easy getting over all that.

His bad cop ways of relating to women may have come to a screeching halt since Lolly came into his life, but she'd inadvertently opened the Pandora's Box of emotions that he'd managed to lock down tight for the past several years.

The exponential growth of the hurt, anger, and excruciating heartache of a ten-year-old boy whose mother had up and left him now coursed through him regularly. But the worst part of all of it was the longing. The acute, desperate longing for something he couldn't convey. Befriending Lolly had caused him to hope, and now that she was with Brooks, he wasn't sure where he was going to put all that.

As Vance started up the long, gradual hill of the old railroad path, the vision of a pink-cheeked, dewy-eyed blonde assaulted him. For the hundredth time, he racked his brain for who she was, this 3-D hologram his mind continually tortured him with. The goddamn thing had ruined all blondes for him because none of them could ever measure up to the…warmth that this vision held.

Tired of wrangling with all the bullshit in his head, Vance did what he'd been doing for the past five years. He turned on the power boosters and got lost in the run.

"Dude. How far did you run?"

Vance pulled up short and blinked. Busy mopping sweat out of his eyes with the hem of his shirt, he hadn't noticed the prepped-out pretty boy sitting on the lounge chair next to his father's pool. Standing there panting and dripping sweat after the punishing run, his eyes darted between the guy dressed up like an Easter egg and the crystal clear water of the pool. Finally, he pulled his shirt over his head, kicked off his shoes, and dove in.

Damn that feels good.

Vance swam underwater for as long as his breath would hold, wondering who the hell that was. The guy had stood up as Vance had approached which meant he had manners…or wanted something… or was scared. Though he didn't look scared. He was wearing a crisp, pink button-down shirt with the sleeves rolled up to his elbows and tucked into a pair of meticulously pressed lime green Bermuda shorts. With a belt that was kinda lame and kinda cool at the same time. Vance needed to get another look at that belt.

As he surfaced he thought he should probably know the guy, right? Brooks probably knew the guy. Brooks—fucking Hero of Henderson.

Vance swam over to where Starched & Pressed was hanging.

"So," he said, folding his arms over the side of the pool. He looked up at the kid, squinted against the sun, and asked, "Do I know you?"

The kid bent down, shaggy brown hair falling over his forehead as he offered Vance his hand. "Davis Williams. Phi Delt from State— like you. I was at The Situation two nights ago for our wet T-shirt contest cleverly disguised as a charity fundraiser, and…well, I'd like to talk with you if you have some time."

"You'd like to talk to me? About what?"

"Well…uh."

Vance pushed himself up and out of the pool in one graceful move, placing a foot on the concrete ledge. "Listen, Davis." Vance felt proud he'd remember the kid's name. *See I can be good at names.* "I was off duty by the time I arrived, so if one of your frat brothers landed himself in jail, you'll have to talk to the officer on duty at the time."

Davis laughed. "Fortunately, after you and Brooks flashed your badges at the door, things stayed fairly sane. So no one got tossed in jail, as far as I know. However," he said with a very broad grin, "it was an epic night in Phi Delt history. More money raised than ever before, and everybody seemed to have a very good time."

"Huh." *Everybody but me.*

"Listen," Davis said. "You don't know me, but I know all about you. And I have found myself in a rather desperate situation, and could use your…expertise. I'm willing to do whatever needs doing to get it."

Vance continued to drip chlorinated water onto the pool deck. He couldn't imagine what this frat boy wanted, but after that sex dream it was clear he needed a distraction, so he was willing to go with it. "All right, Davis."

Look at that. Still have his name on the tip of my tongue.

"Let me take a shower, and then we can talk over breakfast."

Their attention was drawn across the pool as Genevra DuVal stepped out of the French doors leading from his father's kitchen. She wiggled her fingers in a happy greeting at the two of them. They wiggled their fingers back, mesmerized by the smoking-hot brunette in the tiny pink bikini and woven see-through cover-up.

"Yeah," Davis said, his voice sounding tight, "your mom already invited me."

"Dude. That is so not my mother."

"Oh…thank God," Davis croaked.

"I know, right?" Vance pulled himself together and hit Davis in the arm. "Put your tongue back in your mouth and wait for me here." When Davis didn't pull his gaze from Genevra, Vance tapped his cheek none too gently to bring his eyes back toward him. "Hey! You hear me? Right here."

"Got it," Davis said, shooting one quick glance back across the pool. He started moving to his vacated lounge chair. "Don't worry, dude. I'm not going near any of that."

"All right then. Give me ten minutes." Vance smiled as he headed toward his shower. He didn't know Davis Williams and had no clue as to what he wanted. But whatever it was, Vance's heart and soul were damn grateful for the diversion.

CHAPTER TWO

Davis sat on the cushioned lounge chair feeling strangely comfortable in the opulent surroundings. As his gaze surveyed the many multipaned windows across the back of the mansion and the long stretch of lawn in every direction, he considered how welcoming the woman in the pink bikini had acted toward him—a stranger— showing up on her doorstep early on a holiday morning. And as much as he knew Vance had a reputation as a womanizer, which was exactly why Davis was here, the guy was crazy likable too. Of course, being a legend at his alma mater didn't hurt. The guy wasn't just lady-killer handsome; he was also part of the team who had won the College World Series seven years ago. Even more than that, Vance Evans had given a large donation to their Phi Delta chapter the year Davis had pledged. Vance's donation had allowed the frat house to be overhauled and upgraded, the benefits of which Davis thoroughly enjoyed during the years he lived in the house.

Through his musings, Davis heard someone approach from behind, so he stood and turned toward the sound.

The hot, bikini-clad brunette was holding out a fluted glass and smiling invitingly. "I thought you might enjoy some orange juice."

"Awful kind of you." Davis smiled back and took the glass from her hand.

"You wouldn't happen to be the Davis Williams from NC State my daughter Lolly talked so much about, would you?"

"You're Lolly's mother?" Davis asked, his eyebrows shooting sky-high.

"I am," Mrs. DuVal said in a very empathetic and soothing tone. No doubt she was completely aware of the heartache her daughter was putting him through.

"Well, it's a pleasure to finally meet you, Mrs. DuVal." He knew the word, "finally" came out begrudgingly, like he was a terrible loser. Of course, that was just how things stood now, he reminded himself. "I ran into Lolly the other night over at The Situation." And then he stopped himself, because a wet T-shirt contest was definitely not the kind of thing he wanted to bring up to Lolly's mom. He finished by saying, "She looked as pretty as ever."

"Well, aren't you sweet for saying so. Why don't you come join Hale and me while you wait for Vance? We're just sitting down to breakfast and would be grateful if you joined us." She put her arm through Davis' and started walking him toward the table. "It's the only meal they allow me to cook around here, and I tend to go a little overboard."

Davis knew he should be saying no. Vance had been clear. "Wait for me here," he'd said. "Right here." But as the brunette bombshell's body brushed up against his, everything in Davis' head got a little foggy, so he was in no position to stop his feet from moving right along with her. The one clear thought he kept thinking was that this woman was way too young to have a daughter his age.

Way too young and way too curvy. Yes, she looked a whole lot like Lolly. But he would sooner believe them to be sisters rather than mother and daughter. And, while his head was traversing a very slippery slope, he couldn't help but acknowledge that Lolly would never be able to fill out a bikini quite the way this woman did.

Something was way, way off here.

How was it possible that she was Lolly's mother? Lolly, who matched him in age at twenty-three. This woman was nowhere near the age of his own mother. And what was she doing here? Was Mrs. DuVal the housekeeper? The cook? After all, she had answered the door and shown him to the pool to wait for Vance. And if she was the housekeeper and/or cook, did they require her to wear a bikini while she worked? What kind of Playboy Mansion had he stumbled into?

He had so many questions cruising through his brain, but none of them could be articulated politely. So he kept his mouth shut and put one foot in front of the other, sipping his orange juice and trusting that the answers would emerge on their own.

And that's when freaking Bruce Wayne stepped out of those good ol' French doors.

Okay, maybe the guy wasn't Batman, but he was handsome, fit, and rich as fuck by the way he dressed and his obvious command over land, sea, and air. You could tell simply by the way he carried himself that not only the house, the pool, and the grounds belonged to him, but clearly this woman who continued to hold on to Davis' arm did as well.

Well, that explained a lot.

He knew Lolly's dad had died before she was born and that her mother never remarried. So, he was guessing she was shacking up with Batman. And no judgment there. Hell, even *he* wanted to shack up with Batman.

"Sweetheart," Mrs. DuVal cooed as they all converged around the umbrella-topped table set for five, "this is Davis Williams, a friend of Lolly's. Davis, this is my fiancé and Vance's father, Hale Evans."

Fiancé. Well, now. Wasn't Batman one smart son of a bitch?

Davis held out his hand to Mr. Evans as Mrs. DuVal released him and went to seat herself. Batman's grip was firm and his expression was welcoming.

"Good to have you with us," Hale said. "How is it you know Lolly?" he asked cordially as he indicated the chair Davis should take.

Davis shrugged off the question and redirected the subject by complimenting Batman on the beautiful landscape as he sat down. Then he watched as Bruce Wayne popped a cork out of a bottle of champagne and poured it liberally on top of Davis' orange juice.

"It's a big day around here," Hale said. "I insist everyone help me celebrate."

"Well, if you're gonna twist my arm." Davis shrugged.

"Indeed," Lolly's mother said with a smile as Batman winked at her and added a mere dollop to her glass.

It should have felt odd. Davis was a total stranger to the two beautiful people sitting down at the table with him. Yet, he observed again how comfortable he felt in their company. Completely relaxed, as if he'd known them all his life. And, just as he started sinking into that comfort, he felt two large hands land hard on his shoulders as a growl hit the air.

"I thought I told you to wait over there." Vance had arrived shower fresh and mean as a pit bull. "What the fuck? Excuse me, Genevra," he said, nodding across the table at Miss North Carolina.

"My bad," Genevra said brightly, passing a large platter of scrambled eggs, bacon, and sausage to Davis. "I dragged him over. I like company at breakfast."

"Hmm. You don't even know this guy." Vance sat down next to Davis and pulled the cloth napkin down to his lap. "*I* don't even know this guy," he added taking a warm blueberry muffin from the basket in front of him and lifting a knife to cut off a pat of butter.

"He knows The Dynamite," Hale said absently as he dished himself a scoop of grits from a heavy ceramic bowl.

Whatever that meant had Vance's knife stopping in mid-air. He twisted his neck and blinked directly at Davis. Vance's lips thinned as he carefully laid his knife on the side of his plate. Then he sat back in his seat, placed his elbows on the arms of his chair, and carefully folded his fingers together over his torso.

"How, exactly, do you know Lolly?"

So…that meant…Lolly—Dynamite—got it. Okay then.

Looking back, Davis would find humor in the immediate situation. Sitting there, the unerring point of focus of Lolly's mother, Bruce Wayne, and a man who was about as happy to hear this bit of news as he would be to learn someone ran over his dog. *Uh-oh.* The last thing he wanted to do was piss Vance off. Because, if all went according to plan, Vance Evans was the guy who was going to help him win Lolly back.

CHAPTER THREE

Vance was well aware that his voice had an edge to it. That the muscles in his arms were flexing inadvertently with an energy he was actually trying to conceal. If Genevra and his father hadn't been seated across the table, he probably would have tossed Preppy-Wan Kenobi into the pool first and asked questions later. This was far more civilized, he assured himself, given the fact that The Dynamite—as his father so cleverly referred to Lolly—had recently exploded his entire fucking life. And now it seemed she was the gift that just kept on giving.

Davis' eyes drifted first to Genevra, then to Vance's father, and then back to Vance—who hoped he looked like he was waiting patiently for an answer.

"Lolly and I used to date," he said. As if that answer wasn't going to get his preppy ass thrown into the pool.

Vance did his best to maintain an outward calm. He cleared his throat and then smoothed the side of his hand over his lips, holding himself back from leaning forward and getting into the guy's face.

"Date," Vance repeated. "When was this?" he asked, all calm and neighborly like.

"Recently," Davis said, turning his attention to his plate of food.

"How recently?" Vance asked, wondering what the fuck he was doing. Lolly wasn't his girl. Lolly was Brooks' girl. And if anybody should have a problem with this guy it was—

But then the sky opened and the angels started singing. "Holy shit," Vance exclaimed. "Pardon me, Genevra," he added in her direction before he burst out laughing. "You are Milquetoast," he accused Davis with a pointed finger. "*You* are Nice, Safe, and Boring."

Davis' expression deflated.

"Aw, sorry man." Vance slapped Davis on the back, feeling renewed vigor for his muffin. He picked up his knife and started buttering the sucker heavily. He shook his head, having some empathy for the poor bastard, but he couldn't keep the smile off his damn face. "It's just that your unfortunate reputation has translated into a world of good for me and my buddy Brooks over the last couple of months. I don't think I'm spilling any secrets saying that because of you, Brooks has been able to sidestep the land mines of Nice, Safe, and Boring to finally capture the heart of the love of his life."

"Lolly?" Davis groaned.

"Uh, yeah, sorry man. She's picked him. And you...*and I*," Vance acknowledged out loud, looking directly at his father, "are going to have to live with that."

"But, gentlemen, do not despair," Hale said as he took the champagne bottle and filled the flute in front of his son's plate. He set the bottle down and took Genevra's hand, looking at her like she was all he'd ever wanted. "In most cases, the woman who turns out to be the love of your life is not the first one you fall for." He leaned over and kissed Genevra's hand. "So have heart," he encouraged. "And eat up. The love of *my* life is a very good cook."

"Well, you're right about that," Davis said around a mouth full of food.

The poor guy was eating like he'd been living on gruel and stale bread for a couple of years. "Davis," Vance inquired, "are you still at State?"

"Just graduated in May," Davis said helping himself to two muffins from the basket. "Five-year program. A double major in finance and economics. Came out with my undergraduate degree and my MBA all at the same time."

"So you're not an idiot," Vance concluded.

"Except when it comes to women, apparently."

Vance laughed as his father held up his champagne flute and said, "Welcome to the club."

Vance noticed Davis start to say something and then catch

himself, glancing over at Genevra.

"You looking for a job?" Vance asked.

Davis shook his head. "I start in September with a firm in Baltimore, my hometown. But I'd like for you to hire me as a summer intern."

"I'm a cop. We don't do interns."

"You're not much of a cop," Davis said, reaching for the grits, "but you're a hell of an entrepreneur."

"I'm a damn good cop," Vance said defensively. "What the hell do you know about me anyway?"

Davis turned his head and gave Vance a look that seemed to hold up two framed diplomas and a whole lot of common sense. "I know everything there is to know about you, *Vance Evans*."

"Bullshit," Vance said, going back to his eggs.

"I was part of the Phi Delt pledge class when you handed over a million dollars to have the house gutted and renovated."

The cacophony of silverware clattering onto everyone's plates ended in a stunned silence. Genevra and Hale stared at Vance like they'd never seen him before.

Oh, for fuck's sake.

Vance combed his napkin over his mouth before he said with deadly calm, "That donation was anonymous."

"Yeah." Davis glanced around, understanding the faux pas he'd just committed. "Sorry about that. It's just that with the whole finance and economics thing, I was brought in as the accountant on the project. So I knew. That it was you. And then I sort of, you know…"

"What? Stuck your nose into my private business?"

"Yes. Yes, I did," Davis said with growing enthusiasm and not the least bit of apology. "Can you blame me? A twenty-five-year-old fraternity brother who majored in English donates a million dollars. All I kept asking myself is how did he do that? 'Cause I want to do that. So I Googled you and saw that you are on Lewis Kampmueller's KampsApps' Board of Directors. And with just a little digging, I found out that you were Mr. Kampmueller's primary investor. And since his company shot to the moon like a freaking rocket, you made yourself look like a genius and have probably made your initial investment back a hundred times over by now."

"Two hundred fifty," Vance said quietly. "Two hundred fifty times over." The cat was out of the fucking bag, so why not put it out there? He felt his dad lay a hand on his arm.

"What was your initial investment?"

"Twenty-five thousand."

"That was seven years ago," Hale said in surprise. "How the hell did you have that much money, and how the hell did I not know about it?"

"Because your head was stuck up your ass," came the heavily Spanish-accented voice of his grandmother as she approached the table.

All three men stood, but Davis moved to pull out the chair next to him for Vance's exquisitely dressed grandmother who looked just like Sophia Loren. And damn if Vance didn't watch his grandmother give Davis a long assessing look up and down and then a subtle smile and quick wink like she was a cougar on the prowl.

Vance rolled his eyes. Emelina Flores was nothing if not obvious. And she'd accused Vance of…what did she call it? Tomcatting around. Well, apparently that apple didn't fall far from the damn tree.

"Abuela, this is Davis Williams. Davis, my grandmother, Emelina Flores."

Davis looked at Emelina, then at Hale, and then back to Emelina. He said quietly to Vance as all the men sat back down, "There are some seriously good genes running in this family."

"Don't I know it," Vance agreed.

"Madre, I beg your pardon," Hale said as he filled her flute with champagne. "You were saying…about my head?"

"Ah. Yes. Thank you," she said, taking the champagne and toasting the table briefly. "How could you have possibly known about your son's accumulation of wealth when you were constantly gallivanting about the country gathering your own?" she said before taking a sip. "And then had your head up your ass during your brief respites at home." The sound of Emelina talking was melodious, to the extent that anything that came out of her mouth sounded couth and refined. Most of the time, her words were far from it, and Genevra seemed to continuously find humor in that. She spit her orange juice back into her glass. Hale passed her his napkin without blinking an eye.

"Davis, it seems you are getting more Evans history than you bargained for this morning. I apologize," Vance's father said.

"Frankly I'm enjoying the fact that even families who are rich, beautiful, and eternally young have issues. Please, pretend I'm not here."

Genevra choked up another laugh, causing her orange juice to tip precariously. Hale reached over and steadied her hand while keeping his eyes on his mother.

Vance chimed in as if his painful family history was no big deal. "Long story, short, my father's equity investment business has kept him out of town most weekdays—"

"Up until now," his father tossed in.

"Right," Vance agreed. "Up until Lolly's mother caught his eye. Then he managed to find investment opportunities right here in Henderson, where I had *already* been finding money-making opportunities since I was ten years old. Ever since my mother waltzed herself out of town with another man and his daughter, and Abuela moved here from Spain, rescuing my father and me from certain starvation."

"What opportunities did you pursue when you were ten?" his father asked.

"Evans' Mobile Bar and Grille," Vance and his grandmother said in unison.

"That lemonade stand?" His father gaped. "The one you pulled on a wagon behind our tractor?"

"That lemonade stand made me over ten thousand dollars during the three years I was in business. After that it was delivering papers, washing cars, dancing with ugly girls—"

"Wait." Hale held up one hand. "Who paid you to dance with ugly girls?"

"Their fathers, who do you think? I'd hand them their paper, make a hint or two about an upcoming social at the middle school, and bam. Ten bucks a dance. I could rake in three hundred dollars in one night if I marketed my services hard enough. Toward the end of middle school, I didn't have to market anymore. Checks would arrive in the mail to cover the whole damn year. Easiest money ever."

"Except you had to dance with ugly girls," Davis said.

"They all looked like dollar signs to me," Vance insisted. "Besides, with your eyes closed you don't know if you're kissing an ugly girl or a cute one. And face it, not all cute girls know how to kiss."

Genevra's tinkling laughter caused Hale to grin with boyish joy as he clearly forgot what they were talking about and focused all of his attention on her. God, his father was in deep. Which was a good thing. A damn good thing.

The man had changed on so many levels, Vance couldn't begin to add them all up. Gone was the Type A, high-strung, demanding father who was never around when Vance had needed him. In his place stood a loving father, a doting son, and a very indulgent fiancé—a man who had found a way to claw back into his life after having emotionally evacuated it for some twenty years.

Yeah, his mother had pulled a number on the both of them, hadn't she? Well, Vance was glad at least one of them had found his way back.

"So," his father said, interrupting Vance's plummeting train of thought. "After the lemonade stand and the rest of it, you had money to invest when Lewis had his bright idea."

Vance nodded his head and smiled, happy he was there for Lewis. And happier still it had been working out so well for all of them.

"Then why are you still driving that beat-up old pickup and living in my pool house? Don't get me wrong—I love having you here. You are welcome to stay forever. But why haven't you and I discussed going into business together before last night?"

Emelina started to speak, but Hale cut her off. "I know, don't say it. I've had my head up my ass." Everyone laughed, including Hale. But then he got serious.

"I'm sorry, son. I truly am. I have wasted valuable time that I cannot get back. More importantly, I've wasted your time. I was not the father that you needed or deserved. And for that, I'm even sorrier." He took a deep breath then, glancing around the table. He held up his glass of champagne. "To Evans & Evans Investments, Inc. And no more wasted time."

"Hear, hear," they said, everyone clinking glasses.

"So, about that internship?" Davis asked. "I can only give you about six weeks, and you wouldn't have to pay me much. I'm happy to be a gofer as long as I get to pick your brain about business, investing and..."

"And what?"

"And, you know, other stuff in general."

Vance and Hale looked at each other, tilting their heads in the exact same way. "Lolly's not the boss of me," Vance stated, "but she's probably going to hate this."

"Probably so," Hale agreed as a slow, mischievous grin spread across his handsome face.

"But you think it's a good idea anyway," Vance said, "because Davis is crazy qualified."

"Davis is crazy qualified, but, in truth, that's not why I like this idea."

Vance sat back, waiting for an explanation.

Hale looked between his son and his fiancée and then threw his hands up as if he were surrendering. "I admit it. It amuses me to see The Dynamite self-combust." He looked over at Davis. "You don't mind being hired for my amusement, do you?"

"No, sir," Davis laughed. "Happy to have the job. And I will do my best to provoke Lolly, or uh, The Dynamite, into exploding whenever you are around."

"Genevra?" Vance asked.

She held up her hands as Hale had done. "I'm an innocent bystander. I am *not* getting involved."

"Okay, then," Vance said looking at Davis. "You're hired. Now your rate of pay depends on how well you handle our first order of business." Vance pulled out his cell phone and handed it to Davis. "A pool party." Vance looked over at his dad who nodded and smiled. "This afternoon—to celebrate EEI, Inc. Call everyone listed under favorites. Then call around and see if you can get a keg of beer delivered here by 1:00. If not, we'll go pick it up in my truck."

"Done." Davis touched a few keys on Vance's cell. "Okay, listed alphabetically...let's see who we have. First up...well, of course," he said with a slight grudge, "Brooks Bennett. Henderson's Golden Boy. Baseball superstar in high school and college, and...uh, Lolly's latest victim."

Laughter erupted. Even Davis cracked a smile.

"Huh," Davis said, looking at the phone. "Darcy Bennett. Brooks' sister?" He glanced up at the nodding heads. "I knew she was Lolly's best friend, but I never made the connection between her and Brooks."

"She also happens to be Lewis Kampmueller's fiancée," Vance said, "so don't bother calling her directly. Just call Lewis."

"Check that. Definitely looking forward to meeting the illustrious owner of KampsApps. I wonder how much he gave *his* fraternity."

"Lewis isn't exactly the fraternity type," Vance said.

"Really?" Davis lifted one brow. "Because he seemed to thoroughly enjoy being Contest King the other night."

"Right. Might not want bring that up in front of Darcy."

"Okay, then. Next on the list is…Annabelle Devine. Totally hot redhead I tried to hit on Saturday night."

Vance busted out a laugh. "Oh, man. You sure know how to pick 'em. Annabelle—The Keeper of the Debutantes—is the sole property of Duncan James."

"There was no ring on her finger," Davis insisted.

"Which Duncan is trying to rectify as quickly as possible," Vance said. "But I'll give you credit, Dude, you've got some balls. Excuse me, Genevra."

Genevra beamed over at Vance.

Christ, she looks too much like Lolly.

Vance ducked his head. "Go ahead and call Annabelle directly," he told Davis. "In fact, why don't you remind her that you two met Saturday night and tell her she can bring her plus one…or not." Vance snickered. "Duncan was not on my side of the Lolly issue, so as far as I'm concerned, you are welcome to mess with his mind."

"You're the boss," Davis said grinning. He glanced back at the phone. "Let's see, Grace Devine and Tess Devine. Holy Shit! Annabelle has sisters?"

Vance grinned at the enthusiasm of youth. "Tess is my age, an actress, and dates Johnny Wilder so she'll bring him. Great body— likes to show off her cleavage, so whatever she decides to wear to a pool party should be extremely entertaining."

Genevra covered a smile with her napkin.

"Grace is a couple years younger than I am," Vance went on, smiling at Genevra. "Hot, but in a totally covered-up way. Totally kick-ass FBI. Her scary spy-guy boyfriend is probably still in town, so hit on Grace at your own peril. Annabelle, whom you already met, is *the baby*. However, don't get on her bad side. She totally ripped me a new one over the whole tennis incident."

"You mean where you kissed Lolly in front of the entire Club," Davis said. "Kissed her so hard and so long that the grapevine crept all the way to Raleigh with the news. Had me dragging my sorry ass up here to try to talk some sense into her."

Vance shot Davis a look. "Big words for somebody who then hit on Annabelle."

Davis shrugged. "I was trying out my new move."

"And how'd that work out for you?"

"It could use some fine-tuning." Davis admitted, before saying, "Okay, back to the list. Mrs. Genevra DuVal," Davis said, looking up from the phone and grinning at Genevra. "That *is* a beautiful name. Should I put you down for a plus one?" he teased.

Vance looked over at her sincerely. "You will attend, right? All three of you are a part of this deal," Vance insisted, his gaze expanding to include his father and grandmother.

"I wouldn't dream of missing it, dear boy." The Spanish accent lilted over the table. "I have the perfect attire. Trust me. I'll be there with bells on."

"A little nervous about that, Abuela, I am not gonna lie."

Davis grinned before looking back at the phone. "Next up… hmm, Lolly Duval."

"Yeah," Vance moaned, rubbing his face hard with both hands. "Go ahead and delete that contact. For the time being, it's probably best that any communication between Lolly and me go through Brooks or her mother," Vance said, shooting a glance at Genevra.

"In fact, give me *your* phone." Vance took Davis' phone from the table and started playing Pac Man with it. "I'm deleting her from your contacts, too."

"Is that really necessary?" Davis whined. His face contorted as he watched Vance abuse his phone.

"Just giving us a little space from the forbidden fruit," Vance said. "Besides, twisting you into knots is going to be so much fun that neither of us is going to have time to worry about Lolly."

"If by knots you mean manning a pool party filled with hot babes, twist away," Davis said, winking at Emelina before ducking his head and going back to the list. "Hale Evans." He gave Hale a grin. "Check. And, uh," he glanced down and then back up, "Mrs. Flores." He smiled at Emelina again. "I am very much looking forward to your wardrobe choice for the afternoon."

"Jesus Christ," Vance muttered.

"Okay, down to Duncan James," Davis went on. "Can I just delete him from your contacts as well?"

"You gettin' a little full of yourself?"

"I'm the first employee of EEI, Inc. I am feeling the power," Davis proclaimed looking back down at the phone. "Okay, uh, here we are at Mr. Lewis Kampmueller, President and CEO of the current Fortune 100 Company KampsApps. I will definitely call him. There is only one more name. Or sort of name. You've got a Harry The Bartender listed."

"Let me see that," Vance said pulling his phone out of Davis' hand. "I do not fucking believe this," he breathed. "Oops, sorry, Genevra."

"Who is Harry The Bartender?" Genevra asked.

"That guy. That bartender guy at the Club last night. The one with the zany-ass powers and cure-all tequila shots. He's got mad waiter skills. He knows what you want before you do. I've run into him three times, but I never asked him for his number. Lolly thinks he's cute, by the way," he said as an aside to Davis. "I have no idea why he's listed in my favorites, but I'm telling you, if this number works, the guy will probably wiggle his nose and have beer, burgers, and tequila shots appear out of thin air."

"Call him," Hale said. "This party is on me. If he can do it on such short notice, tell him I'll double his fee."

Vance stood and walked a few feet away as the call went through. One ring and then—

"Mr. Evans, how are you sir?"

"Harry? How did you know who was calling?"

"Your picture came up on my phone, of course."

"How the hell—never mind," Vance said, closing his eyes and shaking his head. "Harry, I need a big favor. I'm throwing a pool party this afternoon for about twenty-five guests. We need beer and food. Anything you can do to help me out? I'll make it worth your while."

"Loading the truck now, sir."

"Excuse me?"

"Evan & Evans Investments—caught wind of it last night, sir. I figured there might be some celebrating. I'll be there in an hour to set up."

Vance's mouth moved, but no sound came out.

"It's all right, sir. No need to say anything." And with that, Harry disconnected the call.

Vance wandered back to the table, unable to say any more than, "He'll do it," as he sat down.

"Perfect," Hale said as he kissed Genevra's hand once more. "Start the party at two and it can rage on as long as you want. But at some point, Genevra and I would like to speak with you and Lolly privately."

"Fine," Vance said, "but you don't need to give me another lecture on friendship versus true love."

Hale laughed. "No. I trust we're done with all that. This is about another matter entirely."

Vance looked from his father to Genevra, curious. "Is this about setting a date for your wedding?"

"It is," his father answered with a grin. "We want to do it as soon as possible."

"You do know this is probably going to make Lolly's head explode."

Hale's smile went broad as he stood up and started collecting empty plates. "I'm counting on it."

While Genevra, Emelina, and Hale cleared the table and took themselves elsewhere, Vance listened in while Davis made the calls. When that was done, Vance said, "Okay, now just to amuse ourselves, let's go through and invite everyone's exes. Start with Tansy

Langford. She can't stand me and I feel the same about her, but it will be amusing to watch Brooks and Lolly have to deal with her."

"So she's..."

"Brooks' ex," Vance supplied.

Davis' dimples grew deep. "I like where your head is at," he said.

"Right? And just to piss off Duncan a little more, invite Stubs McKenna, Archibald Reynolds, and Tucker Davenport. During Duncan and Annabelle's first date, Brooks and I kept sending those guys in to interrupt."

"Practical jokes on your best friends. I am your man."

"And, to make it really interesting, go ahead and call everybody listed under Jail Bait."

Just then Hale stuck his head out of the French doors and hollered, "Walk the boy down to the garage and have him pick out a car to use while he's on official company business."

"I've got a car, sir," Davis hollered back. "Thanks, anyway."

"Oh, so you're not interested in driving a vintage Corvette, an Aston Martin One-77, or a 2013 Jaguar convertible, red with white interior?" Vance chided.

"On second thought," Davis shouted back to Hale. "That'd be great." He hopped up from his seat. "Come on, man. Before he changes his mind."

Vance laughed as he stumbled away from the table, having to sprint to catch up to Davis. "Damn, boy, you can run. What position did you play?"

Davis slowed to a jog. "Midfielder."

"Outfielder?" Vance stopped him with a hand out, his insides tightening with concern.

"Noooo, midfield. As in lacrosse—the fastest game on two feet. In fact, since I'm going to be hanging around Henderson this summer, maybe I should offer a lacrosse clinic on the weekends. Seems about time somebody should bring this town into the twenty-first century."

"Dude!" Vance stomped around in pained anguish. "There is so much wrong with what you just said, I don't know where to begin."

Davis laughed. "Just because you and Brooks played baseball a hundred years ago—wait! What the hell am I looking at?" Davis stared at the sight of the long, white immaculate stable. He sounded a little bit dazed as he said, "Your dad doesn't keep horses in there does he?"

"Only horsepower. Come on."

The two of them were like kids at Christmas going over Hale Evans' fleet. The large silver Rolls Royce, the sleek lapis blue Gran Turismo Maserati. Davis didn't understand the nostalgia of the black 1977 Pontiac Firebird Trans Am, having never seen the movie *Smokey and the Bandit*, but he sure fell in love with the 1934 Cadillac with the rumble seat.

In the end, Davis figured the vintage Caddy wouldn't be as much of a chick-magnet as the white One-77 with the red interior. Smart move.

"Is your father serious about this?" Davis asked as he sat in the leather seat and caressed the steering wheel.

"I assume. He needs them driven and he's only one man."

"Yeah, and he's probably always in the Batmobile. What do you drive?"

"My truck, generally. Though I'm fond of the 'Vette. It's got a stick, so it's fun to drive."

"I never learned."

"That so?" Vance asked. "Lolly likes the 'Vette."

Davis rolled his head in Vance's direction and gave him a long, hard stare.

"What?" Vance asked. He watched the kid take in a deep breath, like he was getting ready to spill some deep, dark secret. *Shit.*

"I didn't come here for the business internship," Davis admitted, getting out of the car. "Although I'm happy to have it, and I'll do a good job. But, at the risk of sounding ridiculous, the truth is I came here to learn how to…embrace my inner Vance Evans."

Vance cracked a grin. "Your inner who da what?"

"You heard me. Don't make me repeat it. Though that's exactly how your buddy Brooks put it the other night. He pointed out all the pretty girls in the room and told me to channel *you*. Worked so well I figured he was on to something. Something I needed to learn."

"Where the hell did you run into Brooks?"

"I had Lolly backed up against a wall at The Situation, right before the wet T-shirt contest."

"You? Mr. Nice, Safe, and Boring had Lolly backed up into a wall?"

"I was desperate. I know what a freaking player you are, so I was trying to talk some sense into her—which Brooks actually appreciated. Of course, I didn't realize at the time that *he* was Lolly's new boyfriend."

Amused, Vance rubbed his chin. "Sucks for you."

"Really? You want to compare who this sucks for the most?"

"No, I do not. So let's just get this conversation out of the way, shall we? *You*," Vance said, poking Davis in the chest, "are done with Lolly. *I*," he said, poking at his own chest, "am done with Lolly. Lolly chose the better man. She chose Brooks. No one is winning Lolly back. We are *both* done with Lolly."

"You trying to convince me or yourself?"

Vance pushed Davis out of the garage and up the path to the pool. "So what exactly did Brooks mean by channeling your inner me?"

"If I knew, I wouldn't be here, would I? I mean, he clued me in on the whole nice, safe, and boring routine—"

"Lolly's words, not ours."

Davis' face contorted with a grimace. He shook it off and kept walking. "Brooks said the backing-Lolly-against-the-wall move was priceless, and that was all I needed to know in order to pick up any girl in the room—any girl but Lolly. He made that tidbit abundantly clear."

"Well, that's the only move Brooks needed, but he's the superhero good cop, so one move worked for him. You, my friend, are going to need a few more moves," Vance said as they reached the stone patio.

"Which is the real reason I have landed on your doorstep. To learn from the Great Seducer himself."

"Okay, stop right there, because that's the old me. The new me…." *The new me what?* "Oh, fuck it. Never mind. I helped Brooks over the minefield of Nice, Safe, and Boring, and since I desperately need a distraction, I guess I'm willing to help you, too." Vance looked his protégé up and down. "Tell me about that belt."

"What's wrong with my belt?"

"I didn't say there was anything wrong with it, goddamn it. I just asked you to tell me about it."

"Oh, okay." Davis looked down and patted the brown leather attached to the buckle and then spread his fingers onto the khaki colored background of the needlework that made up the rest. "My mom made it for me as a high school graduation present. It's got my initials, the Maryland flag, NC State's mascot, lacrosse sticks, a lobster, a crab, and a race horse."

"Why the lobster?"

"My family summers on Nantucket."

"You're a rich kid."

"Says the pot to the kettle."

Vance grinned. "How long did it take your mom to make that belt?"

"I don't know."

"Next time you talk to her, ask her. Tell her I like it."

"All right."

"Is your mom the one who dresses you like this?"

"Like what?"

"Like you've attended prep schools since you were five."

Davis swallowed.

"Really?" Vance's grin broadened. "Since you were five?"

"What is wrong with a private education?"

"Nothing, except that you dress like you've got one. And you play lacrosse. And I'm not sure how I feel about you being smarter than I am."

"Not smarter than you when it comes to women."

"Only when it comes to getting laid." He again looked Davis up and down. "I think if we get you a decent haircut and a pair of bad-ass shades this preppy-prep, color-my-world thing you've got going on could actually work to your advantage. Nice and Safe with an edge. Reel them in with a smile and then back their little fannies right up against the wall." Vance hesitated, his eyes searching Davis' face intently. "I don't know...I'm just thinkin'... there has *got* to be more to you than meets the eye."

"Oh! You mean like this?"

In a Ninja blur, Vance felt his legs go out from under him. But before he hit the ground, he was lifted and tossed like a fucking beanbag over Davis' back, and completed a full somersault before splashdown in the center of the pool. He came up sputtering "What the fuck" in protest and awe at the same time.

"Double black belt," Davis said, hands on hips.

"Shit," Vance said, treading water, "I knew there had to be something. The Lollypop know about this black belt thing?"

"Lollypop?"

"Lolly. Did she know you were a black belt?"

Davis shrugged. "I certainly wasn't gonna pull any of that shit on Lolly."

"See," Vance told him, "that was your big mistake."

CHAPTER FOUR

By three o'clock, the shallow end of the Evans' pool was loaded with happy, boisterous bikini-clad and board-shorts-sporting guests playing a fierce game with a beach ball over a net Davis had stretched across the pool. How he'd managed to rig that up so quick Vance would never know, but it sure added to the fun. Even Genevra and his father had been tempted to join in. The prepped-out Ninja continued to be full of surprises.

When the tribe of giggling young bathing beauties arrived in a pack and gathered at the end of the pool, Vance turned Davis in their direction. "See that right there?" Vance said, pointing to all the ponytails and tan lines. "That is your signing bonus."

Davis' tongue fell out of his mouth. He wiped his lips to put it back in. "Jail Bait?"

"At one time they were, and I had to remember that. Now, they're all grown up and ready to play. See the brunette with the long braid? That's Lacy Ray—but some of the guys around town refer to her as *Racy Lay*. And the platinum blonde? I swear to God I only know her as Titty Titty Bang Bang." Vance prodded Davis forward. "They all need a drink, a place to store their loot, and probably some help rubbing suntan lotion on those hard-to-reach spots. You think you can handle that?"

"Handle all that and then some." Davis headed off.

"Figured as much," Vance murmured after him. He saw Brooks then, coming up from the garage all long bodied and broad shouldered. His short copper curls glistening in the sun, his mirrored shades reflecting the light, and his shit-eating grin telling the world that he was now one happy S.O.B.

He ought to be, Vance thought. Not every day you've got the girl of your dreams waking up in your bed for the first time.

Vance had expected the thought to sting, and maybe there was a twinge. But the twinge was short lived when a whole lot of what-the-fuck started stomping through his brain. Because Brooks didn't just recognize Davis. Brooks was over there fist-bumping the guy like the two of them were tight.

Vance watched them exchange words. Davis pointed in Vance's direction. Brooks looked up, surprised, and then offered a few more words before he patted Davis on the back. Brooks proceeded toward Vance.

Here it comes, Vance thought.

"What the hell is going on with you and Pinks?" Brooks asked, throwing his thumb behind him.

"Pinks?"

"Pinks! You know, Lolly's milquetoast."

"His name is Davis. Why are you calling him Pinks?"

Brooks shrugged. "Because the guy had pink shorts on the other night and he's wearing a pink shirt now."

Vance grinned over his beer. "Pinks it is." He shrugged. "Where's Lolly?"

"With Darcy. Probably telling my sister all kinds of stuff that I'd prefer be kept between the two of us. They'll be here soon. It's bad enough I've got to get used to Darcy being in our social circle. Care to fill me in on why I have to be subjected to Lolly's ex as well?"

"What are you whining about? Looked like you were going to lean in and kiss him on the cheek. I expected you to take a swing at him, not shake his damn hand."

"Hey. The guy was trying to talk Lolly out of dating you. That gave us a bond."

"Yeah, well, Pinks is cool. I've hired him as a summer intern."

"Intern? Isn't that code for slave labor?"

"Exactly. Between being a cop, a coach, your campaign manager, and now part owner of EEI, Inc., I need an extra set of hands."

"But the guy lives in Raleigh. If you needed an intern, you

should have hired someone here in Henderson," Brooks insisted.

"The guy showed up on my doorstep at eight o'clock this morning. Your fault by the way."

"How the hell is it my fault?"

"Apparently you told him to channel his inner Vance Evans. So he's come to the source and wants me to turn nice, safe, and boring Pinks into Casanova. But don't worry. I've talked to him, and he's not going to try to win Lolly back."

"You're damn right about that. Lolly is off the market."

"That's what I told him."

"That's what I'm telling *you*."

"Which is another reason I've hired Pinks. Now that you've got Lolly handcuffed, Pinks is gonna fill the void," Vance explained.

"You planning to make him your new tennis partner?"

"Pinks," Vance yelled toward the end of the pool. "You play tennis?"

"Tennis is my middle name," Davis yelled back while applying suntan lotion to Titty Titty.

"There you go. My new tennis partner."

"So you're serious about this. This Pinks thing is for real?" Brooks asked.

"You think Lolly's going to be pissed?"

"Because the guy she shook loose three months ago is your new sidekick? God, I hope so."

"I'll talk to her," Vance said.

"Yeah, and when you do, you'll keep both hands tucked into your back pockets. There will be no more touching, fondling, or kissing Lolly."

"You, buddy, are not the boss of me."

"I'm the Chief when it comes to Lolly."

"Jesus. What are you worried about? She chose you—the Good Cop. Surprise, surprise. And it's not like Lolly is all I ever think about—or you know, shows up in my sex dreams or anything."

"Fucking A—Duncan James!" Brooks yelled. While Duncan crawled out of the pool and dripped his way over to the two of them, Brooks gave Vance a serious glare. "We are getting this thing handled once and for all. I am not kidding."

Annabelle Devine, with her long red curls and her hourglass figure clad in a skimpy white bikini and a floral sarong tied low over her hips, sashayed over and handed her beau a towel. She kissed Duncan on the lips and then turned to give Brooks a kiss on the cheek in greeting.

Duncan dried his face and hands, running the towel over his hair, chest, and body. It was hard not to notice Annabelle licking her lips.

"What's up?" Duncan asked, smiling at Annabelle and bringing her in for a wet hug.

"Could the two of you keep your hands off each another for one cotton pickin' moment?" Vance growled.

"Jealous?" Duncan teased.

"Yes," Vance admitted.

"Which brings me to why I've called you all here," Brooks began. "As you are well aware, the only reason Vance is not sporting a black eye after all his tennis court shenanigans two days ago is because Annabelle did such a fine job raking all his character defects over the coals that I thought a bruised ego would suffice. A bruised ego and his promise to contact Piper Beaumont in the next ten days. Actually, we are now down to seven."

"Jesus Christ," Vance protested.

"Not even he can help you now," Brooks assured him. "Duncan, can you set this up?"

"Absolutely."

"Annabelle, will you accompany Vance so he doesn't get cold feet?"

"I'd be happy to."

"Vance?" Brooks questioned, raising a menacing eyebrow.

Dear God. Why did he ever bring this up? Piper Beaumont was not going to know him from Adam, and he'd just look like a goddamn fool and ruin the one memory of his childhood he relished.

Vance sighed heavily, squeezing his eyes together, knowing there was no way out. If he were in Brooks' shoes, he'd be demanding the same damn thing. Still, he needed to extract some form of payment. "I'll do it as long as you promise to sit down with me this week and make a plan to run for mayor."

"Done. Let's get a beer."

After planting a quick kiss on Annabelle, Duncan turned and cannonballed into the pool. Brooks and Vance headed toward the bar.

"By the way," Vance said. "This Pinks thing? It gets worse."

"How could it get any worse?"

"The dude plays lacrosse."

"Jesus Christ," Brooks cursed. "That sport is like a plague of locusts eating up all the athletes who should be playing baseball."

"Don't I know it."

Lolly, Darcy, and Lewis watched the party from the kitchen, as the girls arranged cupcakes on a pretty tray before taking them out to the food table. As the scene with Brooks, Duncan, Annabelle, and Vance unfolded across the pool, they all stopped what they were doing and watched.

"What's going on out there?" Darcy asked. "Is that my imagination or is Vance looking a little freaked out."

"They are probably discussing Piper," Lolly said, intrigued.

"Who's Piper?" Lewis asked.

"She's that girl," Lolly said as she watched. "The one from fourth grade."

"What?" Darcy said, pulling on Lolly's arm.

"Oh," Lolly looked between two bewildered faces. "Okay. But you did not hear this from me," she said, huddling them closer. "Although, of course, Lewis, Vance would tell you this himself—if you were around more. Hey," she said all bright eyed and happy. "Why don't you two seriously think about moving back to Henderson after your wedding?"

"Stop," Darcy said. "You are starting to sound like my brother."

Lolly laughed. "I guess I do," she agreed. "Brooks finally has me buying into the town revival thing," she said with a smile. "Now that I'm committed to him and to a new business here after I get my master's, I want my best friend to move back home. Pleeeeease," she begged.

"We'll think about it," Lewis said.

"No, we won't," Darcy argued.

"We will if she'll tell us more about the girl from fourth grade," Lewis cajoled.

"Oh. Okay," Darcy said. "Tell us about what is freaking Vance out and we'll…consider it as a very slight, probably-not-gonna-happen possibility."

Lolly frowned.

"It took me all my life to get out of this town," Darcy complained. "Do not ask me to come back and watch you and everybody else continue to fawn over my brother."

"He's going to be mayor some day."

"Of course he will." Darcy rolled her eyes. "Which is why Lewis is moving his business out of New York and back here to Podunk over my dead body."

"Darce—" Lewis tried to cut in.

"It would be so great for Henderson," Lolly cried.

"Oh My God, Brooks has brainwashed you already," Darcy cried in horror. "You were my friend first," she insisted. "You may not throw all of Brooks' Hero of Henderson crap on me just because he gave you an orgasm."

"Oh, God—" Lewis gasped.

Lolly opened her mouth to retort and then slammed it shut and smiled. "Several. Several really good orgasms," she said through a slow grin.

"Enough!" Lewis said, clasping his ears. "You two really need to stop discussing this stuff while I'm standing here. In fact, I'm sure Brooks would agree with me. We don't want you discussing this stuff at all."

"Oh, like you guys never compare notes," Darcy said.

"No," Lewis said, his eyes growing so big they made his nerdy-boy glasses look small. "We do not. You are his little sister, for God's sake. The guy is having a hard enough time dealing with us being engaged. Trust me. We do not discuss…anything." Lewis took a deep breath. "Now please, for the love of God, tell me about Vance so I can go out there and get a beer."

Lolly grinned an apology, feeling sorry for Lewis. "I'm sorry. My fault for getting off topic. Here's the story. Back when Vance and Brooks were asking me to help with their good cop, bad cop images,

Brooks got Vance to realize that he didn't really like women—which was sort of a shock because…you know, the guy is a notorious playboy, and women seem to love him all the more for it. But he seemed kind of desperate to stop all that and asked me to be his friend—to help him figure out what else there was to appreciate about women. Well, as much as I wanted to help him, I'm not a psychologist, and I said as much. That was when he told Brooks and me the story about his mother leaving when he was ten."

"His mother left when he was ten? Just up and left?" Darcy asked.

"Apparently she took up with another man, left, and never looked back. Vance and his dad were in a state of shock. Mr. Evans was so devastated that he couldn't talk about it. So—oh my God, I will never forget Vance telling us this—the two of them would sit on the front porch together, every night. In silence. Looking into the horizon. Longing for her to come back."

"Poor kid," Lewis said. "I mean, I knew his parents were divorced when we met in high school, but I figured it was, you know, normal. Not abandonment."

"From the way Vance told the story, I'm pretty sure it was shock-and-awe abandonment." Lolly nodded, wide-eyed.

They all turned their heads and stared out the window at Vance.

"So what about this girl?" Darcy asked.

"Well, Vance said that no one at school was talking about it either. Not his teacher or the principal or the mothers who helped out in the classroom. He said his whole world had picked up and walked out and no one was acknowledging it. Everyone acted like there was nothing wrong. Like he was fine. He felt invisible."

"I'll bet," Lewis said.

"Well, Piper Beaumont, this girl in his class, noticed something was wrong. She took Vance by the hand one day, and he turned to her and told her everything.

"And then she did the sweetest thing I've ever heard of. She told Vance that she would be sad if her mother left, so she would share his sadness with him. So they took turns being sad. Vance would go and play and be happy for a while, while Piper sat and held vigil for his mother. And then Piper would play while Vance was sad."

"How sweet," Darcy breathed.

"Vance told us it worked. It made him feel like someone cared. Like someone was there for him. Every day he would tell Piper how he felt, and she would listen. He was able to feel better when Piper was around."

Darcy clapped a hand against her chest, her eyes misting up. "Damn it. Now I've got to like stupid Vance," she said.

"What do you mean?" Lewis questioned. "You don't like Vance?"

Darcy waved a hand. "You know, he was Brooks' friend and was just annoying."

"I was Brooks' friend!"

"Yes, but you weren't a hot, muscle-bound athlete dripping sex everywhere you went."

"What the—?"

"What I mean is, you were brilliant and interesting and had those cute glasses and lanky arms and you nodded at me when you walked by on your way to the refrigerator," she said in a dreamy kind of way. "Vance was testosterone on a stick. You were *my* hero of Henderson."

Lewis pushed his glasses back up on his nose as he looked down at Darcy and smiled. "Well," he said, "okay, then." He looked up at Lolly. "Carry on."

"So," Lolly said, noticing that the two of them were still gaga-ing over one another, "the summer break came and Vance thought about Piper every day. He couldn't wait to go back to school to see her, and then…." Lolly trailed off.

"Then what?" Darcy asked, snapping her attention away from Lewis.

"School started and she was gone. Her family had moved out of town over the summer."

"Oh, no," whispered Darcy, clearly horrified.

"Yeah," Lolly agreed. "First his mother and then his lifeline."

"That could leave a guy with some issues," Lewis said.

"Yeah. Brooks figured Vance was either trying to punish all women for his mother leaving him, or he was too afraid to let himself want more than sex. Either way, after hearing that story, it all made sense. And made me want to help him."

"Which you did," Lewis said. "That man's been living like a

monk for months. Frankly, having known the guy since high school, this change is a little disconcerting."

Lolly and Darcy laughed. "I know, right?" Lolly said. "He really wants to change. In fact," she said, brightening, "he used his cop expertise and Google and found out that Piper is a lawyer in Raleigh. So he had Duncan track her down. Only…."

"He got sidetracked with you," Darcy said.

"A little," Lolly admitted. "So he didn't follow through with an introduction. Probably got nervous about stirring it all up again. But I think what we all just saw out there was Brooks forcing the issue."

"Can't blame him," Lewis said. "Now that I know Darcy thought Vance was hot, muscled, and—what did you say? Testosterone on a stick? I say let's get those two reintroduced. Fast."

CHAPTER FIVE

Vance stood with his back to the makeshift bar at one end of the pool and watched the beginnings of a slow summer sunset creep over the scene. There was so much more to celebrate here then met the eye. Certainly there were toasts to the future of Evans and Evans, and clearly his dad was overjoyed that the two of them were now going to be in business together. Which frankly blew Vance away. It would have never occurred to him that his father was interested in doing business together. But over the last several months his father had been staying in town during the week, something he'd never done before, and…well, obviously Genevra had everything to do with the dramatic change. Because Hale Evans had spent the day actually playing with him and his friends. Playing. In the pool. Like he was a freaking teenager, for God's sake. Vance grinned at the thought. And the guy was funny. Really funny. And he was easy to talk to, which God knows had not always been the case.

The love of a good woman, Vance thought shaking his head. It made all the difference where his father was concerned.

He wondered how fast he should move out of the pool house to give the newlyweds some room. Although Abuela didn't seem to be too worried about that. After all, the house was huge, and Genevra had been here regularly since they'd finally announced their affair. Nah, he didn't need to be in any big hurry to pack up and move out. Which was a good thing…because he had nowhere to go.

And didn't that just throw cold water all over this happy little gathering.

"You're only lonely because you're standing over here," came a voice from behind him.

Vance had to smirk. It was Harry the damn Bartender. The one who could see all and knew all. He turned and looked the guy over. Dark hair, probably Pinks' age, a compelling smile that reeled you in, and shiny brown eyes that glistened from behind as if that was where his super powers were coming from. Vance threw up his hands in surrender.

"I'm not even going to ask," he vowed. "I'm not going to bother to ask how you do what you do and know what you know."

"It is a mystery, sir," Harry said as he smiled and offered up one of his infamous tequila shots.

"Like your shots, right? You think tequila solves everything, don't you? Hangovers, first date jitters—"

"And love triangles," Harry interjected, pushing the shot glass closer.

Vance felt himself blink. And blink again.

"Goddamn it, Harry," he cursed, taking the salt shaker held out to him as he licked the spot between his thumb and index finger. "Doesn't a guy get to have any secrets around you?" he said, taking the shot glass, downing the tequila, and sucking on the lime wedge Harry had produced out of thin air.

"What secret?" Harry protested. "Mr. Bennett—Good Cop. You, sir—Bad Cop. Miss DuVal—caught in the middle. It's been the top gossip in Henderson since the tennis court debacle last Friday. I am here tonight to do one thing and one thing only."

"Yeah? What's that?"

"Assure you that all is well."

"All is well?" Vance scoffed.

"All is well," Harry soothed. "All is exactly as it should be. Miss DuVal has made her choice—which has freed you up to look elsewhere."

"Freed me up." Vance said dryly. "To look elsewhere for what, exactly?"

Harry's brow furrowed as he folded his arms over his chest, taking a stance that shot one message and one message only out of those crazy crystal eyes. *You are either in denial or simply a dumbass.*

And neither is going to get you where you want to go.

"Isn't it time to waltz that tray of cupcakes around?" Vance suggested.

Harry's smile broke long and broad. "As long as you got the message, sir," he said before hoisting the cupcake tray like the expert waiter he was and strolling off.

Vance looked after him. *I swear to God I am gonna figure that guy out sooner or later.* And then his gaze shifted to his grandmother who was stretched out like Greta Garbo on a lounge chair. Her Hollywood wide-brimmed hat and bathing attire had lured Harry and other males in all afternoon. The woman was an unconscionable flirt at the age of seventy-eight, and the fact that Grace Devine's rough-and-tumble spy guy was the one sitting on the edge of her chaise now had Vance shaking his head. Shaking his head and wondering how he could incite some kind of argument between spy guy Leo, and black belt Pinks so Vance wouldn't be the only stooge who got tossed in the pool. Of course, the FBI big shot probably had his own black belt.

Yeah, Vance thought, better to save the preppy ninja bit for another day. Though it sure would make for some entertaining action.

Action.

The word had his gaze swinging over to Pinks and the Jail Bait Bikini Team. Vance's eyes shot wide as he took in Pinks with his shirt off. The guy had stripped down to his lime green shorts to get in the pool a while back and was now sporting a heavily muscled chest and sculpted arms as he continued to play host to the lithesome bodies surrounding him. Vance wondered if Pinks even knew Lolly was there. It certainly looked as if Pinks had taken Harry's "freed up to look elsewhere" motto to heart.

He sighed deeply, thinking maybe he should "look elsewhere" as well. Because standing here among the people he was closest to—his best friends and his family—he could feel that insidious and painfully familiar feeling of utter loneliness creep back into existence. And he hated it. It made him do stupid things he noted as he licked his lips, eyeing the swell of Titty Titty's voluptuous display.

Hell, he'd been living like a monk for the past two months trying to break himself of the habit of having to drag a woman home to bed. Because like a fucking girl, he had started waking up and hating himself for it in the morning. So he'd begged Lolly to help him find another way—a better way—to relate to women. And Lolly had worked her magic, because once they started interacting he *wanted* to be a better man. He wanted to be whole. He wanted to leave the needy kid in him behind and be the kind of man a woman like Lolly could love.

"Jesus," he swore under his breath. "Lewis," Vance yelled, calling his buddy away from a conversation with his parents and Tess Devine, Henderson's one and only Broadway star. "How 'bout playin' me in that new video game KampsApps just put out? Maybe you can throw me a bone to help maneuver through the Banshee Bandits and get to the next level."

Lewis pushed his glasses up higher on his nose and said, "Finally, somebody here is speaking my language. Those Banshee Bandits are systematically…."

Vance smiled and patted Lewis on the back, letting him go on and on with all that techno speak Vance didn't give a shit about. As they headed toward the pool house, Vance took one long last look at Titty Titty and assured himself he'd be happier playing video games with Lewis—at least come the morning.

Vance didn't understand half of what Lewis was telling him about how the levels of the video game weren't just stacked vertically, but horizontally and diagonally as well. He was just happy to get lost in the game and stop the downward spiral of his thoughts for a time. Stop the emotional deluge that wanted to spew like a volcano from the depths of his soul. Because somehow, by being friends with Lolly, the wall holding back his emotions had started dismantling itself brick by fucking brick. Until that one insidious emotion called Hope slithered through the wall and scattered its ugly cravings disguised as glorious sunshine throughout his mind, heart, and soul.

Hope—the bane of his childhood.

He had held vigil with Hope. Sat and held Hope's hand while waiting for his mother to come back. Wished the same goddamn wish that she would return on every set of birthday candles. Hope had sat up nights with him, graduated to the next grade with him, played fucking third base with him right up until he won the State Championship. And that's when he realized something.

Hope sucked.

Hope was like the Banshee Bandits. You had to get over it, go through it, or maneuver around it in order to get to the next level—which he had. He'd finally gotten over Hope, and then he had manhandled Longing, shoving those two emotions, along with their nonexistent pal, Joy, into the depths of his being and bricked them up good.

He didn't remember what the ultimate catalyst had been, because life had been good for a while there. His college years had been fun and angst-free. He'd felt normal for the first time in his life. But then—something happened. Something had happened that snapped him in two. Because out of the blue, he became addicted to running, and it wasn't long after that he became addicted to sex. Whatever it was had gone down about five years ago. But apparently he'd bricked that up as well.

Aaaaand just when he'd gotten his head back into the video game, in walked Trouble with her long, lean legs.

"What does it say about a party when the host slinks off to play video games?" Lolly asked, catching Lewis and Vance red-handed.

"That KampsApps makes epic games," Vance said, killing off the Banshee with the golden crossbow. "Besides," he said, focused on the ensuing riot around his avatar, "while Lewis is in town, I need to wrestle all the tricks from him I can."

"Lewis, sweetheart," Darcy cooed from behind Lolly, "drive me out to the lake and remind me why I've agreed to be your bride."

With a few quick toggle maneuvers and a couple of quick button combinations by Lewis, Vance's avatar and team of sidekicks exploded into glittering debris, while the remaining characters on the screen knelt on one knee and bowed to Lewis' avatar. Lewis turned to Darcy and smiled, pushing his glasses up his nose. "Gladly."

"What the fuck?"

"I slipped you and your men an imploding device about three levels ago."

"How the hell did you do that?" Vance cried. He looked at Lewis and then back to the screen. "That was so fucking cool. You have got to show me that move."

"Later," Lewis said, standing and walking Darcy out the door.

"Did you see that?" he asked Lolly.

She nodded, smiling. "Pretty cool," she agreed. "Seems Lewis has his own version of bad cop moves."

Vance grinned, turning off the game system and the flat screen TV. "He does at that," he agreed. "Where's Brooks?"

"He's smoking a cigar with Duncan *and Davis*."

Vance stood, turned, saw the arms crossed over her chest and the set to her jaw and realized he had not discussed Davis the intern—or anything else for that matter with Lolly.

"You mad?" he asked. "Because I'll let him go. The kid is smart, has nothing to do all summer, and can probably help my dad and me out in a zillion ways getting our business shit together, but you just say the word and I'll run his lacrosse-playing ass out of Henderson."

Lolly cocked her head and sighed. Then she turned on her heels, throwing over her shoulder, "My momma and your daddy requested a moment with you and me. Probably about the wedding."

"Wait." Vance caught up to her and grabbed a wrist, turning her around. He pulled her close and held her chin between his thumb and index finger so he could look into her eyes. He searched their depths before asking, "You and Brooks. Are you all right? Did he… treat you okay?"

Lolly's tongue flicked out to wet her upper lip as she nodded her head.

"Because if he didn't, I'll take care of things. You got me?"

Lolly smiled, embarrassed. "He was worth the wait," she admitted. "Everything was just…." She shook her head loose of his hold. "You don't have to worry. Not about Brooks and me."

"All right, then," he sighed, happy for the one woman in the world who had endeavored to become his friend.

"And I told Brooks you and I were not giving up the King and Queen Golf Tournament at the Club. We've won three matches already, two of them hard fought and won in extra holes. We aren't throwing that away."

"Lolly—playing golf takes a lot of time. Time you should be spending with Brooks."

"That's ridiculous."

"Seriously? After the tennis nightmare, our continuing to play golf will make Brooks cranky. And frankly, I can't afford to have the man cranky right now. I want him happy and thinking he's invincible. I want him focused on running for mayor."

Lolly tilted her head and gave Vance an indulgent smile. "Trust me. I will do whatever I need to do to keep the man from becoming...cranky. And his feeling of invincibility will be an inevitable byproduct," she promised.

Vance rubbed his hands through his hair. "See," he said, shaking his finger at her, "that kind of stuff—that shit—has got to stop. Because this thing between us," he said, waving his finger between the two of them, "this friendship we've developed? It's got me feeling like an overprotective big brother who wants to insist you have a chaperone and a curfew."

"A chaperone? And a curfew? Are you insane?"

"As if that's news to you," he retorted. "And guess what?" He stepped right into her personal space. "In no time at all I am going to be your older and wiser step-brother, so you may as well get used to it."

"You are so not my brother."

"I will be soon."

"Okay," Brooks said, clapping his hands together and interrupting the scene. "Usually I'd say let's kiss and make up, but I'm not interested in living through that again. So why don't the two of you go back to your corners and let me play referee. Lolly?"

"Vance thinks I need a chaperone and a curfew."

Brooks ran a hand down his face, clearly trying to compose himself. He looked over at Vance. "Care to enlighten me?"

"I don't know," Vance said throwing up his arms. "I'm starting to feel like I'm her goddamn big brother or something. I want to...you know, make sure she's all right."

"I'm fine." Lolly insisted.

"I know you're fine," Vance shouted around Brooks who now stood in the middle of it.

"I don't need a big brother—I need a friend. My *friend* Vance. The friend I have painstakingly cultivated for two long months," she said, peering around Brooks to Vance. "The same two long months it took me to get an invitation into *your* house." She turned on Brooks. "Here is what I need. I need my *friend* Vance and my *boyfriend* Brooks, just like it's always been. And I swear to God, if the two of you mess this up for me, I'm leaving Henderson and taking House of DuVal with me."

The sound of applause had all three heads spinning toward the door. Hale Evans stood at the entrance to the pool house, his face beaming like it was the best damn day of his life. "Dynamite, that was brilliant. Almost as good as the first time we met."

Lolly turned red and huffed, stomping around him to get out the door.

Hale eyed the two men left in her wake. "Gentlemen, I assume that little explosion has settled whatever awkwardness may have remained between the two of you?"

"Absolutely," Brooks said, clasping Vance around his shoulders. "When it comes to loving Lolly, I just realized I need all the reinforcements I can get."

While Brooks begged off to help Harry and his crew clean up, Hale ushered Vance into his library where Lolly and her mother were already seated together on the plush, down-filled sofa. Lolly shot Vance a look as he walked in, clearly not over the big-brother fiasco.

Well, tough. She was the one who got him feeling again, and right now he felt like her big brother. Deal with it.

He felt his brow furrow as he sat down in an armchair across the inlaid wood coffee table from the women. Genevra looked a little nervous. Smiling, but biting her lip. Eyes bright, he noticed, but wringing her hands in her lap. Setting a date couldn't be that big of a deal could it? What the hell else could they have possibly brought them in here to discuss? He crossed an ankle over a knee and sat back, wondering what was about to go down.

Hale cleared his throat, standing at the foot of the coffee table. He'd changed into a pair of dress slacks and a casual shirt. His hands were in his pockets until he started to speak. Then one hand came out and gestured along with his words.

"Genevra and I have some…rather exciting and, uh…unexpected

news. We wanted to share it with the two of you right away, and since we are all here together…." His father's voice trailed off.

Vance started to smile. Exciting? Unexpected? He knew it like he knew Brooks was going to be mayor. His father had knocked up Genevra DuVal. They were about to announce that the two of them—at the ages of forty-three and fifty-two—were going to have a baby. His eyes shot to Lolly at the same time his hand came up to cover his smile. This was going to be priceless.

Lolly, who looked rather bored and still miffed, finally turned her head and looked at Hale once his silence had gone on too long. "Lolly," Hale said in a very quiet, understated tone, like he was trying to put kid gloves on a sleeping tiger, "your mother and I are going to have a baby."

Vance watched it. He watched the words register and sink in. He watched the lack of comprehension, the disbelief, and then the dawning of the truth. Yep, there it was. The fuse was lit and about to blow. Lolly opened her mouth, staring at Hale. The she clapped her mouth shut and turned an accusing eye toward her mother, who blinked nervously and let out a short laugh under her grown daughter's scrutiny.

"How is this possible?" Lolly said.

It was like watching an implosion in slow motion.

"How could you possibly let this happen again? Once, when you were eighteen—oh well. But now? In this day and age? At *your* age?" Lolly accused, her voice starting to shake. "How did this happen?"

Vance jumped up. "I don't care how it happened, I'm just glad it did." He grabbed his father's hand and pulled him in for a hug. "I have always wanted a baby brother," he exclaimed, his own elation shocking him a little bit. *Really? He always wanted a little brother?* He mentally shrugged. *Guess so.*

He went over to Genevra, who stood and turned toward him, smiling. He embraced her in a bear hug. "I couldn't be happier. For you or for me." Then he whispered in her ear. "Lolly will come around. Be strong."

She nodded her gratitude as he released her, her eyes welling with tears. "Those are happy tears, right?" he asked, making sure that at least the expectant parents were on board with this new turn of events. Genevra nodded again, wiping the tears away.

"Happy. Yes. Very happy," she said, smiling over at his father.

"Well, at the risk of raining all over your parade," Lolly said, "do any of you understand the risks involved when the egg and sperm are ancient?"

Genevra looked at her daughter and blinked. "Ancient?"

"Mother. Acting like an irresponsible, hormonal teenager and looking like you are not a day over thirty does not make your eggs any younger. Face facts. Your eggs are old and Mr. Evans sperm has got to be iffy—"

"Iffy?" Hale protested.

"Which does not make this good news or exciting news, although I certainly will agree it's unexpected. But you know what this really is? This is scary news. Because now you've gone and made Vance all happy, and Lord knows what's gonna happen if this baby comes out with two heads and one long continuous unibrow."

"Ah, Sweetsie," her mother cooed, pulling Lolly into her arms for a tight hug. "It's going to be okay. I've already been to the doctor and things look really good so far. Hale and I are aware of the risks and we are going to take each day as it comes. We are going to do all the recommended tests, and the doctor has assured us that there is no reason not to expect a healthy baby." She pulled away as Lolly wiped a few tears from her eyes. "Sweetsie, whatever is going to happen here, the four of us will get through it together."

Hale cleared his throat. "In the meantime, we are very, very hopeful there may still have been one shining star in the whole iffy bunch."

CHAPTER SIX

One week later, Duncan James stood in a hallway just off the lobby of Raleigh's Wake County Justice Center. He was dressed for court, although he wasn't scheduled. Beside him stood a bright-eyed Annabelle Devine in her signature white business attire, perfectly fit for court. Beside her was one very nervous Vance Evans. He was dressed in an unprecedented three-piece suit that even put his always impeccably dressed father to shame. The man was drawing looks from every female who walked by and a few of the men as well.

The fact that Vance wasn't returning any of those looks spoke plainly to the stress he was feeling. They were all here to meet Piper Beaumont, a woman Vance hadn't laid eyes on since the fourth grade. A woman who was about to be ambushed as far as Duncan was concerned. His colleague, Matt Collins, was standing in the center of the lobby waiting for Ms. Beaumont to come out of the courtroom where she was defending a young client. Matt had assured Duncan that Ms. Beaumont would be able to handle the spontaneous introductions. He went on to say that Ms. Beaumont could handle anything.

In short order, Matt gestured toward them, indicating that he had Ms. Beaumont in his sights. Duncan, Annabelle, and Vance all moved into the lobby to wait for Matt to announce their presence and bring Piper over for introductions. There was a lot of momentum coming from the courtroom. Duncan noticed what looked like a set of parents with their college-aged daughter moving swiftly toward the front doors of the building, followed closely by a herd of dark-suited males.

And then came a bit of sunshine. No, not a *bit* of sunshine, but the whole ball of fire come to earth in the form of one petite, curvy, outlandishly dressed for court Piper Beaumont.

Duncan knew it was Piper because Matt had stepped directly into her path and was talking to her, apparently explaining that he wanted to make an introduction. Piper, in her bright yellow garden party dress and three-inch yellow patent heels, handed her large, yellow tote to one of the three briefcase-toting male lawyers surrounding her. She turned her head to say something to all of them. They nodded and off they went at full stride.

"Is that *her*?" Annabelle said, sounding overly delighted. She moved past Duncan as if compelled to take a closer look. Duncan, apparently under the same compulsion, moved in step behind Annabelle. Admittedly, he was just as intrigued. He only hoped his voice wouldn't come out sounding quite so delighted.

Matt Collins turned to indicate the two of them. "Piper Beaumont," he said. "This is my colleague, Duncan James."

Oh, Duncan thought as he took her hand. *Not a ball of fire at all, but a Kewpie doll come to life.* Yellow-blond curls, large blue eyes, and pink cheeks. Forget her mouth. He couldn't chance another look at her mouth, for Christ's sake. He was standing next to Annabelle.

"Ms. Beaumont." He grinned. "It certainly is a pleasure to meet you." He cleared his throat and then remembered the woman standing to his left. "May I introduce Annabelle Devine? She's from Henderson. Like you."

"Oh, really? Henderson?" Piper asked, gazing at Annabelle as if Annabelle had come from the moon rather than just an hour's drive away. "It's got to be my favorite place in all the world. I grew up there. Well, I didn't exactly grow up there, but I was there through fourth grade."

"I lived there most of my life," Annabelle gushed. "I'm in Raleigh now, but my parents are still there, and I go back all the time."

"Oh, I've been meaning to go back. I keep tellin' everybody that the Research Triangle may as well be the Bermuda Triangle. Once I moved in, I never moved out. Except for college—I did manage to get out of the state for college. But that inexplicable pull, that force of the Triangle, had me back here before I knew it. How is ol' Henderson?" Piper asked. Her southern drawl became noticeably stronger the more she talked to Annabelle.

"Just as lovely as ever. You really ought to come back for a visit. The center of town has been transformed by a few boutique shops and two nice restaurants. There are a couple of small businesses, too. Other than that, I bet you'd find it just as you remember."

"Ms. Beaumont, the reason we're here," Duncan interrupted, "is to reintroduce an old friend of yours *from* Henderson. Maybe you remember Van—" Duncan looked behind him and saw nothing but empty space. "Wait. Where'd he go?"

As they stood gabbing, the lobby area had cleared out. Except for the security detail, they were the only ones left.

Vance Evans had disappeared into thin air.

⁂

Vance's phone didn't buzz inside his pocket until he was halfway back to Henderson. He pulled it out, noted that it was Duncan, declined the call, and threw the phone into the passenger seat of the Corvette. Then he floored it.

At least Duncan hadn't tried to contact him in front of Piper.

It was bound to happen, he thought as he shook his head. Pick up a hundred girls and the odds start to turn against you.

When he saw her enter the courthouse lobby, he'd recognized her immediately. And there was no way he was waiting around for an introduction because she would have recognized him as well. Not from fourth grade, but from a night five years ago when no names had been exchanged. A night in Raleigh, celebrating Cinco de Mayo in a dive bar with a Jimmy Buffet cover band. They'd maneuvered each other into a dark corner and—

"Christ."

He hadn't thought about that incident in a very long time, but boy, it was all coming back to him now. Standing halfway down the bar when she walked in, he remembered her eyes searching the crowd and landing on him. And on him they stayed. He didn't know what he'd done to deserve the attention of a blond-haired, pink-cheeked picture of innocence but he stood his ground willing to find out.

Two drinks and an hour later, she finally navigated her way to him. He'd admired her ability to brush off all the come-ons with such finesse that the sons of bitches still smiled in her wake. She stopped directly in front of him. He looked down, she looked up. He said, "Hello." She said, "Hi." He asked if she wanted to dance. She took his hand and pulled him on to the dance floor. Forty-five minutes later, she had her hands under his shirt and was backing him up against a wall.

"Jesus Christ." He was getting turned on just thinking about it. It's what separated her from every other woman he'd been with. She was the aggressor. She took control the moment she laid eyes on him. He wasn't particularly aware of it at the time, but his body sure recognized it when she started kissing him. All he did was sidle them farther into the dark and then slide his feet out a bit so he wasn't so much taller. She took control of his mouth, her hands holding his head as her sweet tongue swept over his lips. He didn't have to think, plot, plan, or implement. For the first time he was not in control, and he relaxed into it. He enjoyed the sensation of being seduced instead of seducing.

Which is probably why it all went to hell.

That kiss. Her kiss. He'd never been kissed like that in his life. He shook his head just thinking about it. There wasn't anything particularly different about it. There were lips involved, tongues involved, hands—great hands. Her hands were all over the upper part of him. He remembered that.

He remembered she'd physically tilted his head and then moved hers the opposite way. That's when he'd wrapped his arms around her tiny waist, practically crossing them at the elbows, and pressed that luscious round rack of hers to his chest. Once their tongues touched, she opened her mouth farther and he did too.

The feel of her tongue, the moisture of her mouth, the plumpness of her soft pink lips was all so good that he wasn't thinking about anything. He simply allowed the sensations to wash over him. And that magical combination sent him to a place where everything was right with the world. Where his mother still ran her fingertips through his hair as he fell asleep at night. Where Piper's smile greeted him at school every morning.

"Holy fuck!"

He hadn't even known he was kissing Piper at the time, yet his mind went to that place. That comfortable, easy, let somebody else take care of me place. Her kiss took him there. And he'd reveled in it. He had accepted it and enjoyed it until his brain betrayed him by slowly bringing him back to reality. And that's when he remembered that anything that could make him feel this good was not going to be sticking around.

And he hadn't enough heart or soul left inside him to pay that kind of price.

Vance couldn't remember what happened after that. He only remembered the emotion tied to it. Desperation. Self-preservation.

He bet Piper could describe what happened in great detail. That's why he ran today. He didn't ever want her to know that Vance Evans was the one who'd left her standing there.

He had no recollection, but somehow he got himself out of the bar and home. And then—

"Holy shit."

He'd put on workout clothes and gone out for a run. And he'd been running ever since. The fact that he was doing eighty miles an hour speeding away from the current situation did not escape him.

An alert from his cell caught his attention. As he exited I-85 and cruised up the ramp, he reached over and checked the text message from Duncan. At the top of that ramp, somewhere between home and everything else, Vance Evans was forced to stop running.

"*That night in the bar. Cinco de Mayo. She knew it was you.*"

⁓⁓

As twilight deepened, Brooks strolled along the back of the clubhouse and watched as a lone figure on the driving range continuously drove golf balls over and over and over. The driving range was closed, but apparently plenty of balls had been left for Vance to take out his frustrations.

After the call came in from Duncan that things had not gone as planned in Raleigh and Brooks couldn't get a hold of Vance on his phone, Brooks headed to the batting cages. He'd pinned some of his own hopes for Vance on this Piper Beaumont, so Brooks wouldn't have minded spending some time cracking a ball with a bat himself. But Vance was in the middle of the golf tournament with Lolly, so it made sense that he was here. Hiding. Or whatever.

Brooks stood for a while, waiting to see if Vance would give up. But as the minutes ticked by and darkness fell across the green lawns stretching out before him, he took the initiative and walked out to Vance and stood off to the side. Three swings later Vance stopped, looked at the ground, and then started to scuff his foot like he was a pitcher on the mound.

"She's amazing," he said. "More than I could have ever dreamed up." He brought the club up and swung it like a baseball bat. Hard. "I picked her up at The Charlie Horse five years ago not knowing who she was." He stopped for a moment. "Actually, maybe in the back of my mind I did recognize her. Because when she kissed me, I distinctly remember thinking about her smile. Back in fourth grade. The one she waited to give me every morning when I walked into that classroom."

Vance turned toward Brooks, but it was too dark to see his face. "It felt so damn good that I ran away from it. From her. Now, any normal person would run toward something like that. But not me. No, I'm so screwed up I couldn't get out of there fast enough. She was right there in my arms, and I threw it away."

"You didn't know who she was."

"It didn't matter who she was! For the forty-five minutes I was with her, I was happy. So happy I forgot I was me. And when I came down from this rare high, when I remembered that I am the kid whose mother left him, that I didn't matter enough for her to continue a relationship with me, that nothing I did, no amount of money I made, no amount of academic honors, not even winning the fucking College World Series was impressive enough to bring my mother back. When I remembered who I was, I didn't have the courage to be happy. And that is on me."

Even if Brooks had possessed the wisdom of Solomon—even if he'd been able to conjure the perfect words to miraculously heal Vance from the damage his mother had inflicted, he could not have given them voice. The length and breadth of emotion seizing his chest and throat wouldn't have allowed the words to pass. So he did the only thing he could. He strode forward and placed a solid hand on his buddy's shoulder.

CHAPTER SEVEN

Late Friday afternoon, Vance leaned against his father's lapis blue Maserati Gran Turismo with its convertible top down exposing the fine caramel leather interior. Dressed in a pair of jeans, a red V-neck T-shirt, and a pair of leather flip-flops, he watched the courthouse doors some twenty white stone steps above him with his feet crossed at the ankles and his arms crossed over his chest. When he saw Piper and her lackeys exit the building, he took a step forward and tucked his hands in his pockets.

Piper spotted him halfway down the steps and froze.

He watched as she slowly tucked a few wind-blown curls behind her ear while steadily meeting his gaze. His solar plexus tightened as the rest of the world fell away.

One of the men-in-black said something to divert her attention. He watched as they spoke briefly—watched as she checked the time, opened her yellow tote, and dug out a group of files to hand over to one of her minions. With her finger tapping the top of the file, she gave instructions and received a few serious head-bobs.

Then the suits moved off.

Vance reminded himself to breathe as his gaze lingered over Piper, standing alone in the middle of the broad staircase, clasping her pretty briefcase with both hands. She looked soft and vulnerable with her sleeveless yellow dress fluttering about her knees and her yellow-blond curls dancing in the warm summer breeze. Vance drank her in, every memory he ever had of Piper colliding into this one perfect moment.

She raised one tentative hand in greeting.

He did the same.

Then she ducked her head and descended the steps, the end of a curl brushing her lips as she made her way to him. She stopped less than an arm's length away and used a finger to drag the bit of curl away from her lower lip. She took a quick glance around and then focused all her attention directly on him.

"Hi," she said shyly.

"Hello," he responded, taking a short step forward and briefly touching the tip of his index finger to the side of her arm. He caught himself and forced his hands into his back pockets. "Did you come down here to see me or to check out the car?"

She blinked up at him—her eyes pure Carolina blue. "What car?"

Vance licked his lips and let his eyes dart to the right before a slow grin spread across his face. "I'll bet you are very good at your job."

She laughed and came into her full voice as she said, "I am."

"Any chance you have time to take a ride?"

"Any chance you'd let me drive?"

"*This* from the girl who said, 'what car?'" he said, feigning heartbreak as he opened the driver's door for her. He'd have handed over the title if that's what it took to get her to come with him.

Her smile spread from pretty pink cheek to pretty pink cheek. She reached back to slip off one tall, yellow heel and then the other, tossing them on the floor behind the driver's seat. Then she turned to face him, flatfooted.

Oh. Dear. God.

Vance gulped for air. He stood towering over the most petite, most precious, blond-haired, blue-eyed baby doll of a girl, whose lush round curves claimed she was no baby at all. This darling, five-foot-nothing female—looking up at him like he was some freaking A-list celebrity—was all woman. Overtly feminine and softly plump in all the right places—starting right there with those red ripe lips. Something about her being so tiny and standing this close made him want to beat his chest and roar. Because all he could think about was tangling his fingers in all those bouncy curls and dragging her back to his cave.

Hell, yes.

He pushed his hands deep inside the pockets of his jeans, wrestling with his inner Neanderthal while Piper, blissfully unaware of the danger she was in, dug out a pair of sunglasses and a yellow headband before placing her briefcase next to her shoes. The headband made her look all of eighteen, but the dark shades were so damn cool they made her look like she owned the Maserati.

"So…yellow." It was all his lust-addled brain could stammer.

"Annabelle told me it's my signature color. I didn't realize I had a signature color."

"Annabelle?"

"My new best friend."

"Perfect," Vance grumbled, wincing as he shut her door. "Damn Keeper of the Debutantes needs to keep her nose out of other people's affairs," he muttered, moving around to the passenger's side. He opened the door and slid into the luxurious leather interior.

"Key?" She held out her palm. Vance stared at her delicate little fingers and fought back the urge to bite them. Wondering from what scary depths of his rusted-out soul that little desire had sprung from, he dug the rectangular device from his pocket and placed it in the center of her palm instead.

"Hit the button and the key will pop out."

Piper did as directed, smiled and slid the key into the ignition. Then she laughed out loud at the blood-stirring *VAROOM* the engine made. "Wow."

The noise settled him. In fact, Vance laughed at her reaction— happy his father's car could bring such joy. "Just wait 'til you hit the gas," he promised.

And she did—all the way to Henderson. With Vance pointing out the potential speed traps, Piper took full advantage of the horsepower beneath her and drove like she was Dale Earnhardt in a skirt. Vance spent most of the drive glancing over at her and grinning behind his hand. It was a bit disconcerting to observe how much this tiny, yellow feather of a woman loved going fast—loved weaving in and out of traffic and throwing the Mas into sport mode to really move out. Nothing about the way Piper drove was tiny or delicate, shy or hesitant. It was full throttle all the way. It brought back memories of their full-throttle night when they'd been out on the dance floor, her hands all over him—backing him up against a wall.

Two thoughts occurred at once. One, the against-the-wall-thing was *his* signature move, and two, how the hell was he going to get her to do it again?

For forty-five minutes they let the wind whip over them and carry away the summer heat. When Piper asked him to turn up an old rock ballad on the radio, they both sang at the top of their lungs, laughing. The sound of her laughter smoothed over Vance like a soothing balm, and for a moment everything stopped and became crystal clear. Thank God he'd taken the chance to see her today. Thank God he'd found the courage to do it. Because even if this drive was all that there would ever be between him and Piper Beaumont, it would be enough. Because in that one fleeting moment, Vance felt joy.

He directed her off the interstate and into Henderson proper, then down roads and into turns, realizing she didn't remember any of it and had no idea where he was leading her. When she pulled up in front of their elementary school, her baby-blues went wide and that plump, sexy mouth of hers formed an *O*. She looked between him and the front door, and raised her sunglasses to the top of her head. "I remember," she whispered.

It looked nearly the same as it did when they were students here together twenty years before.

"Take me to the playground."

Vance nodded and indicated with his fingers that she should turn the car around and park in the teachers' lot. "It's changed," he warned.

"Not completely," she said, walking barefoot to the swings. "These aren't the exact same swings, but they are in the exact same place." She sat in the rubber seat, both hands gripping the metal links at her sides. Vance joined her, sitting in the next swing over.

They surveyed the grounds as they used their feet to gently sway back and forth. The new playground equipment was just a fantasy to kids of their era, with all the climbing structures, hideouts, and cozy nooks here and there. Slides and monkey bars all made of the latest non-corrosive, non-life-threatening materials.

"You liked the merry-go-round the best," Vance remembered. "You liked to go fast on that, too," he said, throwing her a wink.

"Mmm," she agreed. "But your Maserati doesn't make me near as dizzy."

"My dad's Maserati," he corrected. "I have a very unimpressive, very beat-up old pickup."

"Hmm, a truck," she said noncommittally. And after a silence she asked, "How is your dad?"

Vance looked over at the small group of kids kicking a ball in the field beyond the playground equipment. "He's doing very well, actually. He's getting married again. In fact," he said, and then laughed. "He's having a baby."

Piper bit her bottom lip and beamed up at him. He would have missed it if he hadn't taken a quick look back at her. He got caught up in the warmth of her expression and couldn't tear his gaze away. He felt himself lick his lips.

"You sure grew up pretty," he said quietly, longing to run a finger over her soft, round cheek. He turned his head and pushed at the ground with his feet, moving the swing back and letting it fall forward. "I never forgot what you did for me here, Piper. I want you to know that. Every day, you'd be waitin' on me with your soothing smile. It gave me the feeling that eventually everything was going to be all right."

"And is it?" she asked. "Is everything all right?"

An unbidden smile took hold of his mouth. "Well, at the moment, I can't think of a thing that isn't just about perfect."

Piper blushed. Blushed the prettiest color Vance had ever seen, and it radiated as if somehow she'd been lit up on the inside. Her baby blue eyes twinkled just the same as he remembered. The freckles scattered across her nose seemed to fit his memory too. Her round cheeks were exactly the way he'd always pictured, but her lips...her lips he had trouble reconciling. Because those lips, those luscious, plump, raspberry pink lips had grown full and succulent and were a distraction he wouldn't have known about in fourth grade.

He was staring at her lips when his world fell out from under him.

"I thought about you a lot when I lost my mom," she was saying. "I was a grown woman when she passed from ovarian cancer, and yet it hurt so much to have her gone. I didn't need her fixin' my lunches or to be there when I got home from school. I didn't need her to wash my clothes or help me with my homework. I didn't need her to do anything at all. But I needed her to be. Just be...here for me. Just to know I had that support. That love."

Vance was struggling to catch her words. Trying hard to understand exactly what she was saying. He searched her face for clarity.

"So when she died and I felt that pain, that depth of agony that no one can relate to unless they themselves have experienced it, I thought of you. I finally understood just how bad it really was for you."

"What?" Vance could only whisper.

"That's when I Googled your name."

"Your mother passed away? Piper. I wish...I should have been there for you."

"You were."

He stared at her, confusion swamping him.

"One week after my mother's funeral, I walked into The Charlie Horse intent on blowing off some steam. The first person I saw was you."

"Oh, God." Vance panicked. The events of the entire night fell sickeningly into place.

"I knew it was you because I had seen your picture on the Internet. Your official Henderson Police Department photo came up. I dislike cops, by the way."

"What the—?" Vance felt like his head was going to explode. "What do you mean you don't like cops?" he shouted as he scrambled out of the swing. "And if you knew who I was, why the hell didn't you tell me who *you* were?"

"I was planning to. At some point. It all just seemed to be going so nicely that I didn't want to break the flow. Besides, you kept looking over at me and I guess I thought maybe you recognized me too."

"I didn't. I swear I didn't know it was you." He took a breath and let his face fall into his hands. "Holy shit," he said, scrubbing at his eyes. "Why didn't I know?"

"Vance, it's all right."

He started pacing in front of her, running a hand through his hair.

"It's my fault," Piper claimed, standing up from the swing. "It was wrong of me not to have told you who I was. I'm so sorry about that."

"Piper, just…just…stop talking. Please." He stood with his hands on his hips staring at the ground. "I…I…." He closed his eyes briefly and took a long breath. "Please don't let another apology come out of your mouth." He looked at her intently, willing her to understand. "I'm going to repeat that, just so we're clear. I don't want…no, I *can't* have you apologizing to me. Because what I need to tell you—in order to clear up all this history between us—is something that you had no control over. And I know that."

Vance rubbed a fist over his forehead and began to second-guess himself. "I probably shouldn't—oh hell. You were my lifeline in fourth grade, all right? To this day, I'm pretty sure I would not have survived without you. I owe you more for your kindness back then, than I could ever repay. So…there is nothing I wouldn't forgive you."

Piper nodded her head but rolled her hand in a hurry-up gesture. "I feel like I'm waiting for the other shoe to drop."

Vance looked her in the eye, feeling his whole body succumb to the truth. "I spent every day that summer after fourth grade waiting to see you again."

Piper's breath hitched.

"You were the only one who gave me relief."

"Vance," she breathed.

"Once school started, it took me a good four days to find out that your family had moved out of town. Probably took me another few days to understand exactly what that meant. That you were gone."

"And not coming back," she whispered.

"Just like my mom."

❦

The little boy that Piper had loved madly twenty years ago was standing right there—in front of her—as if time had never passed. The same eyes, the same hair, the same sadness. Only this time, she was the cause—inadvertently.

Unfortunately, inadvertently or not, harm had been done. The logical lawyer side of Piper's brain saw her family's move for what it was to Vance.

Lousy timing.

A double whammy.

A crying shame.

But the emotional side of Piper—the little girl that loved him and never wanted to cause him pain—that side of Piper was knocked out cold.

Bloody.

Beaten.

Lying splattered all over the playground.

She was pretty sure it was her emotional side Vance was reacting to when he uttered a curse and dragged her into his arms just as her legs started to wobble.

"Oh, baby doll," he whispered. The warm concern in his voice swam through her internal hysteria, soothing her distress. One strong arm supported her weight when her legs would not, while a large hand tucked her head close against his chest. He was so much stronger than that little boy she'd loved. Strong physically because she felt like a rag doll with the ease he'd managed to secure her against him. And emotionally because he was taking complete control of the situation. As her brain wrapped around that, her distress abated little by little. She came to understand that he'd been devastated but not destroyed by the events of his past.

"I'm okay," she said, sniffling, testing out the strength returning to her legs. Then she licked her lips and said it again, against his chest. "I'm okay." Her hands came up and pressed flat against his pectoral muscles…strong and solid, like he proved to be on the inside.

She knew Vance didn't want her to apologize. *That* she had heard loud and clear. But she needed to say *something*. She tucked her head and wiped at her nose with her hand, then brushed under her eyes with the base of her palms. She took a deep breath and tried to gather

her scattered thoughts.

"I'm okay," she said again, pulling back a little bit, wanting to remain in the circle of his arms. "I really am. I just...truthfully, as much as I hated moving and as much as I missed you for so very long, I never...ever once imagined how our move had affected *you*."

"You were ten."

"Yeah. Yeah, we were ten." *As if that made us immune to heartache*, she thought, stepping back from his embrace and shaking her hands out as she went. She turned her back to him and tried to rub off any smeared mascara that might be under her eyes.

Vance came up behind her and put his chin on the top of her head. "And now we're old," he grumbled.

That made her laugh. She turned and saw his sad smile. Then he put his hand under her chin and ran his thumb under her eye. "I shouldn't have said anything."

She shook her head adamantly. "Thank God, you did. I would never have connected those dots and...wow...that's a lot of desertion for a little boy to handle."

"I know you didn't desert me."

"That's exactly what I did. Whether I had any choice in the matter or not, and no matter that we were just kids, you were left by someone you...."

"Loved," he supplied.

"And trusted," she whispered. *No wonder he never recognized me. I'm lucky he didn't suppress me from his memory entirely.*

Vance nodded several times. "It's good that you know. I need you to know so that you'll understand two things about that night at The Charlie Horse. First, I know what it feels like to be deserted. So, having...deserted you, after your mother had just died...." He closed his eyes, unable to speak.

"It wasn't like that," she assured him. "I didn't feel abandoned."

"Really? We spent forty-five minutes on the dance floor, shared several mind-blowing kisses, your hands were all over my body and out of nowhere, for no apparent reason, I turned around and left. If you didn't feel abandoned, what did you feel?"

She stared at him for a couple of heartbeats. Then surrendered the truth. "Heartbroken."

Vance's hands fell to his sides. "Oh," he said gently. "I'm so sorry."

Piper came and took his hand, reminiscent of exactly what she'd done in fourth grade, and walked the two of them over to a picnic table. They sat down facing each other. "You said there were two things. Two things you wanted me to understand about that night at The Charlie Horse."

He was looking down at the table. At his finger rubbing back and forth over the wood. "I...ah." He turned his head and looked far afield. He had planned to tell her about their kiss. Try to explain to her exactly how good it felt. Tell her how it had conjured up her memory and the memory of his mother. Explain to her what that had done to him and why he ran.

"Can you...." he said, turning his attention back to her. "Can you stay for dinner? I'd like my father and grandmother to meet you."

"I...of course! Of course. I would love to meet them. It's just," she said, blinking those big, blue eyes, "I'd like a chance to freshen up first. I want to be at my best when I meet your Mighty Abuela."

Vance laughed. "My Mighty Abuela? Is that what we called her?"

"I don't remember what we called her. I just know we feared her. And that she fed you turtle soup."

"Well, she's mellowed a bit since then," he said as they stood and started toward the car. "She only bites the heads off of turtles once or twice a week these days."

CHAPTER EIGHT

"Do you speak Spanish?" Vance asked Piper as he drove them away from the elementary school.

"No. Why do you ask?"

Vance's cell phone was already at his ear when he grinned at her and started talking. *"Abuela, si no te importa, me gustaría invitar a alguien especial para cenar con nosotros esta noche. Sí, es una mujer muy hermosa. ¿Quieres que yo lleve algo? Vale. Por favor, le dices a papá que saque un buen vino. Se va a arreglar un poco aquí en casa. En breve llegamos a tu casa. Nos vemos en media hora. Gracias."*

"That is really unfair," Piper complained.

"I know." He grinned.

They pulled into the long length of garage disguised as a stable and Piper stood up in the passenger seat before they came to a stop. She raised her sunglasses and took in the surroundings. "There sure is some kind of horsepower in here. Wow." She looked over the Corvette, the Trans Am, the Rolls Royce, and the rest of his father's fleet and gawked. "You are crazy rich," she said, exiting the Maserati and taking her briefcase from Vance.

"My dad is crazy rich. And generous enough to let me play with his toys."

"How do you choose?" Piper wondered, walking down the length of the garage and taking a good look at all the autos. "Why did you choose the Maserati today?" she asked as Vance tugged at her hand to get her to leave the garage and head up the stone path.

"It draws a lot of attention."

"Good choice," she said with a laugh.

Each step up the hill revealed more windows sprawled across the back of the house to their right. Vance watched her process it all. The house, the lawns, the beautifully landscaped pool and Jacuzzi that lay beyond their feet as they came to stand on the stone patio. Piper looked toward the triangular wood and glass pool house on their left. "Did you have all of this when I knew you?"

"We had the land and my dad had the vision. We had a nice house back then, but nothing like this."

"It's breathtaking."

Seeing it through Piper's eyes, Vance agreed. He nodded, leading her over to his pool house.

"I've lived here since I came home from college," he said, opening the door and leading the way into the well-appointed living area. He stood to the side, watching her take in the large flat screen TV, the sectional sofa, the huge ottoman, end tables, and lamps all in shades of blue and tan. From where they stood, she'd be able to see his small kitchen and table in the back. "At that time, my dad would be gone all week on business, so it was a way to be here for my grandmother and still have my own space. Abuela and Dad have done their best to pretend I live on the other side of town. But fortunately, I'm always welcome across the pool."

Vance motioned her toward the open double doors of his bedroom. "The bathroom is in there. If you need anything, check underneath the cabinet. If it's not there, I'll run next door to see if I can find it."

"Wow," was all Piper said when she walked into his bedroom. "Wow," he heard her exclaim again when she opened the door to the bath.

Vance smiled. It felt good to *wow* Piper.

He sat down on the couch and checked his phone for messages. No one knew he'd gone to Raleigh to see Piper. Hell, he hadn't known he was going until he was halfway out of town. There were plenty of messages from Pinks and Duncan. While he read through them, the idle part of his brain started to wonder about his father's reaction to this unprecedented act of bringing a woman home to dinner.

He caught movement out of the corner of his eye and looked

up to find Piper standing in the doorway holding girly supplies. "So, who is she?" she asked.

"Who is who?"

"Whoever is spending the night here on a regular basis?"

Vance looked down at his phone, continuing to scroll through messages as he said, "I haven't had a steady girlfriend since college. And I don't think that lasted a semester."

"Well, then what is all *this*?"

Vance brought his head up and started to pay attention. He noticed a curling iron, a bag of fancy toiletries, an electric toothbrush, and he especially noticed the Costco-sized box of condoms. "I'm not a monk," he said slowly.

"So...you're not a monk, but you haven't had a steady girlfriend since college?"

Trouble was brewing. He felt it. And like a dumbass, he allowed his mouth to hang open while he nodded his head.

Piper took a long look at the box of condoms, probably noting the variety of textures and flavors along with the fact that they were almost gone. "What? Are you like a man-whore or something?"

Vance fell back against the cushions in shock, rubbing a hand over his mouth trying to hide his embarrassed amusement. How the hell was he supposed to answer that?

Piper stomped her foot. "Vance Evans, that is disgusting!" She looked at everything she was holding and grimaced. "Ick." She turned, curls flying, and took off toward the bathroom. He sprung off the couch to follow, getting there in time to witness her shoving all the stuff back under the sink and slamming the door of the cabinet.

"Piper," he started.

"What?" she snapped, looking up at him.

God, she is cute.

"I'm sorry. I've led a misspent youth." He tried not to grin, but the expression on her face was so perturbed he couldn't help it. "Listen, if it helps at all, I am truly trying to change my ways."

"Right," she muttered, digging into her briefcase and pulling out a small cosmetics bag and her purse.

"I am. My buddy, Brooks, will tell you. The only girl I'm involved with now is his girlfriend, Lolly. And that's so I can learn to appreciate women for…other things. You know, be friends."

"That is such bullshit."

"What?" He feigned shock. "Piper Beaumont, how does an ugly cuss word like that come out of a pretty little girl like you?"

"I know worse," she said, scrubbing her face with a fresh washcloth.

"Look, I don't want to start throwing blame around, but if you'd just told me who you were five years ago, my reputation with the ladies would be less than half of what it is today."

She stopped and stared at his reflection in the mirror. "Is that true?" she asked. "Would you have stayed—that night? If you had known it was me?"

Vance let out a long breath as he tucked his hands into his pockets to keep himself from pulling her to him. "Piper, I've been looking for you since the last day of fourth grade. If I had known it was you in my arms that night, I can't imagine that anything could have dragged me away. In fact…."

When he didn't finish, Piper prompted, "In fact?"

Vance shook his head and glanced at his watch. "You just get ready. We'll talk about this later," he said, moving from the room and heading back to the living area.

Piper stared blindly into the mirror, basking in Vance's words.

"I've been looking for you since the last day of fourth grade," he'd said. "If I'd known it was you…nothing could have dragged me away." Those perfect words had soothed her instantly—turning her insides soft. She smiled at her reflection, happy to know that she had not been alone in her memories, but that Vance had remembered her, too.

Piper went back to scrubbing her face, hoping to untangle the windblown mess of her hair quickly. She was very curious to meet his family.

Twenty minutes later, Vance opened the French doors of the main house and motioned for Piper to step inside. The sun was starting to set, bringing shade to the patio and allowing things to cool off. Still the air conditioning inside the expansive kitchen brought relief. Piper moved in front of Vance who had exchanged his

T-shirt for a casual, white linen button-down.

Seated at the tall countertop, three faces glowed with anticipation and delight, welcoming Piper in a way that immediately put her at ease.

Vance started the introductions as they all stood. "Piper, this is my grandmother, Emelina Flores, my father, Hale Evans, and his fiancée, Genevra DuVal. Everyone, I would like you to meet Piper Beaumont, my very best friend back in fourth grade."

Piper noticed awareness hit both Vance's father and grandmother when he mentioned fourth grade. Which is why, she supposed, Genevra moved first, coming around her fiancé to clasp both of Piper's hands.

The woman smelled of roses and happiness. "It is lovely to meet you," she said. "I'm not sure I'd remember any of my classmates from fourth grade."

"Obviously, she's quite special." Mr. Evans slid in between them, taking her hand and looking her right in the eye. "Piper," he said gently, cupping her hand in his, "we are honored to have you in our home."

"Thank you," she managed, licking her lips. She felt a little tongue-tied. Mr. Evans' gorgeous face was terribly disconcerting.

Fortunately, he turned her toward the Mighty Abuela, which may have proved sobering if not for the sudden embrace she found herself in. Vance's elegant grandmother held her close and murmured something in Spanish, then released her quickly and stepped back, eyeing her up. "Now this is a celebration," she declared, clapping her hands together with a delighted smile on her face. "Old friends are the best friends, no?" She swung her gaze toward Vance. "We will make you feel so at home you will never want to leave."

Piper thanked her. Thanked them all for allowing her to join them on such short notice. Then she accepted a cold glass of wine from Vance and struggled to gracefully pull herself up onto the tall counter stool. All the while she was being peppered with questions.

Vance sat down next to her and put his hand up to stop the barrage. "Let's all give Piper a moment to breathe, shall we?" he suggested. "It's only been a couple hours since we reunited, so maybe it would be prudent for Piper to simply tell us what she might like us to know about herself."

"Okay," she agreed, "and then I get to ask the questions."

Vance laughed. "Good luck with that."

"Well," she said, feeling incredibly conspicuous being the subject of all of their bright, optimistic gazes. "I fell in love with Vance in fourth grade—"

Vance snorted, his grandmother sucked in a shocked breath, Genevra beamed from ear to ear, and Vance's dad's eyes glistened over a jubilant smile.

"And then my parents moved me and my brothers to Chapel Hill, which I just hated at first, but grew to like after making new friends. I went to a private girls' high school, which I also hated at first. Don't get me wrong. I liked my parents just fine, I just hated all the stuff they were doing to me."

Everyone laughed.

"While everybody else wanted to come to Chapel Hill for college, I saw that as my opportunity to leave. I picked a school in the middle of nowhere, Miami University in Ohio. Oxford, Ohio— nothing but corn fields and fifteen thousand kids looking for a party.

"I wanted to be an actress. But through a series of unfortunate events, I decided my talents were needed elsewhere. Which required me to stop partying and put my nose to the grindstone so I could get into law school."

"You're a lawyer?" Hale asked, his brows raised high.

"I am," she stated. She didn't mind his disbelief. Knowing full well that she looked like a blond Betty Boop, she'd come to expect his reaction. And she often used it to her full advantage in court.

"And you should see the boy band following her around, doing her bidding," Vance said.

"Boy band," Piper snickered. "My firm likes to indoctrinate the new male lawyers by making them work for me," she explained. "I don't dress or act like tradition mandates, so once they come to respect me, they don't have a problem taking orders from anyone else in our firm."

"Are you a litigator?" Genevra asked.

Piper nodded as she sipped her wine. "I do one thing and one thing only," she said, setting her glass gently on the granite. "And I do it very well."

Hale leaned over the counter, placing his chin on his hand, curious. "And what is the one thing?"

Piper shot an anxious look toward Vance, figuring he may as well hear it now and hear it from her. Lord, she hoped he still had that same sense of humor. "I defend college students. From trumped up and ludicrous charges."

"Really?" Vance said, his brows raising as he sat up tall on his stool and crossed his arms over his chest. "Trumped up and...what was that? *Ludicrous* charges?" He loomed over her, appearing two parts amused and one part incredulous.

"Yes, exactly." She smiled into his handsome face, not about to play false.

Vance ran a hand down over his mouth, trying, she thought, to hide his amusement. "Care to enlighten us further?" he said, holding out his hand toward the rest of his family.

"Very well." She spoke to the table at large. "I represent the type of cases where if a—" she shot a quick glance toward Vance, "—a police officer had used a little bit of common sense, asked pertinent questions, and judiciously issued a warning instead of whipping out his handcuffs, the entire incident could have ended where it began. Thus saving the kids, their parents and the judicial system a whole lot of time and angst. So, I only take cases with certain parameters. Which means I have clients spread throughout the Research Triangle and beyond. With all the colleges in that area, there's a lot of business."

"Thus, the 'I hate cops,' comment," Vance murmured.

"I never said *hate*," she corrected. "But I'm a defense attorney and have good reason not to be overly fond of them."

"Although you make a pretty good income off of the ones who don't use good judgment," Hale teased.

"It is the cross I bear," she said, grinning and lifting her wine. "I'm certainly not unaware of the irony."

When there were no follow-up questions, Vance glanced around the table. "Really?" he asked. "Is no one going to ask the obvious question here?"

When there was no response, Vance groaned, "Oh, for God's sake. Piper." He turned his whole body in her direction. "Please tell us all what happened back at good ole Miami that put you on your Trumped-up and ludicrous soap box."

Ha. Like that was *ever* going to happen. She pulled out all the charm her momma taught her and fell into the thickest Southern accent she could muster. "Why now, look at me going on and monopolizing this entire conversation. Forgive me, Miss Emelina, because in truth, I'm just dying to hear all about where you came from in Spain and how difficult the transition was when you arrived in Henderson."

While Vance's grandmother blushed and touched the back of her updo, the rest of the room chuckled softly and let Piper get away with egging Emelina on to tell her story. Vance, she noticed, seemed more content than she'd expected, throwing her a quick wink over a devastating smile. *Oh, Dear Lord,* she thought suddenly, bracing her heart. *Vance Evans continues to be one slippery slope.*

<hr />

Dinner was served outdoors amid candlelight. The breeze had kicked up just enough to make it pleasant. The conversation flowed easily and after dinner no one seemed in a hurry to leave the table. Genevra announced she would be preparing breakfast in the morning and hoped to see Piper there.

"I look forward to it," Piper said, at the same time Vance said, "She's not staying."

Piper looked at Vance like he'd just told her there was no Santa Claus.

"I can stay," she assured him quietly. "I'd like to stay."

"I'll be driving you back to Raleigh tonight."

Abruptly the three older adults stood as one and began clearing the table. Piper stood too and started to help until Vance captured her wrist and dragged her from the table.

"Piper, you can't possibly stay here—with me—tonight."

"Why not?"

Sputtering in disbelief that he would actually have to spell out the obvious, Vance said, "Well, for one, there is no way I'll be able to keep my hands to myself." He ticked off his index finger. "I also happen to be a cop, and for some mysterious and undisclosed reason you have a big issue with cops," he said, ticking off his middle finger.

"In addition, less than two hours ago you called me a man-whore." He ticked off his ring finger and then held the three of them up, wiggling them back and forth. "Take your pick."

Ms. Beaumont, the defense attorney, held up her hand. "Have I asked you to keep your hands to yourself?" she questioned, and then answered, "No. Because I've been crazy about you for twenty years," she said, folding over her thumb. "*And* you left me in the middle of the dance floor lusting after you for the last five." Down went her index finger. "I may not be crazy about cops in general, but if you refer back to argument number one you'll understand why I'm willing to make an exception in your case," she said, closing finger number three. "And, while I agree that the man-whore thing is generally disconcerting, there is something to be said for experience." Down went finger four. "As well as never running out of condoms." Finger five. "I believe, Officer Evans, you are clear out of arguments."

CHAPTER NINE

If Vance could have hit a pause button and gotten life to hold still for just a moment, he would have called Brooks on the phone and begged his forgiveness. Because up until this very moment, he had not understood why Brooks had continually gone out of his way to keep Lolly out of his bed.

Now he understood completely. It was simply self-preservation.

Right now—standing here, drinking in her pouty lips and soft, pale skin—Vance was willing to do just about anything to keep Piper in his life. Including keeping her out of his bed.

He'd rather be friends.

Friends had no reason not to see each other on a regular basis. Friends could even fight and make up. Friends forgave each other. Lolly taught him all that. Friends got to know each other, figured things out together, shared secrets, hopes, and dreams.

He needed to build that with Piper. And once the foundation of friendship was strong enough to stand against any random act of his insanity, then he'd take it to the next level and make her his own. He needed her invested heavily so whenever it did go to shit, it wouldn't be easy for her to walk away.

He did not want her walking away.

Abandoning him.

Again.

"I'm not arguing," he insisted. "I'm simply inserting the stuff you're so fond of, a little common sense. Today has been amazing. Piper, you're amazing. But I've just found you. You probably have somebody back in Raleigh you need to shake loose and—"

He saw it in her eyes.

"What? There's a dude back in Raleigh?" *Of course there was. No woman who looked like her was sleeping alone. Fuck! And here he was talking her out of spending the night with him. Freaking moron.* "Piper?"

"Okay. All right. Yeah," she said starting to back down. Starting to walk toward the pool house. "But I can take care of that with a phone call, really." Then she hesitated for a moment. "Maybe two."

"Two?"

"No more than three. Three calls and I'm good to go," she said, stepping inside his place.

Vance broke out in a cold sweat. "You're sleeping with three different guys?" he asked very quietly so the pounding in his head wouldn't detonate.

"No! Oh, my God, I'm not like you." Piper rose from gathering her purse and briefcase. "I have two dates on my calendar. Just dates. One will be easy to brush off. The other, well, we've been dating a little bit, so he's probably not going to be too happy."

Vance understood completely. *Poor son of a bitch.* "And the third?" he inquired.

Piper sighed as she sat down on the couch. "That one is a little complicated, so okay," she said, capitulating, "I'll stop throwing myself at you. But you know," she frowned, "a girl can only take so much rejection. Leaving me on the dance floor and now this." She looked up at him with her baby blue eyes and laid her heart on his coffee table. "Vance, do you at least find me attractive?"

Vance had to concentrate to keep his feet riveted to the floor. One move toward her and it would be all over. "I'm working very hard trying not to think about how," *fucking hot,* "attractive you are."

"Suppose I refuse to tell you where I live?"

"I'm one of those pesky cops, remember. I already know where you live."

"What if I simply refuse to get in the car?"

"Again, the ugly cop. We're trained to muscle a hundred pounds of fluff around."

She looked so beaten down and forlorn that his heart nearly

broke. He crossed the distance between them and crouched down in front of her. "Come on," he said gently, taking one of her fingers and shaking it a little trying to bring the life back into her. "We'll take the Rolls and you can snuggle up with me while I drive. And while you're doing that, you can text me the names of those three guys you're going to be kicking to the curb first thing tomorrow. Just in case I need to follow up with any of them."

"I don't wanna take the Rolls," she sulked.

"Aww. Everybody wants to ride in the Rolls," he coaxed.

"I wanna take your truck."

Now why'd she have to go and say a thing like that? Vance thought as he did the one thing he hadn't done since the two of them were ten.

Vance Evans dropped his heart straight into Piper Beaumont's hands.

An hour later, Vance had his arm tucked around a sleeping Piper, sitting in his truck in front of her condominium building. The woman smelled like a nectarine dipped in honey—sweet, succulent, and playful. He looked down to see her sweet cheek nestled against his chest. He felt her succulent curves under his arm as he held her close. And he longed to playfully entwine his fingers in her blond curls. Instead, he slowly placed a kiss on the top of her head. Then he laid his head back against the headrest and closed his eyes, relaxing into this one perfect moment of unequaled contentment.

His mind drifted—suspended and blank. And then, slipping into his one moment of sheer contentment came the question: *If my mother had not abandoned me, would I be sitting here with Piper now? Would Piper have ever meant so much?*

Piper had done her best to fill the gaping hole in his heart back then. She'd nurtured him when no one else would. And it had helped him heal. Piper had meant so much to Vance because he'd suffered that loss. And being with her today was everything he could have hoped for when he'd set out to find her.

And more.

Because she wasn't just his savior in fourth grade. No, she was also his hologram. The one who'd haunted him with its playful and easy emotion. The one that caused him to steer clear of blondes, knowing they would never measure up. And now that he realized Piper had been the temptress at The Charlie Horse—well it all finally made sense.

Now he understood why he'd gotten so damn lucky that night— why he was the one she came to. Because she knew who he was. And perhaps the reason her hands and lips provided a pleasure so acute it caused him and his chicken-shit heart to run screaming from the room was because deep down inside he knew her, too. And remembered that she'd left him.

Inadvertently. Not of her own free will.

His logical mind understood that clearly, but his damn heart kept responding with a "fool me twice" warning. He must have tensed up at the thought because Piper stirred against him and opened her eyes.

"Home?" she asked, blinking off sleep as she sat up beside him.

God, she looked like Goldilocks. All warm and sweet and resembling far more the classmate than the temptress.

"Stay right there," he whispered. "I'll come around and get you."

"Are you at least going to kiss me goodnight?" she asked sleepily as she climbed out of his truck. Honest to God, the question startled him because at the moment she looked about twelve fucking years old.

He held her yellow briefcase and took her hand, walking them slowly to the front door of the building. Maybe it was time he confessed about why he'd run off on her. "How 'bout I tell you about the most amazing kiss of my life. It happened about five years ago. It was Cinco de Mayo—"

An immense figure loomed up out of the shadows of the condominium's covered entranceway. Vance stopped walking, but Piper kept moving forward. "Just ignore him," she whispered, as if having some genetically enhanced ape rise from the bushes was not a problem. "Evening," Piper said quietly, nodding politely to King Kong as she stepped up onto the landing.

The guy was huge, with a big square head sitting on big square shoulders. His menacing gaze traveled over Piper before merely flicking toward Vance. Vance thought about Pinks—his new black-belt sidekick—sort of wishing he was here at the moment.

Piper did her best to ignore Kong, but the ape positioned himself in her way, folding his arms over his chest and becoming an immovable object. Vance watched as King Kong forced his little Goldilocks to step around him to get to her door.

No way was that shit going to fly.

Vance threw out his chest, stretched his six foot two frame to six foot three and got right up in the ape's personal space.

"You the door man?" he questioned.

"Nope," Kong replied.

"Do you live in this building?"

"Nope."

"Well, there is a no loitering sign on that door. So, if you're not the doorman, and you don't live here, I suggest you move on." He finished by pulling out his badge and popping it into Kong's face.

"Really?" he heard Piper exclaim from behind Kong. "What are you going to do next? Pull out your handcuffs?"

A yellow twirl of lightning flashed in front of Vance as Piper stepped in between him and the brute.

"Officer Evans," she started, glaring at him like she was some irritated school teacher.

What the hell?

"This man is standing here, minding his own business. He's not creating a scene or disturbing the peace and he doesn't appear intoxicated or homeless."

Oh! I get it. Ms. Beaumont the lawyer has arrived.

"And what do you do?" she asked rhetorically. "You declare him a loiterer, shove your *badge* in his face, and demand he vacate the premises. As if you, a small-town cop, have any jurisdiction here."

And didn't that just piss him off.

"You've got to be kidding me. Piper—"

She whirled around, offering Vance her back as she stood between him and Kong, digging something out of her briefcase. She handed it to the ape. "If he arrests you, call me. I'll be your lawyer, free of charge."

Kong took the card and then looked up into Vance's face and smiled. *Sucker.*

Vance was busy staring Kong down until he heard the door

open and shut behind the ape. That's when he realized Piper had left him standing out there. He sprang into action, sidestepping Kong, but the damn door locked on contact, leaving him to stare through the glass at Piper's sweet little backside swinging quickly down the hallway.

He banged on the door, yelling, "Piper!" and heard the words "Go home Vance" drift behind her as she disappeared.

Vance threw up his arms. "What the fuck just happened?" he said aloud, turning to find himself stuck out in the dark with Kong.

The ape turned a little human when he started to laugh. "I take it this is the first time you've run up against Ms. Beaumont," he said.

Vance just stared wild-eyed, not knowing what to say.

"She's not a fan of cops," Kong said.

"Yeah," Vance said, rubbing the back of his neck. "I get that."

"I think pulling your badge was the thing that set her off."

"Ya think?"

Kong laughed again, but it was more in camaraderie than amusement. "You should try going up against her in the courtroom. At least out here she cut you quick. Didn't toy with you like you were some damn mouse—dangling you by the tail over the open jaws of a cat."

"You've gone up against her?"

Kong held out his hand. "Officer Dash Stevenson. Her favorite mouse."

Vance shook the guy's hand. "Vance Evans, small-town cop with no jurisdiction," he said. "So what were you doing out here?"

"I've lost fifteen cases to that woman. Good, solid cases. Yet she makes me look like a first-rate asshole in front of the judge and occasional jury every single time. Recently I hit my breaking point and have been throwing out a few opinions of my own. Although you saw how well that's working. Tiny little thing could care less. And now she's offered to be my damn lawyer," he said, holding up her business card. "How am I supposed to stay pissed off at her now?"

Vance grinned at the change of heart and at the same time stood in Kong's shoes. He could well imagine Piper tucked into some frilly little dress, tossing her blond curls around while playing coy for the judge and flirting with the jury. They'd look over at Kong and see exactly what he'd seen five minutes ago—a threat and a bully. She'd make her case by inserting her so-called common sense and logic and then doing a fancy tap dance around the defendant's idiot behavior and the actual law that had been broken.

Poor bastard.

Still. "So, are you planning on retaliating?"

Kong shook his head in the negative. "No. Not unless I can catch her speeding," he said, starting to cheer up. "Then all bets are off."

⁊⁊⁊

Piper leaned back against the door to her condo, shutting out Vance Evans and all thoughts of his glorious looks and smoldering appeal. She took a couple of deep breaths, doing her best to disconnect from her emotional turmoil. "After all this time," she muttered aloud, setting her briefcase beside the couch as she entered the cozy living space.

Her apartment was neat and cheerful. Annabelle Devine would love it, Piper thought, looking at the overstuffed upholstery done in splashes of color where yellow was featured prominently. At the moment, Piper found it hard to drum up any enthusiasm.

Usually she loved coming home to her place. It wasn't large, but it was hers and it was paid for, as was everything in it. Like the boutique-sized old-world dining room set complete with its bijoux chandelier which she passed on her way to the bedroom.

She sighed when she hit the double doors and leaned against the jamb as she gazed at her favorite piece of furniture. The queen-sized sleigh bed with its carved footboard and headboard wasn't dressed light or frilly the way one might expect from Ms. Piper Beaumont. By comparison, it was rather tailored and elegant in shades of green and ivory silk. It looked soft and inviting, until she blinked. Then it just looked lonely.

She allowed her heart to sink just a little, her body to ache for the want of his touch. Of all the things Vance Evans could have grown up to be, "He had to be a cop," she said aloud. She had been so hopeful when she saw him standing at the bottom of the courthouse steps today, because she had fantasized about a scenario just like that for the past five years. Yet her hopes had been dashed the moment Vance pulled out his badge.

Because when he pulled out his badge, it took her right back to college. Right back to that terrible, awful, no good, horrible night.

Classes hadn't even started yet. It was only her third evening on campus and she was excited to have been invited by a friend of a friend to her first college party. Piper was coming out of the darling gingerbread-style house right off the edge of campus. Blissfully unaware of any peril, she stepped into a sea of happy freshman while carrying a can of beer.

That's when the overzealous cop, arriving out of the blue, made a beeline across the lawn and through the crowded party, zeroing in on her. Probably because she looked so damn young. He was tall and lean, and his expression was downright gleeful when he pulled out his badge and shoved it in her face. Then he took ahold of her arm, swung her around, and cuffed her in front of everybody.

Well, everybody who wasn't underage and hadn't scattered into the wind.

The cop cuffed her before he asked to see her ID. He cuffed her before he took the time to notice that the can of beer she had been holding was unopened. He cuffed her before she could explain that she was simply carrying the beer to an older coed who was of age to drink it. And Piper was too scared and too caught off guard to protest any of it.

She was in the back of his police car, heart pounding, panic rising, before the cop finally realized the beer had never been opened and she couldn't have consumed any of it. She could tell he wasn't happy about that turn of events.

It was at that point he decided not to take her to jail, but to write her a ticket. He told her she'd have to appear in court, but that things should go her way since she'd been cooperative. Then he took the cuffs off and let her go.

Only, things did not go her way.

Not only was she immediately infamous campus-wide for being the first freshman "arrested" that semester but, due to the fact that her parents were already *generously* stretching their finances to send her to college out of state, she did not ask them to fund a lawyer for her day in court. Piper assumed it wasn't necessary to spend eight-hundred dollars or more on a lawyer since the cop had told her things would go well for her and it wasn't actually her beer. Not that she wouldn't have liked to drink a beer—she was a college student after all. But being charged with possession made it sound like she was hawking marijuana, for goodness' sake. She just needed a chance to explain all that. So, she decided to face the judge alone.

Big mistake.

She learned a valuable lesson that day. Lawyers are very, very important to uninformed college students.

The judge had a full docket that day of what he seemed to consider *pampered rich kids*, and the cop who had caused Piper all this angst stuck to his facts without once mentioning the unopened beer or her cooperation. And since Piper didn't have a lawyer by her side arguing that she hadn't been given a breathalyzer, that the beer can in question was unopened, and that her record was clean, the judge threw the book at her.

He didn't care about her honest responses. He simply looked at the charge of possession and put her on probation until she turned twenty-one. Then scared her to death by telling her that she now had a *permanent record*, and that if she so much as got caught jaywalking before she turned twenty-one, he'd throw her in jail for *thirty days*.

And that did not include the five-hundred dollar fine, the three-hundred dollar court costs, the drug-and alcohol-awareness classes she was now required to attend, or the six months of community service he gave her on top of it all.

Her college experience went to hell faster than Grant took Richmond. Piper ended up lonely, sitting in her dorm room most Friday and Saturday nights while her new hallmates trotted off to parties and rush events. She was too scared to venture out, not wanting to chance temptation only to meet up with another cop who could make her life any more miserable.

She was embarrassed, she was angry, and she was frustrated beyond anything she'd run up against before. For weeks, her mind cried out with the "it's not fair" scenario. Out of sheer boredom and with way too much time on her hands, she decided to arm herself with knowledge of the law to protect herself and her friends from any future mishaps. Had she understood her rights and the law, and had the confidence to point them out that night or in the courtroom, events would have gone differently. She was convinced of it. As it happened, the events of Piper's first Friday night in college changed the course of her life permanently. All thanks to a tall, lean, overzealous, I'm-pulling-out-my-badge-and-throwing-my-weight-around cop.

And she had just watched Vance Evans do exactly the same thing.

Officer Stevenson might be big and intimidating, but Piper had known him a few years—and the truth was the man was nothing but a giant teddy bear. She'd run into him working with kids' charities where they'd shared a few laughs and even a couple tears trying to ease the plight of Raleigh's underprivileged children. At the moment though, she was definitely on his shit list because she'd gotten George Howling off with a hand slap—which even Piper had to admit was not what the kid needed—but she did not want to get into a debate over justice in front of Vance. So, as frightening as it may have seemed to have someone that big waiting on your doorstep, Piper had not been alarmed. She knew who Dash Stevenson really was.

It was obvious that a whispered, "just ignore him," did not convey any of that to Vance, however.

"Why does he have to be a cop?" she moped.

It's so extraordinarily unfair, she pouted, propelling herself toward her walk-in closet, *because so much else about the situation couldn't be more perfect.* Starting with Vance himself, she thought as she tugged down the zipper of her dress, stepped out of it, and tossed it into the dry-cleaning basket. Tall, dark, and yummy, like he'd been all those years ago that night at The Charlie Horse. Gorgeous dark hair worn just a little too long. Emerald eyes that could hypnotize a woman into doing just about anything. "Obviously," she grumbled as she pulled a nightshirt over her head. After finding all that crap left in his bathroom, clearly she wasn't the only female willing to drop her panties on the dance floor for him.

She flicked on the light as she entered the bathroom and thought it had been for the best—Vance dumping her in the middle of their romantic liaison. She took a headband and pushed the curls out of her face, turning on the faucet and waiting for the water to get hot.

It all would have worked out just fine, she sighed, *if I hadn't been spotted.*

She scrubbed her face clean, releasing that thought for the thousandth time and letting it slide down the drain. She'd been living with the consequences of that night for a long time now—and had accepted them—or so she thought, as she dabbed on some moisturizer and ran a brush through her curls. Of course a day like today would undoubtedly bring it all back, she supposed. And as she crawled underneath the covers, remembering her time with Vance's grandmother, father, and Genevra DuVal brought an unbidden smile to her lips.

She laid her head on her pillow and allowed herself to bask in how welcome they'd made her feel. She grinned as she thought of Mr. Evans' quick wink, Emelina's sweet hug, and Genevra's warm smile—each of them completely enthralling in their own way. And so happy to meet her—obviously assuming that she and Vance had some kind of a relationship that warranted her presence among them.

Ooooh Lord. Vance.

In the five years since she'd seen him, there were subtle differences that caused a striking effect. Starting with those crazy biceps—like the guy pumped iron in his sleep. The moment she had wrapped her hands around one, she thought she was going to drool. Around Vance she felt like an adolescent at a boy band convention—and that boy band comment about her male first years *had* been funny. And that was another thing—he still had the same sense of humor she'd fallen in love with back in fourth grade.

Piper reached over to turn out the light. As she snuggled onto her side and closed her eyes, she was immediately reminded of leaning against Vance during their long ride home.

Even though she started out acting cool and aloof because he was taking her home, Vance didn't put up with any of that crap. Once he got behind the steering wheel of his truck, he reached across with both arms, and pulled her over to his side of the bench seat without so much as a "Come here" or a "Please."

And didn't that just set her desire soaring?

The man smelled like cloves and oranges—rich, spicy, and extravagant. His body was hard and firm, and she spent a fair amount of time wondering what he'd look like with his shirt off, in a pair of low-riding board shorts, dripping wet as he got out of that pool he lives beside. For all that dark hair and tan skin, he wasn't covered in manly fur. Just a respectable amount of hair ran down his forearms. She wondered about the hair on his chest and then the hair on his legs. He was solid and he was strong, handsome to a fault.

And he was a cop—a cop with a badge. One he pulled out and flaunted the first chance he got.

Piper turned over and groaned into her pillow. It was for the best, she tried to assure herself. His running out years ago, leaving her on the dance floor. *Yes, it all would have worked out just fine,* she sighed, *if I just hadn't been spotted.*

Or…if she hadn't given in to the irresistible temptation that had always been Vance Evans.

CHAPTER TEN

Sprawled out on his stomach, Vance pulled his pillow over his head when he heard the door to the pool house open.

Not interested.

It was Saturday morning and he didn't have to play cop. Until he smelled Genevra's famous breakfast being served poolside, he was not interested. The only thing he might drum up interest for then was a pitcher of Bloody Marys, a stack of pancakes, and a lounge chair where he could spend a long, hard day working on his tan.

Fuck running.

Brooks was right—running was for spandex-loving freaks. Running every damn day since he'd left Piper at The Charlie Horse had done nothing but bring him full circle. And here he was, all by his damn self—again.

So unless The Lawyer Beaumont was the one coming through his door to apologize for her freaking *"Really? What are you going to do next? Pull out your handcuffs?"* comment, he was not interested.

"Vance?" Lolly whispered.

Unless of course it was Lolly.

Now wide awake, Vance tossed off the pillow and rolled over to find The Lollypop and Henderson's Golden Boy standing at the end of his bed.

"Y'all finally decide on that three-way we talked about?" he said, propping himself up. "I might be a little rusty, but I hear it's like riding a bike. So, hop in."

Lolly squealed with laughter, bouncing onto his bed as Brooks threw out his patent "Fucking A."

The Lollypop bounced over, kissed him on the cheek and then stole both his pillows, propping them up against the headboard as she sat back against them. She was dressed for summer in a tiny little red skirt, a white eyelet halter top, and her hair tied up high in a pretty red bow.

"We came for the details." She tapped his sheet-covered thigh. "Start talking."

"Details?" Vance scoffed, throwing a look at Brooks he hoped conveyed that he needed to get better control over his woman.

Brooks simply shrugged. "Sue me," he said. "I'm curious, too."

"Let me guess," Vance said, pulling a pillow out from behind Lolly and leaning back on it himself. "Genevra called you."

"She did," Lolly acknowledged. "And she thought Piper was faaab-ulous."

"Faaab-ulous?" he repeated.

"Yes, faaab-ulous. That's exactly how she said it. So we couldn't wait to come over to find out if you thought Piper was faaab-ulous too."

"Just to be clear," Brooks interjected, "I could have waited."

Vance smiled at his buddy. "Yeah, I think I got that."

"So, are you happy?" Lolly went on.

Vance turned his head and smiled at her. "Of course, I'm happy."

"I mean are you happy about Piper?" she pressed.

"I'm happy about you…and Brooks…and Dad…and Genevra… and baby brother Brody."

"Brody?"

"Yeah. Brody."

"You know this may not be a brother."

"No. Let's have a brother. You'd be okay with a brother, right?"

"I'd be okay with a healthy anything—"

"Great, because I want a brother. A brother named Brody. And now that that's settled, I'm officially happy."

"But weren't you even happier last night with Piper?"

"Parts of last night made me too happy."

"Too happy?"

"Right. Plain old happy works better."

"So you are afraid? Of being too happy?"

"No. I'm afraid of being unhappy."

"Well, if Piper is so faaab-ulous, then why are you worried about being unhappy?" Lolly questioned.

"Because as faaab-ulous as Piper is," Vance imitated, "she doesn't like cops."

"Good thing you're not much of a cop," Brooks said over his trademark grin.

"You'd think that would finally be working for me, wouldn't you?" Vance said. "Turns out, Piper brings out the cop in me. Last night I actually became the quintessential bad cop."

"So?" Lolly asked. "Don't tell me Piper didn't fall for all your innate sex appeal and completely disarming skills of seduction."

"I am standing right here," Brooks claimed.

"You know what I mean," Lolly soothed, throwing Brooks a sultry look.

"Okay, and now I'm the one right here," Vance retaliated. "In my room, in my bed. So stop with the blatant 'I'll take care of you later' looks, all right? That is not helping."

"Sorry," Lolly said. "Now tell us all about Piper and what you mean when you say she doesn't like cops?"

Vance opened his mouth to speak and then remembered what he hadn't told Lolly—which was the best part about finding Piper. He angled his head and gave her a tender smile, taking her hand in his. "She's the one," he told her.

"The one?" Lolly said, her eyes going big.

"She's the vision—the hologram that's been haunting me. I had no idea. Until I saw her."

"Piper is the blonde who has ruined you for all other blondes?" Lolly asked amazed.

"She is," Vance said, remembering how Piper had released his inner caveman. "She's like this sweet, feminine, delicate little China doll that I just want to pick up and carry off and…." he finished with a growl.

"What hologram?" Brooks said, his voice escalating as he spoke. "What vision? And why the hell does Lolly know about this and I'm just hearing about it now?"

Torn from his potent memory, Vance looked over at Brooks as if he'd just asked the dumbest question in the world. "Lolly and I are friends," Vance said with the "of course" insinuated.

Brooks dropped his jaw into a what-the-fuck expression. "Really?" he asked. "And you and I are…?"

"Well, we don't talk about this stuff," Vance defended.

"Since when?" Brooks yelled. "We talk about this stuff all the time."

"Look. It was just this thing—this 3-D vision of a pretty little blonde that appears in my head, especially after I've taken some random woman to bed and woke up regretting it. I told Lolly about it when she asked me why I didn't do blondes—and the reason I don't do blondes is that none of them ever measured up to this hologram and the emotion that it embodied."

"So you've been carrying around a picture of Piper in your head for years and didn't even know it," Brooks stated.

"Correct. And, interestingly enough, that Cinco de Mayo thing was apparently not such a coincidence. It turns out Piper knew exactly who I was. Which is sort of insane that she didn't divulge that bit of information before she stuck her tongue down my throat."

"Why didn't she?" Lolly asked.

"I think she thought I knew her too."

"You mean all this time she thought you walked out on her, *knowing* it was her."

"Up until yesterday."

"Well, was she happy to see you or pissed you had left her hanging in the bar?"

"She was happy to see me. I mean, she wasn't crazy about finding all the evidence of my overnight guests in the bathroom there. She even called me a man-whore. I told her I've been celibate for eons now, so I'm going to need backup on that from you two."

"Eons," Lolly scoffed.

"Hey," Brooks countered, "it's all relative. For him, it's been eons."

Lolly rolled her eyes.

"She had all of us eating out of her hand at dinner. But you already know that," Vance said, nodding his head toward Lolly. "And she wasn't very happy that I was taking her back to Raleigh last night. Seemed she was ready and willing to pick up right where we left off in The Charlie Horse."

"And you had a problem with that?" Brooks asked in disbelief.

Vance spread his hands and shouted toward the ceiling. "What the hell have we all been working on these last two months if not making me a better man? Of course I had a problem with that. This is Piper we are talking about, for God's sake. I do not want to screw this up."

"How could you possibly screw it up?" Brooks yelled back. "The one thing you know how to do where women are concerned is to give them an orgasm."

"Well, what about that friends thing Lolly and I have been working on so damn hard, uh? What about appreciating women outside of the bedroom?"

"You've already been friends with Piper," Brooks countered. "You already appreciate who she is. She's your fucking hologram, for God's sake. She's the one you want to take to the next level—the one you want to take to bed and leave panting for more. Trust me. You take Piper to bed, you are not going to regret it in the morning."

Vance folded his arms over his chest and looked between Brooks and Lolly. "I'll admit the evening would have ended better if I'd given the woman what she wanted. Because with me trying to be the good cop, disaster ensued. And now, being any kind of a cop is apparently a huge fucking problem."

"Okay, so explain to us about the cop thing? Why doesn't she like cops?" Lolly asked, moving closer to Vance so Brooks had room to join them on the bed.

"God, I wish I knew." Vance tucked his arm around Lolly's shoulders and brought her closer as Brooks' huge body stretched out on the other side of her. "She makes her living defending high school and college kids from what she calls overzealous cops. It's a thing with her. Apparently a big thing, because last night when we were confronted with this enormous NFL type loitering on her front step and acting like he had an axe to grind, I pulled out my badge and told him to get lost. The next thing I know, Piper—no, not Piper actually, but *The Lawyer Beaumont*—is in my face, calling me Officer

Evans and throwing lawyer speak around like it was confetti. Then she hands the guy her card and tells him that if I arrest him, she'll be his lawyer, pro bono, right before she flounced her pretty little ass into her condo, locking me out and telling me to go home."

Vance looked between Lolly and Brooks who both stared at him open-mouthed. "I know!" he said. "And get this. She literally called me a small-town cop with zero jurisdiction—in front of the goddamn linebacker I was trying to intimidate."

Both Brooks and Lolly dissolved into hysterical laughter. Vance couldn't help but join them.

"Oh, man," Brooks sighed, wiping tears from his eyes. "Of all the times for you to pull out your badge. You never pull out your badge."

"I know, right? I hardly ever carry the damn thing. But by some colossal twist of fate, I not only had it in my pocket, but apparently I couldn't wait to show it off."

There was a knock on the door and without thinking Vance hollered, "Come in."

"Hey," Pinks said as he came around the bedroom door, clipboard in hand, "since you went AWOL on me yesterday I need to go over a few things—"

The poor guy took one look at Lolly in Vance's bed and pulled up short, sputtering. "Perfect. Just perfect," he said before he started yelling at all three of them. "Maybe I am nice, safe, and boring, but whatever the hell is going on here has clearly crossed the line into kinky. Jesus, I'd like to rip my eyes out."

"Oh, My God," Lolly cried. "I'm completely dressed."

"Well, *he's* not." Davis said, pointing at Vance.

Vance flicked a look to Lolly. "The Ninja's got a point."

"And you," Davis said, poking a finger at Brooks. "What kind of a man lets his girlfriend crawl into bed with a guy like that?"

"Hey," Vance said. "I represent that."

Lolly snickered at the same time Brooks began to defend himself. "Dude," he yelled back at Pinks. "You think I'm happy about this?" indicating the three of them in bed. "This is exactly what Tansy warned me about."

"Tansy?" Lolly said.

"Yes, Tansy," Brooks growled. "She said that as long as you and I planned to adopt Vance, the three of us would be very happy. But I swear to God, I did not picture this."

"Tansy? Tansy Langford?" Pinks asked. "Glad you brought her up, because *that one* is becoming a problem. Who the heck is she anyway?"

"Brooks' ex who ran off to some big city. Recently came crawling back with her tail between her legs," Vance explained.

"Well, your father has gone and hired Tansy Langford to be the office manager."

"What?"

"She was there yesterday directing the furniture delivery. As if I couldn't figure out where the hell the furniture should go," Pinks said.

"Christ Almighty," Vance said. "That woman hates me." Vance threw off the covers and dragged his legs out of bed. He tugged at his boxers to make sure he didn't expose himself to the audience gathered in his bedroom before he stood and headed into the bath. "Why the hell would he go and hire Tansy of all people? She's probably going to undermine me at every turn. Do we even need an office manager at this point?" Vance asked Pinks through the crack he left in the bathroom door.

"Not while I'm around. Apparently she approached him at the pool party and told him about her resume. Told him she was detail oriented and a hard worker. That she was smart enough to run the place so that neither one of you ever had to set foot in the office if you didn't want to."

"Then why the hell do we need an office?" Vance asked around a mouth full of toothpaste.

"Marketing," Pinks responded. "You need your name on the door in the center of town. You also need a place to meet with clients. Not that your bedroom isn't a great gathering spot," he went on, "it just might seem a bit casual to some."

Vance smiled in spite of himself. Pinks The Ninja was all right.

"What are you going to do about Piper?" Lolly hollered from the bedroom.

"Who's Piper?" Pinks asked.

"Piper's the reason he went AWOL on you yesterday," Brooks told Pinks.

"Ah, the plot thickens," Pinks said. "Not sure that bed is going to be big enough for four."

Vance wrapped a towel around his hips and opened the door to lean against the jamb. "So, what am I going to do about Piper?" he asked. "The truth is, the cop issue is not really a problem. I mean with Evans & Evans starting up, coaching baseball, and Brooks' mayoral campaign on the horizon, I could drop my badge off tomorrow and never miss it." Vance looked over his tribe and made a decision. "But Piper doesn't know that." He smiled. "She probably thinks I'm a full-on, full-time, twenty-four-hours-a-day cop.

"Brooks, you said it yourself. It's time to take this to the next level," Vance went on, feeling more certain as he spoke. "Piper and I are already friends. In fact, she told my father she fell in love with me in fourth grade. She's seen me at my worst—leaving her stranded five years ago and then again with Duncan just last week—and she still got in that car with me yesterday."

"Because you were driving a Maserati," Pinks remarked.

"A totally bad cop car," Vance insisted.

"Yes, but once you pulled out your badge, she locked you out and told you to go home," Lolly reminded him.

"That happened after I'd already made the mistakes of taking her back to Raleigh and refusing to kiss her goodnight. Trying to be the good cop backfired…big shocker there…because if there is one thing everybody in this room has learned, it's that when it comes to romancing a woman, the only good cop is a bad cop. So from now on, I intend to be a very bad cop."

"What if she refuses to see you?" Pinks asked.

"Now that'll just play right into my plan, won't it?" Vance smiled.

⁓౿∽౭∽⁓

Piper had only thought about Vance Evans seven times during her Saturday morning ritual. She thought that was pretty darn good since thoughts of him had kept her up half the night.

Propped up in bed with a cup of coffee and the laptop she used strictly for play, she'd spent a couple hours creating her latest Pinterest board—part of her Dream Home Collection. This one, entitled Bake

Me a Cake, had been inspired by Vance's father's house. She'd never seen a kitchen quite like his, and while she'd dined with the Evans family, she kept wondering how odd it would sound if she offered to cook a dessert for them—in their kitchen.

So instead, she'd spent the morning creating her own virtual kitchen. Now the new Pinterest board housed pictures of fancy cabinetry, painted lava stone countertops, unusual sinks, pretty hardware, La Cornue ranges, and every baking luxury a closet pastry chef could want. A lime green Cuisinart food processor, a turquoise blue KitchenAid mixer, pretty floral tin canisters, crystal cake plates, rustic pie plates, marble rolling pins, playful cake pans, and vintage-looking aprons all provided such delicious torture that she ended up pulling up her recipe files with the intention of baking something delicious.

She wondered if Vance was a sweets eater, and if so, did he prefer dark chocolate to milk chocolate or no chocolate in his dessert at all? Not that she should worry about it, she thought as she scrolled through her recipes. He was a cop, and a man, so she would probably never hear from him again…at least not for another five years. Ah this! She had wanted to try the Meyer Lemon and Olive Oil Chiffon Cupcakes with the Lemon Poppy Seed Curd for a long time. Poppy seeds and lemon curd, what's not to love? Then she picked out an old favorite to go with it. Butterfinger Fudge Cookie Bars would do the trick.

Just in case she'd have someone to serve them to—Crap! She had a date tonight. She had told Vance she was going to…what did he say? Kick them to the curb? But really, it wasn't like Officer Evans was all that interested in her anyway. He was sweet and— she sighed—wonderful when they were on the playground together talking about old times, clearing the air about Cinco di-Saster and wanting to introduce her to his family. And he did want her right up against him in that god-awful truck of his. She laughed out loud at her thoughts. There really was something about a truck.

But other than that, he hadn't touched her too much during their time together. And when she threw herself at him—well, that was ego deflating for sure. She sighed loudly as she got out of bed and headed toward the shower. Breaking a date with cute-boy Danny seemed like a really dumb idea. At twenty-nine and counting, her biological clock was ticking. At the rate Vance Evans showed up in her life, her ovaries were going to be on borrowed time the next time he crossed her path. Besides, he'd already been the catalyst that caused her to toss her dream away with both hands once. She'd be a fool to sit around and wait for him to do it again.

CHAPTER ELEVEN

Right after Vance ordered Pinks to make up a pitcher of Bloody Marys and before he joined everyone poolside for breakfast, he picked up his phone to call Piper. That's when he realized he didn't have her number.

How the hell is that even possible?

He'd been with women less than five minutes and gotten their damn number. How could he have spent hours with Piper and not have asked for hers? He shook his head as he scrolled through his contacts. He was slipping, right when it started to count.

He texted Annabelle—being as she was Piper's "new best friend"—and kept it short and sweet.

"Need Piper's number."

He added a *thanks* hoping to fend off any curious phone calls. He just wanted her to text him back, plain and simple.

Of course, he didn't manage to get out his door before the phone rang. "Goddamn it! All I want is the woman's—" *Oh. Duncan.* Vance picked up. "This better be you," he said.

"It's me," came Duncan's voice. "Annabelle is texting the number. But I've got big trouble that needs handling and you're the man for the job."

After Vance agreed to handle Duncan's big trouble, he looked for Annabelle's text. Piper's number was there, thank God. He quickly stored it and then pressed the number and waited while her phone rang and rang. Eventually her sweet voice sang in his ear asking him to leave a message and wishing him a pleasant day in the prettiest southern accent he could imagine.

He cleared his throat. "Piper, it's Vance. I—uh, am calling to apologize for last night and I sure wouldn't mind the opportunity to do it in person. Give me a call, please. I'll be waiting to hear from you." He disconnected and noted the time.

His father, Genevra, the Big Em, and the rest of the merry misfits watched him expectantly as he strode around the pool and approached the umbrella-covered breakfast table. Lolly was the one to voice the question that was so obviously on everyone's mind.

"Did you get ahold of Piper?"

Christ Almighty. When did his personal life encompass this many people?

"No, I did not," he said, taking a seat beside her. "However," he looked up and smiled, "I did talk to Duncan James and have a juicy tidbit that may satisfy you until the next installment of Piper-gate." He reached for the platter of pancakes and bacon as he went on.

"It seems Duncan's twenty-one-year-old brother has gotten himself into some hot water," Vance explained with a wry grin. "Duncan didn't give me any details, but whatever the hell happened has his parents in an uproar. They've banished the kid from their summer community and have shipped him to Duncan for babysitting. Duncan's law firm has no room for a new intern, so he was wondering if Evans & Evans could use another hand. I told him to bring him up. I figure if he's a pain in the ass, we can stick him with Tansy. That ought to make the boy's life a living hell."

"Now what in the world do y'all have against Miss Langford?" Hale asked.

Vance waved off the question. "Never mind that," he said, "because here's the best part. Duncan's brother's name is…Jesse James."

A collective laugh erupted. "You're kidding," Genevra said.

"No, and I swear to God I'm going to get the kid a gun belt and one of those cap guns that looks like a pistol from the wild-west and make him wear the damn thing. I've got a ninja and an outlaw working for me. Tell me this is not a great summer."

"Mmm, with a name like that," Lolly said, raising her eyebrows while grinning at her mother, "I can't wait to meet him."

"Well, as one who is quite familiar with scandal, I'm certain to make him feel right at home," Genevra said.

"We'll put him in the guest room next to Davis," Emelina suggested. "The two of them can embrace their inner outlaw while playing pool boy for me."

Vance tucked his tongue into the side of his cheek and eyed Brooks directly. "You see what's going on here, don't you? These three have yet to lay eyes on the kid, but because he has a bad cop name, they are all salivating."

"Which means you have your work cut out for you keeping the kid out of trouble," Brooks said.

Vance stretched his head from side to side. "I'll put Pinks The Ninja on him. Seriously, you should see this guy's moves," he said, pointing to Davis.

Lolly burst out laughing. When Davis and Vance threw her incredulous looks, she stopped. "You're kidding, aren't you?" she asked.

"I'm a double black belt," Pinks informed her. "So no. He's not kidding."

"Davis," Lolly said in a breathy that's-amazing-you're-my-hero voice.

"Aaannnd we're out of here," Brooks declared, standing and dragging Lolly out of her seat. He threw her over his shoulder and smacked her on the butt, walking off as the table broke out into a round of chuckles.

"The man knows how to handle his woman," Vance laughed. "And since when is Pinks staying in the house?" Vance asked, looking at his intern.

"Since I found him sleeping in his car just outside of the gate," his grandmother told him.

"My lease was up in Raleigh," Pinks explained.

"Geez, I was wondering how the hell you seemed to be on the job twenty-four seven. Okay. Jesse James bunks with you." Vance looked at his dad. "This okay with you? Turning your place into a home for lost boys?"

"If your grandmother is okay with it, I'm fine. Frankly, it's a joy to have this place full of life for a change."

"Abuela?" Vance questioned.

Emelina's eyes sparkled. "Please," she said, "it will be more fun than when Genevra's brothers-in-law raided our wine cellar."

There was plenty to discuss over breakfast concerning Hale and Genevra's upcoming nuptials. Labor Day weekend had been the original date, but now with Brody the baby bump due to make an appearance, the wedding had been pushed up to the third Saturday in August. An enormous tent would be erected right on the estate and everyone was given an array of assignments to pull off the gala event in just five weeks' time.

During the discussion, Vance checked to make sure his phone was turned on, hoping he'd have heard from Piper by now. The words, "Go home, Vance," started to echo in his mind, making him edgy.

In the middle of the lively discussion on how to best utilize Tansy Langford, one where Pinks seemed particularly full of ideas, Vance excused himself to place another call to Piper. He walked to the far side of the pool and stood off the patio, in the grass beneath the shade of a tree.

Again her phone rang and rang. Eventually her voicemail picked up, forcing Vance to leave another message.

"Piper. It's me again. Listen, I really am sorry about the badge thing. Obviously it sets off a nerve with you—a nerve I don't want to be associated with. I'm normally not much of a cop, but last night I guess I was being a little overprotective. I didn't realize you knew King Kong—I mean, Officer Stevenson, so…Okay, again, I'd like an opportunity to talk to you in person, maybe over dinner tonight. Give me a call," he said hanging up. He added an exasperated "I'll be waiting," after the fact.

He wandered back to the table, shaking his head in the negative at the expectant faces.

Three fucking hours later, Vance fought for control as he laid another message on Piper's voicemail.

"Ms. Beaumont. I had no idea who that guy was or why he was standing on your front porch," he said. "What I did know is that he could have disabled you with one whack to the side of your head. So there was no way—in hell—I was leaving him outside your place with you in there alone and me on my way back to Henderson. If flashing my badge was going to help get him gone, I was happy I had it on me. Now, if you have an issue with me watching out for your welfare, then the two of us have a big problem. Almost as big of a problem as you not calling me back." Vance flicked off his phone.

He stood perfectly still, thinking.

Never in all his thirty years had he called the same woman three times in one day.

Hmm.

When it came to women, he had more instincts in his pinkie than most men had in their whole damn body.

Damn straight.

After a few more moments, he nodded his head and said aloud, "Okay then. Bad Cop it is."

The Henderson Police Department had gone casual for many of their routine duties. Instead of the traditional uniform, the bike patrol and officers working certain community-related events could wear the Navy blue sports shirt with the department logo and a pair of khaki pants or shorts, depending on the weather. So Vance hadn't actually had his full standard-issue cop getup on for a very long time. He stood in front of the mirror in his bathroom now, marveling at how adding more weight training over the last year had caused his uniform shirt to strain at the buttons running down his chest. It made him look like a fucking body builder—and kind of a tool.

He turned from side to side, checking out his physique in the mirror. Eventually, he decided the body builder fit worked in this situation, enhancing the bad cop image he was going for. If he was going to be throwing his weight around, he may as well show it off, too.

He borrowed a cruiser from the precinct lot. A completely AWOL move and one that would probably cost him dearly unless he could convince Dudley Do-Right—The Crown Prince of Henderson—to cover for him. It wasn't like he and Brooks hadn't pulled a few pranks over the years. He just hoped this one turned out well.

Piper hadn't answered her phone all day and he did his best to stay away from that thought as he drove into Raleigh. He refused to try her again, so when he pulled into her parking lot and found a spot up front facing the building, he simply got out and rang her bell.

Again, no answer.

He didn't know what he expected, other than she'd actually have had the decency to call him back. So he sat in the cruiser and read *Planning Local Economic Development: Theory and Practice*, one of the pile of books he and Brooks were reading to help them formulate a plan for economic prosperity in Henderson. He took notes, watched people come and go from Piper's building, tried not to look at the clock too much, and then tried not to think about it being a fucking Saturday night at eleven o' you've-got-to-be-kidding-me p.m.

He went over their conversation yesterday in his mind. There wasn't just one guy she had to shake loose. There were three guys and…what had she said? One of them was complicated? Apparently pulling out his damn badge last night had nixed kicking these guys to the curb. Because it was becoming pretty fucking obvious that Piper was out with one of them now.

Vance sat there incredulous. Stewing. Because when Pinks had suggested Piper may refuse to see him, he didn't give it much consideration. She was his hologram, for Christ's sake, and they had clicked on so many levels yesterday. But no calls back, and clearly she had plans tonight—

Headlights shown quickly through the cruiser as a car pulled into the lot and parked several spaces down. Vance heard car doors slam and muffled conversation before a couple came into view, walking on the sidewalk in front of the building and now directly in front of him.

Sure enough, Piper was being escorted by some average-sized asshole with long, blond surfer-dude hair. And she was smiling up at him. The dumb fuck was grinning from ear to ear, no doubt figuring he was about to get lucky.

So not happening.

Vance let them make their way onto the fateful porch steps where it all had gone to shit the night before. His finger was firmly planted on the boom-whoop button, which he hit the moment surfer boy settled both hands on Piper's hips. For a single second, the lights flashed and the siren sounded, and Vance let himself enjoy the bottled-up glee that spouted forth when the stunned couple separated as if caught holding a stolen bag of cash. He exited the vehicle, puffed his chest out, and sauntered forward, digging down into the depths of his bad cop image.

◦◦◦

Piper had run into Officer Dash Stevenson at the grocery store earlier that day, and had seen him again just before cute-boy Danny had escorted her into Poole's Diner for dinner. Since he'd given her a nod both times, she wasn't particularly concerned. But she was ready to put her foot down at him showing up here and interrupting her date again.

But the officer coming out of the dark wasn't the big jughead. And Piper didn't have to see his face clearly to know exactly who it was. She couldn't say whether it was the curve of his biceps or the McDreamy cut of his hair, but she didn't have to process his athletic stride to know that Vance Evans was back in Raleigh.

And didn't that just give her a thrill?

She tried to stifle a smile as he approached, because really, this was an invasion of her privacy after all. And cute-boy Danny didn't deserve whatever he was about to get. But watching Vance move forward slowly and deliberately, with that sexy smirk on his face that boded nothing but trouble, Piper felt her heart thump a little harder.

I am in way over my head.

Cute-boy Danny turned toward Vance and asked the inevitable question. "Problem here, Officer?"

Vance stopped his approach with one foot on the bottom step, looking up at the two of them. "Well, I'd like to ask Ms. Beaumont a couple questions, if that's all right," he said. "Seems we have a communication problem." He directed his gaze at Piper. "Your phone in good working order, Ms. Beaumont?" he asked, coming up the steps to the landing.

"I'm-m, I'm not sure," Piper stuttered, trying to remember the last time she handled her phone. "I'm—oh! I left it in my bedroom, charging this morning. Forgot to put it back in my purse when I ran out to do errands." She felt herself smile as hopeful awareness dawned. She knew she was flirting—right there in front of cute-boy

Danny—but she was so tickled with the thought that Vance had called her, she just couldn't help tilting her head toward one shoulder and asking, "Did you try to call me today, Officer Evans?"

"I did," he confirmed, smiling back. "Three times. So you see, it was rather urgent," he said, licking his lips and pulling himself back into cop mode. He turned toward Danny and held out his hand.

"Vance Evans," he introduced himself. "And you are?"

"Danny Bruce."

"Where ya from, Danny?" Vance asked all friendly-like as he shook her date's hand.

"West Coast, originally," Danny answered. "San Diego area."

"That right? Big surf out there?" Vance asked.

"It's pretty crackin' most of the time."

Vance nodded his head, grinning. "Crackin'," he repeated. "And what do you do around here?" Vance asked.

"I'm a lacrosse coach at Carolina," Danny said proudly.

"Lacrosse?" Vance questioned. "Is that like…a real sport now?"

When Danny drew his head back, looking perplexed, Piper stepped in. "Don't mind Officer Evans, Danny. He played baseball at State."

"America's favorite pastime," Vance insisted, and then Piper watched him shake his head in surprise and turn a hundred-watt grin in her direction. "Why Ms. Beaumont, I had no idea you followed my career at State."

Piper looked to Danny. "Officer Evans and I were in fourth grade together," she explained. "He's practically my brother."

"I'm not her brother," he told Danny.

"Well, I mean, you're like a brother to me," Piper explained.

"No. No," Vance said obviously becoming a little irritated. "I'm nothing like a brother to you."

Piper shrugged. "You're a little like a brother," she insisted.

"Danny," Vance said, pulling out his badge and flipping it open. "I'm gonna have to borrow your date for just one minute. If you would hold on to this for me," he said, handing him his badge. "We won't be long." He looked at Piper and said, "Ms. Beaumont? A word, please." Vance's arm stretched out to indicate the stairs.

Piper smiled obligingly, stifled a giggle, and headed down the steps, following the walkway out toward the sidewalk. Vance caught up to her and grabbed hold of her upper arm, steering her to the left, out of Danny's line of sight. When they came to a stop behind some large shrubbery, Vance gently turned her to face him.

"Piper," he said quietly, stepping in close and causing her to look up at him. "When you check your phone tonight, there are going to be three messages from me. And when you hear them," he said, gently cupping her cheeks between his palms, "I want you to remember that this is what I was trying to say."

Piper saw him lean down, her eyes fluttering shut just before she felt his lips touch hers. Tenderly, he kissed her lips with exquisite slowness, such gentleness, as if she was precious and important, something to be savored and appreciated. As if there was nothing more enticing than the bow of her top lip or the plumpness of her bottom one. His kiss was delicate, unhurried, and full of emotion. She simply followed the flow of it, kissing him back, basking in the feel of his hands on her cheeks, the softness of his touch. Her entire focus was on the feel of him against her lips and face, until he drew his mouth over her cheek.

"Cut Danny Boy loose," he whispered against her ear, sending chills down her spine. "Call me when it's done. Then come to Henderson for breakfast around the pool tomorrow."

He ducked his head and stepped back. His hands drifting from her cheeks to her shoulders and then down to her hands. He curled his fingers in between hers and pulled her forward, turning them back toward Danny. Before they came into view, Vance dropped her hand and straightened his shoulders.

Piper followed along in a blissful daze. The unhurried tenderness of his kiss lingered on her lips, so potent she wondered if any evidence remained. She had to clasp her hands together to withstand the temptation of running her fingertips over her mouth.

She wasn't the least bit upset that Vance had told her to cut Danny loose. It was as if she'd been hypnotized by his kiss, and his quiet suggestion was entrenched so deep inside there could be no fighting it. She watched as Vance retrieved his badge, said goodnight, slid inside the police car, and drove out of the parking lot.

When she turned to Danny, she said the only thing she could think of. "He was right. He's not anything like a brother."

CHAPTER TWELVE

Piper waited forty minutes to call Vance.

"I have a confession to make," she said.

After several heartbeats, Vance said in a low and controlled voice, "I'm listening."

Piper took a deep breath and blew it out. "I really, really want to bake something in your father's kitchen."

"You want to what?"

Her words tumbled forth as she paced around her bedroom. "I was planning to camouflage this as a request to contribute to brunch tomorrow, but the truth is, from the moment I saw that gourmet kitchen with that La Cornue French range I haven't thought about much else. I have this amazing cinnamon roll recipe that I make from scratch. I can bring everything I—"

"You cook?"

Piper had to pause a second to collect her thoughts. She honestly didn't understand his question. "Of course, I cook," she said. "But I'd rather bake. There's something about rolling out dough or mixing up batter, decorating a cake—"

"Piper!" Vance interrupted. "How long ago did Rock Surf leave?"

"Rock Surf?"

"Your date. Danny Boy."

"Oh," Piper said, taken aback. "I don't know. Pretty much right after you left, I guess."

Silence.

"Vance?"

"Piper," he said quietly, "I asked you to call me after he left."

Piper blinked a couple of times before a slow smile dawned. She stopped pacing and sat down on her bed. "Officer Evans, were you worried that your persuasive skills hadn't done the job?" she teased.

"I almost turned around twice," he admitted.

Piper flopped onto her back, laughing. "I came upstairs, changed clothes, daydreamed about cooking in that kitchen, and then I listened to your messages. I'm sorry I didn't pick them up earlier. Although…."

"Although?"

Piper rolled onto her stomach and lowered her voice. "I did kinda love you crashing my date," she said. "And as much as I hate to admit it, you sure look good in your uniform."

Vance chuckled. "I'm glad it worked out as it did then."

"Mmm, me too." She flipped over. "So what about tomorrow? Will you indulge my fantasy of preparing food in that five-star kitchen?"

"Piper, rest assured I'd be happy to indulge all of your fantasies."

"Ha. Since when? Last night you couldn't get me out of your place fast enough."

"Yeah, well you can just forget about last night. Last night I mistakenly thought it would be a good idea if we took some time to get reacquainted—to get to know each other as adults before I started indulging your fantasies. I didn't realize I was going to have to take a number and wait in line for a date, let alone to get you to call me back."

"Vance, all kidding aside, I'm terribly embarrassed about the way I threw myself at you. My only defense is that I got caught up in you appearing out of the blue, leaning against a Maserati, and whisking me away after all this time. I mean, when does stuff like that actually happen to me?"

"I'm here to serve."

Piper covered her eyes and stifled a groan. Because if Vance had any idea how often she'd imagined him coming after her and demanding they finish what they'd started at that bar—

"I got caught up in the fantasy, just like I did at The Charlie Horse on Cinco de Uh-oh—reading far more into the situation than there actually was." She sighed. "I'm not usually a flighty female, but when it comes to you, I have a very active imagination."

"Well, doesn't that sound promising."

"But you're right, of course. We do need to get to know each other as adults. Because when you pulled out your badge last night, it really struck a nerve."

"Yeah, and that's something you and I are going to have a little chat about, eventually. In the meantime, I'll do my best to come to terms with the fact that you make cinnamon rolls from scratch. Are we talking Pillsbury Doughboy, or Cinnabon?"

"Pffft. Don't make me laugh. Cinnabon wishes they had my recipe."

"I swear I don't know another woman my age who has any idea how to boil water. Lord knows Lolly doesn't cook."

"Lolly?"

"Lolly is my one and only female friend, other than you."

"Ah. And you and Lolly are how close?"

"Close."

"Close, as in the two of you have been intimate?"

"Not that close."

"So you've never slept with Lolly?"

"Nope."

"Did you want to?"

Silence.

"So you want to sleep with Lolly?"

"No. Lolly is my best friend's girl. Now before I knew that, I may have wanted to sleep with Lolly. But now that Lolly is sleeping with Brooks, and Lolly's mother is sleeping with my father, and I'm coaching Lolly's ex-boyfriend on how to pick up women, it's gotten a little complicated. So no, I have not, nor will I ever, sleep with Lolly."

"Hmm."

"Hmm, what?"

"That's a lot of Lolly going on."

"Which is why I'm very eager to add a little Piper to my life. And Lolly is eager as well. She knows our story."

"Our story?"

"Fourth grade, Cinco de Hell No, and you locking me out last night."

"She knows I locked you out last night?"

"Yes, because Genevra called her after dinner and told her that you are faaa-bulous. She couldn't wait to get the details."

"Genevra thinks I'm faaa-bulous?"

"They all do. My father, the Big Em, everyone. So getting kitchen privileges shouldn't be a problem. What time do you want to arrive?"

"Early. The dough needs to rise."

"Okay. Bring your bathing suit if you'd like. It's going to be hot and we can spend some time around the pool."

Piper sucked in a breath remembering her fantasy of him shirtless, in board shorts, dripping wet. "Officer Evans, you are playing right into my hands."

Pulling into the circular drive of the Evans Estate, Piper was supremely glad she'd finally traded her law student VW Bug in for her new I-am-on-the-road-to-success, sporty scuba blue Audi TT. She passed the beautiful carved wood front door and parked, stepping out from the beige leather interior and lifting her sunglasses to admire the mansion before her. *Wow.*

She checked the time, wondering if anyone would be awake at eight o'clock on a Sunday morning. It was likely no one but Vance knew she was coming since their conversation had ended after midnight last night. However, with her focus on that incredible kitchen and perhaps having the space to herself for a little while, she opened her trunk and started to fill her arms with supplies.

As she maneuvered her bounty toward the front steps, the door miraculously opened and standing in the threshold was a young man, shower fresh and handsome with thick brown hair. His surprised expression was replaced by an engaging smile as he jogged down the steps.

"Hey there," he called, coming forward, dressed in pastel Madras plaid shorts and a white button-down. He immediately relieved her of the overflowing grocery bag and the two flat pans clutched in her right arm. "Are you here to help with Sunday brunch?" he asked.

"I am," she said, gifting him with a smile while readjusting the rest of her supplies in her arms. He walked around her, grabbed the last bag out of her trunk and slammed it shut.

"I'm Davis. Davis Williams. I'm here to assist in any way I can," he offered, coming back to her side and pointing toward the open front door. "I'm a double black belt in karate by the way," he added as he fell into step beside her.

"Really?" Piper said, turning her impressed expression toward him.

"It's true," he smiled. "Inside this nice, safe exterior lurks the skills of an assassin." He winked at her. "Just wanted you to know there's more to me than meets the eye."

Piper gave a short laugh, immediately enamored. They stepped into the marble foyer, a circular balcony edged with a scrolled wrought-iron banister and short sets of stairs heading up on the right and left. Through the wrought iron she could see into the lower level of the mansion. She followed Davis up the right set of stairs onto a carpeted landing, glanced into the luxurious dining room to the right, and then followed him into the kitchen.

Davis set her supplies on top of the expansive kitchen island, the one she'd been dreaming about for the last thirty-six hours. It was topped with granite, but not like any she'd seen. It was blue, similar to a robin's egg, but richer with shades of lapis and pearl. She settled her wares on the smooth surface and ran a hand over it longingly.

Davis immediately started unpacking her bags.

"You don't have to do that," she said, starting to help him. "I don't want to keep you."

"Suddenly church doesn't seem so exciting," he said, smiling. "The heathens are still asleep. Since I'm the only Catholic in the bunch, I like to get up and out so I'm back before the entertainment begins."

"Entertainment?" Piper asked, curious.

"Oh, yeah. This place is full of entertainment. I've been here a couple of weeks and the one thing I've begun to understand is that you never know who is going to show up next."

"So, seeing me in the driveway?"

"Just played into my expectations," he said as he lifted two heavy mixing bowls out of a bag. "You didn't need to bring all this. I'm pretty sure somewhere in all these cabinets they'd have exactly what you'd need."

"I'm trying hard not to impose," she said as she turned the French range to preheat, inspecting it inside and out. "I'm not even sure they know I'm here," she said, standing up and smiling. "I'm kind of forcing the issue because I wanted to roll out dough on this granite and bake in that oven."

She pulled her apron from a bag and lifted it over her head, wrapping the strings around her back and tying them in the front. When she turned around, Davis was right there backing her up into the corner of the counter by the oven. She put a hand on his chest and let out a nervous laugh as his hands pressed against the edge of the counter on either side of her waist. He bent down so they were eye to eye.

"As I mentioned before, I'm here to assist you in any way I can," he said quietly. "Now, perhaps you'd like to tell me your name so we can become better acquainted."

Piper could hardly speak around her nervous grin. The double black belt had captured her attention in a way she hadn't expected. He was delightfully charming and obviously playful. She noticed his eyes eventually landed on her mouth, which caused her to lick her lips self-consciously and answer him quietly. "I'm Piper Beaumont," she said.

"Piper Beaumont," he said, testing her name with a smile. "That's a pretty name. Piper," he repeated. "Where have I heard…." Suddenly Davis straightened. "Damn." He stepped backward and held his hands in the air. "You're the one they've been talking about," he accused.

"Really?" she said, overeager and delighted. "What have they been saying?"

"Hmm," Davis thought. "Well, they were all in bed together when I walked in and—"

"Stop! Who was in bed together?"

"Vance, Lolly, and Brooks," Davis said. "Yesterday morning I walked in on them and I believe they were talking about you."

Piper blinked a couple times as she held her breath, telling herself she hadn't heard him correctly. "What do you mean 'they were all in bed together?'"

"Oh. Not like that—although I have to admit when I first walked in I thought it was just like that," Davis said, leaning toward her. "Because, you know, they are close. Really close. And I just wasn't sure exactly what the three of them have worked out. At first I was disgusted, because really—Lolly's not like that. And Brooks, hell, Brooks isn't like that either."

"And Vance?"

"And Vance what?" came the smooth baritone from her left.

Piper turned abruptly to find Vance coming through the French doors. He was dressed in running attire and using a towel to wipe sweat from his face, brow, and neck. He came forward and smiled. "Sorry I'm late," he said as he leaned over and touched his lips to hers without getting his sweat-laden body too close. "Did Pinks show you in?"

"Pinks?"

"Davis here."

Piper's head was spinning, unable to remember Davis' name or what they'd been talking about now that Vance was standing in front of her in his skintight spandex shirt. His hair was slicked back, his biceps were bulging. The definition of his chest and the flat plane of his torso were causing heart palpitations. And the exposed parts of his tanned legs that extended from loose, long shorts were firm and shapely, covered lightly in dark hair. Even his ankles were sexy, she thought as her gaze traveled down, and his socks and running shoes were nothing if not just plain cute. *Dear Lord.*

Davis came to her rescue. "We were just getting acquainted. I was offering to help."

"He mentioned you were in bed with Lolly," Piper said, still feeling caught inside some sort of stupor.

Vance turned his head in Davis' direction. "Well, thanks for that, buddy," he said as if Davis had done him a favor. "That was probably a huge help."

Vance turned back to Piper and wrapped the towel around his neck, holding on to both ends. He nodded his head back toward Davis. "Smart. Ninja-fied. Obsessed with Lolly," he said in way of explaining.

"What about you?" she asked. "Are you obsessed with Lolly?"

Vance leaned his head toward his shoulder, looking at Piper with a gentle smile. "Not anymore. She's got a place in my life and she's not going anywhere. I'm happy with that."

"You love Lolly." Piper said it as a statement.

"I do," Vance admitted, clasping Piper gently by her upper arms. He spread his legs to make himself shorter and looked into her eyes. "I love Lolly. Lolly and I are having a baby brother together. And we are very excited. We are also standing up for our parents at their wedding. And Lolly takes care of my boy, Brooks. These days he's a lot less tense and angry. There's nothing not to love about Lolly. Just ask Davis here."

Piper looked over at Davis.

"Yup. Hard not to love Lolly," Davis agreed.

"Does Duncan love Lolly?" Piper asked, bringing her gaze back to Vance.

"No. Duncan does not love Lolly," Vance said. "Duncan loves Annabelle. But Annabelle loves Lolly, so ipso-facto…. Now my dad, he really loves Lolly. He calls her Dynamite."

"Dynamite?"

"Because she has a tendency to explode."

"She didn't do that when we were dating," Davis said.

"You didn't know how to light her fuse," Vance replied without taking his eyes from Piper.

Davis stomped off in a huff but Vance said to Piper, "Don't worry about him—he's doing fine."

Piper shook her head quickly as if trying to return to her first concern. "But you—you…love Lolly?"

"I do. She found a way to help me stop abusing myself and others—which probably started around the time I ran out on you. I am a different man standing in front of you today because of Lolly. So, yeah, I love Lolly and frankly…you should too."

Piper simply nodded. What could she do? "Okay, then," she said, resigning to jump on the bandwagon.

An hour later, Piper was greeted with a surprised laugh as Genevra appeared in the kitchen looking as lovely and cheerful as a morning rose. "To what do I owe this pleasure?" she asked delightedly, offering

Piper a happy grin. Then her gaze landed on the length of rolled-out pastry sprinkled with a combination of butter, cinnamon, sugar, and nuts. "Wow," she said, her eyes going wide. "That looks amazing."

Piper started to roll one of the long ends of the pastry, feeling a little self-conscious being caught red-handed in the beautiful kitchen. "I hope you don't mind," she said, sending Genevra a shy smile as she worked. "Vance invited me to breakfast and I took advantage of that as an opportunity to cook in this kitchen. I'm a closet baker, and the kitchen in my condo is a bit cramped."

Genevra held up her hand. "Say no more, I completely understand. Which is why I insist on cooking breakfast here. Isn't it wonderful?" she asked with renewed amazement, looking around as if she'd never been here before.

Piper laughed. "I see we are cast from the same mold."

"Mmm. The kitchen in my cottage is old and tiny. When I'm in here, I feel like I'm the host of a cooking show. I'm inspired to create."

Piper expertly finished rolling the length of dough into a long log. Then she dug out a string of dental floss. "What are you going to do with that?" Genevra asked.

"I found if I try to cut the sections with a knife, they flatten and warp." She slipped the center of the string underneath one end of the dough. "But, if I cut with the floss…" she said, crossing the ends over the top and pulling tight, demonstrating as the floss cut through, "…I get a nice, round bun to bake."

"Perfect," Genevra said, looking on and admiring the now-exposed cinnamon swirl. "Can I try?" she asked.

"Sure." Piper handed her the floss and watched as Genevra cut the next cinnamon bun off the end of the roll.

"One more." Genevra laughed. "This just works so well."

As the two women cut the long log into a dozen jumbo-size rolls and carefully transferred them onto two jelly roll pans, they chatted about similar recipes and what else Genevra planned to make for breakfast.

"Vance and his father don't eat a lot of grits, but Davis and I love them, so I always make those," Genevra said. "Emelina's favorite breakfast is Eggs Benedict, and I have an amazing Béarnaise recipe which she enjoys, but she also has a sweet tooth, so your cinnamon rolls will please her to no end. I think we should go ahead and start the grits on the stove, fry up a lot of thick-sliced bacon and put it all in the warming drawer until your rolls are ready. Then at the last minute, we'll scramble up a platter of eggs adding a little feta and green onion for flavor."

Piper smiled realizing Genevra had made her mammoth cinnamon rolls the focal point of the meal. She was as gracious as she was beautiful, Piper thought. And if Lolly was anything like her mother, Piper was sure she'd love her indeed.

The women worked together, sharing cooking strategies and recipe tidbits. Emelina came in elegantly made up for a social event with her hair beautifully coiffed, wearing a loose pair of white linen slacks and an orange gauzy top. And when she recognized Piper standing in her kitchen draped in a splattered apron, she clapped her hands together in delight and declared that a round of Mimosas would be just the ticket.

As Piper sipped her champagne cocktail, slivered the onions into chives, and chatted merrily with the older women, she felt at once a great longing for her own mother, and a bubbling joy at being included here so completely.

When she began transferring her fresh-from-the-oven cinnamon rolls onto a large, elegant platter and drizzling them with a thin vanilla-enhanced icing, Emelina left to set the patio table with placemats, cloth napkins, and silverware. Piper turned toward the windows, her breath catching as she spied Vance coming from the pool house.

As if aware of her fantasy, after having "pumped iron" and showered, he was dressed in board shorts and nothing else. Oh, he had a shirt in his hand, Piper noticed, but the blue Hawaiian flowers printed on his white swim trunks rode low on his hips as he sauntered—as if in slow motion—along the pool, giving her exactly what she'd longed for: a glimpse of Vance without his shirt.

Her lips parted in awe at his tanned torso, her eyes noting the curve of his broad, muscled shoulders and how they pinched before spreading into well-defined biceps and lengthening into solid forearms. One part of her mind immediately went off on a merry tangent imaging those arms drawing her to him, sliding around her, pulling her close. She felt her body flush in tingling response as her eyes traveled over the sleek expanse of his chest.

Sculpted pectoral muscles over firm abdominals, for God's sake. And the man walked around like this was no big deal. Her own breasts ached and, out of the corner of her eye, she noticed Genevra had come to stand by her side.

"He really is quite something," Genevra offered, sounding as enraptured as Piper felt.

Piper let a long sigh escape, feeling at ease with the woman by her side. "I'm literally having trouble forming a thought," she said honestly. "I believe I am stupefied."

Genevra gave a short laugh. "That's exactly how it started for me with Hale. We were supposed to be discussing business and I couldn't get my head out of the bedroom."

Piper gave a short huff of acknowledgment and turned, wiping a tear from her eye. "He's far more than I can handle," she said, trembling. Shocked by her own response, she busied herself with the rest of the icing.

"Piper," Genevra called softly in wonder. "Surely you don't believe that," she said, laying a comforting hand on her back. "Vance is just a man, albeit a darn good-looking one." A laugh broke forth from both women.

Piper sniffled. "He's a lot of man," Piper insisted, "and the two of us have history which hasn't been thoroughly disclosed."

"Bah," Genevra waved her concerns away. "The two of you have today. Enjoy that. Be present for that." She pulled out the warming drawer to retrieve the bacon.

"How the hell did I get this lucky?" boomed a voice at the end of the kitchen island.

Piper lifted her head to find Hale Evans' joy-filled expression.

"Sticky buns the size of my head, more bacon than is bound to be good for me, my gorgeous fiancée pregnant and practically barefoot in my own kitchen—I am in heaven," he exclaimed. "And Piper, I'm assuming by your sunshiny presence, the boy has yet to muck things up. My pride is almost unmanageable."

Piper allowed herself to be caught up in his joviality. With a brilliant grin, she lifted the heavy platter and carried it to him, happy when he started to salivate. "They are cinnamon rolls," she corrected haughtily. "But I do have a sensational sticky bun recipe I'd be happy to come back and bake for you."

"By all means." He lifted the platter from her hands and headed out onto the patio.

Smiling, Genevra directed her to take off her apron and pointed down the hall to the powder room. "Wow him," she ordered. "It'll take a few minutes to get everything on the table, so I want you to put your bathing suit on. If you didn't bring one, I have one you can borrow."

Piper stood frozen in a daze. "Are you sure?" she whispered, untying her apron. "That might be a little...much for breakfast."

"Fight fire with fire," Genevra suggested. "Besides, hitting him with a one-two punch ought to even the playing field."

"One-two punch?"

"Your cinnamon rolls and that body in a bikini. Trust me. If he's anything like his father, the upper hand will be yours."

CHAPTER THIRTEEN

When Vance saw his father lay Piper's cinnamon rolls on the large umbrella-covered table, he leaned toward his father's ear and said, "She's a lawyer who likes to bake. And from the looks of it, she's apparently good at both."

Hale straightened and licked his finger which had managed to find its way into a pool of icing at the edge of the platter. "It's just a crying shame she's so unfortunate looking."

Vance bit back a smile. "I'm doing my best to overlook it." He clapped his father on the arm. As Hale seated his grandmother, Vance moved toward the kitchen and was met at the French doors by Genevra, who thrust a platter of eggs and bacon into his hands.

"Take these and sit," she commanded. "Piper is powdering her nose and will be out in a minute."

Pinks arrived next with a tray containing tall, slim glasses, an ice bucket, and a glass pitcher of Bloody Marys. "I'm trying a new mix," he said to the table at large. "It already has horseradish in it, so everyone take care." He glanced around. "Where's Piper?"

"She'll be out shortly," Genevra said, indicating the men should sit. "Let's go right ahead and begin, shall we? I'm sure she doesn't want the food to cool."

"Genevra, here is a Virgin Mary for you." Pinks handed her a glass. "Miss Emelina, here's yours just the way you like it. I've added Genevra's shot to yours, making it a double bloody—or a double Mary, whichever you prefer."

"Bound to make you doubly merry, Abuela," Vance said as he

took a glass from Pinks. He stirred the red concoction with the long, leafy celery stalk and then took a hearty sip, which he proceeded to sputter out of his mouth and down his white T-shirt as he tried to swallow, breathe, and stand all at the same time.

The scrape of his chair against the stone pavement brought curious gazes, and soon the entire table joined Vance in watching the playful vision of femininity that was one Piper Beaumont make her way out the French doors and over to the table.

All three men stood, mouths agape, napkins in their hands, as Genevra and Emelina eyed one another and carried on filling their plates as if nothing out of the ordinary was happening.

Vance was stunned speechless as he took in Piper's striking appearance. Her hair, held in place by shiny, little clips, was tucked up into a hot, curly mess on top of her head leaving the slender column of her neck temptingly exposed to the sun's rays and, dear God, his mouth. She wore a cover-up that did anything but, as it was crocheted in loose stitches with a plunging V-neckline. The teeny-weeny polka-dot bikini underneath that tangle of string was mesmerizing for what it exposed. Her waist—tiny and tucked, tempting him to try to circle it fully with his hands. Her cleavage—full and lush, tempting his mouth and hands at once. Her thighs—sleek and enticing, tempting his groin to stir without remorse.

The bit of fabric also stirred his imagination for what it did manage to conceal. His mind began undressing her, trying to solve the mystery of the shape of her breasts, the hue of her nipples, and the color and texture of the hair at the juncture of her thighs. He imagined the two of them on a deserted white-sand beach, him laying her down, stripping her naked, and exploring her succulent body with his hands and mouth.

"Snap out of it," his brain shouted as he stood daydreaming like a drooling simpleton while his father pulled out the chair between them and helped Piper be seated at the table. "Get a fucking grip," he told himself as he felt his tongue drag over his lips, his napkin dangling in front of his shorts. But his brain had been short-circuited and he continued to stand even though Piper was seated beside him and reaching for something on the table.

When she looked up at him in question, with those plump,

raspberry-colored lips straining toward the level of his crotch, it took every ounce of self-discipline he possessed not to outwardly groan. He didn't trust himself to speak, but managed to place a hand on the table and lower himself carefully into his chair. He reached for a glass of water and drank it down, noticing that across from him, Pinks had donned his new pair of shades. Sunglasses so dark that no one could see where his eyes landed. It irritated Vance to no end that Piper was seated across from The Ninja. His foot lashed out and struck the asshole in his shin. "Eyes on your plate," he ground out quietly, hoping the conversation around him swallowed the remark for all but Pinks.

The Ninja glared at him as if his feelings were hurt, but Vance didn't feel an ounce of regret. He was staking his claim.

Before Vance's blood pressure could spike and blow off the top of his head, a gentle hand landed on his forearm. He felt his eyes close and the tension ease throughout his body, immediately soothed. It was the touch he remembered from all those years ago, and if he had been alone, he would have cried like a baby, letting the emotion of its return surge through him. Because the touch Piper bestowed on him now performed the same feat of magic it had in the weeks following his mother's abrupt departure. When there was no one else willing or able to comfort him, it was her touch that had found a way.

He forced his mind to reach for solace. Then he nudged his emotional state into gratitude, and when he was able to fully feel it, he turned his attention to Piper and granted her a small, intimate smile.

Her baby blue eyes twinkled over a hesitant grin, as if she had cause to be unsure of herself where he was concerned. He wanted to tell her everything right then. About her touch and its overwhelming effect. About how he remembered it so strongly from twenty years ago. How it was probably the one memory that had led him to seek her out after all these years. And how her touch was most likely what had triggered his panic attack the night he left her on the dance floor five years before.

Instead he leaned down and lightly kissed the spot between pink cheek and delicate ear. It must have tickled because she tucked the spot against her shoulder and rubbed as she let out a short laugh.

The sound loosened the invisible restraints confining his limbs, and he reached a hand behind her bare neck and stroked the tender skin with his fingertips.

He was in deep and it scared him. Piper was his childhood savior and his hologram. As he stared across the table at his father's fiancée who glowed with carefree happiness as she chatted about the latest wedding plans, Vance wondered if he'd ever be able to make Piper feel like that. Make Piper want to tie herself down to the likes of him. A broken man looking to be made whole.

Christ Almighty. A broken man looking to be made whole? Vance cringed inwardly. *What a fucking drama queen.*

He needed to lighten up and he needed to do it now. Taking hold of his Bloody Mary, Vance downed the sucker. He refilled it to the brim also freshening Piper's. By way of apology, he topped off Pinks' while he was at it. A little alcohol on a Sunday morning never killed anyone—even if he was on duty later that evening. Which reminded him that Piper had kicked Danny Boy to the curb and shown up for brunch because Bad Cop had told her to as only Bad Cop could. So he doubted that a sniveling confession about the soothing power of her touch would go a long way to enhance the state of his manhood in her eyes. Yeah, he'd best keep all that to himself for now. If Bad Cop was the one who had the woman hooked, he better rely on Bad Cop to reel her in.

Gradually, the shock of Piper's smokin' hot body on Vance's nervous system eased from a volcanic blast down to a simmering pool of lust settling in the center of his swim trunks. At least his brain had begun to function enough for him to chime into the conversation now and then, and to actually taste the complexity of Piper's soul-stirring cinnamon rolls. The accolades shouted from all ends of the table were not exaggerated. Apparently Ms. Beaumont not only had a talent for winning cases and making grown men weep, but her culinary skills, at least when it came to sugar and pastry, were also off the charts.

The breakfast passed pleasantly with most of the focus directed at Piper, although the catalyst that had precipitated her law degree remained a mystery. Eventually Emelina enlisted The Ninja's help with clean-up while encouraging Hale and Genevra to sit and continue conversing with Piper and Vance.

"Well, I'm just going to have to come out and ask," Piper said, sounding a bit apologetic. "But for the life of me, I have not been able to figure out how Davis fits into this family."

"No?" Hale teased. "You haven't figured out that Davis is my future stepdaughter's ex-boyfriend who arrived on our doorstep uninvited, yet talked himself into a nonexistent internship while secretly planning to win Lolly back or, at the very least, to learn how to seduce the pants off a myriad of other unsuspecting young women? I mean, what could be more obvious?"

Vance was fully amused by the look on Piper's face, a cross between shock, horror, and incomprehension.

"He's darling," Genevra defended. "We've adopted him as one of ours. And while I have no idea if he's managed to seduce the pants off anyone, I can tell you that he's been indispensable around here. He's taken over a significant role in the planning and execution of our wedding."

"But mostly he works for my dad and me," Vance said, bringing Piper's attention around to himself. He took one of her hands in both of his and began stroking her narrow, little fingers, realizing he and Piper hadn't talked much about anything beyond their shared past. "We've recently gone into business together," he explained. "And in just a couple of short weeks, Davis has found us office space, managed to have it renovated, cleaned, and furnished, and has hired a graphic artist to come up with a logo, which he's having made into a very large shingle for us to hang outside the door. The Ninja is smart, aggressive, and is doing just fine with the ladies." He glanced over at Genevra. "He's not winning Lolly back, but I think he's made his peace with that."

"So when will I get to meet the infamous Lolly?" Piper asked.

Genevra glanced up and nodded her chin toward the space behind the rest of them. "I think now is good a time as any."

❧

Piper turned her head in unison with Vance and Hale. Looking beyond the swimming pool, she watched as two heads crested the top of the hill, followed by shoulders, then bodies and legs in turn.

Piper noticed the couple chatted animatedly while swinging clasped hands between them. They walked toward the pool, but their faces were directed toward one another, oblivious to being the center of attention.

"Lolly and…?"

"Brooks," Vance said. "Brooks Bennett. Best friends since high school. He and I played baseball together here and at State."

"Mmm." Piper returned her attention to the ones on approach. Brooks Bennett was big and handsome with short copper curls, broad shoulders, and a square jaw. He wore navy board shorts under a loose fitting T-shirt and on his feet were athletic shoes.

"He's been the Golden Boy of Henderson for longer than he cares to remember," Vance offered. "The good cop to my bad. And with me as his campaign manager, he'll be running this town in just over a year. We're putting together a plan to inspire economic growth with low rent and tax incentives for new and existing businesses."

Lolly could easily imagine Brooks Bennett as the mayor of Henderson. And, like the rest of the men she dined with, she could plainly see that he was in love with Lolly and not afraid to show it.

His wide grin showered affection over the tall, lean brunette whose hair was pulled into a high ponytail and tied with a red bow. Lolly's short red shorts showed off the length and shape of her legs while her white tank top clung to her long, thin torso. She was athletic and only resembled her mother in facial features and coloring. Where Genevra was soft, round, and elegant, Lolly was firm, strong, and pretty.

It was about then Lolly noticed the table full of onlookers. She waved and then tossed Brooks' hand aside, breaking into a run. Brooks ran after her, picked her up, and threatened to dump her into the pool. With a shriek, she clung to him and ducked her head into his shoulder. Piper smiled at their fun, standing as they approached. Brooks placed Lolly back on her own two feet.

Brooks noticed her first, stopping and adjusting his stance as he settled in front of Piper. His muscular legs were spread wide and his large hands were clasped in front of him as he looked her over with an appraising grin. "This?" he said, shooting a quick but pointed look toward Vance. "*This* is Piper?"

"Piper?" Lolly said in awe, raising her sunglasses and setting them on her head. "Why…" she stumbled, searching for words, "you're…perfect. Isn't she?" she asked Vance, her eyes big and bright.

"She is," Vance agreed.

Lolly took her hand as Vance introduced them. "Piper, this is Lolly DuVal, my…well, my friend and soon to be stepsister. Take your pick. And this is Brooks Bennett."

Brooks couldn't get close because Lolly was standing directly in front of Piper, smiling at her like she was the last of a species thought to be extinct.

Piper couldn't imagine why she was being held under such bedazzled scrutiny until Vance stepped in to explain.

"Forgive my friends," he said, as he moved to stand closer to her side. "They have heard the legend and seem a bit starstruck."

"The legend?" Piper looked at Lolly and Brooks in turn as they grinned down at her.

"About fourth grade," Lolly said, nodding her head. "When you saved him from utter despair, allowing him to be happy while you took on his sadness. He told us that when you held his hand, it was that simple human—"

Vance's hand clasped over Lolly's mouth. "Aaaaand that's enough," he decreed.

But Lolly pulled his hand down below her mouth spouting, "And you're his hologram—" before Vance shut her up again.

Vance looked behind him and addressed Brooks. "This is a disaster. You know that, right?"

Brooks simply nodded, beaming his broad grin.

Vance leaned down and whispered in Lolly's ear as his green eyes held Piper captive. "Lolly," he said calmly, "Piper and I are in the process of getting reacquainted. It would be helpful if you would control any further outbursts regarding things told to you in confidence."

Lolly nodded. "Sorry," she said, as Vance removed his hand.

"I'm his what?" Piper asked immediately.

"His hologram!" Lolly enthused, only to find her mouth captured once again.

Hale howled with laughter as he got up. "Gentlemen, you have met your match. Son, if you've anything to confess to Piper, I suggest you drag her off and do it now. Or better yet, let Lolly handle it for you. The two of them seem able to communicate at the speed of light."

A muffled response was captured under Vance's hand. Both women dissolved into giggles over the absurdity of the situation, eyeing each other with gleeful anticipation of what the two of them could reveal to one another. It was in that moment that a bond was formed and Piper had to agree with everybody else.

There was nothing not to love about Lolly.

CHAPTER FOURTEEN

While Lolly and Piper chatted and laughed together stretched out on side by side lounge chairs, Brooks and Vance dangled their feet into the water at the far end of the pool, enjoying their view of the bikini-clad bodies. They had shed their shirts and splashed water on their torsos as the heat of the day became real.

"It's probably good they're getting along," Brooks offered.

Vance laughed. "You think?" he said, taking a long pull on a bottle of water. "Piper already has Annabelle labeled as her new best friend. Lord knows the two of them couldn't have gotten on any better than this." He pointed to the women. "Frankly, what's going on over there is just downright scary."

"Only because Lolly knows too much and is indiscriminately sharing it with your new girlfriend," Brooks jeered.

"Thanks for that."

"Just keeping it real," Brooks said, laughing. He ducked his head toward the water, but raised his eyes to covertly stare at Piper through his sunglasses. He lowered his voice. "Annabelle and Lolly may be a handful," he acknowledged, "but this one, with a body like that, yet so tiny you wanna pick her up and put her in your pocket—Christ. You're gonna be running interference left, right, and center. I cannot—for the life of me—imagine how you kept sweet, voluptuous Tinker Bell out of your bed the other night."

"Oh bro, that was nothing but sheer panic. Being that she's Piper—*and* the hologram. She's not just the one that got away; she's the one that got away twice. So, sue me for being a pussy and trying to think with my head and not my dick. It worked for you, didn't it?"

"I suppose," Brooks said, "but Tinker Bell is far from twenty-three, and I'm guessing she knows exactly what she wants. Frankly, it's a fucking miracle that all that sweet, soft, and vulnerable doesn't have a ring on her finger. Lolly may have been willing to knock her head against a brick wall for a time, but if you're interested in Tinker Bell, my advice would be to start a full-court press—now."

Vance appeared taken aback. "Listen," Vance said. "If this is about me staying away from Lolly—"

"No. No," Brooks insisted. "This has nothing to do with Lolly. This is about you. About what you need. Look, when I heard Piper was a lawyer, I figured she'd be a cool distraction but ultimately a long-term dead end. Because you don't need to be knocking heads with a woman who throws metaphorical punches for a living no matter how brilliant, beautiful, or savvy she is. But what you do need is that," he said pointing toward Piper. "A woman who likes to make pastry into poetry. A woman who is charmingly sweet and eager to like your crazy friends and family. Just five minutes in Piper's presence and I totally got why she's your hologram. She's sweet and has this whole nurturing side to her that you not only need but crave."

"Because my mother sucked."

"Well," Brooks said, "I wouldn't have put it that way exactly, but yeah." He nodded toward the girls. "Think for a minute about why you started to fall for Lolly. And I'm not talking about the bullshit physical stuff or the competitive insanity you two share."

Vance threw Brooks a pained expression.

Brooks held up his hands. "Fine. We won't talk about this."

After a few quiet moments, Vance moved his arms behind him and leaned back onto his hands. "Lolly talked to me—like I mattered," he admitted. "She didn't leave, even when I was a classic asshole. She wants me to be happy."

"She cares about you," Brooks expounded. "There is genuine affection there—so whether you are a classic asshole or not, nothing you can do or say will alter it. And that is something none of us can get enough of. Piper did that for you in fourth grade, which is why you never forgot her."

"Yes," Vance said, shifting his weight forward and wiping his hands against each other. "But we're not in fourth grade anymore, are we?"

"She likes you, and by some stroke of luck she's also available, so take advantage of that. I don't need to remind you there is more fun to be had now that you two are all grown up."

"She doesn't like cops," Vance grumbled. "Although..." He brightened. "She didn't mind Bad Cop busting up her date last night."

"Probably because you didn't throw your badge around."

"Oh, I threw the badge around. The badge is going to be thrown at every opportunity."

"Strange dating tactic."

"Love me, love my badge," Vance declared.

"You do remember you're not much of a cop, right?"

"Apparently I'm all cop when it comes to Piper. I swear to God, when she slipped off her heels to drive the Maserati, and I stood towering over her looking down into those baby blue eyes and all those Goldilocks curls, something in me just...." Vance turned the palms of his hands face up and rounded his fingers into claws, growling. "It was primal and urgent, and yeah—if I could tuck her into my pocket and keep her there I would."

"A Piper Pocket Doll," Brooks stated while bringing a water bottle to his mouth. He stopped it midway, noticing the trio walking up the path from the garage. "Well, what the hell do we have here?"

Vance's head shot up, a slow smile spreading. "I do believe our outlaw has arrived," he said getting up to greet the newcomers. Annabelle veered off toward Piper and Lolly, but Duncan James kept coming and so did all the long hair and loose limbs by his side.

"Jesus," Brooks said. "What the hell is with all the pink shirts?"

"I don't know," Vance grinned, watching Jesse James and his raspberry Izod saunter towards them. "But The Ninja clearly needs to see this. Pinks!" he yelled.

Davis descended from the French doors with a dish towel in his hand. "Get a look at this," Vance said, indicating the two James brothers as they approached. "Now that dude knows how to wear pink," he told him.

"Makes me think we're missing out on something," Brooks said. He looked across the pool and swore. "Fucking A. Would you look at that."

All three women were sitting up and taking in the scene as if Jesse James had walked off the cover of *Men's Health*. Their faces were bright and eager, their mouths stilled for the first time in an hour. Brooks looked again at Duncan's brother and tried to see him through their eyes.

The kid exuded cool. And it had little to do with how he dressed because, for the love of Christ, he was dressed like a sloppy Pinks. Colorful, prepped out, and even had a fucking lacrosse stick laid over the black duffle bag he carried. *What the hell was this? An invasion?* But from the worn flip-flops on his feet to the slicked-back hair and sunglasses, something about the way this kid carried himself with a tossed-about confidence gave him a magnetism that couldn't be missed at fifty paces. Jesse James was coolness personified, and with his likable grin, he drew you in, male or female.

Even Brooks, who claimed Vance Evans—the great seducer—as his friend, had never seen anything like it. He grinned broadly as he reached out his hand to welcome the boy to his clan.

Vance and Pinks responded likewise, with Pinks throwing out some mumbo-jumbo about the evil sport that was killing the quality of high school baseball. Thank fuck Vance had the sense to shut the two of them up before Brooks changed his mind and ran them both out of town. He still wasn't certain about Pinks' motives anyway. Although Brooks had to admit the guy was certainly likable.

"I'll take you inside to meet the family," Vance was saying, "and then The Ninja here can show you to your room."

"The Ninja?" Jesse asked, the right side of his lip lifted into a crooked smile.

"Double black belt," Pinks explained.

"Sweet." Jesse fist bumped Pinks.

"Yeah, sweet," Duncan said, dragging in a shitload of sarcasm.

"Bro." Vance laughed in the face of Duncan's surly glare. "Lighten up. It's a great day when Brooks and I finally get to meet the other James brother. Whatever The Outlaw's done, he starts with a clean slate here. We are all about the do-over and, trust us, we've got it covered," he assured the eldest James brother.

"So, what the hell did you do to get yourself kicked out of Nirvana?" Vance asked, turning his attention to Jesse.

Jesse snickered and nodded at the term. He scratched his unshaven jaw and looked a little chagrined as he said. "My heart has grown overly fond of a seventeen-year-old."

Duncan nudged his brother from behind. "Tell 'em the rest."

Jesse jerked his head and sighed. "We were caught in a compromising position."

"Dude!"

"Oh, man."

"Son of a—"

"Relax," Jesse told them. "It was consensual and days before her eighteenth birthday. On top of that *I* was not the aggressor, so you all can just stand down."

"Stand down?" Brooks asked pointedly while taking two slow, deliberate steps into The Outlaw's personal space. "Just so we're clear." He pulled off his sunglasses and tapped them against Jesse's chest. "Henderson is my town. My Nirvana. Everyone who lives here is like family to me. So while you happen to be a guest in *my* town, you do not so much as fucking *smile* at a female until Vance or I have checked her ID."

Brooks was met with silent anger straining to be released. If the kid was gonna blow, Brooks wanted to know now. "You got it?" he barked.

"Roger. That." Jesse spat.

"Ooookay then." Vance stepped in between the two of them and turned Jesse by the shoulder. He looked back at Brooks as he shoved Jesse toward the house. "Struck a tender nerve, did it?" he asked, scowling at Brooks. "Very impressive bad cop moment, however." He motioned for Pinks to follow him and then pointed to Brooks and Duncan. "You two chill. I've got this."

Brooks watched them go.

"He talking about you and Lolly?" Duncan asked.

Brooks faced his buddy and told him the truth. "Summers were always the hardest with Lolly and Darcy running around the house in nothing but bikinis. Fortunately, I was so much older, she was rather oblivious." He flipped his head toward Jesse's back. "How much trouble are we looking at here?"

Duncan shrugged. "I wish I knew. He's had no disciplinary issues in college that I'm aware of, and didn't have any in boarding school. The only time he seems to find his way into trouble is when he's under the same roof as my mother."

"The judge?"

"That'd be her," Duncan acknowledged. "The two of them have been pushing each other's buttons for years. I can't figure it out."

"What about your dad?"

"Dad and Jesse are cool. Dad didn't take the incident lightly, but even he thinks my mother is overreacting."

"Is the girl's family pressing charges?" Brooks inquired.

"No. Nothing like that. She turns eighteen next week, and she's crazy about Jesse. The sticky part is that our family has known her family for years. Actually, for generations, because my mom grew up with both of her parents every summer, and all of the grandparents knew each other socially. The kibosh has been put on this budding romance mostly to stop the spread of gossip. Because if you think Henderson's bad, shrink this town down to three-hundred houses and stick them on a gated peninsula. Henderson doesn't know the meaning of the word gossip."

"Doesn't sound much like Nirvana to me," Brooks said.

"I never thought so. Although Jesse is in love with the place. Kinda like you are here. So, Mom sending him away for the rest of the summer? It's kind of like you being banished to New York City."

"Dear God," Brooks shuddered. "Okay, I'll go a little easier on the kid. But this thing—with the girl?"

Duncan shook his head. "He's not talking about it. And his cell phone has been confiscated. Which leads me to believe—"

"That it wasn't all about sex," Brooks finished.

"No," Duncan agreed, his expression a little sad.

"Age may be just a number, but at her age, it's the law," Brooks said. "Probably best the two of them are separated for awhile."

"My mother's point exactly."

"So the mission is to drum up a little interest in age-appropriate girls?"

"Couldn't hurt," Duncan said. "And putting him to work would be an added bonus. The only thing Jesse has to put on his resume is camp counselor."

Brooks looked around the pool, the grounds, and the three pretty ladies sitting across the way. "It's starting to look like we could actually use one of those."

◈

Jesse James laid across the queen-sized bed tossing a lacrosse ball up and down. The overly zealous dude named Davis stuck his head in the door and asked, "Aren't you going to unpack?"

Rolling to a sitting position and flinging his legs over the side of the bed, Jesse stared at Davis. "What are you in for?"

"In for?" Davis laughed. "Like this is a prison? Hell, I bartered my way into this place. Originally for the love of a woman." He had the grace to look sheepish. "But, now I've landed this primo internship with a budding empire and I get to watch Vance up close and personal." When Jesse raised one eyebrow, curious, Davis went on. "Not like that, douche bag. The guy happens to be great with women and I'm…not. So," he said, with a self-deprecating grin, "the real internship is learning how to shake my nice, safe, boring persona."

Jesse's smile grew slow and eager. "You don't say?"

Davis tossed his chin toward Jesse's stick. "What position?"

Jesse looked down and grabbed the long handle. "Defense. You?"

"Middy. Played on the club team at NC State."

"I play for Princeton."

"You get in because of your grades or your lacrosse?"

"Both."

"Cool. Good season?"

"Beat Hopkins. Suffered a crushing defeat from Yale."

"Dude."

"I know," Jesse said, cradling the ball in the net of his stick. "Makes no fucking sense, does it?"

"None whatsoever. I'm from Baltimore by the way."

Jesse's interest perked up. "Really? I've got a lot of friends in Baltimore."

"Let me grab my stick and we'll throw the ball around. See how many degrees of separation there are between us."

"I'm down with that," Jesse said, following Davis from the room. "Why do they call you Pinks?"

"I was wearing pink shorts the night Brooks found me backing his girlfriend, Lolly, up against a wall. The same Lolly that used to be my girlfriend."

"Seriously?" Jesse asked. "I know he and Duncan are good friends, but that guy's an asshole."

"Farthest thing from," Davis corrected him. "But I'll let you figure that out for yourself. Although," he said, stopping just before they headed outside, "he's not a fan of lacrosse."

"Because he's some freaking baseball god. Yeah, I've heard the stories," Jesse said with a complete lack of enthusiasm.

"Okay. Good. Well, we don't want to piss him off, but since Henderson is in the dark ages without any sort of lacrosse program, I'm thinking of offering weekend clinics to introduce the game."

"I thought you said you didn't want to piss him off," Jesse smirked.

"Well," Davis said, smiling, "I don't mind pissing him off a little."

CHAPTER FIFTEEN

Vance dove into the pool and Piper's eyes followed his blurred form as he swam underwater toward her. She sat at the top of the circular cement steps with her legs calf-deep in the water and watched as his long-fingered hands and well-defined arms pulled his body up the steps. His hands touched her feet and then circled her ankles. She glanced over her bent knees as his head and upper body emerged through the surface of the crystal-clear water. And just like earlier that morning, the sight stole her breath as she marveled at the fullness of her fantasy come to life.

Water sluiced from Vance's hair down over his muscular shoulders and chest, leaving sparkling droplets in places that tempted her tongue. She covered her mouth instead.

"Why are you smiling?" he said, as a slow grin showed off white teeth which were dramatically enhanced by his midsummer tan.

She lowered her hand and leaned her face toward him, begging to be kissed. His body stretched forward, complying with a slow peck.

"Are we dating?" she asked him, licking at the water he'd left on her lips. "Lolly and Annabelle want to know."

"Yes," he said. "We are dating exclusively. Now come into the water so I can put my hands on you."

"You want to put your hands on me?" she asked over a cheeky grin.

"Constantly."

"I'm not a strong swimmer," she said, unfolding her legs and standing on the step.

Vance took her hand and began pulling her into the water. "I'll be sure to keep a tight hold on you then," he said through an easy smile.

She allowed him to lead her down the steps. "I mean, I can swim fine. I just don't…do that." She tossed her chin toward the laps Brooks and Lolly were doing up and down the length of the pool.

Vance glanced over his shoulder. "Oh," he said, bringing his attention back to Piper. "*Nobody* does that. They're just showing off."

She found footing on the last step and felt Vance's other hand skim around her waist underwater. He dragged her off the step and fully into the pool. Just a few paces forward, the water drifted above her shoulders, and she reached for him in an effort to keep her head above water.

"I've got you," he said quietly, pulling her up and against his chest, wrapping both arms around her lower back. An effervescent heat tingled behind her chest as she slid against his naked torso.

She circled her arms loosely around his neck and smiled, finding herself looking down at him for the first time. "This is nice."

"Very nice," he agreed. "I'd like to kiss you again but…." He gestured toward Duncan and Annabelle coming out of the pool house, having changed their clothes. "I'm afraid I'll forget this is not a private party."

"Mmm. Maybe you'll invite me to one of those sometime," she said, licking her lips as her eyes scrutinized his deep green irises.

"You got it," he said, pulling her down a bit so that the juncture of her thighs grazed briefly against his erection.

"Wow," she whispered wide-eyed, reaching to pull a wayward curl from her face.

"Been that way since you marched out of the house in a whole lot of nothing. Christ, you about gave The Ninja and me a heart attack."

"You deserved it. Who shows up to a family brunch wearing a swimsuit and bulging muscles?"

"Bulging muscles, huh? Sounds like a year of pumping iron in order to motivate my team has really paid off."

"Mhm. Must be some team," she commented. She felt his hand

drift over her backside. "I don't do laps and I don't lift weights," she confessed, gnawing on her bottom lip. She watched over Vance's shoulder as Lolly's long lean muscles kicked and pulled at the water. She looked back at Vance. "I'm not like Lolly. I'm not very athletic."

Nudging her with his chin, he scooted her face to the side and whispered against her ear. "If you can wrap your legs around my waist, you are athletic enough for me."

"Like this?" she offered and curled her short legs around his middle, hooking her ankles behind him.

He spouted a half choke, half laugh. "Exactly like that," he said, reaching behind him and unhooking her legs. His hands slid from ankle to outer thigh, causing the heat she'd felt stirring in her chest to cascade and gather deep in her core. His soft, silky touch was tantalizing, and she immediately understood why he'd dislodged her.

"Sorry. I keep forgetting this isn't a private party."

"Me too," he said, playfully placing a kiss on the tip of her nose.

"Hmm," she purred, just as she heard the patter of running feet and then felt a huge splash. She pushed herself away from Vance as an enormous shower of water soaked the two of them mercilessly.

"Sorry, Piper," Annabelle called from poolside as Piper spit and blinked while scraping sodden curls from her face. "I told him not to do it, but Duncan thinks a cannonball is the height of summer hilarity."

"It is," Duncan agreed, beaming at the disaster he'd made of Piper's hair. "If you don't want to get wet, stay out of the pool," he chided, diving under and heading to disrupt the two serious swimmers.

Piper scrambled to the steps where she began pulling all the clips from her hair, reinserting them to hold her curls back from her face. Then she dove back in and dragged Vance with her to help dunk Duncan under the water.

Splashing and chaos followed, and it didn't take long for all three men to look toward the glorious redhead lounging in her white bikini, high and dry and reading the latest edition of The Trident, her sorority's alumni magazine.

Duncan said quietly. "I will pay you good money if you throw that woman into the pool."

Piper gasped.

"Shh," Duncan said, eyeing her directly. "You know nothing."

Piper smiled her acquiescence as Vance and Brooks took the bait and slowly maneuvered their way to the steps. In a flash, Duncan had a hand wrapped around Lolly's mouth, preventing her from warning Annabelle. He lowered a brow at Piper again. "She could have warned you about the cannonball," he reminded her, which convinced Piper she could enjoy the antics guilt free.

After a shriek, a scramble, and some very loud full name enunciating, Annabelle Devine—Keeper of the Debutantes—landed fanny first in the pool. She came up surprisingly serene, her beautiful red hair as vibrant wet as it was dry, the ends still curling around her shoulders. And although her face was soaked, not a drop of makeup had smeared. She did however shout and fall ungracefully backward in the water as Duncan's head came up between her legs, trying to get her to perch on top of his shoulders.

"Come on, baby, let's try that again," he urged, pulling at one of Annabelle's long, graceful arms. "You can do this," he said cheering her on as he ducked under the water once again. This time he managed to hold on to Annabelle's thighs tight enough for her to find balance on top of his shoulders.

"Chicken fight!" Duncan yelled, and Brooks answered the call by diving under and bringing Lolly up on his large shoulders in one smooth step. The two of them looked like a giant alien transformer compared to Duncan and Annabelle and instead of putting her arms out and wrestling with Lolly, Annabelle covered her face and screamed as Lolly pushed her easily off Duncan's shoulders and back into the water.

Brooks laughed until his side hurt, still carrying Lolly on his shoulders. "Annabelle, that was just downright embarrassing," he shouted.

"Pool antics are not my forte," she said allowing herself to be brought back up on Duncan's shoulders. "But I'm a quick learner, so you two can just bring it."

Duncan smiled with pride and said, "That's my girl," as he did his best to help Annabelle stay on his shoulders.

Piper felt herself pulled back against Vance as she watched the antics. His chin rested on her shoulder. "I wouldn't mind having my head between your thighs, but there is no way you and I can compete with that," he said as Annabelle and Duncan fell back into the pool as one.

Piper blushed and laughed. He released her then, skimming his hands around her waist as he maneuvered in front of her and slowly backed her into the wall of the pool. He stood flat-footed with his legs spread, his feet on either side of hers. She bobbed on the tips of her toes and found herself drowning in the smoldering emeralds of his eyes. "Vance?" she said, as the chicken fight renewed behind him.

He leaned down and she closed her eyes, a well of chemicals releasing into her system, bubbling up from her midsection and heating her from the inside out. His lips touched hers in a soft caress as his fingers tickled her bare skin from hip to waist under the water. Her head went light and dizzy, and she centered herself by laying her flattened palm against his chest and feeling the heavy thud of his heartbeat beneath all that muscle.

He teased her lips as he did her body, barely touching anything at all but making her feel to the power of ten the impact of his unhurried and elegant assault. It was bliss wrapped up inside gentle torture and so exquisitely what she longed for that tears came to her eyes.

No longer aware of the sunshine, the pool, or the wild thrashing and lively curses flowing around her, Piper was enveloped in a cocoon of Vance Evans' gentle doting—her senses honed in exclusively on the velvet tips of his fingers, the rich plushness of his lips, the luxurious scent of his aftershave, and the scant taste of chlorine left on her lips by a light caress of his tongue.

She heard him suck in a deep breath as his lips trailed from hers. Her eyes fluttered, then a few beats later, opened to his heated stare. He sank down into the water then, moving a few paces back, bringing a dripping hand down the center of his face, and then shaking the drops off like a dog would toss water from his fur.

"How many others—" he started, but it came out harsh and gruff. He immediately stopped himself, closed his eyes, and seemed to fight for control. "What I meant is, how many dates, with men," he clarified, "are left on your calendar?"

Piper felt her smile go wide, her eyes locking on to his handsome face. "One," she said, and then she pushed off the wall and floated toward him feeling giddy and playful. "You want to know when it is?"

Vance's expression was stern as he pulled her around and cradled her in his arms. "You plan to keep it?"

"Only if you're going to come in, guns blazing, and bust it up."

"If you're keeping it, I'll definitely be busting it up."

Piper couldn't help the devious grin that pulled at her when she remembered how enticingly Vance had coerced her into sending Danny home. But eventually she relented. "I suppose that would be sort of mean, wouldn't it? To my unsuspecting date."

"Hey, you cannot be held responsible for the actions of a small-town cop with no jurisdiction."

Piper bit her lip and shot her eyes wide open, looking at Vance.

"Yes, those were the words you used in front of King Kong Friday night."

"King Kon—? Oh, Vance," she stuttered, between horrified laughs. "I'm—I'm sorry." She giggled and then stilled her mirth with a hand over her mouth.

"You should be," he scolded. "Those words have been branded over my pride. Trust me, I'll be dragging all that around for a very long time."

"Oh." She reached up and touched his cheek with her fingertips. "Forgive me. That was nothing but my pride getting in the way."

"Hmm." He eyed her suspiciously.

"I'll go ahead and cancel my date."

"Probably for the best. Speaking of, any sign of King Kong yesterday?"

"You mean Officer Stevenson, right?" At Vance's quick nod, she went on. "I saw him twice. Once while running errands and once while out with...you know—on my date. It was probably just coincidence. I'm guessing he lives in the area."

"Okay. What if we find out exactly where he does live, make sure it is a coincidence?"

"Vance, I really don't think there's a problem."

"I tend to agree," Vance said. "In fact, I like the guy. He gave me a little insight and—"

"Insight? What kind of insight?"

"Oh, Lawyer Beaumont," Vance warned, cocking his head and looking at her as if he were seeing her in a new light. "I have been made well aware of your courtroom antics."

"Antics?" She furrowed her brow. "There are no antics," she insisted.

"Oh, I can well imagine the antics," he scoffed. "Officer Stevenson related how you dangle him and his ilk like mice by the tail. Teasing and taunting and then making them out to be overzealous bullies in front of the judge."

Piper felt her cheeks flame. "I do not."

Vance's brows shot up into his forehead. "Really? I know how I felt when you laid me low for pulling out my badge."

"That was different."

"Maybe. Maybe not."

Piper blinked and saw all of her court appearances run like a movie reel inside her head. None of them gave her pleasure. All she felt was the anger every case stirred up inside.

"Baby doll," Vance said, pulling her out of her thoughts. He stroked a gentle hand over her cheek and kissed her lips. "I was teasing," he soothed. "You are good at your job. I wouldn't have told you that if I had thought it would upset you."

It had upset her. She didn't realize she made Officer Stevenson feel like a dangling mouse. But even if she had? She shook it off and worked up a false smile. "I'm okay." She waved it off.

"Are you sure?" Vance searched her face with genuine concern.

She felt her lungs constrict and tears well up into her eyes. She dipped below the surface of the water to cover it up as her mind groaned for the second time that day, *I miss my mother.*

When she emerged, Vance and she were being pounced upon by his friends, taunting them to join in their play. So they did. And though she was treated cautiously at first, eventually one good dunking by Brooks broke the newcomer barrier and she became a prime target for abuse, which strangely went a long way to soothe her aching soul.

Piper knew she shouldn't have agreed to poolside cocktails with Lolly and Genevra after Vance and Brooks headed off to work. But she was crazy about Genevra and eager for more of Lolly. Plus there was no reason to race back to Raleigh. So she showered and changed into the sundress she'd worn that morning, figuring one cocktail wouldn't hurt.

And it didn't, until Emelina insisted that since Hale was taking The Ninja and The Outlaw out to dinner, Genevra, Lolly and Piper should join her at the Henderson Country Club. Once there, Emelina ordered a bottle of her favorite Spanish wine and a glass was placed in front of Piper with a wink from a cute young bartender named Harry.

She vowed to sip it slowly and only drink half, but as the outrageous details of Genevra and Hale's whirlwind romance were dished up, along with Lolly's hilarious side comments, Piper forgot all about her hour-long drive back to Raleigh.

The laughter continued throughout dinner, and another bottle was opened and poured as they lowered their voices and eagerly shared past romantic mishaps, with Emelina winning the prize for the most outrageous and entertaining stories. Piper was grateful they never pressed her for information about Vance, especially the night five years ago when their chance encounter had changed the course of her life forever. In the back of her mind, she hoped that one day she'd be able to share that mishap with the same level of gaiety Genevra and Lolly shared the lack-of-condom stories that granted Genevra her two pregnancies.

Piper marveled at how mother and daughter could laugh and joke together over their adventures in life, and even though Piper expected that dreaded ache in her heart over the loss of her mother to burst forth at any moment, the longing did not come. She was content to simply be included, admiring the relationships in front of her.

CHAPTER SIXTEEN

The call came in at nine o'clock.

Sitting in the same police cruiser he'd commandeered to break up Piper's date the night before, Vance was literally spying on a group of teens gathered at the lake. His job was to do a drive-by and investigate only if anything seemed off. The group was small and peaceful. Just a bunch of kids sitting on the end of tailgates, probably talking, laughing, and enjoying being out of the house. But once Vance saw those very distinguishable Henderson High baseball caps, his curiosity was piqued and a strong sense of responsibility kicked in.

Those boys were his boys, and he wanted every one of them—even pain-in-the-ass Johnny Mac—to live long and prosper. That kid was too tall, too good looking, and too confident to have his arms around two different girls and not have it lead to trouble. With Brooks' wrath over Jesse James' sexual indiscretion ringing loudly in his head, he was not interested in having any sort of replay of that with one of his boys. And unfortunately for Johnny Mac, he was too easily identifiable. Vance was debating where the responsibilities of being a coach ended and being a cop began when his cell phone vibrated against his ass. He was surprised at the name on the screen.

"Harry!" he said as he picked up. "You trying to drum up business for your tequila shots?"

"I haven't poured one yet tonight. Figured that meant you were on duty. How are you this evening?"

"I'm fine, Harry. What can I do for you?"

"Well, I'm calling because I had the pleasure of meeting Ms. Beaumont at the club tonight."

"Is that right?" Vance said, his brows lifting. "How the hell did she end up there?"

"Your grandmother, sir. Ms. Beaumont was her guest for dinner along with Mrs. DuVal and Miss DuVal. I had the pleasure of waiting on the ladies, and I think it's safe to say they were all having a very good time."

"Hmm," Vance said, rubbing at the back of his neck, his forehead creasing. "One bottle's worth of a good time or two?"

"Now you know your grandmother, sir. She's a fine hostess. I opened two bottles of her favorite wine and Ms. Beaumont enjoyed her fair share. I'm not saying she was stumbling around drunk, but she's such a tiny little thing that even with the large coffee and bottle of water she requested for the ride home, I'm still a little concerned. If anything happened on my watch—"

"I'm on it," Vance said as he started the car. "How long has she been on the road?" He checked the time as he pulled out of the gravel parking lot.

"She's just walking out the door now."

"Harry?"

"Yes, sir?"

"I owe you one."

Vance clicked off his phone and cursed under his breath. "What the hell is she thinking?" He rubbed a knuckle back and forth over his lips as he drove, the gravity of the situation sinking in, causing his chest to tighten and his fears to explode. What if, after finally finding Piper, she managed to get herself hurt or worse over a couple glasses of wine? His stomach clenched at the thought. He pounded the steering wheel with the heel of his hand. "Drinking and driving? For Christ's sake, Piper, you're a fucking lawyer."

He drew in a long, seething breath. "I'll tell you what," he said on the exhale. "The lady wants jurisdiction, she's going to get jurisdiction." He reached over and flicked on the siren.

Planning to cut Piper off before she hit the interstate, Vance drove quickly, debating how to handle the confrontation. Like Harry said, she was a tiny little thing—couldn't weigh much more than a hundred pounds. Anything more than a glass of wine an hour would surely cause her to blow more than 0.08. A DUI was a big fucking deal in this town and any other, and it pissed him off to no end that Piper would put herself and others in jeopardy like that.

"Jesus!"

And where was Genevra? How the hell could she let Piper get in a car and drive back to Raleigh?

Vance was not happy—not happy at all. In fact, he was reaching a level of outrage he didn't know what to do with. He literally had to talk himself down. He turned off the siren once he started backtracking to the club, scrutinizing every car he passed looking for her sexy little TT.

When he reached the gates of the club his gut was so twisted in knots that he wanted to get out and hit something. Just punch a good, solid dent into the hood of the cruiser. Because as bad as the situation was, now that he'd somehow missed Piper, he had zero control over the outcome one way or another. If another officer stopped her, he couldn't intervene, and if they didn't....

"Goddamn it!"

Before he turned around to try to chase her down, he made a quick, jerky turn onto Country Club Drive, just to make sure she didn't have an accident in the damn parking lot. There wasn't but a handful of cars left in the lot. And would you believe it? The first one he spied was hers.

The jolt he felt course through his body was different from any other kind of relief he'd ever experienced. It was visceral. And in the time it took him to pull over and exit his vehicle, it threw water all over his sense of indignation and just about shut down his brain altogether.

His senses, on the other hand, had gone animalistic—alert and finely tuned. He noticed the Audi was not running, that the interior light was on, and the driver's seat was adjusted back from the steering wheel. Piper's head was bent low, maybe looking at something in her lap. As he drew close, he smelled coffee and citrus. Heard the dull beat of music. He caught himself just before he grabbed the door handle and yanked it open, realizing that she'd be startled if he did.

He stopped everything and simply stared. Thinking.

Then he slowly backed up, got in the cruiser, and drove back out of the drive.

Two hours later, Vance finally got what he'd been waiting for. Piper's car came out of Club Drive and turned to head out of town.

He rubbed a hand across his smile. All was right with the world. In fact, he thought as he started the cruiser and put it in gear, everything was just about fucking perfect.

He let Piper drive out of the neighborhood and down a stretch of secluded road before he flipped on his siren. Probably scaring the shit out of her, he thought. But he'd make it up to her. He'd happily make it up to her.

He pulled over behind her, shut down the siren and lights, and took his time exiting his vehicle. Her window was down as he approached the driver's side, and as he set his forearm on the top of her car and leaned over with a big grin, she turned and slapped him in the face.

"What the—?"

"That is not even funny," she shouted.

He rubbed his cheek, thinking it was a little funny. He tried to stifle a grin when he spoke, realizing she'd just played into his bad cop hands. "Neither is assaulting an officer. Now I'm going to have to ask you to step out of your car and keep your hands where I can see 'em."

"Vance!"

"There is no *Vance*," he said, wagging a finger at her. "You're dealing with Officer Evans now. Small-town cop with no jurisdic— Oh. Wait a minute." He held his hands out to the sides, jostling them toward the ground where he looked around at his feet. "Would you look at this?" He gave Piper his best dumb-shit, southern-boy smile. "I am actually standing in a *whole lot* of jurisdiction."

"Good Lord," Piper muttered.

"So," he said, sauntering forward and placing his hands on the edge of her door, "instead of flashing all of your fancy business cards around, I suggest you do exactly as I say, or you're going to find your big-city ass in a whole lot of small-town trouble."

"Are you even on duty?"

"Would I be driving that thing if I weren't?"

Piper's round cheeks drew taut, her plump lips flattening into a tight line. Vance watched as all the sparkle evaporated from her eyes and the soft, gentle temptress, who'd mesmerized him all day, turned into her job.

"Officer Evans," she snapped, her southern accent disintegrating with all hints of playfulness along with it. "It is highly unconscionable to use the power of your position to pull over a citizen without just cause."

Yeah, that bullshit is so not gonna fly.

It was like Friday night with Kong all over again, and there was no way in hell he was letting her pull that shit again. Ever.

"Piper," he said, leaning in, his voice low. "Get out of the car—now."

Her seatbelt snapped back. The Lawyer Beaumont did her best to stare him down as she exited the car, but Bad Cop did not relent. His emotions had been strung out too far over the last several hours and, on top of that, he shouldn't have to work this damn hard to get the girl to do what he wanted!

"Hands up against the car."

She stood firm, arms crossed over her chest, glaring at him as if those baby blues had the capability of turning him to stone.

He stepped forward, spinning her around to face the car. She gasped as he gripped the bare flesh of her shoulders, the contact immediately shooting energy from his hands to his chest.

Goddamn.

He closed his eyes and forced himself to take a deep breath. The lush citrus perfume of her hair and body mingled with the pine that surrounded them. The heat of the day had given into the comfort of night, and he found himself on a dark, secluded country road—a ball of raging desire battling back the caveman who longed to break through and take over.

He wanted Piper back. The soft, docile woman whose touch soothed and eased him. He wanted to coax her playful spirit to life. Remind her who she really was. So in measured increments, he released the hold on her shoulders until nothing but his fingertips were left to swirl lightly over the tender flesh. As she continued to yield, he let his fingers begin a slow trail, glancing oh-so-gently down the length of her arms, feeling goose-bumps rise underneath his touch. He let his fingertips glide around the circumference of her wrists and then scratched his nails lightly along the tops of her hands. He felt resistance drain from her fingertips, the tension melting from her arms, leaving them soft and compliant as his fingers closed around her wrists.

He allowed his chest to bump against her shoulders as he drew her arms out to the side and then on up, encouraging her hands to settle on top of the car. He stretched his palms flat over the backs of her hands, his bare forearms resting on top of hers. Every nerve ending from his knees to his shoulders stood alert at the soft, supple feel of that mere twenty-four inches of skin-to-skin contact.

Dear God, what would it be like to lay his naked body against her soft, pliant flesh? He sucked in a breath through his teeth, the very thought of it making his blood heat.

His voice was rough, jagged, and barely audible as he forced it through his dry throat. "Spread your legs," he ordered, his foot instinctively feeling the space between hers. His lower body stepped closer and he straightened. Then he whispered over the slight hollow where firm shoulder transformed into tantalizing neck.

"This is just a game, Piper." He wondered at what had turned his sweet, unselfish classmate into a fractious lawyer. "Play along with me," he coaxed. He kissed the spot below where his lips hovered. "No real cops. No real lawyers. Just you and me, playing a game." He wrapped his fingers in between hers and gripped her hands. "Okay?" he whispered against her ear. Her breathing had become labored, and when she nodded, her curls caressed the side of his face. He turned his head, sinking his nose into her hair and growled.

He twisted her around to face him, his lower body leaning in, pinning her against the car. He caught her face between his hands and kissed her lips as he asked, "Have you been drinking?"

She nodded her head as a submissive squeak erupted. He continued to kiss her lips, the corners of her mouth, and her jawline as he interrogated her.

"Wine?"

"Ah-humm," she purred.

That made him smile. "Good wine?"

"Mmm." She tilted her head back to give his mouth better access to her neck.

"Jesus, Piper," he whispered against her neck. He pressed his weight more fully against her while his fingers caught themselves up in her curls. His blood was burning him from the inside out, raging with a desire to feel her beneath him. He untangled his hands and spread them, gripping the top of the car. His mouth sought hers, his lips wanting more, his body hard and firm pressing up against her, then easing back. "Open for me," he said against her mouth, his tongue playing at the seam of her lips. Her lips parted enough to let his tongue slip through and he groaned as the moist warmth assaulted his senses. That first slide of tongue against tongue blew a fuse collapsing his mind into darkness, while the sensation of it reached out and cupped his balls.

Piper's body unfurled, awakening and responding to the masculine energy that sought to plunder. Her breasts had never felt more sensitive, fuller, or more near bursting with the longing for large hands and demanding lips to caress and soothe the ache within. Her hips released and expanded, her pelvis offering itself up for communion. She was aware of the softening between her thighs, of everything opening and growing damp. Her scent a welcoming call to the strong, demanding, undeniable force pressed so dearly against her body.

Her jaw went slack at the first touch of his tongue, her mouth relinquishing all control to his pleasure. She sighed beneath his groan, seeking to cater to his every whim. Only her hands were tense, clutching the shirt at his sides so that he could not pull away. So that he could not run.

So he could not run.

The trembling started in her heart, and Vance must have felt it the moment she realized what was happening. How he was so in tune to her she couldn't figure, although perhaps the tensing of muscles as the panic began to consume her was his clue. Instead of open and compliant, she felt her body closing, as if every internal organ was bracing itself for the shock of disappointment.

"Fuck," she heard Vance whisper over the top of her bent head. "Piper? Baby doll? What the hell just happened?"

"I'm sorry," she said, shaking her head. He gripped her chin between his fingers and raised her face so she'd have to look him in the eye.

Those green orbs worked hard to bank his lust while they searched her eyes for an answer. "You were right there with me. I know you were. Why the sudden change?" His face masked nothing. He was dumbfounded and earnest in his inquisition.

If she had any thoughts of trying to shrug this off, looking at him now set all that aside. Vance was not a boy who could be put off with some flimsy excuse. He was a man—with a man's heart, a man's needs. He stood before her full of integrity, and she needed to honor that and match it fully.

She licked her lips and blinked back the emotion threatening to puddle in her eyes. "I was," she agreed. "I was right there with you." She laid a hand against his chest, stroking her thumb over his heart. "And it felt really good." She swallowed. "But then I remembered… back at the bar…the night you…ran."

"And?"

"And…I don't know…I sort of went into a panic attack, afraid you were going to do it again."

Vance's mouth hung open in exasperated disbelief. His hand lifted toward her only to fall and slap against his thigh. He looked away, his body huffing in frustration. And when he looked back, his features were strained and tense. His eyes shifted across her face. Finally, he took a step back and said, "Go home."

"Vance—"

"Piper, it's late. The reason I stopped you was to thank you for taking the time to sober up before driving home. The rest of this," he said, waving a hand between them, "is clearly nothing but a train wreck. I've already apologized for running out on you—*five fucking years ago*—and I refuse to continue to be kicked in the shins for whatever some asshole cop did to you back in Ohio."

Piper's lungs constricted and the top of her head tingled as she watched him turn and stalk away. She searched for something to say that would stop him, but her mind was void of all words. Just empty space between her ears and a deep sense of grief saturating her body.

But then Vance turned of his own volition and stomped back to her. Her heart clung to a bit of hope until he started in. "You never should have been a lawyer," he said with such vehemence it caused her to shrink back. "That is not who you are. You are soft and sweet, kind and gentle. That lawyer you channel? She's nothing but a simmering pot of anger ready to boil over at the least provocation. You changed the entire course of your life to pay back one fucking cop. Well, I am not him." He stalked off to his car, pulled a U-turn, and left her standing on the side of the road.

Alone.

Piper assumed she was in shock. During the entire ride home her mind remained alert but glaringly empty, cut off from the rest of her body, which grew wearier by the mile. She pulled into her building's lot around midnight and saw Officer Stevenson sitting on the front steps. Her first thought was to rip him a new one, but as Vance's words, "nothing but a simmering pot of anger" echoed through her, she fell deeper into fatigue.

Leaving everything packed in her trunk, she dragged her purse out of the passenger seat and made the trek to the front steps, surprising herself by climbing the stairs and sitting down next to the giant.

"I'm sorry," she said quietly, then leaned her head against his huge arm and sobbed like a baby.

CHAPTER SEVENTEEN

To say Piper suffered through the week from hell was putting it mildly. Her schedule was jammed with court appearances in Raleigh, Durham, and Chapel Hill as all the rowdy and ridiculous senior shenanigans caught by the cops during graduation week finally landed on the court dockets. Most of the infractions were minor, nothing that a hundred other students had gotten away with the same night of her clients' unfortunate incarcerations. Public intoxication, public urination, possession—that one pissed her off the most—disturbing the peace, failure to heed first warning, blah, blah, blah into a relentless menagerie of cases she'd manage to get dismissed or reduce to fines while in her sleep.

The interesting ones, including the very titillating public sex charge where her clients were caught with their pants down humping loudly in Duke's Rubenstein Library, would take a little more of her ingenuity. Especially since her clients weren't just having sex surrounded by rare books and artifacts, but were alleged to have spread out specific materials and had sex *on top of* rare books and artifacts. Apparently they were history majors.

At every court house, Officer Stevenson stood outside the front doors as she entered and was there when she left, watching until she drove off in her car. Sometimes he was in uniform and sometimes he wasn't. They never exchanged words. Most of the time there was simply a brief nod, although by the end of the week Piper was surprised to be on the receiving end of a wink and a smile more often than not.

She didn't understand why the man was following her, because if his intention was to do her harm or argue about the justice system, Piper surmised he would have done it Sunday night when she was most vulnerable. Instead, he'd placed a heavy arm around her while she cried, letting her tears soak through the side of his shirt. She had found a measurable level of solace there on the steps beside him, and she felt that solace whenever she laid eyes on him now.

Her minions sensed her tension at the onset of Monday morning, subduing their light-hearted banter and stepping up to volunteer in big ways and small. They were eager to help, so she let them, pleasantly surprised by their vast and varied capabilities. By Friday, she was asking their opinions for more than simply directing a teachable moment.

Thursday night she headed to her childhood home to have dinner with her widowed father. Thursday evenings were their time together, and usually she treated him to a new recipe she would prepare in his kitchen and leave him with a new dessert treat or two. This week, she surprised him with Chinese carry-out, explaining about her busy week and not about her inability to empty out her car's trunk of her baking supplies and facing the havoc those memories would inevitably bring.

It was a long, exhausting week, arriving at the perfect time to keep Piper's mind off of Vance and the three-day roller coaster ride he'd sucked her into. So when her last case ended at four thirty Friday afternoon, she decided to head into the office instead of going home. Home was quiet with no distractions. At home she might have to actually consider the things Vance had said. The office had a long string of emails and messages demanding her attention. The office provided distraction from the insidious thoughts bumping up against the outer edges of her mind.

⁀෧⌇⌇

After leaving Piper by the side of the road Sunday night, Vance poured himself three shots of tequila and slept through the night. He was grateful for the dull, nagging ache in his head the next morning because it kept him from thinking too much on his five-mile run and then while he lifted weights alone in the high school's training room, which also served as his office. He finished up some paperwork left over from baseball camp and then headed home to shower. Since he had spent much of the previous week lamenting over blond curls and a well-rounded ass, he dressed himself in casual business attire and decided it was time to get down to work.

The scene he walked in on at the recently furnished offices of Evans & Evans Investments was exactly the kind of thing he needed to get his head back in the game.

"That is not your job," Pinks was saying, his index finger tapping the center of the desk where Tansy Langford sat. "Your job is to sit here, answer the phones, and look pretty in case someone walks in off the street."

Whoa, Pinks. Vance's eyes shot big and round as he clasped a hand over his laugh so he would not disturb the trouble getting ready to explode in front of him.

"What are you?" Tansy questioned. "Some kind of *Mad Men* wannabe? Sit here and look pretty?" She stood and placed her hands flat on the desk, leaning toward Pinks. "Are you fucking kidding me?"

"Nice potty mouth, Yacht Club. Not exactly the image E&E Investments is trying to project."

Yacht Club?

"As if you and your lacrosse stick add any value around here."

"Since E&E will be sponsoring Henderson's first annual lacrosse clinic with our name plastered across the back of every T-shirt, we'll just see what kind of value add my lacrosse stick can be."

Sponsor what?

"Maybe if you knew how to handle your dick as well as your stick, Lolly wouldn't have dumped you."

"Leaving you a clear path to stab your cold-hearted talons into Brooks' unsuspecting back."

"Well," Vance said, stepping forward with a broad grin. "If this isn't quite the lovers' quarrel."

The two who had come to a standstill with their faces mere inches apart, stepped away from each other with utmost haste. Tansy resumed her seat at the desk, straightening her blotter and touching the bounty of red Sharpies sticking out of a pencil holder. "I'm sorry you had to see that," she said contritely. "It won't happen again."

Vance shook his head, looking Tansy over like she was a life form from another planet. "No, no, no," he said adamantly. "That shit is not going to fly in this office."

Tansy looked up at him, startled. "What?"

"You *hate* me," he told her.

"I don't…*hate* you."

"Yes. You hate me, and I'm okay with that. Been okay with that for a whole lot of years now. So just because you now work for my father, do not think you have to start sucking up to me. Because, I'll tell you what. That, I would really hate."

"Vance, I don't just work for your father."

"Yes, you do."

"No," she said cautiously, "I work for both of you. I am completely capable of running the office and being the executive assistant for both of you."

"But I've got Pinks, here," Vance said pointing at The Ninja. "He's my man. I give him orders, he gets the job done. Pinks and I speak the same language. We understand each other."

"Oh," she said, nodding her head and smiling indulgently. "It makes perfect sense for you and Davis, I mean Pinks, to work together—you two being over-grown frat brothers and all. But know that if you ever need something of actual importance taken care of, I'm here for you."

"Actual importance? Like ordering lunch?" Pinks said.

"Or making coffee?" Vance added.

"Maybe being in charge of the Famous Amos Cookie Baker I'll be ordering off of Amazon this afternoon," Pinks said. "You can put it on the credenza behind you and just swivel your chair around when fresh cookies are required."

Vance chuckled and gave Pinks a high five. "See?" he said to Tansy. "An idea man." He turned to Pinks and said, "Seriously. I want one of those."

"I'm on it," Pinks said, reaching for his backpack and pulling out his MacBook Air.

Tansy looked up at Vance as he sat on her desk. "Not that it hasn't been a pleasure, but what the hell are you doing here?"

He spread his arms wide. "Isn't it obvious? I'm working."

"Working?"

"Yes, working. We need an office calendar. I want to schedule some meetings." Vance noticed that Tansy pulled at a notepad and took up one of her pens, which surprised him in a good way. "What's with all the red Sharpies?"

Tansy glanced at her pens. "George W. Bush had his black Sharpies, I have my red ones."

"George W. Bush?"

"Forty-third President of the United States."

"I know who the man is. I just didn't know you two were close."

"We're not close. It's just...."

"Just what?"

"Nothing. The two of us prefer Sharpies, okay? Now about those meetings?"

"Right. I'd first like to meet with you, Pinks, and Dad. With the wedding coming up, Dad's head is on Genevra and the honeymoon and nothing else. The three of us need to find out what he's left hanging out there business-wise that we may need to follow up on in his absence. He's taking his bride to Europe for a month or more, so we need to get with him now and see what's what."

"When are you available?"

"I'm...available," he said slapping his hands against his thighs. "I'll get whatever schedule they have for me over at the police station and let you know."

"How 'bout you give me the name of a contact person over there, and I'll let you know."

Vance sat up straighter, a little taken aback that Tansy could actually be helpful to him. "Even better. Call Carol Milton. Do you know her?"

"Yes."

"Okay, and since I've got nothing going on at the high school this time of year, E&E is my priority. But don't book me for anything on Tuesday nights."

"Why? Is that your poker night or something?"

"Or something."

"What?"

"I teach English as a Second Language at the library."

Tansy burst into hysterics. "Oh, my God. That is classic."

"Pinks!" Vance yelled, getting off Tansy's desk.

Pinks came running. "What's up?"

"Tell your secretary where I am every Tuesday night."

A broad smile cracked Pinks' face. "My secretary? I like the sound of that." He rubbed his hands together and looked over at Tansy with glee. "He tutors at the library—English as a Second Language."

"You're serious." Tansy's eyes went wide in disbelief first and then in apology as she looked between Pinks and Vance. Then her countenance changed completely. "Oh, your grandmother," she scoffed. "You didn't even have to take Spanish."

"No. I didn't have to take Spanish because I was already fluent."

"Big deal. Start speaking Russian or Chinese. Then I'll be impressed."

"How about you start impressing me with your ability to focus on work? Once you've got that first meeting set up, I want to schedule another with Pinks, The Outlaw, and Brooks."

"Fine. What's this about?"

"It's about brainstorming Brooks' campaign platform. Hey, what city did you run off to anyway?"

"Dallas."

"Really?" Vance raised his brows. "And how did you like it?"

"I liked it just fine, thank you."

"Tansy," Vance said in all seriousness. "You could be a valuable asset to Brooks' campaign. It wouldn't be a bad idea to have a woman's point of view about Henderson and what this town needs. Since you ran off and then crawled back with your tail between your legs, you have a perspective we could use. I'll call Lolly and see if she'd mind."

"Call Lolly?" Tansy spouted. "Brooks does not need permission from Lolly to include me on some brainstorming team."

"No. But I do," Vance said. "Lolly's my friend and she's going to be my stepsister. So the last thing I'm going to do is piss her off."

"Fine," Tansy sighed, rubbing her forehead.

Vance smiled, standing in Tansy's shoes for a moment. "You didn't think this thing through, did you?"

"You mean that I'm going to be working for Genevra and Lolly DuVal now too? No," she admitted. "I did not think this all the way through."

"Well, Tansy," Vance said, pushing Pinks in front of him as he headed down the hall, "cry uncle and I'll be happy to purchase your one-way ticket back to Dallas. Maybe George W. is looking for an assistant."

On Tuesday afternoon, Brooks beat down the door of the conference room where the E&E Investment team meeting was happening. He shoved Jesse James in front of him and held up a slew of pink flyers, ranting and raving about the sorry state of American sports as he threw them across the table.

Vance picked one up and read, "Free Introduction to Lacrosse. Girls and boys. All ages. No equipment necessary. Saturday, July 31 from 10:00 to 12:00. Henderson High soccer field." He looked over at Brooks. "I take it you have a problem with this?"

"And you don't?"

"The Ninja and Outlaw are entrepreneurs. I'm not going to squash their dream."

"Their dream? You are the fucking baseball coach. What happens when Skip Lewis and Johnny Mac decide they are tired of standing around in the outfield and want to trade in their gloves for—for—"

"A real man's sport?" The Outlaw supplied.

"Fucking A," Brooks cursed. He looked in earnest at Vance. "You're killing me here. You and your band of merry men," he said, pointing between Davis and Jesse.

"Merry men?" Vance scoffed. "I believe you are referring to my Superheroes."

"Super-what-oes?"

"Welcome to training camp. These two are helping us set the ground work for saving Henderson. Since intern is such a generic term, we came up with superhero. Has a nice ring to it, don't you think? We're still working on a tagline."

"And a website," Pinks chimed in.

"A website?" Brooks shouted at Pinks. "With a picture of you decked out in pink tights and a pink cape with a big P on your chest? And this one playing cowboy with a gun holster and black hat?"

Pinks looked at Jesse. "We could totally rock that."

"Dynamic Duo" Jesse agreed.

"Holding lacrosse sticks," Pinks added.

"Goddamn it, Evans," Brooks shouted.

"What the hell are you so worried about?" Vance asked. "Their flyers are pink, for God's sake. Girls are invited. No self-respecting baseball player is going to show up and venture into the dark side."

"Well, just to make sure, you and I are going to be there displaying our State Championship trophy."

"Hey! That's intimidation," Pinks said.

"You got that right. We've been cultivating this varsity team too long to have you super-yahoos come in and bust it all up."

"Okay," Pinks said. "You want to protect the integrity of your team, and I respect that. I mean, as a local sports hero and this town's next mayor, you'd like to see all kids involved in sports. Look what it did for you, right?"

"Fucking A," Brooks mumbled under his breath.

"And since so few can actually earn a coveted spot on Coach Evans' elite, championship-winning baseball team, as mayor you'd like to cultivate more opportunities to teach sportsmanship and fight childhood obesity. As mayor, you know that because of Title IX, women's lacrosse is the fastest-growing sport throughout colleges and universities today, creating more scholarship opportunities for women. And as mayor, creating opportunities for the entire population of Henderson is not only a goal, it's your personal tagline." Pinks deepened his voice as if he were a television announcer. "Creating economic opportunity for our town and our families. Brooks Bennett, candidate for mayor."

"Ba-da-bum," Jesse finished.

Silence.

Brooks looked between Pinks and Vance, his mouth hanging open. Finally, he said, "How the hell can I argue with that?"

"I'm not sure you can," Vance laughed. "Here, let me walk you out. Jesse, sit in on the rest of this meeting. You and Pinks can distribute the rest of those flyers when we're done," Vance said as he turned a rather stunned Brooks and pushed him through the door.

"What the hell just happened in there?"

"The Ninja is smarter than I am," Vance admitted. "Which

makes him a fucking genius compared to you."

"He reeled me in with the 'saving the integrity of our team' bullshit and suddenly lacrosse is now going to single-handedly save Henderson."

"No. We are going to save Henderson, but it's looking more and more like Pinks would be an asset to the team. I'm pulling Tansy in on it too."

"Tansy?"

"She's smart, she's a woman, and she's lived elsewhere."

"Who are you and what the hell have you done with my friend? You hate Tansy."

"I hate her a lot less now that she's not going to be your wife. And since Dad hired her, we may as well put her to work. I'd like to get everyone together for a day-long brainstorming session tomorrow. I want ideas on paper, I want them prioritized and then we'll divide them up and start researching strategies for implementation. When the day comes that you announce your candidacy, you will have in your back pocket a well-thought-out, detailed, step-by-step strategic plan to stimulate the economic growth in Henderson. There will be no empty campaign promises from the town's Golden Boy. You will come off as smart as Pinks, only taller and better looking."

"Absolutely. And I'll be standing next to our Championship trophy when I do it. You can count on that."

The rest of the week bloomed with the kind of work Vance had longed to do. He felt his father's enthusiasm as Hale explained the ins and outs of his investment strategies with each of the companies he owned. They discussed which ones were running at optimal profit, which ones could use an influx of time or money to enhance profitability, and which ones no longer made sense to own. Vance was amazed at the attention and consideration his father gave his own opinions. The two of them had a lot in common, but it was clear they brought different skill sets to the table, skills that should prove complementary to one another.

On Thursday night, the two of them sat alone in the dark poolside, enjoying a prized Scotch from Hale's collection along with hand-rolled Cuban cigars. They sat quietly, exhilarated by the prospects of their shared business ventures. Both feeling good about the conscious decision they'd made to support the town of Henderson with their capital, time, and expertise. As the evening lengthened, Hale eased back in his chair and said, "I'd like to share something with you, if I may."

Vance puffed on his cigar and nodded.

"I had a revelation, if you will, while I was traveling about eight months ago. I was on this plane and noticed I was weary. Really bone-tired. I knew it wasn't the work or even the travel because if anything, that stuff energizes me. I hoped it wasn't my age," he laughed and took a pull on his cigar.

"Of course," he said, blowing smoke into the night, "anybody with a degree in psychology could have told me the problem. Even though your mother had left years ago and life had moved on, I had not. All this time I had been carrying around a lot of extra baggage wherever I went. I carried sorrow in my heart, anger in my chest, and guilt on my shoulders. I'd been carrying around hurt on my back and resentment in my mind, and I never once set it down. Of course I was weary."

Hale took a sip of his Scotch, and Vance didn't say a word. He didn't want to interrupt his father now that he had finally started to talk about the aftermath of his mother's departure.

"I decided right then to put it all down. To let it all go. I decided I needed to find a reason to forgive your mother. And the miracle was that immediately after I decided to forgive her, the answer came to me. Without your mother, I would never have had you.

"And you, my boy have been my greatest joy." Hale reached over and rattled Vance's arm, making him smile as he stared into his snifter. "From the moment you were born to that first shoebox full of money you made. From the first time you picked up a bat to when you started defying curfew. Every time I see your face it makes me happy. You have been my reason to work hard. My reason to come home. My reason to buy another damn car, because I get to share it with you," he laughed.

"Now, there isn't a woman around who comes with any guarantees." He let that thought hover in the air around them while he sipped his Scotch. "You and I," he said, pointing at Vance briefly with his glass. "We probably deserve a few guarantees after going through what we've been through. But we aren't going to get them. We can't love enough, do enough, give enough, or be enough to guarantee that we won't ever have to feel that way again.

"Unfortunately. Unfortunately, for us, we have to be willing to risk feeling that bad again. It's that simple, and it's that hard. Genevra DuVal was available to me the day your mother walked out. But I spent twenty years being blinded by anger, hurt, and fear. The moment I gave all that up, there she was.

And my only regret—my *only* regret—is that I didn't figure it out a whole lot sooner."

Hale sipped his Scotch while Vance mulled the story over in his mind. He had a couple regrets.

"Dad," he finally said. "I'm glad you found Genevra."

"She'd been there all along. Just waiting for me to get out of my own way."

"Hmm," Vance said noncommittally, and took a drag on his cigar.

"Figure out a reason to forgive your mother. The rest will take care of its self."

Vance had only thought about leaving Piper standing on the side of the road in the dark about five times over the course of the week. Five times an hour, that is. Which was pretty good, considering her body haunted his dreams every damn night.

Of course the upside to that was that *Lolly* was no longer being conjured up in his bed, Vance thought, so at least that was something.

He hadn't had to give voice to what happened between him and Piper Sunday night because with Lolly and Genevra AWOL taking care of wedding plans, neither of them were around to ask. And if Brooks or Pinks mentioned anything, he was able to shrug them off and change the subject. Vance knew his father was talking about Piper of course, but what really scared Vance was what Annabelle was going to do to him when she heard Piper's side of the story.

Because although Vance stood by what he'd said to Piper, he wasn't enough of a moron not to realize his method of delivery was spectacularly ill-timed and unfair, and that leaving her in the middle of the road at night was just plain wrong. Hurt, fear, and frustration tended to do that to a guy.

And make that frustration with a capital F. Because having his body pressed up against Piper's didn't just feel good, it felt soul-stirringly, mind-blowingly good. Add to that the fact that he hadn't had anything pressed up against him since the night of Lewis' engagement party three months ago and his frustration at Piper's sudden change was increased tenfold.

No wonder he blew a fucking gasket.

And now as Friday's happy hour and the weekend were about to commence, Vance felt as if he were dangling by one hand off the sheer side of a cliff. He didn't know if he wanted to continue the struggle and reach for the edge with his other hand and hope he had the strength left to drag himself up, or if he should simply give in to what felt like the inevitable and fall back into the valley from which he had attempted to climb out.

Either he was fixing this with Piper, or he was going to get laid. *Christ.*

He phoned Brooks.

"I'm about to do something stupid," Vance said. "And since Lolly will probably cut my balls off when she finds out, I'm giving you the chance to talk me out of it. Meet me at the Club."

CHAPTER EIGHTEEN

Harry The Bartender had served Vance a second shot by the time Brooks walked in. The two of them watched Brooks glad-hand his way through the tables, smiling his big grin at everyone, spreading sunshine all over the damn place. It made Vance wonder why he bothered to work so hard on Brooks' campaign. If the guy so much as hinted that he'd like to be mayor, Vance had no doubt the town would carry him on their shoulders to the Mayor's office, toss the incumbent out on his ear, and place Brooks in it. Then they'd commission a crown to be sculpted, declaring him king at the swearing in.

Vance glanced at Harry.

"King does have a nice ring to it," Harry agreed.

Vance pounded his fist on the bar and growled. "I did not say that out loud. How the hell do you do that?"

Harry waved him off. "It's certainly not rocket science."

"What the hell does that mean?" Vance said, but he was interrupted by Brooks.

"Sorry I'm late," he said. "You manage to hold off stupid 'til I got here?"

"Yes, but after two shots, stupid is starting to look a lot like a good idea."

"I hear ya," Brooks said before he downed his shot. "Mmm. God, that's good. Harry! Hit me again."

"Really?" Vance said. "What stupid thing are you trying to work into a good idea?"

"Third Base," Brooks said after a long "Ahhh" following his second shot of tequila, "if there is one thing I'm learning, it's that when it comes to the Final Frontier, stupid is standard operating procedure."

"Final Frontier?"

"That one, sweet morsel of womanhood that is so perfect, so satisfying, once discovered all you can do is settle in and stake your claim."

"So, Lolly's…lady parts?"

"Are making me crazy. I enjoy staking my claim."

"And it's made you stupid."

"So stupid that the words, 'Anybody can finish off your momma's wedding dress, but you're the only one who can finish me off,' actually came out of my mouth."

"Dear. God."

"Yeah. Like I said, stupid."

"Harry! Two beers, please. And do me a favor," Vance said, handing Harry his phone. "Call Pinks. Tell him to fill up the big cooler, grab The Outlaw and my truck, and pick us up in an hour." Vance looked at Brooks. "Tonight you and I are taking the S.H.I.T.s to the lake."

"The shits?"

"Super Heroes in Training."

Brooks laughed so hard he fell off his stool.

Boom, boom, boom—one email after another was quickly read and then answered or discarded. Piper was on a roll as seven o'clock on Friday evening turned into eight o'clock and then nine. She was handling things with speed and alacrity, staying at the office to open and delete the slew of emails she'd let pile up in her inbox for close to a month.

The last emails she went through were not personal, but general interoffice blasts. She liked to know what was happening with the rest of the firm and reading and deleting the string of emails served that purpose. She was close to the bottom of these, feeling genuine relief at having taken the time to get through them. With three to go, she read and deleted one, causing the next to open automatically.

It was a picture taken in the maternity ward of a hospital showing off the family portrait of a young father, mother, two-year-old son, and their brand new baby daughter.

Piper's breath caught at the sight of the photo, her body tense and tingling, unable to move. She knew she should just hit the delete button, but her eyes latched on and devoured the precious expression on the toddler's face and then the pink baby bundle in the woman's arms. "A boy and a girl," her heart sighed. The longing she felt was poignant. The connection she felt, keen.

Because those precious little ones could have been hers.

There had been a time when she was busy planning her wedding to the man in the picture, and in just five short years he'd fulfilled their dream of a family—with another woman. He now had what she'd always wanted. Children to dote on, a family to raise. A household to love and care for. That's what the two of them had planned together. It was her dream. It was his dream. And she had taken that dream and thrown it away with two hands.

Because her mother had died in the middle of it, and Vance Evans had shown up at exactly the wrong time.

⚬⟞⟜⚬

Back in Henderson, it was the perfect July night—less humid with an actual breeze—for an impromptu by-the-lake party, and the crowd kept gathering. Brooks and Vance sat on the tailgate of Vance's truck, the large cooler vertical between them. They were situated far enough away from the action that their cop personas would not spoil anybody's fun, but close enough that they felt like part of the party. They kept their eyes on Pinks and The Outlaw as the two did a meet and greet, working their way into the good graces of the Henderson faithful.

Newcomers were unique and welcomed, especially if they were connected to an influential family. It seemed from the look of things that Davis Williams and Jesse James—two boys from the North— were taking Henderson by storm.

"So you gonna talk about why you can't take your eyes off of Racy Lay's ass?" Brooks asked.

"Been in a drought for a long time now," Vance said, taking a swig of his beer. "Just admiring the view."

"Bullshit. It's becoming pretty apparent I'm here to talk you out of taking an unsuitable woman into your bed."

Without taking his eyes off of Racy's ass Vance said, "I cannot confirm or deny. Besides, it looks like I'd have to fight Pinks off. And who's to say that Racy Lay is unsuitable?"

"Lolly for one. Annabelle for another. And who am I forgettin' here? Uh…oh yeah, a lady by the name of Piper Beaumont. Pretty little thing, about this tall," Brooks said holding his hand five feet from the ground, "tiny little waist, fabulous tits, and an ass that would kick the shit out of the one you've been staring at. Any of that sound familiar to you, idiot?"

Vance shook his head and met Brooks' WTF stare for about a tenth of a second before he had to look away.

"Start talking or I'm out of here," Brooks threatened.

Vance ran his hand over the back of his neck, groaning. "Just too much bullshit between us," he said. "She's as screwed up as I am."

"Well, who the hell isn't?"

"You aren't. Lolly isn't."

"Like hell. I walk around this town pretending to be the answer to everybody's prayers because the jackass superstar that came before me let everybody down. And Lolly—Lolly has named her business after her jackass father who refused to marry her mother. Everybody's screwed up and we are all in this together. So lay it on me. What the hell is so blasted wrong with Tinker Bell—Goddess of the yellow polka-dot bikini and pastry chef extraordinaire—that you aren't doing your damnedest to get into her pants right now?"

"Well, that's just it, isn't it? Piper—the real Piper—is practically perfect in every way. She's exactly as I remember in grade school. Sweet. Kind. Caring. But *The Lawyer Beaumont,* who Perfect Piper pretends to be, is an angry, aggressive bitch on wheels. I pulled her over on her way out of town Sunday night just to tease her, and she was not amused."

"No one has ever been amused when I've pulled them over."

"I'm telling you when that switch flips, she doesn't even look like the same person. A total Dr. Jekyll and Mr. Hyde. She treats every cop who crosses her path like he's a link to whatever the hell happened to her in college. And I am no exception to that rule."

"So you—not being much of a cop and with everything else you're involved in—are letting your badge get in the way of hooking up with your hologram? What part of that makes any sense to you?"

"Being a cop is part of me. If she can't handle that part of me, she certainly isn't going to be able to handle the rest of my bullshit."

"What rest of your bullshit? This *is* your bullshit. If your mom gave birth to the fucking Prince of Wales, she *still* would have walked away. Her leaving was not about you. Grow up for Christ's sake. If Piper has a problem with cops, be the cop who helps her get over it. Fucking A." Brooks pulled out his cell phone and started hitting buttons.

"What are you doing?"

"I'm taking my own damn advice and texting Lolly," Brooks said. "Telling her I'm an ass and I want a do-over. And if you don't pull out your phone right now and start texting Piper about what a truly classic ass you were to pull her over when you *knew* she had issues with cops, then I'm gonna…."

"You're gonna what?" Vance challenged.

"I'm gonna let you take an unsuitable woman home tonight and then drop Lolly off at your doorstep first thing in the mornin'. If you think Piper's a headache…."

"Pftt. Like I'm afraid of Lolly."

"Blow me. We're both afraid of Lolly. There's only one man in the entire world not afraid of Lolly, and he's marrying Lolly's mother."

Vance had to smile at that. "You know, if things work out for you and the Lollypop, my father will be your father-in-law. Which means I'll be your brother-in-law."

"And with Lewis marrying my sister, he's already my brother-in-law." Brooks stopped texting and looked up for a moment. "Fuck Piper," he said, going back to his texting. "Nab one of Annabelle's sisters so we can hook Duncan into the network too."

"Yeah, I'm going to pass on that."

Bing!

Brooks looked at his phone, his broad grin spilling over his face. "Check this out."

Vance looked at the picture of a short, pink dress. "So?"

"That's the trench coat Lolly had on the night she came to the precinct to seduce me. The *only* thing she had on. But it got all botched up because her uncles ransacked your father's wine cellar, remember?"

"That, I will never forget."

"When the dust settled that night, I told her I wanted a do-over with her in the trench coat. She must have read my text about a do-over and thought that's what I meant." Brooks began texting her back.

"You aren't setting her straight are you?"

"Hell, no. I'm telling her to put it on and come pick me up." He finished texting and held his arms out wide. "Look what can happen when you admit you're an ass," he said, his eyes lighting up with humor. "Now stop being a pussy and admit what an ass you were to Piper."

Vance pulled out his phone. "Fuck that. I'm gonna tell her I want a do-over."

CHAPTER NINETEEN

Piper sat there, numbly staring at her ex-fiancé's family. She didn't cry. She felt too empty for that. But she stared and stared and contemplated the evidence of how much his life had expanded in five short years compared to how her own life had stayed the same.

Sure, she was good at her job, but it was never who she had planned to be. She had planned to be the woman in the hospital bed, in love with her new baby and her sweet family. She didn't plan to be the little lady lawyer who had pissed off enough cops that one of them felt it was necessary to be her unofficial bodyguard.

Dear God.

That was it, wasn't it? That's exactly why Officer Stevenson had been following her around lately. *He* didn't mean her any harm, but apparently he knew someone, or several someones, who did.

Ohmigod.

All those insidious thoughts she'd been holding at bay flashed as brightly as neon signs. Vance was right. She had been taking her anger and frustration out on every cop she came up against because of a single incident that happened twelve years ago. She had set out to get even for an injustice that had been done to her, and look where that had landed her—all alone and working on a Friday night.

She checked her watch—*Oh, God*—and worked quickly to shut down her computer and gather her things. Poor Officer Stevenson was probably standing around outside the office or waiting for her to show up at home. How the hell was she going to fix this with him?

She heard her cell phone ding, alerting her to a text message, but she didn't have time to check it. She needed to find out if her suspicions were true. Mostly, right now she needed to get home safely, so Officer Stevenson could be free to live his life.

She grabbed up her yellow patent leather tote and headed for the door.

❦

Vance checked his phone for the eighth time in an hour. He waited a full beer later to check it again. Nothing but his glaring *"I want a do-over"* message hanging pathetically out there in cyber space.

And what the hell was Piper supposed to say to that?

So Vance texted what he should have texted the first time.

"Piper. How badly have I messed this thing up?"

Because that's what he needed to know. Could she overlook all he'd barked at her at a time when he was feeling particularly vulnerable?

Holy Jesus. And now I need to stop being a pansy and start having a good time.

For the love of God, he needed to lighten up.

"Pinks!" he called, hopping off the dreaded lonely tailgate to join the party. Pinks—ever the Boy Wonder—showed up immediately and fell into stride. "Which one have you got picked out?" Vance asked.

"Which one what?"

"Which one of these babes are you hoping to see naked?"

"Jesus, dude. That is not how I operate."

"Which is exactly your problem. I've watched you all night talking and laughing and having a good time, and that's great if you're Brooks Bennett and running for office. But if you want to get laid, you need to focus."

Davis stopped in his tracks. "Are you serious? Is this a one-on-one Vance Evans How to Pick Up Girls and Enjoy a No-Strings Sexual Encounter Workshop?"

"Isn't that what you came to me for?"

"Hell, yeah," Davis said, tucking in his shirt and running his fingers through his hair. "About damn time you get around to teaching me something I don't already know."

Vance smirked at that. The kid wasn't wrong.

"Okay. First, stand still a fucking second and survey your domain. Running around and being all things to all women is not going to get you any of them. Pick one out. The one you really want to rub up against, not the one you want to take home to Mommy."

"Roger. That."

"Then, take your time and study what's going on with her—who she's talking to, who she's looking at. Is she the shy type, hiding behind her girlfriends? Or is she drinking a little too much, attracting attention by dancing on a tailgate and looking for a different kind of party? And it doesn't matter where on that scale your point of attraction falls. You just want to get a good feeling for what's going on with her before you insert yourself into her present reality."

"Insert myself into what?"

"Her reality. Her awareness. The easiest way to do that is to watch what she's drinking and be right there the moment she needs another. Be her hero; offer a cold beer, or even a bottle of water. The night gets chilly, you offer her the blanket out of the back of your truck."

"I don't have a truck or a blanket."

"Just an example, douche bag. It's eighty fucking degrees. Try using that double-degree brain of yours. All I'm saying is to be observant, stay close, and look for your opportunity. If she drops something, pick it up. If she wants to dance, take her hand and lead her onto the dance floor. If she stumbles over her own two feet, catch her. You want to make an impression, and you want it to be personal."

"Ahhh," Pinks nodded, the dawn of understanding lighting up his eyes. "This isn't rocket science, is it?"

Vance smiled. His little intern was growing up. "No," he laughed. "It is not rocket science. The biggest mistake is lack of focus. Women want to be the only one you have eyes for. So pick one and zero in."

"All right," Pinks said clapping his hands together and zeroing in. "Anything else I need to know?"

"Got a condom in your pocket?"

"Uh—"

"Gotta adopt that Boy Scout motto—always be prepared," Vance said, pulling out a condom from his back pocket and handing it to Pinks.

Pinks looked at it and then raised his head. "You got another you can give me?"

"Jesus, kid. Why would I be carrying around two condoms?"

"Hey, you're Vance Evans. If you don't carry around two, who does?"

Vance slapped Pinks affectionately on the back. "Point taken. Now get in there and back some cute piece of ass up against a truck."

"I will not let you down," Pinks said.

Vance watched him go, his smile eventually fading. He ran a hand over the nape of his neck, looking around at all the women at his disposal and trying to stave off that old feeling of loneliness. "Piper, Piper, Piper," he whispered. "Are you gonna respond or is this about to get ugly?"

He pulled out his phone to check it again just as a voice floated to him from behind.

"I enjoyed your pool party after the Fourth," Lacy said, using her sweet southern accent to nail him right between the thighs. "The first time I'd ever been invited to the Evans estate. I'm not sure I had the chance to thank you properly."

Vance turned, offering up his best smile. It was like a knee-jerk reaction he just couldn't help. "Why, Miss Lacy Ray, what would a pool party be without you and your pretty friends showing up in those tiny, little swimsuits?"

Her eyes dipped to the ground, and Vance was pretty certain she was blushing, even if he couldn't see it in the dark.

"It was nice of you to have Davis call us," she said. "He was a good host."

"Yeah. He—he was helping me out. He's a good kid. In fact, he's...right over there," Vance pointed, hoping like hell she'd follow after Pinks and leave him the hell alone.

"He is a good kid," she agreed. And then Vance actually felt her working up the courage to say, "But, I'm more interested in a man."

Goddamn it.

Vance clenched and unclenched his fist, standing his ground while Young and Appetizing tried to reel him in. He cleared his throat.

"Lacy, honey, how old are you?"

"I'm twenty-two."

Almost Lolly's age.

"Who'd you come out here with?"

"I drove," she said. "I'd be happy to give you a ride home."

"Wouldn't you be stranding some of your friends?"

"They'd find rides."

He hesitated.

"You could ask Davis to take them home in your truck," she suggested.

Vance turned his head to survey the party, not really seeing anything. Racy Lay had a reputation, and there was not a man alive who would blame him for taking her up on her invitation for the kind of ride she was offering.

All right, maybe Brooks would blame him. Brooks would tell him that Lacy is one of those girls he shouldn't be messin' with. And that was probably true. But where was the Golden Boy when he needed him? Easy to be holier than thou when you were gettin' some on a regular basis.

Still.

"Lacy, trust me on this. You don't really want what you seem to be asking for, honey."

"Ha—"

"I know you think you do," he said, pulling out his phone. "But I'm actually waiting on a—"

Lacy's hand landed on his ass. Not up high, but waaay down low. Felt a little more like the inside of his thigh. Right next to where his semi-retired nuts were all tucked up nice and quiet inside his jeans. But with Lacy Ray's fingers a breath away from the two of them, they were now howling at the moon, begging to be set loose and yelling at their buddy Johnson to start swingin' his stuff around.

The disconnect from his brain was immediate.

Vance reached behind Lacy and placed a hand on the exact same spot of her body and squeezed, bringing her right up against him in an "I mean business," kind of way.

"I'm telling you right now. My heart does not get tangled up in this kind of...ride," he said.

Lacy licked her lips. "I'm more interested in your hands."

"Is that so?" He smiled. "Who are you trying to piss off?"

Lacy shook her head. "Nobody. I'm just looking for a real good time."

"Well, darlin', I just happen to have one of those in my back pocket."

⌒⌒⌒⌒

Piper didn't actually see Officer Stevenson, but there was a squad car that followed her all the way home. If she could be sure that he was doing the following, she would have gone up to the window and spoken to him about all this. Instead, she headed quickly into her condo building, not wanting to take the chance it was some other cop she had inadvertently pissed off.

Once inside her bright little apartment, she emptied her purse onto the kitchen countertop and snatched up her phone. She'd call Raleigh's main police station and see if they'd put her through to Office Stevenson, wherever he may be.

She pushed the button and the text message indicator flashed.

She read, *Vance Evans. "I want a do—"*

"VANCE," her heart sang out. Vance, Vance, Vance, Vance, she chanted in her mind as she opened up her phone and read his two texts, the first of which had come in hours ago. "How did I miss this?"

She reread the texts.

"I want a do-over."

And, coming in a couple hours later,

"Piper. How badly did I mess this thing up?"

How badly had *he* messed it up?

Piper's heart melted—just softened up and dripped off all the animosity she'd been feeling toward Vance. Because where she stood in this moment, it was so glaringly obvious that he'd only told her the truth. In fact, she had known it when he said it, but didn't have the fortitude to face it, acknowledge it, and deal with it.

But, boy, did she have to do all of that now.

She texted back, "I'm the one who is messed up. Call me. Please."

She started to place a call to Officer Stevenson and then stopped and went back to texting Vance.

"A do-over sounds wonderful."

⌒⌒⌒⌒

Standing in between Lacy's legs with both of his hands underneath her ass, Vance rubbed the bulging seam of his jeans against the seam of her short shorts while practicing the art of kissing in a very focused and calculated way.

He didn't notice the vibration of his phone.

But seated on the hood of her car, her legs circled around his hips, Lacy did.

"I probably wouldn't mind all that vibratin' if you'd put your phone in your front pocket," she told him.

Vance pulled away. "What?"

"Either turn your phone off, or put it in your front pocket where it'll do me some good."

Vance felt for his back pocket, planning to turn the damn thing off. He pulled it out, feeling for the off switch as he went back to Lacy's lips.

"Holy shit!" he said, not only pulling away from Lacy's lips, but scrambling out of the iron-clad embrace of her legs. He looked down at his phone and read Piper's two texts. When he looked up at Lacy and remembered what he'd just been doing, he felt physically ill. And it must have shown.

Lacy took off her flip-flop and threw it at him.

When his mouth dropped open but no explanation came out, she hopped off her car, picked up the flip-flop, and hit him with it.

"What? I tried to tell you I was waiting for—" he said, starting to laugh in the face of her fury.

"Vance Evans, you suck!" Lacy said, stomping away.

He thought better of a snide retort and let the girl go. He turned in the other direction and dialed Piper back.

"Piper!"

"Vance," she said, sounding breathless.

There was silence while Vance tried to calm his heart, desperately wrenching himself out of the black hole that Lacy represented and moving into the sunshine that came with thinking about Piper. "Baby doll," he breathed into the phone. "Forgive me."

"I like the idea of a do-over," she said.

"Yeah, I know. That's—that's what I'm trying to do here."

"No. I mean, I want a Cinco de Mayo do-over."

"Cinco do-what?"

"Tomorrow night at The Charlie Horse—same bar, same premise—just you and me five years later."

"Same premise?"

"Yes. You standing there…being *you*, and I'm…."

"Looking to blow off steam?" he suggested with a snicker.

"I'm…." She stopped talking and Vance heard her sigh. "I'm… looking for the love of my life."

Vance swallowed.

"I'm your man. See you tomorrow night."

CHAPTER TWENTY

The moment Vance woke up Saturday morning he told himself he was too happy to go for a run. Piper was giving him a do-over and that was all he wanted to think about. He did not need a run.

Because a run meant he had something inside him that needed to get out. And what happened last night between him and Lacy Ray was not something he needed to run out. Five minutes of his lips on top of Lacy's did not constitute tying himself up in knots of guilt. No, he was not going for a run he told himself as he pulled on his athletic clothes and laced up his Nikes.

God fucking dammit!

He ran an extra mile just to shut his guilty conscience up.

He stood bent over with his hands on his knees, panting. *Lolly DuVal has ruined me forever. I didn't know the meaning of the word guilt until she came into my life. And right now the whole thing is pissing me off.* He went and pumped iron until he was too tired to worry about anything anymore.

After showering, Vance took on the next problem of the day. He was scheduled to work tonight. So either he was finding someone to take his shift or he was turning in his badge earlier than anticipated because there was no way in hell he was missing this night with Piper.

He was sitting on his couch taking care of that when the woman who was suddenly the bane of his existence crashed through his door, uninvited.

"Get out," he shouted at Lolly. "I am not in the mood for whatever holier-than-thou crap you are planning to feed me this morning."

"Oh," she shouted back at him. "And don't think I don't know why. There is a picture being texted all over town of you sucking face with Lacy Ray."

Vance felt himself go white. A picture? How the hell is there a picture? And, oh Jesus. If Annabelle Devine got a hold of that picture, it was only a minute and a half before it would show up on Piper's phone. "Fuck!"

Lolly burst into hysterical laughter.

"What the hell?"

"There's no picture. I just heard about everything from Davis and wanted to give you crap."

"This is all your fault," he accused, shaking his phone at her. "Now I'm telling Piper everything. Confessing it all, this minute. And if she doesn't go through with our do-over tonight, it is on your head."

"How is you being stupid my fault?"

"Because I feel guilty! And I didn't ever feel guilty until you came into my life. You and your Lollypop nonsense about what there is to like about women outside of the bedroom."

Lolly grabbed his phone out of his hands.

"Jesus, you're getting on my nerves," he said.

Lolly let the room stop vibrating around them for a moment before she said as calmly as she could, "Piper doesn't need to know about last night."

"No," he agreed. "But if she should ever find out...."

Reluctantly Lolly handed his phone back. "I guess I'd want you to be the one to tell me. But, listen. Blame it on your deep despair over not having heard from her all week...and the alcohol. Tell her you and Brooks were tying one on because I was being a self-centered bitch."

Vance lifted a brow.

"I'm exaggerating the circumstances to help you out."

"Right," he scoffed. "Where is Brooks anyway?"

"At his place. Still in bed."

Vance lifted two brows.

"Yeah. Me being a self-centered bitch worked out really well for him."

"Lolly."

"Yeah?"

"Thanks for taking care of my boy."

She smiled.

"Now get the hell out so I can text Piper."

"If you have a problem, I'll call her. She loves me."

"Of course she does," Vance muttered as he heard her shut the door. Without hesitation, Vance started texting Piper.

"In an effort to clear the air before tonight, I have a confession."

He sent that off and immediately a text from Piper came in.

"I'm listening."

"Oh, so now you're listening." Vance muttered to himself. "Where the hell were you last night before I ventured back into man-whoredom?" He should just call her and talk this out. But he didn't trust his stupid mouth, so he texted again.

"Last night when I thought all was lost, I had a five-minute indiscretion."

"Only lasted five minutes? You must be terribly embarrassed."

"Very funny. Do you need the fully clothed details? Or are you gonna let me off easy?"

"That depends."

"On what?"

"On how upset you get when I tell you that I sobbed in Officer Stevenson's arms for an hour Sunday night."

Vance read the words twice before he threw his phone through the doors to his bedroom and fell back against the couch, stringing a foul-mouthed litany together about a motherfucking, cocksucking, overgrown ape.

"Jesus fucking Christ," he shouted toward the ceiling.

He bounded up to retrieve his phone, found it in the middle of his unmade bed, and dialed Piper.

"I'm going to need a little more information," he said with as much control as he could muster.

"Like what?"

Vance took his phone from his ear and made a face like he wanted to kill something. He pulled himself together and asked, "Like, were you in his goddamn bed while you were sobbing in his arms?"

"Vance!"

"Piper!"

"Of course not!"

"What do you mean "of course not?" You told me you were in the asshole's arms. What am I supposed to think?"

"It wasn't like that. He was sitting on my front porch when I got home. After what you'd said to me that night, I felt so bad about the way I've been treating him in court that I sat down next to him to apologize. But all I could do was cry. He was kind enough to put his arm around me and just…be there."

Goddamn it! He wanted to throw his phone again. He really did.

"Vance?"

"Hmm?"

"Say something."

"Say something? Okay—how 'bout this? I *hate* that I was the jackass who made you cry. The only thing I hate worse is that Kong was the one to comfort you."

What he stopped short of saying was that what was good for the goose was in no way, shape, or form tolerable for the goddamn gander. He didn't just hate the thought of another man touching her. He couldn't physically tolerate it. The caveman in him was beating his chest and looking around for a big fucking club. And apparently the caveman decided it was time for him to start talking.

"Piper, I appreciate you telling me. And while we are clearing the air, I will go ahead and tell you now that I plan to track down Kong so the two of us can have a little chat."

"Vance, I think he's protecting me."

"From what?"

"I think I've pissed off one too many cops."

"Piper, it's your job to win cases and get your clients off."

"Yes, but the way I do it, I make it personal."

The zero jurisdiction comment she'd thrown at him resonated in his brain, slowing him waaaay down.

"Yes, baby doll, you do."

Vance heard her sigh. Then he heard a catch in her breath. *Damn it.*

"Piper, I'm…sorry. I…."

"You were right," she sobbed. "That is not who I am. That is not who I want to be," she sobbed some more and then sniffed. "They're just doing their job, but I get so personally…absorbed in the case it's like I'm the victim all over again."

"I know, baby. I know. Listen, I've got to tie up a few loose ends here, and as soon as they're done I'm coming to Raleigh. I'll take you out for a nice dinner and we can talk all this out. Until then, I don't want you thinking about any of it, okay? Just…stay in your apartment and…be safe. I'll talk to Officer Stevenson, and we'll get to the bottom of this. The three of us will figure this out, together."

"Vance, I need our night at The Charlie Horse."

"I know. You need me to finish what we started. I get it. You need me to stick around and not leave you stranded."

"Yes, that too, but I—"

"I am on board with all of it. Believe me."

"Good. So we'll turn Cinco de Nothing into Cinco de Satisfaction."

"You are singing my song."

"You'll be there when I walk in around nine."

"Piper, under the circumstances, I think it'd be better if I just pick you up."

"Oh, my God. What part of the term "do-over" do you not understand? This is important, Vance, vitally important. I need you standing in the middle of the bar trolling for chicks or whatever you were doing five years ago when I walked in. And bring those legendary moves with you. I am not kidding about this. You will act like you have no idea who I am—until I tell you—which is the part that makes it a do-over."

"Wait. Let me get this straight. You, Piper Beaumont—the girl who has a huge issue with cops—wants Vance Evans, Bad Cop to show up at the do-over."

"I do. I really do."

"Okay, but I warn you. I'm a little rusty."

"Apparently there were five minutes last night that prove otherwise."

"Well, thanks so much for that reminder."

"I'll see you around nine. There's a good band playing tonight, so the place should be just as crowded."

"Piper," Vance said, dropping his voice low and grinding out every word, "I remember every minute of that night. You came in looking for trouble and you found it. You were the aggressor and the do-over I'm interested in is with that girl. With Naughty Piper. And, just so we're clear? There will be a shot waiting for you at the bar."

He hung up before she could respond.

CHAPTER TWENTY-ONE

Piper's heart was racing a mile a minute as she pulled into a parking spot and exited her TT. She was late. Unintentionally late, but she was a good half hour behind schedule because it took every ounce of courage she had to get dressed and then walk out the door. But if Vance wanted Naughty Piper, she was determined to give him Naughty Piper.

Normally she'd wear a tank top under her slinky yellow dress because it was so low cut in both the front and back that any bra would be overly exposed. Tonight she'd psyched herself into going braless and tankless. And now, as she felt "the girls" *bounce* across the parking lot, she knew her nipples were unapologetically announcing to the world exactly where they were.

So be it.

Tonight was not for shrinking violets. Tonight was for reinventing what had begun so well and ended so poorly.

Shoulders back, bright-eyed, she drew forth her most flirtatious smile and shined it brightly at the hulking bouncer who moved to open the door. He returned her smile with a knowing grin—like he knew she was looking for trouble and had come to the right place. She was surprised when he signaled one of the bartenders and said, "Sonny over there will take care of you."

Piper thanked him, slowing her roll as she stood and surveyed all The Charlie Horse offered. The dark wood bar with its shiny brass trimmings ran the length of the room to her right, and tall tables ran down the wall to her left. In front of her was a carved-wood railing open to the sunken floor below. A boisterous crowd filled it completely. Beyond it was an ancient stone wall with two separate archways leading to the dance floor and the band, which had already started to play.

And in the center of it all stood Vance Evans, even more striking then he'd been five years earlier.

Piper mentally licked her lips at the notable changes. Five years ago, the man had been gorgeous by all accounts. But tonight he was a full-grown male—all sexy and hard bodied—with no boyish features left over from his youth. His dark hair was styled back from his forehead and his facial features were hard and angular. No hint of lankiness remained from his baseball days. His body now owned every inch of his height. His clothes were current and expensive, and he wore them well. He had a short glass in his hand and stared at her over the edge of it as he took a slow sip of the amber liquid. She felt the intensity of emotion radiating from his eyes. Like a sleek and agile black panther, Vance Evans had just found his prey.

Her body responded with a groundswell of desire, the fallout drifting like spent fireworks all the way to her toes. She turned her attention to the bartender named Sonny, walking toward him and gifting him with the same smile she'd given the bouncer.

"*Miss* Beaumont," Sonny said in greeting.

It'd been a long time since anyone had called her "Miss" Beaumont, and it had a noticeably softer and less edgy feel to it than Ms. did. The way he'd said it—the way it felt—it was like coming home. She fluttered her lids and smiled. "Hello, Sonny."

"The gentleman who ordered this sounded overly confident you'd know who it was from," Sonny said, placing the pretty little tulip glass in front of her.

She smiled, delighted with the yellow liquor and the sugared pansy attached to the rim. She had to stop herself from taking a picture.

"The gentleman was born overly confident," she said. "And I'm quite sure you and I are standing in his natural habitat."

Sonny winked as she saluted him with the miniature stemware. She took it and maneuvered along the bar to the set of stairs, stepping down into the capacity crowd to make her way toward Vance.

And just like before, he watched her come.

Confident is an understatement. He had no idea who I was five years ago, yet even then he knew I was coming for him.

Piper had to admit. That cocky part of Vance? It turned her on. And she'd be foolish to deny it. Inserting himself into her date with cute-boy Danny last Saturday—hot. Whisking her off and kissing her own will out from under her—doubly hot. Just thinking about it got her motor running. She emerged in front of Vance turned on and eager for whatever was going to play out. She basked in his easy, seductive smile, just like she had five years ago. And just like before, he looked down at her, smug and curious, and said, "Hello."

Holy God.

It was a sexy hello, full bodied, deep voiced, with an edge of eagerness, and it slid over her skin leaving tingles in its wake.

Feeling a slight bit of vertigo, she licked her lips as she looked up into his emerald eyes and smiled. "Hi."

He leaned down and spoke close to her left ear. "I've been standing here a long time waiting to taste that shot."

She offered him the first sip.

"That's not what I mean."

Her brow furrowed.

He leaned in that much closer. "Baby doll, I have seen you in action, so I am not buying the sweet and innocent thing."

Piper grabbed his shirt and stood on her tiptoes, putting her nose right up against his neck.

Lord, he smells good.

Opening eyes she wasn't aware she'd closed, she played the game. "I'm sure I have no idea what you mean," she said, exaggerating her southern accent on purpose, but noticing that her words were a little shaky—just like she was feeling. So she punctuated them with a flick of her tongue against his neck.

"Drink the fucking shot," he growled.

She smiled against his neck. Mr. Smooth had his limits, she thought, wondering just how far she could push him. Slowly releasing her hold on his shirt, she backed up just a tad. Turning her head to the right, she raised the tiny glass and took a tentative sip. The liquor was smooth with a bite, lemony and powerful. She upended the glass and swallowed the rest.

Immediately, she felt his fingers dance along the back of her scalp, turning her face toward him. Her mouth came under assault as Vance's tongue plunged in and stroked her own. He slanted his mouth more fully and pressed the arm that held his glass against her back, pulling her around and square against him. Her mind reeled back five years, thinking that it was no wonder she got caught if this was how it had been between them—standing in the middle of The Charlie Horse in the center of Raleigh on a big night out. But she didn't have to worry about that now. In the back of her mind, she considered how ironic it was that she hadn't for a moment thought of her fiancé the last time. Yet, the ramifications that had followed were so dire, she thought of him now.

She pushed against Vance's chest to break the kiss.

When he quirked his brow, she looked him square in the eye. "I've a confession to make."

"I'm not your priest." He moved in for another kiss.

"It's about Cinco de Mayo," she said against his lips. "Five years ago."

"Baby doll," he whispered, kissing her lips, her cheek, her lips again. "The only thing that matters is what is happening now."

He was right. She'd been living in the past. But ooh, she was moving forward tonight, she thought as his tongue took a leisurely swipe along the tip of hers. Tonight she was laying down all the guilt and shame and indulging once again in her wildest fantasy—Vance Evans. "Just don't leave me," she whispered.

"What?" he said, leaning his ear toward her mouth.

She captured his earlobe lightly between her teeth and scraped his flesh as she pulled her mouth down and off. If he ran away this time, she'd know where to find him. "My name is Piper Beaumont," she said with her lips pressed up against his mouth. "And I've loved you for a very long time."

That caused him to growl and pull her hard against him, her nipples smashing against his chest, his hard-on blatant against her abdomen. "Jesus," he said. "I need to get you on the dance floor." She took his hand and led their way through the crowd, heat spreading up through her neck and face, down through her chest and core. Her little clutch was taken from her hand. When she looked back, she saw Vance hand it off to someone behind him.

"Pinks," he offered. "I brought The Ninja for protection."

"Protection?"

"In case Officer Stevenson took the night off."

She nodded, hoping like hell Officer Stevenson was nowhere around. Same for anyone else she knew in her lawyer persona. She'd left angry and frustrated Ms. Beaumont at home and brought Naughty Piper along for the ride. But the thought of Naughty Piper in public again brought out a bit of panic.

She whirled around and pressed a hand against Vance's chest to stop his advance. But he kept on coming, pushing her backward into the darkness, into the noise, and into the middle of the wild crowd that made up the back room of The Charlie Horse. They blended into the action as she took stock of what was happening around her. Nobody paying too much attention, everybody worried about their own good time. Fine then. She'd do likewise.

She pulled Vance to her, eager to get lost in his lips and out of her thought pattern. He accommodated by wrapping both arms around her and meeting her demanding mouth with his own. He wasn't gentle, he wasn't calculated, he wasn't coaxing a damn thing. He was taking.

Lust consumed her. The more she gave, the more Vance demanded. She upped their game, and he'd raise it again. On the dance floor. Surrounded by…everybody. Suddenly, an icy beer was shoved between them, causing them to suck in their breaths and break apart.

Pinks stood beside them, two long-neck bottles dripping with condensation in his hands. "You two are not alone," he said. "Now let's get a little space in here," he chided. "A little something to cool you two teenagers down. For God's sake, act your age will you? Not like you're a couple of virgins at the senior prom."

"What?" Piper looked at Vance, shocked. "You're not a virgin?"

"Cute," he said with a grimace, taking the beer from Pinks.

"Thanks," Piper told Pinks. "I owe you," she said, lifting the beer out of his hands.

"The band is good," Pinks said with a toss of his head toward the stage. A slower, gentler-paced song started to play. "Enjoy it. Dance. It's early yet. You've got all night."

"Okay, Mr. Nice, Safe, and Boring," Vance said. "Back the fuck off or I'm calling in The Outlaw and tossing your ass off duty."

"And that's going to hurt my feelings how?" Pinks said, stepping back and getting lost in the crowd.

"You're paying him to be here?" Piper asked.

"I pay him for everything," Vance said doggedly. "Come here," he said, pulling her to him again. "The Ninja's right, we've got all night. It's been a long week without you in my life. I went a little hard trying to make up for lost time."

They swayed together to the music, sipping their beers, talking now that the noise level had lessened, the crowd had diminished. She had one hand on his shoulder, he had one hand on her hip.

"In my own defense, I will simply plead the fifth."

Vance smiled. "You and your lawyer speak. Are you gonna get over me being a cop? Or do I have to get you sloppy drunk, drag you into my jurisdiction, arrest you on some trumped up charge, and then incarcerate you, hold you captive, and torture you until you change your mind?"

"Now, see," she drawled, "you've just gone and made it all sound so darn appealing. If the first cop had looked like you do and tortured me the way you have in mind, I probably would have gone on to become an actress."

"If the first cop had done what I plan to do, I'd have to shoot him."

"Avenging my honor?"

"Erasing his memory."

A slow grin stretched itself across her lips. "Mmm, what could you possibly have planned?"

"First, I'll have to bring you to justice for public nudity."

"Public nudity?"

"I could ask any guy in here who is not wearing a bra and every drunk one of them would point directly at you. Your body is this close to inciting a riot."

"Really?" she asked, her eyes lighting up. "This close?" She held his gaze as Naughty Piper lifted her hands above her head and started circling her hips slowly to the beat of the music. "I've never... actually...incited a riot," she said, moving in a slow circle, looking back at Vance over her shoulder. "I'm sort of looking forward to it."

"Go ahead and have your fun, baby doll. Penalties accrue," he warned.

She backed into him, rotating her hips. He took a long pull on his beer as he placed a hand—fingers splayed, palm flat—possessively against her stomach. She felt his thumb nesting between her breasts, his little finger resting on her bikini line. He pressed her back against him, hips moving to the beat of the music. He seemed reasonably restrained while her whole internal warning system went off and then began to melt. She reached one arm back to curl around his neck, a beer still clutched in her other. She felt his mouth fall to the side of her neck and his chin scrape against her shoulder. His kisses were light and teasing, and she let her eyes close, let herself get carried away with the music.

"If we were alone, I'd strip you naked to your waist," he whispered in her ear.

She tilted her head back and responded. "If we were alone, I'd let you."

She felt him smile.

His hand slid sensuously over the waist of her dress as they kept dancing.

His words were low and rough. "If we were alone, my hands would be making a long, slow study of your naked and voluptuous feminine charms."

She smiled. "If we were alone, I'd like that."

He took another pull on his beer, used his chin to tilt her head in the opposite direction, and leaned down to kiss the other side of her neck. "There's a rumor going around...that I'm good with my hands. But what I'm really good with is my mouth." He sucked gently on her neck and sensation shot everywhere as if to prove his point. "So when I get you alone," he said licking close to her ear, "I'm going to show you just how talented my hands and mouth can be." When she tried to move her head to respond, he nudged it back. "Everywhere."

She lifted her head back against him, craning her neck so she could see him. "That's a lotta of talk for a guy with your reputation."

"You think I'm playing?" he growled.

"I think talk is cheap," she teased.

She was spun around, dragged up against him, and then felt all of his long, hard length rock against her.

Dear…God.

So besotted with the yearning pulsating through her body, she was being backed up before she knew what was happening. Her back hit a wall—a corner. A dark corner. A corner no one paid attention to because it was tucked around the arched entrance to the room and further hidden from view by a broad, square floor-to-ceiling column. The band started playing a rock ballad and the room vibrated with bass.

"Take a sip of your beer."

She complied, and he took it from her, setting both their bottles on the floor.

"Put your hands over your head."

Yeah, right.

"Aww, baby doll, you think I'm kidding," he said in an isn't-that-cute kind of voice, taking up her wrists, bending her arms at the elbows, and pressing the backs of her hands against the wall by her shoulders. He leaned in for a kiss. A slow, sensuous they-should-be-alone-in-a-bedroom kiss. His mouth controlled the action while he kept his feet and body at a distance. Slowly he rode her hands up along the wall until they were extended high above her head. He gripped both wrists in one hand and then pressed his forehead firmly on that hand, allowing his eyes to look down at Piper.

Her vision was engulfed by his torso. She was only able to witness the length and breadth of his chest. She licked her lips as she watched it rise and fall. When she felt fingertips drifting down over her bare arm, she lifted her head. She watched as they skimmed over the surface of her flesh, all the way down to the sensitive skin of her underarm, and then farther, moving slowly, sensuously over the silky material at the side of her breast.

"You've been teasing me too long." His voice was low and husky. He kissed her wrists held high above her head. "Every night this week, I'd wake up hard thinking of you." He slowly pressed his lower body against her to emphasize his point. The back of his free hand drifted brazenly across the front of her dress, her nipples catching against his knuckles. Piper leaned into him when he turned his hand over and tested her flesh. His hands were amazing, the caress so tantalizing that Piper welcomed the fondling without protest. Sucking in a breath, she closed her eyes as his fingers went rogue.

She opened her eyes when Vance lifted his forehead and turned his head to look behind him. "Pinks?"

"I've got your back," came the reply.

"Best wingman ever," Vance muttered, bringing all his attention back to Piper. "Where were we?"

His mouth descended by increments, so slowly she watched it come. She let her lips soften, welcoming him. She felt the pressure ease off her wrists as his tongue slipped inside her mouth and a sound of pent-up tension drifted from her. Her arms drew down the wall bit by bit, her fingers finding their way onto his shoulders and then into the curl at his nape. It was a lengthy, inviting make-out session against the wall in a dark corner of a crowded room. And every aspect of it encouraged her body to yearn for more.

His fingers heated her skin as they caressed her throat, leisurely sliding down the exposed flesh of her neckline, and then stole inside her dress to cup a breast. Vance groaned appreciatively against her mouth and the thrill it created within her allowed him to continue. He pulled her right hand from his neck, easing it down to lay at her side. Then he reached up with two fingers, tugging at the shoulder of her dress.

His eyes dared her to stop him before he glanced down into the gaping neckline of her dress and looked his fill.

Her breathing accelerated, the heaving of her chest giving evidence to that. "You're going to get me in trouble," she whispered.

"Naughty Piper loves trouble," he said, looking unabashedly down her dress. She felt completely naked when he pulled at the waistband. No doubt it allowed his gaze to travel the length of her torso, spy her lacy lingerie, and see all the way down to her naked thighs. He sluggishly dragged his gaze up to her face, letting her dress fall back into place.

"I'd like to take you home now," he said quietly.

She blinked a couple times, deciphering his words gradually

because the chills running over her body were dumbing down her brain.

"Piper, please don't make me beg."

She smiled at the thought of Vance Evans begging for anything. "What about Pinks?"

"He'll take whatever car we leave behind." Then he flashed her his big, seductive grin. "I brought my truck," he said, dangling it out there like bait.

"I love your truck."

"I know."

She touched a fingertip to his smooth bottom lip. "I'm thinkin' there's a lot we could take care of in that truck."

He captured her finger with his teeth. "I'm thinkin' you're right," he said around it. "You willin' to follow me out of here or am I gonna have to drag you?"

I'll follow you. Anywhere.

"You willin' to dance with me back at my apartment?" she asked.

His weight leaned in, securing her against the wall. He dropped his head and whispered against her ear. "I'm willin' to make *you* dance." He pushed his hand up her thigh, under her dress and stroked a thumb over the front of her lace panties for emphasis.

Her body did respond by dancing.

"You want me to get you off right here?" he breathed against her ear. "'Cause I can do it," he promised. He rubbed his pelvis against his hand, which was caught against damp lace, right on top of her aching need. His thumb stroked her slowly, up and then down.

"Stop," she whispered, but her body moved against his thumb.

"I don't think so."

"Not here," she pleaded.

"Right here."

"Oh, God."

"No…just me, Piper." His thumb slid underneath the lace and lay on top of her tight, damp curls. "Say my name."

She bit her lip, determined to stop the insanity, at least until they got inside his truck.

Vance licked her lips imitating the slow draw his thumb made at the same time. "Naughty," he said as he kissed her. "Naughty," he said as his thumb teased just the right spot. "Piper," he whispered against her cheek. "Say…my…name."

"Vance," she panted. She couldn't help herself.

She felt him smile against the corner of her mouth. "Now," he said, "tell me you want me to finish this right here…" his voice dipped even lower, "in public." His hips started a slow cant, pressing his thumb even more intimately.

Piper's breath hitched, and she laid the back of her head against the wall.

"Breathe, baby doll," he said slowly. "That's why we're here. To finish what we started. Let me finish this. Let me finish you."

She wanted to weep with longing, and although she knew exactly where she was, and did actually care about it, she was too caught up in her own pleasure to stop it.

Vance pressed his right knee between her legs, sliding them apart. "That's it," he said, easing his thumb along her damp center. "Jesus, Piper," he breathed against her temple. "Do I do that to you? Make you soft and wet?" He kissed her head. "Or is it you, just being so damn perfect?"

She whimpered.

"Take all the time you need, baby. I've got this."

His touch was languid. So soft, so light, yet sooo potent.

"There's no place I'd rather be," he assured her, not only in his whisper but with a slow kiss to her temple, and in the leisurely way his finger tantalized.

Her jaw went slack and her pelvis eased against him.

Vance pressed his thigh up and in, giving her leverage. "Whatever you need."

She rocked again, and then a breath caught way back in her throat. Vance's mouth came down on hers, pulling her breath and emotions up and out while his thigh pressed against her. She made a small adjustment, caught his thumb right on the nub of built-up longing and rode his thigh and then the wave as her body shattered against him and against the wall—literally between a rock and a hard place.

Her arms were around his neck, her mouth frantic under his lips, their bodies locked up tight when she started to come to her senses. When her breathing started to slow, when her muscles started to collapse, when the roaring in her ears started to quiet.

When sanity returned.

CHAPTER TWENTY-TWO

Vance felt her tap his chest. Three times. Three quick taps and then he stepped back. Piper didn't look him in the eye when she said she needed her purse, that she wanted to go to the ladies' room. Vance turned around and found Pinks with his back to them about five feet away, leaning against the column, further protecting them from onlookers. He reached out and tapped Pinks on the shoulder.

"Piper needs—"

Pinks held up the little clutch without turning around. Vance took it and gave it to Piper. He thought he heard her say she'd be right back, but he couldn't be sure. The music was loud, and she still wasn't looking at him.

Vance watched her go, walking up to stand next to Pinks. He rubbed his jaw, a sinking feeling settling in his stomach.

"She's bolting, isn't she?"

"Yup."

"And you're sure because…?"

"The restrooms are that way," Pinks said pointing in the opposite direction from where Piper headed.

"And what's that way?" Vance asked, pointing after Piper's trail.

"The back door."

Goddamn it.

"You seem a little relaxed for my wingman."

Pinks held up a key fob. Vance grabbed it out of his hand, smiling. In its place popped a laminated card that looked a helluva lot like—"Piper's license?" Vance said in wonder, grabbing that up too and studying the picture and the birthdate, memorizing it all. "Best fucking wingman ever," he said, clapping Pinks on the back. "I'll give her a few minutes. Let her clear her head."

"You gonna tell me why she left you holding your dick?"

Vance smirked. The kid was not wrong.

"I'm serious," Pinks said, finally looking at him. "Do I need to defend her honor? Because I will take you down if you took advantage of—"

"Simmer down, Bruce Lee. She's fine—we're fine. She's just a little frazzled, that's all. Bad Cop coaxed out Naughty Piper. And trust me, Naughty Piper had a very good time. But once the fun was over, I'm pretty sure The Lawyer Beaumont started shouting a whole lot of 'What the hell is going on here?' inside Perfect Piper's head. So…you know…all three of them bolted."

"Do you hear yourself?" Pinks questioned. "Do you have any idea of what you're talking about?"

"God, I hope so," Vance said. "Come on, I'll buy you a beer."

Piper stood beside her car digging around in her clutch, unable to find her key fob. She took everything out and put it on the hood of the car, but still no key. She huffed and closed her eyes, trying to remember exactly what happened when she'd parked hours before. She'd been late and in a hurry. It was possible that the key fob somehow got left in the car, although she was pretty sure the car wouldn't have locked if that were the case. Still, with the parking lot so dark, she couldn't see much as she peered into the driver's side window. She yanked on the door handle over and over, desperate to get in her car and drive out of here. She needed to put a little distance between herself and insanity, although the way she was starting to shout at her precious little TT, it seemed insanity had surely taken root.

Trying to remember a trick to get into locked cars, she sought out a credit card and shoved it between the window and the edge of the door, hoping somehow, someway that would trigger the lock. If she could just get inside the damn car—

"Ma'am, step away from the car."

Piper twirled, startled, and then breathed deep when she saw two police officers approaching. "Oh, thank God," she said relaxing back against her door. "Do either of you have one of those long, narrow thingies that can pop a lock? I think I may have left my key in the car," she explained. When they weren't immediately forthcoming, she took the time to focus on their faces.

"Officer Millhouse, Officer Kreber." Even Piper noticed the immediate change in her tone—abrupt, condescending. "I didn't recognize you in the dark."

"Step away from the car," the taller officer repeated.

"This is my car."

"Maybe it is, maybe it isn't. We're going to need some ID."

"As if you don't know who I am."

"Oh, Ms. Beaumont, we know *exactly* who you are."

"And what is that supposed to mean?"

"That we have no idea whose car this is. I'm afraid we're gonna need some proof."

"Then help me get into the car so I can show you my registration."

"Let's just start with your license for now," Officer Millhouse said, taking a slow step into her personal space. "Officer Kreber will run a quick check, and we'll see what's what."

"What's what? You mean if there are any outstanding parking tickets or anything you can use to detain or humiliate me."

"Look at that, David, she's smart even outside the courtroom," Officer Millhouse said over his shoulder. "Ms. Beaumont, your license."

"Fine," Piper said. She scooted out to the side to avoid touching Officer Millhouse or having to suggest that he step back. She moved toward the pile of debris on the hood of her car, going through her wallet first and putting things back into her purse as she sorted through the rest of it. She stopped for a moment trying to remember if she'd had to show her ID to get into The Charlie Horse.

She had not.

Suddenly she knew exactly where her key and license were.

She turned around to the two cops and said, "I've been robbed. My key and my license have been stolen. If you'd be so kind as to follow me inside, I'll point out the perpetrator and you two can slake your bloodlust and make an arrest."

"You've been robbed?"

"I have."

"Is your wallet missing?"

"Ah," Piper stalled as she looked into her purse and stared at her wallet. "No. No, thankfully my wallet has not been stolen. Only my key and my license."

"That seems odd to me. Does that seem a little odd to you, David?" Officer Millhouse asked.

"Very odd. Probably should take a drive over to the police station and sort all this out there."

"Ms. Beaumont, please, step this way," Officer Millhouse suggested pointing to the waiting squad car. "We'll just run a quick check, maybe test your blood alcohol level, see where things go from there."

"Look," Piper scolded as she pushed herself off of her car and stepped forward, "I know what you're doing, and I don't find it amusing."

"Well, that's good, because the last thing we're trying to do is amuse you," Millhouse growled.

"No. You're trying to intimidate me."

Officer Millhouse stepped forward, looming over Piper. "And how's it working so far?"

It's starting to work pretty darn well.

"Hey!" an overly cheerful voice hollered from the back door of the bar. "Piper," Vance said as he jogged over. "I found your keys."

He came up on the scene with eyes only on Piper, immediately raising a hand to gently stroke her cheek as he looked into her eyes. "Sorry about this," he said quietly.

His gentle touch, the sound of his voice, just his presence and concern had the lawyer in her standing down, mellowing slowly but surely into Piper—just Piper.

Vance turned and held out his hand to the two cops behind him. "Hey," he said with a good-ol'-boy smile on his face. "Vance Evans." He pulled his own badge out of his back pocket and flipped it open. "Henderson PD and personal friend of Ms. Beaumont's."

"Personal friend?" Officer Millhouse said, his eyebrows shooting sky high. "That's rather hard to believe. She's not a big fan of cops."

"And you two don't seem to be doin' much to change her mind," Vance said in a light-hearted tone. "What's the problem here?"

"We'd like Ms. Beaumont to take a breathalyzer test."

"Yeah, that's not happening."

"Says who?"

"Says her date."

"Is this true? Is he your date?" Officer Millhouse looked around Vance to ask Piper.

She nodded her head.

Millhouse looked Vance up and down. "She didn't mention a date when we caught her breaking into this car. Is this yours?"

"It's hers," Vance said.

"I need some proof," Millhouse insisted.

Vance pointed the key fob toward the driver's side door and clicked the lock. Piper moved around to the other side and rummaged in the glove compartment for her registration. She handed it to Officer Kreber, who took it and asked for her license. Piper glanced over at Vance. Vance pulled it out of his front pocket and handed it over.

When Officer Kreber started to head back to the squad car, Vance stepped forward and stopped him with a low-timbred disquisition.

"Trust me, bro," he said. "You do not want to get into a pissing contest with me because you have an axe to grind with a distractingly beautiful lawyer. Buck up for God's sake. She can't possibly win 'em all. Your turn is bound to come soon. But this," he said, gesturing toward Officer Kreber, "this right here is nothing short of police brutality. And if you think you've lost something to her thus far, just wait until she drags your ass to court with the entire Collins & Reese law firm behind her. Not to mention your own Officer Stevenson and the entire Henderson Police Department. We may not have jurisdiction," he said, with a pointed eye toward Piper, "but we do have Ms. Beaumont's back."

"Henderson? Hey," Officer Kreber asked, "do you happen to know a guy by the name of Brooks Bennett?"

"As a matter of fact I do," Vance nodded.

Office Kreber stepped in and started poking Vance in the chest to accentuate each word. "Best game ever. The guy threw a no-hitter to win the College World Series for State. I fuckin' love that guy."

"Is that right?" Vance said, a big, broad smile across his face.

Piper let it go only a couple seconds before she said, "If it wasn't for Officer Evans making a diving catch of a line drive near third base, Brooks wouldn't have had that no hitter. So you can thank him for that."

"You played third base?" Kreber said, moving to give Vance a high five.

Sports, Piper thought. She didn't get it, but it certainly brought men together like nothing else.

"Hey, why don't you and Officer Gang Bang here drive over sometime this week and let Brooks and me treat you to Skippers BBQ. Best damn pork you'll ever taste. We'll rehash the win and share a few beers. Call it an interdepartmental meeting. Brooks will love that. Besides, I'm sure you city boys could help us out with a few suggestions on how to keep graffiti from taking over the center of our little town."

The two policemen exchanged a look, clearly liking the idea of BBQ, but hesitant to capitulate and let Piper off the hook.

"Look," Vance said in an easy tone, "we're all on the same side here. Well," he corrected with a short laugh, "the three of us are on the same side, and Ms. Beaumont is holding up the constitution by providing counsel to the accused. It's her *job*, and she's obligated to do it to the best of her ability." He held his hands out to the side in a helpless gesture. "She just has a helluva lot of ability. In fact, I bet you didn't know that besides getting college yahoos off with a hand slap, she makes the world's best cinnamon rolls."

"She cooks?" Millhouse said inside a disbelieving grunt.

"Swear to God," Vance said, holding up his right hand. "The most amazing combination of cinnamon and butter you'll ever sink your teeth into."

"Well, who doesn't like a good cinnamon roll?" Kreber grinned.

"Piper?" Vance coaxed, tossing a hand toward Officer Kreber.

"What?" Piper said, shaking herself from the trance Vance's smooth talking had lulled her into.

Vance gave her a wide-eyed, get-with-the-program look. "You like to cook, right? Maybe you'd like to ask when King Kong and his buddies Gang Bang and State Fan would be available for you to stop by their precinct with some of your mouth-watering pastries."

"Oh! Right," Piper said, looking over at the men in blue. "A peace offering...not a bribe," she said, warming to the idea. "I didn't realize how rough I've been on y'all and...well, now that Officer Evans has opened my eyes to a few things, I think I'm going to take some time off and reevaluate my approach in court."

She thought she saw them both take a deep breath. *Good God, was she really that bad?*

Officer Kreber stepped forward and handed her back her license and registration. "I'll look forward to your cinnamon rolls, Ms. Beaumont. Y'all go on and have a good night." He and Officer Millhouse nodded toward Vance and left.

Piper watched them go, her head reeling from the obvious truth. Like some ridiculous comic book character, she'd managed to become a hero to the outlaws and an enemy to the crime fighters. How the hell did that happen? She looked over at Vance, the real hero.

"You saved the day," she told him. "Swooped in here offering up free donuts to a bunch of overworked cops and just like that...saved all of us a lot of time, money, and heartache."

"We men have fragile, fragile egos." He stepped forward and settled his hands on her waist. "Soothe a few ruffled feathers and maybe the next time they're faced with a bunch of silly coeds, they'll think about what you really stand for and insert a little of your common sense." He leaned down and kissed her on the forehead. "Of course, if it actually works out that way, it's going to affect your bottom line."

She could see Vance's emotions shift then. Watched his shoulders tighten as his eyes narrowed in on her. She felt him grip her waist a little tighter. "Were you runnin' out on me, baby doll?"

Piper allowed her forehead to settle against his chest. She breathed him in and let her arms wrap around him, letting his body support her as she sagged into his strength, and into the truth. "I wasn't so much running out on you," she said on a sigh, "as I was running from the ridiculous woman I become when I'm around you."

"Hmm," Vance said, gently stroking the back of her head. "You mean Naughty Piper? That's a shame really, because as much as the boy in me loves Perfect Piper and the cop in me has mixed emotions about The Lawyer Beaumont, the man in me? Well, that one is really into Naughty Piper."

Piper gave a short laugh before bringing her head up and pressing a hand against his chest, creating some space between them. "I've always considered myself a serious woman," she said, as Vance took a step back, letting his hands drift from her. "I mean…I do realize I look like a cross between Goldilocks and a Playboy Bunny, and I admit I've played that up so my adversaries misjudge my intelligence. But…in *most* things, I've considered myself a serious woman."

Vance moved beside her and leaned against the car, putting his hands in his pockets. "You're a serious lawyer. Your record in court proves that."

"Those officers wouldn't have pulled that crap on a serious lawyer, and what I let happen on the dance floor in there was ridiculous."

The night around them fell heavy and quiet, the parking lot devoid of activity. The silence drew out, and after a while Vance pulled his hand from his pocket and reached down to hold on to hers. He rubbed his thumb across the back of her hand. His voice was low and cautious. "You running out on us?"

"No," she sighed, leaning her head against his shoulder. "Just coming to terms with the truth."

He kissed the top of her head and whispered, "You're not ridiculous. You're brilliant, refined, and sensuous with hints of naughtiness. And as much fun as I was having with Naughty Piper, if you want to keep her all buttoned up, then I'm down with that."

"Oh, God," Piper moaned, realizing that there was no way she wanted to keep Naughty Piper buttoned up. "I am *completely* ridiculous."

Vance chuckled into her hair. "You're a little ridiculous. But all women are a little ridiculous."

She should have taken offense and made a case for her gender, but she didn't have the energy. Besides, if the shoe fit….

"And men are assholes," said Vance, "especially those two bozos. And me for lettin' you come out here alone."

"Maybe it's all for the best. Bribing them with baked goods," she sighed. "From angry lawyer to Suzy Homemaker," she grumbled.

Vance pulled her around in front of him, tilting her chin up so she'd look him in the eye. "Piper, you're not a ridiculous woman. You waited two hours to sober up before driving yourself out of Henderson last weekend. It was an asshole move to pull you over, especially knowing your issue with cops."

She held up her hand. "I overreacted. And you were right. About everything."

"Well, now." Vance grinned. "There's a first time for everything. And that was pure dumb luck because all I really wanted to do was kiss you goodnight." He leaned forward, still grinning and pressed his lips to hers in a gentle kiss. A happy kiss, she realized and smiled right into it.

If Vance Evans could be happy after what he'd been through, who was she to cut herself off from all that happiness had to offer.

CHAPTER TWENTY-THREE

"I like kissing you," Vance whispered against her lips, letting his fingers bury themselves in her hair. God, he did. He really, really did. Her lips were ripe and succulent. Her mouth warm and sweet. The touch of her tongue against his own had the power to make him come without any other physical stimulation. Not that there wasn't plenty of that.

While he leaned against her car with his legs spread wide, he pulled her curvaceous body tight up against him, making it easier to get his mouth on hers. He loved that she was tiny and round, that her overt femininity brought out the caveman in him. That her soft and pliant skin made him harder in all the right places. She fit into his arms, between his legs, under his mouth, like no other woman. She was perfect. Perfect Piper. And he let himself get lost in their kiss for a while before his mind started working on a way to make her his.

Because he wanted Piper.

For keeps.

He wanted Piper in his bed. And not just tonight. He wanted her in his bed night after night after night after night. He wanted Piper in Henderson. He wanted to build her a kitchen, one that would make his dad's look puny. He wanted to give her a kitchen she would never want to leave. With a bedroom right down the hall that he could drag her into and kiss her like this while her pastries baked.

Because Piper had comforted him when his mother walked out.

And five years ago her kiss had reminded him how good life could feel.

And she climbed into the Maserati simply because he showed up, forgiving him for running out on her twice.

And because she chose his beat-up old truck over the Rolls.

And she knew that he had caught the line drive that saved Brooks' no-hitter.

"Whoa," he said, pulling his lips from hers, blinking back the sexual haze. "Piper?" he breathed. "How did you know about the line drive?"

He felt her hand curl into the fabric of his shirt, trying to pull his lips back to hers. She shook her head. "What?" she whispered. Her sweet pink cheeks were flushed, her hair was all messed up and sexy, and her gentle blue eyes were dazed.

"Baby doll," he breathed against her lips. "You told Officer Kreber about the line drive during the World Series game. How did you know about that?"

She shrugged, nestled right into him, and whispered, "I was there."

Blink. Blink.

"You were…there? What do you mean, you were there?"

"I was there."

"You weren't there."

"I was there," she insisted. "I was in Johnny Rosenblatt Stadium in Omaha, Nebraska, the day NC State won the College World Series."

"Wha—? Wh—? How?" he sputtered, not comprehending.

She buried her face in his shirt, nuzzling her nose against his chest. He felt her breath through the light fabric as she muttered something unintelligible.

"What?" he asked, pushing her from him.

She pressed back in and muttered something else.

Vance couldn't help himself. He burst out laughing.

"What's so funny?" she grumbled, finally pulling her head out of his chest.

"I don't know," he said. "I just…I just feel good. Piper, you are the gift that keeps on giving."

"Right," she said as if she were rolling her eyes.

"Piper, you are like this shiny, little box, all wrapped up in yellow and gold, and I was content to simply walk by it now and again. But now, I get to open the lid from time to time, and every time I do, there's a precious and unexpected jewel with my name on it."

He needed to buy her a diamond. A big one.

"Baby doll, it doesn't matter whether you were at the game or not. That fact that you know where it was played and that I made a diving catch—" He laughed again. "Even my father didn't make it to that game."

"I was there," she said softly. "I was there because you were playing, Vance. I was at your State Championship game too."

That brought him up short. Took all the joy right out of him. He let go of her arms and stood up straight, every bit of humor leaking from him. "Piper." He felt like he'd been robbed. "Why didn't you make yourself known?"

"I had intended to," she claimed. "But when the final out came, everything erupted in chaos. Everyone started rushing from the stands and onto the field. I couldn't see you in the crowd, so I climbed to the top of the stands to try to spot you. And I did. I saw you. I even called out to you and waved as you came by. There was a moment when I thought you heard me. When you looked up and saw me. And then…."

"Then Lolly's cousin, Molly, jumped into my arms, wrapped her legs around me, and stuck her tongue down my throat," Vance said in defeat, remembering the scene well. That girl was nothin' but trouble.

"Well, I didn't know her name," Piper said quietly, adding a shy smile. "But I didn't feel confident enough to step into whatever was going on between the two of you."

"You have no idea how much I wish you had," He sighed heavily. "And here I thought I was the one looking for you all these years."

"Mmm, Vance Evans." She wigged those luscious tits up against him as she burrowed herself back into his arms. "You don't know the half of it."

"I want to know all of it," he growled, taking her plump little bottom into his hands and pulling her hard against him. Jesus, she was hot. He dropped his mouth on top of hers and did his best to swallow her whole. Every fiber he possessed, from his knees to his neck, wanted to sink into Piper. Just lay her down and show her what the caveman in him could do.

"I came to an eighth grade dance," she said into his mouth. But he wasn't really listening. He was all about the kissing as he tried to figure out how he was going to make love to her in her little TT.

"I asked you to dance, but you didn't have time."

Not her TT idiot. Your truck. She loves your truck.

"You said that to me. You said, 'I'm sorry. I wish I could, but I don't have time.'"

No talking, Piper. Just kissing. Just…stop… Vance's head snapped up. "What the hell did you just say?"

"My friend, Tansy Langford, was so mad at you for not dancing with me that she dragged me out of the dance to go home and do our first shots."

"Wait-wait-wait-wait-wait-wait-wait." Vance didn't know which appendage he wanted to grab first, because both his head and his dick were about to explode. "Tansy? Langford?"

Piper had the audacity to tilt her head and make her eyes go big, like he had the missing piece to life's ultimate puzzle right in his hands.

"She was in our fourth grade class."

"Tansy?"

"Our parents were close. I saw her often during those elementary years after we moved. She knew I liked you. Finally my parents let me go spend the weekend with Tansy so I could go to the eighth grade dance."

"You were at a fucking dance? Piper!"

"Well, don't get mad at me, Fred Astaire. I asked you to dance, but you were more interested in every other girl there."

"Oh, just kill me now," Vance groaned, rubbing his hands through his hair and then behind his neck. "Piper, their fathers paid me dance with those girls. I was so blinded by dollar signs that I didn't know you were there. *Again.* How many times have you been standing right in front of me and I didn't know it?" he shouted.

"Well, imagine how that's made me feel," she shouted back.

Silence.

Black night. Cool air. Quiet parking lot.

And the girl of his dreams, his precious, sweet, little blond hologram was standing within an arm's reach. She had never walked away from him willingly, and far more important than that, he now knew she had always come back.

I love you.

Vance wanted to shout the words. He wanted to tell Piper Beaumont right then and there that she was his and he wasn't going to let her out of his sight again.

Instead, his mouth formed the words, "Come to Henderson. Take the time off of work you were talking about and spend it in Henderson. With me."

"What? Vance," she said as she came into his arms willingly, laughing. "I just can't take a vacation…to Henderson."

"Of course, you can." He began kissing her neck. If he could coax her into letting him put his hand up her dress in The Charlie Horse, this was going to be a piece of cake.

"What about my first years?"

"You've been hogging them all summer. Let them help somebody else out."

"But where would I stay?" she whispered, starting to get lost in the moment—just like he was.

"Handcuffed to my bed," he suggested.

She giggled against his lips.

He smiled and told her how much it would mean to him. How incredible having her back in Henderson would be. Except he didn't tell her with words. He told her with his mouth…and his hands… and she promised him she would come, with her sighs and her lips and her fingers in his hair.

CHAPTER TWENTY-FOUR

Piper woke up Sunday morning early and alone.

Now how the hell did that happen?

She'd spent a long time kissing Vance, laughing with him in the parking lot, but even after his earlier threat to drag her out of the bar and his joke about handcuffing her to his bed, he didn't attempt to talk her into going home with him or work himself into an invitation to her bed. No, he'd spent all his time manipulating her into agreeing to take two weeks off from work and spend them in Henderson.

Which was completely absurd.

While she agreed she had the unwanted attention of Raleigh's police force raining down on her at the moment, she did not feel compelled to leave town until this little "tiff" ran out of steam. Which was Vance's suggestion while he took his time kissing the side of her neck and skimming his magic hands over her backside.

And although she had told Officer Millhouse that she was taking some time off to reevaluate her courtroom demeanor, no specifics had been planned. Vance kept insisting those specifics would only take her a phone call to work out as he'd run his fingertips through her hair and kissed her lips like he was enjoying his favorite ice cream.

And as he continued to press all those…nice…soft…buttons, he slowly convinced her that they needed quality time to get to know one another again and that coming back to the place where it had all started made complete sense.

And it had.

Until the sun came up.

Let's face it. While kissing Vance she'd probably agree to anything, but in the light of day, the idea seemed far-fetched and foolish. Henderson wasn't a vacation destination. There was no lakeside resort. Where would she stay for two weeks? She certainly wasn't moving in with Vance. And what would she do? Lounge beside his father's pool like some hired escort waiting around until he needed her...lips again?

Ridiculous.

And why was he only after her lips? That made less sense than any of it. Especially after he'd coaxed her hand down to his groin. It was abundantly clear the man didn't have a problem in the testosterone department. She thought for sure he'd be draggin' her over to his truck, right before he opened the door to her car, gave her one last, lingering kiss, and then shoved her into the driver's seat and told her he'd see her later.

"Are you kidding me?" she said out loud.

The man was nothing but a tease. And in protest, she decided that from now on, she was going to be the one playing hard to get.

The phone rang, interrupting the downward spiral of her thoughts. "Hello?"

"Ms. Beaumont," came Officer Stevenson's husky voice. "Should I be flattered or frightened that you're so desperate to get a hold of me that you've called my superior officer three times? And what is with this message from your boyfriend, who I understand is calling me King Kong."

"Oh." Piper was mortified. "Officer Stevenson, he means no disrespect. Vance calls every—"

His chuckle stopped her explanations. "It's all right. I'd much rather be King Kong than Gang Bang."

"Well, Vance does like nicknames, but he's not exactly my boyfriend."

"Your sleeping buddy then."

"No." It came out as sort of a sigh before she could stop it. "I'm beginning to believe he doesn't think of me like that either."

"Sweetheart," Officer Stevenson said, "we all think of you like that."

"I—uh. Wow." Piper was stunned.

"Did that just come out of my mouth? I am soooo sorry. Forget I said that. I was out late last night and…well, why don't you tell me what's going on."

That would probably be a good idea, if Piper could remember what she wanted to talk with him about. Right now her mind was blank and spinning.

Officer Stevenson filled in the silence. "And what is this I'm hearing about cinnamon rolls?"

Oh…right. "While I was working late at the office Friday night, something occurred to me," she started without preamble. "You following me around last week wasn't because you were irritated with me, was it? It's because everyone you work with is irritated with me. You were playing bodyguard."

Silence.

"I'm right, aren't I? And it's okay if you don't want to spell it out. Officer Kreber and Officer Millhouse did that well enough last night. Vance suggested I try to soothe y'all with my cinnamon rolls. Which I'm happy to do. I'm just sorry that I've been…."

"Been what?"

"Taking my revenge out on every police officer except the one I'm really mad at."

"Huh. And what's his name?"

"I don't even remember," she sighed.

"What'd he do?" he asked quietly.

"He…did his job," she said, relenting—her eyes finally being opened. "I was a silly college freshman, and he was just doing his job."

"And you had to go to court?"

"I did. And I did it without a lawyer. And things went very, very badly for me."

"And that's why you became a defense attorney."

"Yes."

"And that's why you represent the kids."

"Yes."

"Well…you are very good at your job," he said.

Piper dissolved into hysterical laughter. "So good I'm a pariah to law enforcement."

"I wouldn't say that. But I wouldn't go two miles over the speed limit if I were you either."

"So the cinnamon rolls?"

"Might help."

She laughed again. "Okay. I get it. I'll start sucking up a bit. But seriously, how much danger am I in, if you feel the need to be my bodyguard?"

"The reason I'm your bodyguard is because I was the idiot who started the whole Bust Ms. Beaumont campaign in the first place. It was my big mouth that led the charge against you after you got that asshole, George Howling, off. But after you handed me your card offering to be *my* lawyer, and then cried on my shoulder, well, hell, I felt like the worst kind of gangster. That's when I shifted gears and started running interference. Ms. Beaumont, I can't apologize enough."

"You just did, Officer Stevenson. Thank you. When's the best time to catch you, Kreber, and Millhouse at the precinct?"

"Shifts change at four. You can get everybody coming or going then."

"Duly noted. Now don't you worry one more minute about me. I'll take it from here."

"Yes, ma'am."

Piper hung up the phone wishing her little kitchen had a whole lot more space.

An hour later, she was elbow deep in flour when her phone rang again.

"Hello?"

"Piper, this is Genevra DuVal."

"Well, what a pleasant surprise," Piper said, smiling as she rolled out dough. "How are you?"

"Just as good as good can be," Genevra said in that sweet southern style that reminded Piper of her momma. "I'm just a tiny bit frazzled at the moment with all the wedding preparations. Which is why I'm calling. To ask a huge favor. You see, I've ordered our wedding cake from the one woman in town who makes them, and although her cakes are truly delicious, she can only make it so big. And when I asked that she make two, well, she looked at me like I'd gone and lost my mind. She's about a hundred years old," Genevra said in a conspiratorial tone, "and her one cake will never feed everybody unless we cut it up into itty bitty pieces."

Piper laughed.

"So, Lolly suggested a groom's cake. Well, you know I just fell in love with the idea because if there was ever a groom who deserved a cake, it's Hale. So I went on the Internet and, Piper, you cannot believe the brilliant, creative, whimsical ideas people have come up with for groom's cakes. And now…well, I can't make up my mind. But that's okay, because with this crowd, it wouldn't hurt to have three or even four different groom's cakes rounding out the dessert table."

"I love the idea," Piper said.

"Yes, but to pull that off I'm going to need your magical powers in the kitchen. Please say you'll help me."

"Oh, Mrs. DuVal, I think you know I'd be more than happy to bake cakes in that kitchen."

"Piper, thank you so much. And please call me Genevra. You and I are already bonding in the trenches, aren't we? Now is there any chance you'd be able to drive over here and let me take you to lunch? We could meet at Henderson Country Club and put our heads together. I'll bring my computer and show you what I'm thinking."

"What time?"

"Noon?"

"I'll be there." Piper smiled as she hung up.

❧❦❧

Vance propped himself up on Brooks' desk and swung his legs back and forth beneath him, waiting for his buddy to get his head out of the Sunday paper and acknowledge his presence. It only took two fingers reaching for one of three remaining Krispy Kreme donuts to get Brooks to growl.

"Jesus Christ, you've already had three."

"Get your own damn donuts," Brooks said into the paper.

"Well, how 'bout buying an entire dozen next time? Bring in a few to share with your coworkers."

Brooks took a deliberate look behind him at the completely empty police precinct.

"Goddammit, you know what I mean."

Brooks folded the paper as he sat up. "I do indeed. But what I don't know is why you are here trying to get your hands on my donuts when they should be coasting over Tinker Bell's mighty fine lady parts."

"I…uh, actually…I don't have a good answer for that."

Brooks' brows shot up.

"I don't," Vance admitted. "There was a time last night when all I wanted to do was rush her into my truck and…you know, get 'r done. But she's Piper, and she's…."

"Your hologram," Brooks finished.

Vance smirked.

"Yeah, yeah…she's the one that got away, twice," Brooks said as he yawned.

"As it turns out, she's the one that got away about five damn times," he told Brooks, regaling him with the stories of Piper being close enough to touch when Vance didn't know it.

"Fucking A," Brooks said. "She was in Omaha? For the World Series win?"

Vance shook his head along with Brooks because he still couldn't wrap his brain around that one. "Oh, and guess who her best friend was in grade school. Tansy…Langford."

"Tansy?" Brooks spit out, clearly shocked.

"I know. Seems their parents are still close friends, although Piper hasn't seen Tansy in years."

"Okay, that is just plain weird."

"Don't I know it. So, listen." Vance made the tone of his voice as easy and natural as possible. "I'm going to head to New York City tomorrow. I thought you might want to come with me."

"You're kiddin' right? Why would I *ever* want to set foot in New York City?" Brooks squinted at Vance like he didn't recognize him. "And why the hell would you? Our mission is to make Henderson great in every way that New York City is not."

"Yes, that's our plan and that's what we're gonna do. However, there are a few things you can buy in New York that you just can't find in Henderson. And our buddy Lewis has a contact in the Diamond District, so I'm going to set up a meeting."

Brooks blinked several times. "You can't be serious."

"I am perfectly serious."

"Third Base," Brooks said real slow. "I'm gonna need you to give me a urine sample."

"What? Why?"

"Clearly you are on a drug that's making you impotent and insane all at the same time."

"Oh, like you don't want to put a ring on Lolly's finger before she heads back to grad school."

"We aren't talking about me. We are talking about you. And you've known Piper for…what?" Brooks consulted his desk calendar. "Ten days? And you weren't speaking to her for five of them."

"Well, I'm not a complete idiot, for crying out loud, I'm not actually going to ask her to marry me for…you know, some reasonable amount of time yet. But let's face it. I love her. I always have. So I just want to be prepared for the unlikely moment she decides she loves me back."

"You love her? You love Piper? And I'm not talking about little fourth-grade Piper. I'm talking about the cop-hating lawyer."

"Me…loving Tinker Bell…surprises you?"

"It's darn quick."

Vance shrugged. "She picked my truck over the Rolls. What kind of girl picks a beat-up, piece-of-shit pickup over a goddamn Rolls Royce?"

Brooks sighed. "Your kind of girl."

Vance spread his arms wide as if saying, "there you have it."

"Still," Brooks cautioned.

"Look, Piper cared for me more than my own mother did when we were ten. Four years later, she came back to Henderson and asked me to dance, where I promptly blew her off because no one was paying me to dance with her. Four years after that, she came to watch us win State and got an eyeful for her trouble watching me rub up against Molly DuVal. And still four years later, she showed up in freaking Omaha, Nebraska, which was more than my guilt-ridden father even managed to do. Then, after leaving her standing all alone in The Charlie Horse five years ago, and without one word of apology from me for any of it, she dropped everything she was doing, got in the Mas, and drove to Henderson without asking one question."

"Fucking A."

"I won't find another girl like Piper. And I certainly am not waiting another four years to make her mine."

"You haven't even taken her to bed yet."

"Oh, and like that's bound to be a big disappointment."

Brooks laughed. "Well, hell. What are you waiting for? Get the damn ring, put it on Tinker Bell's finger, and drag her ass to the altar. But why go to New York, for God's sake? We have a perfectly fine jeweler here in Henderson."

"Trust me," Vance said. "What I plan to put on Piper's finger cannot be found in Henderson."

"Jesus Christ."

"So are we going to see you out at the Club this afternoon?"

"To watch you and Lolly celebrate another championship win? No, thank you. However, as Chieftain, I am sending my military leader, Annabelle Devine, over to make sure there is no monkey business this time."

"Great, because I need to talk with Annabelle."

"About what?"

"I want Piper to take some time off work and spend it in Henderson. So she can fall back in love with this place."

"And you?"

"Hey. What's not to love?" Vance teased, spreading his arms out wide and looking down at his physique. "I've got Genevra in on the deal, and I need Annabelle in on it too."

"What about Lolly?"

"Lolly can't keep her mouth shut."

Brooks' big grin spread from cheek to cheek. "When you're right, you're right."

"Piper's having lunch with Genevra at the Club at noon. She'll make sure she stays to watch the end of our golf match. Then I'll get her to hang in for whatever The Ninja and The Outlaw have planned at The Situation tonight."

"What the hell is that anyway?" Brooks asked.

"I have no idea, but they've asked us to be there and bring friends, so we're gonna do it. Duncan is showing up too."

"It's a Sunday night, for God's sake."

"Jesus, dude. It's summer time, and how old are you anyway?"

"Says the guy who doesn't have a shift until Thursday."

"I've got three other jobs and a covert mission to run. And with all the ground work the S.H.I.T.s are doing on your campaign, it will not kill you to show up for them and drink a beer on a Sunday night. Ah—you know what? Don't bother. I'll get Lolly to show up instead. Since I've been helping Pinks toss off his cloak of nice, safe, and boring, I'd like to see what Lolly thinks of him now—since she's his age and can still handle a good time on a Sunday night."

"Fucking A."

"You're dating a young one. You can't get old."

"You know what's making me old? Your father…marrying Lolly's mother…is making me old. Because now Lolly's not just consumed with creating fashions for NC State's Fashion Week, but she's also creating her momma's wedding gown and whatever the hell she's planning to wear to that gala event. On top of that, Annabelle is making me old because she and Lolly aren't waiting to start The House of DuVal and their debutante gown business until *after* Lolly graduates. They are doing it now. Business cards, brochures, advertising—the works."

"So you're blaming my father, Lolly's mother, and Lolly's business partner for making you old."

"I am."

"Because you can't blame Lolly."

"Exactly."

"And you're not really getting old, you're just tired. Tired of waiting around for Lolly's free time."

Brooks stared at him like he wanted to knock some of his teeth loose.

Vance leaned in close and quieted his voice. "Remember the night Lolly found out she was illegitimate? Remember how wound up she was about all that and how she wanted to get a little tipsy and dance it off? Remember how she started taking her clothes off and you had to sling her over your shoulder and drag her out of the bar and into your truck?"

Brooks nodded.

"Well, she might be feeling a little wound up right now, don't you think? Might need to let off a little steam. Sunday night or no, this could turn out to be one of the best nights of your life."

Brooks rolled his head and loosened up his shoulders right before he said, "I'm in."

CHAPTER TWENTY-FIVE

Davis stood at one end of Henderson Country Club's pool and lowered his sunglasses to the bridge of his nose. The long, tall, blond thorn in his side was all stretched out on a lounge chair twenty-five feet away, decked out in a navy blue bikini with gold trim. Bossy, mean, pit bull of a woman who he couldn't get off his mind.

Nice, safe, boring Pinks wanted to walk over there and douse her with water. But The Ninja…The Ninja wanted her every which way but loose.

"Goddamn women," he muttered to himself as he started walking in her direction." Can't live with 'em, can't live without 'em. Apparently."

He stood at her side, blocking her sun just for the fun of it.

"Step aside, little man," she said after opening her eyes.

Yeah. Not happening.

He sat his preppy ass down on her lounge chair, forcing her to move her fabulous legs over. Then he grabbed the opened paperback off the little table next to her and looked at the cover. "*Worth the Weight* by Mara Jacobs," he read. "Now this book looks like fun." He pointed to the naked male and female feet gracing the cover. "I had you pegged for more of a dark, sad memoir kind of girl."

"Why? You don't think I like to have fun?"

"I think if I poured water on you, you'd melt."

She smirked. "So I'm a wicked witch."

"Somethin' like that," He put her book back, clapped his hands together, and looked around the pool.

"Isn't this a members-only club?" she chided.

"Not if you know the right people," he said. "You busy tonight?" he added not looking in her direction.

"I'm busy having a family dinner here. It's my grandmother's birthday."

"Okay, then." Davis got up to leave.

Tansy reached out and grabbed his arm. "Wait. What'd you have in mind?"

Davis stood above her liking the feel of her hand on his arm. He cocked his head in a gesture of nonchalance. "Jesse James and I are planning a little something at The Situation. You should drop by when you finish eating cake."

"I should?" Her voice sounded dubious.

"If you're…interested."

She dropped her hand. "Interested in what exactly?"

"A little fun," he said before he walked away.

⁓⊂⟶⊃⁓

After their lunch, Genevra and Piper stood beneath the shade of a large oak tree in their lady-like sundresses, watching Lolly and Vance hit their approach shots on the tenth fairway. Genevra explained this was the finals of the Club's King and Queen Golf Tournament and it had taken six victories to gets them into this match. Piper noticed that Lolly looked focused and tense, while Vance sauntered up the fairway with an easy loose-limbed grace.

"I don't play sports," Genevra said quietly, leaning toward Piper. "Lolly's ability and competitive spirit came from her father. He was the proverbial captain of the football team. Only he wasn't captain for long." When Piper looked at her questioningly, Genevra whispered, "Too many missed practices, missed curfews, and general misbehavior."

"I see. Was Vance like that?"

Genevra shook her head in the negative. "I've been told he was a rule follower when it came to academics and sports."

"But not women." Piper smiled.

"No, no rules when it came to women." Genevra grinned. "But it's no secret he's been fairly straight-laced this summer."

"I understand that has a lot to do with Lolly."

"She's helped him see a different side of things."

After a long silence, Piper admitted, "It's not like he hasn't laid a hand on me, but he's definitely not rushing me into bed either."

Genevra turned her head to look at her directly. "Then he's treating you differently. Which makes you special."

"Special in a good way or special in a...you know...*delicate* way?"

Genevra laughed. "Special, as in you are far more important to him than any other woman has ever been. He tried to seduce Lolly the first time he met her."

"And she resisted all that?" Piper was amused.

"Only because she had a date with Brooks lined up that night."

"Well, I haven't been able to resist all that since I was ten. But Vance seems to be having no trouble resisting all this." She pointed a finger up and down her body.

"Don't kid yourself. If he's anything like Hale, he is simply trying not to make a wrong move—afraid you'll walk away. The first Mrs. Evans really did a number on those two."

"Hmm."

Genevra took a deep breath and sighed. "So is it wrong that I silently thank her every day? Because if she hadn't walked out, I would never have Hale."

Piper gave a short laugh. "Well, I don't know whether to thank her or curse her. My lifelong obsession with Vance has done nothing but knock me around."

"Luckily, at twenty-nine you have time for things to improve," Genevra assured her. "It took me until I was forty-three to find Hale, and now I've got this precious bonus gift too." She patted her belly.

Piper looked at Genevra's little tummy and felt a terrible yearning inside her own. "I want kids," she whispered.

"You'll have them," Genevra said, patting her arm.

The sound of approaching footsteps turned their attention as Vance came up on them, smiling. He kissed Piper on her lips as he took both of her hands in his. "Hello," he said quietly.

"Hi." She smiled up at him.

"Lolly and I are up two with eight to play. Stay and watch us win."

"I—I wouldn't miss it," she said.

"Great. And, there's something big happening in town tonight, so you'll stay for that too." He squeezed her hands before dropping them and heading off toward the next tee.

Piper watched him go.

"Was that a little bossy?" Genevra asked with a smile. "That seemed a little bossy."

"Yeah." Piper licked her lips. "If he'd simply asked, I would have told him I have to get back. But…apparently…bossy works for me."

Genevra expelled a long breath. "Lord, don't I know it."

Two hours later, as Lolly and Vance were one up with one to go, a crowd had gathered in golf carts and on foot. Duncan and Annabelle were snuggled up in a cart. Annabelle looked like she was heading to a cover shoot, and Duncan seemed unable to keep his hands off her. Clearly they were fans of Lolly and Vance, not golf fans in general. Vance's grandmother, Emelina, was decked out in flowing attire, driving her own golf cart with a drink in her hand. Brooks walked along with Piper and Genevra—Genevra whose hand was now held tightly in Hale's. Pinks and Jesse James kept to themselves as they followed the action along with a couple of dozen curious club members.

The mood was friendly, the crowd responding with shouts and applause. Vance's demeanor had tensed up considerably, and Lolly was continually focused on her next shot. It was obvious the two of them wanted to win, badly.

It was also obvious Brooks just wanted it to end.

And when it did, Brooks breathed a noticeable sigh of relief as Vance gave Lolly a quick hug before shaking hands with their opponents and coming off the green victorious. Lolly, exuberant, raced to Brooks and jumped into his arms. Vance, with a big satisfied grin on his face, eyed Piper as he paid and tipped the caddies. Then he came over, shook hands with his father, kissed Genevra's cheek, and then took hold of Piper's hand, rubbing his thumb over the top.

He gazed at her intently, conveying his immense satisfaction not only with the victory, but that she was there to witness it.

"You're the champion," Piper said softly.

"And you're my trophy," he said back.

Mmm, yeah.

Lord, Piper thought with a sigh. *I truly am a ridiculous woman.*

Annabelle and Duncan drove over in the golf cart. "Celebration on the upper patio?" Annabelle suggested.

"Sounds like a plan," Vance said without taking his eyes off Piper.

"Piper, can you stay?" Annabelle asked.

"She can," Vance answered.

"We'll get a table," Annabelle said.

Vance pulled his eyes from Piper. "Order champagne," he told Annabelle. "Have them put it on my account."

"Tequila for the men." Duncan's voice carried behind him as the golf cart sped off.

"Champagne and tequila," Piper said, lifting a brow. "Sounds like quite the celebration."

"It did take us seven victories," Vance said. "How did lunch go with Genevra?"

"I really like her," Piper admitted. "She's like this perfect mix of a friend and a mom. Both of which I'm grateful to add to my life." They began a slow stroll toward the clubhouse. "And she had some ingenious ideas for the groom's cake. I think the two of us are going to have great fun working together to pull it off."

"So does that mean you'll be at the house baking during your two-week vacation?"

Piper threw him a dubious look. "It means, at the very least, I will be in that magnificent kitchen all day next Saturday."

Vance pulled her arm to slow her progress. Then he spun her in front of him and placed his hands on her hips. "I want you to come to Henderson."

"I'm already here."

"I want you to stay."

That made her smile. "Vance, I'm not averse to spending time in Henderson, you have to know that. But I'm not shacking up with you in the pool house for two weeks. That would just be...embarrassing."

"You're kidding, right? Genevra hasn't spent a night at her place in months."

"They're engaged. They're getting married in a matter of weeks."

"Yes, but what's going to be truly embarrassing is when everybody realizes it's a shotgun wedding. Genevra's *second* shotgun wedding."

Piper quirked a brow. "Lolly and Genevra shared that with me the night your grandmother treated us to dinner. I have to admit I saw Lolly's point. It's kinda crazy to wind up with an unexpected pregnancy in this day and age."

Vance shrugged. "I'm getting a baby brother out of it."

"They know it's a boy?"

"*I* know it's a boy," he insisted. They started walking toward the clubhouse again. "How do you like the name Brody?"

⚜

It wasn't just five o'clock somewhere. It was five o'clock at Henderson Country Club during the heat of July, and the bartenders were busy. Harry appeared as he usually did—out of nowhere—with his tequila shots beautifully presented and placed before everyone around the table. Vance noticed Harry set a shot in front of Genevra with a wink, as if he knew her secret but didn't want to create cause for suspicion.

Lolly downed her shot and immediately reached for her mother's, which made Brooks flash a glance at Vance. Vance simply grinned back. Brooks was in for a hell of a night.

A tall ice bucket arrived, dripping with condensation and filled with Vance's bottle of champagne. And, as Harry popped the cork on that, another waiter arrived with what the men really wanted: ice cold beer. Eventually, an iced tea in a cocktail glass was set before Genevra, and when Emelina arrived, Harry had her Long Island Iced Tea ready as she sat.

There were toasts to Lolly and Vance, the champions. There were toasts to Lolly for her efforts in civilizing Vance. There were toasts to the newest Henderson businesses, House of DuVal and E&E Investments, and toasts to the S.H.I.T.s and their top-secret event at The Situation.

There was a toast to Piper, as the returning Hendersonian, and a toast to the Richmond-bred James brothers who were now honorary citizens. There was a whispered toast to the new Mayor of Henderson and an uncharacteristically uncouth toast given by the Keeper of the Debutantes which resulted in riotous laughter and caused a good many eye to drift toward the Evans/DuVal table.

Vance clasped Piper's hand underneath the table and knew he'd never been happier. Having her in the mix made it complete.

As Emelina left to meet friends for dinner inside and Hale took Genevra by the hand, eager to have her to himself at home, the S.H.I.T.s excused themselves and headed off to do whatever they were planning. That left the three remaining couples to order up appetizers and another round.

"Piper, I finally signed up for Pinterest," Annabelle said. "Lolly and I can definitely use it as a marketing tool. Though when I looked through your 'Bake Me a Cake' Kitchen I saw how it could be a sort of a personal bucket list as well. Wouldn't it be amazing to put all that together someday?"

"Put all what together?" Vance asked, pulling on a nacho.

"Piper's dream kitchen."

"What's this?" Vance asked Piper.

Piper turned all of her sunshine in his direction, causing his heart to hammer hard inside his chest. "One of my boards shows all the elements I would put into my dream kitchen," she said.

Vance's curiosity was piqued. He needed to know all about Piper's dream kitchen because he planned to build it for her.

"And what exactly is Pinterest?"

"It's a social media thing, with pictures. You sign up for a free account like Facebook, and then you create boards and fill them with pictures from the Internet."

"Huh. And how does Annabelle get to see your dream kitchen?"

"She just follows me. I'm going to follow her back, because she and Lolly plan to pin pictures of their House of DuVal creations."

"Thus the marketing tool," Vance said, trying to figure out a way he could follow Piper's boards without losing his manhood.

"It's fun. Harmless fun, unless you get caught up in it and spend an entire morning pinning things rather than working."

"Well, when you take your two-week vacation, you'll be able to do all the pinning you want." He finished his sentence with a kiss to her lips.

CHAPTER TWENTY-SIX

Piper wasn't exactly tipsy when they arrived at The Situation, but she literally squealed when she saw Jesse James with an electric guitar strapped to his body and his hand strumming at the strings right where his "hoodle" would be. Never mind the microphone in front of his oh-so-sexy mouth. The kid might be eight years her junior but if Vance weren't in her life, she would definitely do him.

And so would Lolly, apparently, because the two of them pushed and shoved their way to the front of the packed and wild crowd so they could be at the edge of the stage to watch Jesse sing. Screaming like school girls probably would have been embarrassing if they hadn't had those shots, the champagne, and a couple of beers. As it was, they weren't the only females crowded up close and screaming as Jesse sang Toby Keith's "Get Drunk and Be Somebody" and then changed the words to "Should Have Been a Cowboy" to "Should Have Been an Outlaw" with some very explicit lyrics thrown in.

When Lolly got a look at the drummer, Piper thought she was going to convulse with shock. There was her nice, safe, boring Pinks in a black T-shirt with muscles bulging, banging the drums like a freaking badass and singing backup to Jesse's Outlaw. Piper couldn't help but look over for Brooks' reaction, finding him and Vance at the bar. Brooks was not happy, not happy at all, but Vance was laughing his ass off.

All of a sudden, Piper was grabbed from behind and whirled around. It took her a couple seconds to recognize her old friend, Tansy Langford, and to hug her tight. They couldn't talk over the band and the crowd so they just danced together, along with Lolly, singing and screaming and carrying on like they were preteens at a One Direction concert.

Piper hadn't had this much fun in about five years, so she didn't look at the clock, she didn't turn down a shot, she didn't think twice when Lolly whipped off her red camisole top to dance around in her red bra alone. Of course, that's when the Killer of Fun shoved his way through the crowd on the dance floor, whisked Lolly up over his shoulder and carried her out the back door of the bar.

Brooks Bennett. Spoilsport.

With Lolly down, Piper turned to Tansy to continue dancing the night away, until she noticed that Tansy was licking her lips in a very suggestive manner, staring down one unlikely, prepped-out drummer. Holy Mother of God. Piper actually feared for Pinks, afraid Tansy was going to eat him up and spit him out and enjoy every last minute of it.

She noticed Pinks didn't share that fear, staring right back at Tansy as he rocked out on the drums. Those two were headed for a showdown.

When the last note was played, Piper watched in awe as Jesse James, God of the Henderson Cover Band, took off his guitar to the roar of the crowd, jumped down from the stage, wrapped one arm around her waist, and pulled her tight against his twenty-one-year-old body.

She thought she'd die.

It took about seven seconds to realize The Outlaw was stealing a kiss and then all hell broke loose as Jesse was spun around and punched in the jaw by none other than Officer Evans.

"What the hell?" Jesse stammered, staying on his feet and reaching up to check for blood. "Dude," he shouted at Vance but pointed at Piper. "She has *got* to be older than twenty-one."

Pinks jumped from the stage in the middle of the scene and pushed at both of Jesse's shoulders. "She's his," Pinks said, moving Jesse out of harm's way and soothing him as he went. "That's Piper. That's Vance's woman."

The term "she's his" caused a tickle to crawl up Piper's cheeks. Piper turned her most flirtatious smile on Vance and batted her eyes.

"Is that true? Am I your woman?"

"Well, I sure as hell don't want you kissin' anybody else," he said, his chest pumping. Duncan and Annabelle arrived as the DJ began to spin his albums and the party continued.

"Did you know about this?" Duncan asked with a big grin on his face. "Did you know about this band?" he asked Vance.

"Did you know your outlaw of a brother just had his tongue down Piper's throat?" Vance shouted.

"What?" Duncan said, confused.

"Okay, let's move this to the back room," Annabelle directed. "Come on. Let's get out of this crowd."

Vance grabbed on to Piper's hand and the four of them maneuvered through the crowd, winding their way to the last room of The Situation where the atmosphere was much quieter. They found an empty table and, although there were four chairs, Piper snuggled into Vance's lap and wrapped her arms around his neck. He seemed a little surprised, but she liked the way his hands were rubbing up and down her sides.

"Jesse and I have never been introduced," she said, grinning into Vance's handsome face. "Don't blame the kid. I'm afraid I made rather a spectacle of myself."

Vance groaned, obviously not eager to shift blame.

"I'll make it up to you," she said, "if you let him off the hook."

"Grrrr. Fine. The Outlaw is off the hook. But you are not. This happy look all over your face is making me crazy. You *like* that you were the one he picked out of the crowd."

"Yes," she admitted without remorse. "My feminine pride adores that he picked me. I'm turning thirty, I am reveling in the fact that he picked me. So suck it up and look over at your buddy Duncan and tell him the kid is off the hook."

Vance's sigh seemed a bit exaggerated, and Piper could tell that he was really okay with all of it, probably after having gotten one good punch in. Vance looked across the table at Duncan and told him Jesse was forgiven.

And then Duncan, the cannonball kid who had already messed up her hair once this summer, had to go and open his big fat mouth.

"Piper, I didn't realize you had been engaged to Scott Swanson. I actually know him from law school. Nice guy. I didn't realize he used to be with Collins & Reese."

"Wait-wait-wait-just a goddamn minute." Vance slapped his hand down on the table. "What do you mean, engaged?"

When Duncan realized his mistake, it showed all over his face. His eyes immediately shifted to Piper's and pleaded for forgiveness. It was obvious he had meant no harm. It probably hadn't crossed his mind that she'd have kept that from Vance.

Duncan began to stutter. "I—I…God, I'm sorry."

Annabelle reached out to stroke a soothing palm over Vance's hand, firm and hard on the table.

"Vance, it was years ago and probably never crossed Piper's mind to tell you."

"You knew too?" Vance accused Annabelle.

"Duncan told me. He didn't think it was a secret, obviously, and like I said, I'm sure Piper—"

But her words were cut off by the scraping sound of a chair as Vance stood up and Piper found herself falling. Hitting the floor hard.

CHAPTER TWENTY-SEVEN

"Ouch!"

Vance tried not to let her cry of pain affect him. Tiny little thing that she was flailing around the dirty barroom floor, her dress all wrapped up around those sweet little thighs.

His instinct was to pick her up and cradle her in his arms, protecting her against everything and everyone, but he forced all that down because his itty-bitty self-esteem in the women-who-I-love department was smarting at the news that she'd been goddamn en-*fucking*-gaged to some asshole lawyer who asshole Duncan knew from his supersonic asshole Carolina fucking law school.

Goddamn, he hated surprises.

Surprise! Your mother left.

Surprise! Lolly's dating your best friend.

Surprise! Piper was the girl who kissed the shit out of you on the dance floor.

Surprise! The girl you love more than life itself wants to marry someone else.

Or maybe she didn't, that evil villain Hope cried out to him. Maybe Piper broke her engagement because she realized there was only one man for her. Him.

Yeah, right. Sucker.

No, it could have happened, he tried to convince himself, stepping aside as Duncan and Annabelle pushed him out of the way to help Piper off the floor.

He watched as Piper came up wincing, as Annabelle glared at

him, as Duncan looked around for another beer. Finally the three of them stopped fidgeting and stared at him, waiting to see how he was going to handle this.

Well, let's see. He'd already punched one James brother tonight, so the idea of making it an even two felt kinda good. He'd like that, getting rid of a little aggression on a lawyer.

And punching Duncan would definitely take care of Annabelle, because she'd be all "oh, my sweet baby Duncan" nursing him back to health. Maybe. That one had a mouth on her and a vocabulary she wasn't afraid to use. The last time they clashed, his ego had come out torn up and beaten near to death. *No, thank you.*

So, he directed his attention to the one who he'd already decided he couldn't live without and tried to channel whatever he could from Lolly's "How To Treat Women Outside the Bedroom" lectures.

Goddammit all to hell.

He watched as Annabelle turned and told Piper, "Come on, we'll take you home."

Like hell.

"No...no...no," he said in defeat. "I apologize. I'm sorry. I just...wasn't...aware." He eyed Piper, letting her know that this was all her fault. "Annabelle, you might want to cut me some slack here. Finding out Piper was engaged is a bit of a shock." He looked over at Duncan. "Thanks for that by the way," he said. "I'm sure Piper appreciates your interest in her love life."

"Piper, I...." Duncan stumbled.

"I tried to tell him the other night," Piper said to Duncan. "This is not your fault."

"The other night when?" Vance scoffed.

"The other night when I said I had a confession to make and you told me that you weren't my priest," she shouted.

"I said that?" he asked, trying to remember.

"Yes. I even told you it had to do with our night at The Charlie Horse five years ago, and you said a do-over—"

"Okay. That's it. Party's over," Vance said. He took hold of Piper's hand and drew her out of the clutches of Snoopy One and Snoopy Two.

"You two," he said to Duncan and Annabelle. "You go find some other poor couple to bother. Piper and I need to sort this out—alone."

"Now is probably not a good time to—"

"Now," Vance insisted cutting Annabelle off. "It's going to happen right now."

They all stood still for a moment, silent. Finally Vance pulled Piper after him and headed to the emergency exit at the end of the room. He slammed his palm up against the handle and pulled her into the night.

Then he shoved her up against the brick wall, leaned in, and took her mouth in a desperate kiss. He felt her hands squeeze themselves between them and push against his chest, but that was too damn bad. He had no interest in anything she had to say. Unless it was "Take me now against this wall."

Annnd here I thought things couldn't get worse. He pulled himself off Piper and backed up with a curse.

He watched as she panted, her back still pressed against the exterior wall of The Situation. Her eyes were shut tight, like she was trying to suppress tears—and just like that—all the fight went out of him.

Because he loved her. And the last thing he ever wanted to do was hurt her. He stumbled forward, planning to throw himself at her feet and beg her forgiveness.

"I'm sorry," she whispered. "I'm sorry you found out like that."

He pulled her to him, encircling her neck with both his arms, rocking her gently from side to side, combing a hand over her curls. "It's none of my business," he said. "I overreacted, and in truth, it's none of my damn business."

That's when she started to cry.

Christ. Trying not to be an asshole apparently only makes me more of an asshole.

"Piper, please, baby doll, forgive me. I'm an ass but I'm working hard at not being so much of one. I need practice and, baby, there's no one to practice on but you. So please, stop crying and help me do the right thing here. We can go back inside and dance. Have another drink. Just forget that Duncan ever brought it up. The truth is, I don't care if you were engaged to some lawyer. I'm just very relieved you didn't marry him."

Piper sniffed and brought her head up to peer at him through the ring of his arms.

"It was your fault I didn't marry him," she scolded. "Completely your fault."

"Good," he said, tucking her curly head back against his chest. "Happy to hear it."

She pushed back and he gave her a little more space within the circle of his arms. "Don't you want to know why?"

"I don't know," he said cautiously. "Do I?"

She bit her bottom lip and leaned her head to the side. Then she shrugged. "It's out there. We may as well…face it."

"Oh, God. I do not like the sound of that."

"Well, it has nothing to do with you. I mean, it has everything to do with you, but it mostly has to do with me and my flimsy adherence to a basic morality clause."

"Morality clause?" He knew he wasn't an idiot, but he had no idea what she was talking about.

"You know. Once you get engaged, you aren't supposed to stick your tongue in some hot guy's mouth, even if you have been overly obsessed with him since you were ten."

All Vance could do was blink, because he still had no clue what she was saying.

"Vance. That night I walked into The Charlie Horse planning to blow off a little steam? I was in the middle of planning my wedding to Scott."

"Oh," he uttered. "Oh!" he said as the night replayed in his mind. "You were engaged? How engaged?"

Piper lowered her brows. "What do you mean, "how engaged?" I was engaged. The wedding was months away. We had it all planned. I was going to quit my job. We were going to have kids. I was as engaged as you can get."

Vance shook his head, not comprehending. "So what happened?"

"What do you mean, what happened? You happened, you stupid jerk. You were standing there and I'm like 'Oooh, there's Vance Evans. He must have heard about my mother and, like my knight in shining armor, has come to save me from my sad, sad self.'"

Vance felt happiness drain from him. "Oh, Piper."

"Yeah, I was a complete romantic fool and after I saw you standing there, I didn't think about Scott once the entire night. In fact, I didn't think about Scott for two days after you left me standing on the dance floor, until he arrived at my parent's house and asked for his ring back."

"Jesus."

"Well...I deserved it."

Vance angled his head, so sorry for her and so happy for the bullet he dodged. Maybe there was a God.

"You ever going to cheat on me?"

She shook her head no.

"Okay, then. Why don't we go get it on in my truck?"

Piper burst out laughing.

He pulled her to him. "That was not supposed to be funny."

"It's just, I started to despair that you didn't want me like that."

That had Vance bursting out laughing. "Baby doll, I assure you, I want you just like that," he said leaning down to brush his lips against hers. "I want all three of you like that. Only I get a little nervous when I think about taking sweet, precious...." He kissed her again. "...Perfect Piper to bed. 'Cause she left me once, and one false move may make her do it again," he confessed his fear against her lips. He ran a hand through her hair and looked into her eyes. "And maybe I feel a little more comfortable thinking about getting Naughty Piper naked, because I know how to handle that one. But she's my hologram—the one no other blonde can measure up against, and that kiss she laid on me five years ago was so right that I turned chicken shit and ran out on her, so...."

He kissed her gently, letting his arms drift over her back, feeling her silky skin, stroking her luscious curves. When his hands brushed against her backside, he groaned, squeezing his fingers into her plump bottom and hauling her lady parts up tight against his growing need. "And then we have The Lawyer Beaumont." His voice dropped low and husky. "Who'd probably have me arrested before I finished doing all the dirty things I fantasize about doing to her." He licked his lips before using his tongue to mate with her mouth, wanting desperately to press her back up against the wall. He cut the kiss off before he lost control. "So, yeah," he said, breathing heavily, staring right into her eyes, "I want you that way. I've just been a little preoccupied about messing things up."

She came in close, snuggling into his arms, her fingers opening his shirt so that she could kiss the spot on his chest that was level with her lips. "You can't mess things up, Vance," she breathed against the hair of his chest. Looking down at the top of her head, he watched as she kissed him again.

Oh, he could think of a few ways he could mess this up.

"I fell in love with Fourth Grade Vance before he ever needed Perfect Piper."

He smiled at that. He'd have given anything for it to be true.

"It was the day Willie Prescott brought in his Popsicle-stick log cabin for show and tell. It was pretty big and glued to a large piece of cardboard. I don't think Willie had but a couple of friends, but he was proud of his work and he did a good job talking about it in front of the class. We all thought it was cool.

"Later on, some bully bopped the whole thing out of Willie's hands and it blew apart all over the hallway, right as the entire fourth grade started heading to the cafeteria. Before the teachers could react, before anybody did anything, you gave a loud whistle and shouted for everyone to stop where they were. Then you made everyone pick up the pieces of Willie's log cabin, and during lunch you had an entire tableful of kids helping Willie put it back together.

"I don't know if you were Willie's hero that day, but I do remember that that's the day you became mine."

Piper lifted her head, her heart shining deep within those baby blue eyes.

Oh dear God, she's done it to me now.

Vance couldn't speak, he couldn't breathe. But he was her hero. So he held on to that.

She ducked her head again, addressing his chest. "Can I remind you of somethin' nice you and your mother did together?"

He rubbed his hands over her back thinking that would be a refreshing change of pace.

"And maybe this is the reason I felt your pain so acutely when she left, because I remember this better than anything." She kissed his chest again, her fingers toying with the hair there. He kept watch over her blond curls as she spoke quietly.

"It was your birthday, and your mother brought in cupcakes. They were special because the girls' were pink and yellow, and the boys' were blue and green. And there was a Hershey Kiss on each. But the best part…the best part was that she had written each of our names in icing on our own cupcake. Even the teacher's."

Vance remembered.

"When I asked you why your mother did that, you told me you'd asked her to. That even though it was *your* birthday, you wanted everyone to feel special." Piper dropped her voice to a whisper. "How was I not going to fall in love with that?"

She kept using that word.

That big word that both scared and intrigued him. She'd used it when she met his grandmother and she'd just used it now.

"Vance, you were funny—just had a way with words. And even back then you had a nickname for everybody. You always won the spelling bee, you were the best reader in the class, and I never played dodgeball because you threw the ball too hard. But the best part about Fourth Grade Vance was that you had a smile for everybody. You were a happy kid."

"God, Piper," Vance sighed, taking a step back. "I don't ever remember being a happy kid."

"You laughed all the time," she insisted, shaking her blond curls.

"How do you remember all that?"

"I remember everything, Vance. I remember far more of you being happy than you being sad. Grief is a part of life. And you had the misfortune of going through it way too early. But that sad kid grieving for his mother is not who you are or who you've ever been. You have always been Vance Evans, the boy I loved for more reasons than I can name."

The boy she loved.

Past tense.

But it was a start. Something to build on.

"Piper," she heard him whisper, standing tall in the night. "Piper…I," he stammered, moving in closer. She saw his focus narrow to her shoulder, "I…" he began again, distracted, reaching out with a single finger, touching her shoulder, and then lazily trailing it down her arm. The sensation was light and hypnotic, and it echoed inside her chest.

"I want…to…." His words tapered off as his gaze followed the slow advance of two fingers sliding back up her arm, leaving a delicious sort of tingling in its wake. Like a domino effect, those sent other tingles all over her body.

He whispered the words, "I thought maybe it'd be best…" as he watched, captivated by the way his whole hand now glided over her skin from bicep to wrist. "God, you're soft," he breathed, raising his gaze to meet her eyes.

The usual emerald green had darkened to a smoky shade of forest, and she was taken in by the intensity of his stare. She felt his hand ease up her arm, linger over her shoulder, and move on to caress her neck. Every place he touched heated, causing her breathing pattern to accelerate. His palm slid across her cheek. "Mind if we continue this discussion in my truck?"

With one brief nod, Piper found her hand caught up in Vance's vise-like grip pulling her behind him, behind The Situation, and over to his truck. He propelled her into the passenger seat, slammed the door, and was climbing in the other side before she had a chance to fully exhale. Bossy really did work for her. She threw herself at him as he grabbed for her in turn, her mouth landing on his, his mouth taking them both to the next level.

He pushed her from him once, holding her at arm's length, breathing heavily for a few counts before relenting and pulling her back to him.

It thrilled her when he couldn't decide whether he wanted to kiss or talk. "You…." he'd say. "Piper…." he'd call. "I swear to God," he'd exclaim, all the while pulling her mouth back under his, using his tongue, his teeth, and his lips to convey what he couldn't quite get out.

He wanted her. Really, really wanted her. And when his hands finally found her breasts, she pressed herself farther into him and moaned her appreciation for him finally getting around to that.

"Christ, Piper," he groaned into her mouth as he laid her down across the bench seat of his beat-up truck. He followed her down, his mouth on her neck. His hands on her breasts. His tongue and teeth tickling her skin. She felt his hot breath as he labored over her throat.

"Tell me to stop," he panted. "Tell me to stop," he pleaded as his thumbs roused her nipples under their cotton covering. "We don't want our first time to be here," he insisted even as his hand pulled one of the straps of her dress down over her shoulder.

"Okay," she whispered. "You're right," she panted, loving his weight on top of her, his hands, all the attention he was giving her body. "We don't want our first time to be...oh God," she said as he put his mouth over the nipple he'd just uncovered and sucked mightily.

The intense pull she felt down deep inside almost had her coming. She grabbed his dark head in her hands and held him to her. "Just...maybe...we could...take the edge off." He sucked again and in response she bucked her pelvis against his rock-hard abs.

She felt his hands slide down her sides and crawl up under her dress as his teeth and tongue toyed with her nipple. One of her legs was stuck beneath him and against the back of the seat, but her right leg was able to be released from the fabric wound around her knees. She let it fall to the side.

His hand eased up her thigh and scooted over her bikini underpants. They were damp and that must have turned him on because he moaned, which caused her to buck against him again, and this time his thumb got caught in the way—like the night before—perfectly. Right on that spot. Right where everything was focused. Twice more she raised her hips. Twice more he rubbed his thumb over her in just the right place as his mouth drew in her nipple and sucked hard.

She tried not to squeal as the orgasm ricocheted around her body. She held her breath and locked her lips tight, but some sort of sound came out as she shuddered beneath him. In the end, her arms flailed around from Vance's head to his back, flopping where they would as she whispered, "Oh God. I'm sorry. I just...couldn't...stop myself."

Vance loomed over her, his arms stretched up on either side of her hips. His smile was broad when he looked at her and said, "Now why would you ever want to?" He tucked his head and plucked a few kisses from her lips.

She slid her arm between them then, her hand easing down the front of his pants. "Dear God," he said lifting his lips from hers. "Piper—Oh, Christ," he said as she smoothed her palm down the increasing length of his shaft. "Damn that's nice." His body started moving against her palm and she didn't try to do anything special. She just let him slide his taut erection up and back, using her palm and fingers. "Baby doll," he said with his eyes closed, his body moving, "you have…no idea. Your hand…feels…so good. Christ!" He opened his eyes, looking down at her while he kept moving.

"Are you sure?" he asked. "Because things are about to get messy."

Piper licked her lips, adding a little more resistance to his stroke. "Go ahead." She smiled. "Mess me up."

CHAPTER TWENTY-EIGHT

Monday morning, Vance woke up alone.

With a smile.

Because after years of meaningless sexual encounters and close to three months of celibacy, a hand job from his hologram was as close to heaven as he'd ever been. Given that, along with everything else that had transpired between him and Piper last night, it could probably sustain his soul for weeks to come. Although he wasn't sure he'd be able to keep from tossing that tiny little temptress on her back the next time he saw her. Which was going to be Thursday. Three days from now.

He smiled, remembering how much fun he'd had tucking her luscious little body into her sporty TT while throwing around some Bad Cop orders as he stole a kiss and copped a feel. He told her he'd be leaving for New York today on business. He told her that she was to *wait* until Thursday afternoon to deliver her butter-and-cinnamon laden bribe to King Kong and the gang. He wanted to escort her in and out of the precinct so that all of Raleigh's finest would know Vance Evans, small-town cop with zero jurisdiction, had her back. Then he suggested, well, maybe it was more like insisted, that she have her bags packed and her lawyer business wrapped up for her two-week vacation to Henderson.

She didn't give him a promise, but he didn't need one. Piper Beaumont was coming to Henderson with him one way or another.

For the first time he could remember, he got up and ran for the sheer pleasure of moving his body after a good night's sleep. He went to the high school, lifted weights, ran home, showered, packed, and was standing on the doorstep of E&E Investments turning his key in the lock before eight AM. *God, it was good to be alive.*

"Whoa," he said as he came up short, looking at the scene before him. "What do we have here?" he whispered in glee, slowly walking toward the desk and shooting glances around the rest of the reception area.

Prim, proper, ball-busting, Tansy Langford, was completely passed out and practically falling out of her chair. Her upper body was sprawled across the top of the desk, one arm cushioning her head, which lay limp and heavy. Her face was a mess of smeared eye makeup and, to make the whole thing just that much more perfect, she was drooling.

Vance took out his phone and snapped a picture.

On closer inspection, Vance realized she was wearing the same clothes he'd seen her in the night before, only now half the buttons on her blouse were torn off and the rest were askew. He couldn't be sure, but it looked like her leather skirt might actually be on backwards. Her shoes were missing, two of her fingernails were broken, and her long blond hair looked like squirrels had wrestled in it.

This day cannot get any better.

He took another picture just for the fun of it.

That's when he heard sounds coming from down the hall and went to investigate. There were no lights on, but he definitely heard something moving inside the conference room. Vance quietly opened one of the double doors just a crack and peeked in.

Oh. No, you didn't.

"Pinks!" Vance whispered, stepping quickly into the room and closing the door behind him.

There was Davis, on top of E&E's brand new conference table— moaning—trying to roll onto his side from his back.

"Are you out of your mind?" he whispered as he took in the scene. A double D bra lay on the rug at his feet, there was skimpy girlie underwear a few paces down, Pinks' badass black T-shirt was tossed in a corner, and, *good God,* a pair of boxer briefs had landed in the chair Vance considered his. Even the belt Vance coveted, the one Pink's own mother had handmade for him stitch by stitch, was cast aside at the end of the table. Thank goodness The Ninja had his jeans on, although his fly was only half zipped. Vance groaned, not wanting to be a witness to anything that came flying out.

"For the love of God—Tansy?" Vance asked, squinting his eyes in disbelief.

Pinks rolled all the way over—groaning—now lying flat out on his belly.

"Tansy Langford?" Vance could hardly wrap his head around it. *Why would anyone want to—?*

"I couldn't help myself," Pinks mumbled as he tried to push his body off the table. "It was either kill her and throw her body in the lake, or you know, try to fuck her to death."

"Well, you about damn succeeded," Vance said. "She's passed out on her desk with her clothes in tatters. Why the hell did you bring her here?"

Now in a sitting position, with his legs draped over the side of the table, Pinks rubbed a hand along his jaw and looked at Vance. "Where the hell else was I going to take her? I certainly wasn't going to sneak her into your father's house, and I didn't trust myself out by the lake. I would have just as likely drowned her as…you know… this. God, I ache all over," he lamented, moving his arms, trying to loosen up his muscles.

"Gee, the conference table isn't as soft and cushy as your bed?"

Pinks gave Vance a deadpan stare. "It won't happen again."

"What won't happen again? Sex on my conference table or sex with Tansy Langford?"

"Both," Davis said as he stood up and tried to find his equilibrium. "It may have taken all night, but you can be damn sure I have worked that woman out of my system."

"All night?"

"Yeah, well," Pinks said as he bent over to pick up Tansy's unmentionables and stuffed them into his back pocket, "there were a lot of…issues the two of us needed to work out."

"Like which one of you *tops* the other around here?" Vance smirked.

Pinks smiled. "Something like that."

"Jesus Christ, dude. Whatever happened to nice, safe, and

boring?"

Pinks picked up his T-shirt and rubbed it over his face. Then he eyed Vance and sighed. "I do believe she literally sucked it all out of me."

"Dear God," Vance said, staring at The Ninja. Finally, he shook himself out of his stupor and pointed to the doors. "Get the hell out of here. Take the back way out, go get yourself cleaned up, and when you come back, walk in here like you own the place. Do not let Tansy Langford get the upper hand—in any of it."

"Right." Pinks nodded, pulling on his T-shirt and grabbing his belt.

"I have something I need to discuss with Tansy before I head to New York."

"New York? What the fuck is in New York?"

"God, you're starting to sound like Brooks."

"Yeah? Give me two years and *I'll* be the mayor around here. Golden Boy, my ass. Did you see me on those drums last night?"

Pinks started whipping his ninja hands around like there were drumsticks attached.

"Yes, I saw," Vance chuckled. "The whole damn town saw. I don't know how you and The Outlaw did it, but the place was packed, and your little band is a huge hit."

"You think that was packed? Wait until you see how many show up for our lacrosse clinic next weekend."

"Pinks—Jesus—do me a favor. Steer clear of Brooks until I get back."

"He's scared, right?" Pinks said with glee. "Afraid I'm going to win Lolly back," he teased. "I saw her on the dance floor last night. She liked what she saw. She likes Pinks, the Ninja Drummer," he said raising his brows up and down.

"You are not winning Lolly back."

"I know," Pinks said sincerely. "But it sure is fun to yank the Golden Boy's chain."

"It is indeed. Now get lost so I can wake up Tansy and use all this to my advantage."

"See how all this worked out for you?" Pinks said, as he headed out the door. "I set 'em up, so you can knock 'em out of the park.

What the hell are you gonna do without me?"

"I don't know," Vance muttered to himself as he turned down the hall toward Tansy. "I truly do not know."

～◦∞◦～

It was the feeling of drool running down Tansy's cheek that woke her up. That and the fact that her head, right arm, neck, and shoulder all ached like she'd been hit from behind. She scraped her face over her arm and then began pushing herself into a sitting position when… Bam! The chair rolled out from under her, and her ass hit the ground. But not before her chin struck the edge of her desk with such force it sent shockwaves of pain coursing around her skull.

Owwwww, she thought, wailing inside and squeezing her eyes shut against the crazy pain. *Where the hell am I? I don't deserve this.* She started to cry—planning to curl herself into a ball and drown herself in tears. But the laughter coming from some distant place, somewhere outside of the hell she was presently ensconced in, alerted her to the fact that she was not alone.

Fucking Davis.

She opened her eyes and rubbed her chin, checking for blood and loose teeth. From under the desk, she could see a pair of fine leather loafers and a pricey pair of trousers seated across the room.

Holy shit!

She scrambled off the floor, smoothing down her skirt and trying to straighten her hair as she prepared to face Hale Evans.

When she looked up and saw that it was Vance, she let herself collapse into her chair with a sigh of relief. "Thank God, it's only you," she said, closing her eyes and letting her head fall back to the desk.

"That's right," Vance said quietly. "It's only me." He stood and walked toward her. "Only me and my phone."

She opened her eyes and stared at the cell phone he held out. There was a picture of a homeless woman collapsed in the streets. He flicked his finger across the screen to reveal another picture of the woman taken from a different angle. *That poor soul. Somebody needs to clean her up.*

"Tansy," Vance whispered as she brought her hand up, feeling for a lump on the bottom of her chin.

I should put some ice on this. I cannot be walking around town with a puffy, black-and-blue face.

"Tansy," Vance said again, drawing her attention and pointing to the picture on his phone. "I need your help with something and I want it kept confidential."

"I'm not doing it," she said. "I mean, I'm happy to make a donation and work in a soup kitchen, but don't ask me to make over that poor wretch." She flipped a finger at his phone. "I am no miracle worker."

Vance looked at his screen and then hooted with laughter. "Tansy. This picture was taken twenty minutes ago. It's a picture of you."

She blinked a couple times and leaned forward for a better look. As the full extent of her passage through Hell dawned, she heard Vance say, "Now, unless you want this blasted across all forms of social media, I suggest you agree to help me."

She moaned, dropping her head back to the desk. "I'll do anything you want," she said. "Except touch you. I refuse to touch you."

"I'd have to be roped and gagged," Vance said, putting his phone in his pocket. He sat on the edge of her desk.

God, I hate when he does that.

"Well?" she said. It wasn't exactly that she hated working for Vance. It was more that she couldn't stand to look at him. She rolled her head to the side, trying to see what women saw in him.

"I finally understand why you've hated me all these years."

"Is that right?" she said, pushing herself up and folding her arms over her chest.

What the hell?

She looked down at her braless torso and saw that there weren't but a couple buttons holding her shirt together.

"Yeah, nice office attire," Vance said. "But I'm going to need you to focus right now because I have a plane to catch, and as far as you're concerned, your job and your…reputation…." He patted the pocket that held his cell phone. "Depend on how well you can pull this off for me."

"Spit it out, oh Great and Powerful Oz," she snarked.

"Piper Beaumont was a friend of yours in grade school."

"Yes, Piper Beaumont." Tansy nodded gingerly so the pain in her head wouldn't upset her stomach. "Saw her last night for the first time in ages."

"Right. But back in eighth grade, there was a weekend she spent with you where she asked me to dance, and I promptly blew her off. I'm guessing that pissed you off and you've never forgiven me for hurting Piper's feelings."

She gasped, shocked that he would know that.

"I get it," Vance said. "And now maybe you understand how I felt when you moved out of town leaving Brooks holding his dick."

"It's not the same," she protested.

"Yeah, yours was worse. Way worse. And I'll tell you what," Vance said, getting up off her desk. "I hate the idea that you've had your big grubby man-paws all over my boy, Pinks. If this is some kinda scheme to upset Lolly—"

"Lolly? Ha! And you can just stop right there, Casanova. You are not the boss of me."

"Really? You might want to take a look at who is signing your paychecks, Big Foot. Because that is exactly what I am."

There were literally no words to describe the amount of pain she was in.

"Look," Vance said. "Snubbing Piper was rude and I apologize. In fact, I'd like to make it up to her. And in order for me to do that, it would be helpful if I could take a look at her Pinterest account."

"Just…sign up and follow her boards," Tansy said. "I think even you can handle that."

"Tansy, please, work with me here. Just set up a Pinterest account for me under an assumed name and make it look legit. Then send me the password or whatever I need so I can snoop around Piper's stuff. I'm curious about this kitchen she's dreaming up, and I figure it might be a good way to get to know her a little better. See what she likes."

"You want me to help you get insider information on Piper."

"You've got a problem with that?" he said, flicking her picture at her again.

She winced. "I guess I don't really have a choice now, do I?"

"Nope. And thank you," he said as he started moving toward the door. "Anything you want from New York City? Something from the Big and Tall Girls' Collection at Barneys?"

"A new job," she shouted after him.

"Call Lewis Kampmueller. I'll put in a good word," he shouted back.

CHAPTER TWENTY-NINE

Piper pushed open the double glass doors of Collins & Reese Thursday morning and nearly dissolved into a puddle.

Standing before her was the most handsome, most polished hunk of male glory she had ever witnessed, and it was obvious by the intense and hungry look in his eye that he was there for her. Only her.

Tall and immaculate in his custom-made three-piece suit, Vance Evans was the poster boy for health, wealth, and playboys the world over. He didn't look like a cop. He didn't look like a highly paid lawyer. He looked like a man in control of his own destiny. The way he held himself—legs apart, hands clasped behind his back—screamed authority, power, and clout. His presence dominated the room, and within all the hustle and bustle of the morning office activity, there wasn't a single person, male or female, who didn't slow down and notice all that sovereignty.

As if in slow motion, people moving through the lobby area took notice of Vance and then followed his gaze to Piper. Then they noticed Piper and followed her gaze back to Vance. In the back of her mind, Piper considered the spectacle they were becoming. Yet she was powerless to do anything about it, because she was so stunned at his presence, so stunned at the sight of him, and so trying to control her own response to what had to be the world's largest aphrodisiac.

He grinned, broke eye contact for a second, and then crossed the Persian rug between them, rubbing a knuckle over his lips.

"Miss Beaumont." He smiled down at her, blocking her view of everything else. "If you continue to look at me like that, I'm likely to drag you into the nearest storage closet and ruin your reputation."

Have at it.

"I've missed you," he whispered.

"The nearest storage closet is right down the hall," she whispered back.

He gave a soft laugh. "Piper, walk me to your office."

She did as she was told, leading him down a long hallway to the right, around a corner and back to her small, windowless office. He closed the door behind him and she burst into giggles. "What are you doing here? Dressed like that?"

"Isn't this the way your new clients dress?"

"No." She shook her head adamantly. "That is not how anyone dresses. Now you're the one who is inciting a riot."

He came forward and put his hands on her waist. "This is what I wore the day Duncan set up an introduction. I wanted to make a good impression on my old friend, Piper."

"Oh—" she breathed. "You have made quite an impression."

"Good. So when can I take you away from here? Noon?"

"Noon?"

"Your vacation, Piper."

"Yes, well, about that—"

A tentative knock on her door interrupted them. "Come in," she called.

The face of her dearest colleague poked through, grinning. "Mind if Katie and I come in and meet the handsome man?"

Piper waved her in. "Vance, these are my good friends, Gracie Wills and Katie Winslow. Ladies, this is Vance Evans, my friend from fourth grade."

"You all know about fourth grade?" Vance asked putting out his hand, dazzling Katie and Gracie with his debonair looks and out-of-control sex appeal.

"Did he look like this in fourth grade?" Gracie asked Piper as she shook Vance's hand.

"He's never looked like this," Piper said.

"I've suited up in the hopes of bending Piper to my will," Vance said. "She's promised to take a two-week vacation starting today, and I'm here to make sure that happens."

Piper shook her head at her friends. "It's not going to happen," she whispered.

"Oh, it's going to happen," Vance insisted. He turned to Gracie. "Who is the managing partner here?"

"Ms. Jeffries. Would you like me to inquire when she's available?"

"Gracie!" Piper scolded.

"Yes, I would," Vance said, grinning.

"Vance, that's ridiculous."

"I don't think it's ridiculous." Gracie turned and headed out the door. "I'll be right back."

"She just wants to do your bidding because you're dressed like that," Piper said, pointing a finger up and down his long, lean body.

"Which is exactly why I dressed like this," he said. "I was hoping for your cooperation, but I'll be happy to bend the entire firm to my will in order to get you out of here for a couple weeks."

"How can I help?" Katie asked.

"Piper, how can Katie help?" Vance asked, looking at her pointedly. "Can she take care of the first years while you're gone?"

"Well, I can certainly reassign them easily enough. That's my job," Katie said.

"Perfect," Vance said. "And why don't you join us for lunch? Gracie too. My treat."

"I'd love to," Katie said, turning to leave. "Around noon?"

"Noon works for me," he said, turning to Piper.

"Noon is fine." Piper wondered how she'd lost control of her own free will.

The door closed behind Katie. Vance, who now stood with his hands in his pockets, cocked his head giving her an inquisitive stare. "You're playing hard to get."

"I'm trying not to be ridiculous."

"I like ridiculous. Ridiculous makes me hard."

"Vance!"

He stalked her slowly. "Piper, I'm taking you out of here one way or another." He reached into his back pocket as he backed her up and pulled out a pair of shiny handcuffs. They dangled in front of her, swinging to and fro. "I'm a cop, and I'm not afraid to use them," he said as her back hit the wall. "Twenty years is a long time to wait to see if we are going to work this thing out," he said, reaching for her left arm and cuffing her wrist.

"Oh."

"I am done with waiting," he said, his lips coming to hover over hers. "You're coming to Henderson. You're staying with me. Bad Cop is going to coax every secret out of The Lawyer Beaumont while Perfect Piper bakes cakes in my father's kitchen and Naughty Piper prances around in skimpy little underwear."

"You've been thinking about this, have you?" Piper couldn't help but be amused, although she noticed her heart was definitely trying to beat its way out of her chest.

"The three of you have been keeping me up nights." He reached around her back and clipped her other wrist into the cuffs.

With her hands bound behind her back and Vance's arms braced against the wall on either side of her head, Piper should have been a little more nervous about somebody walking in. But she couldn't remember ever being so turned on.

Vance leaned down and kissed her lips. Then he turned his head and kissed her again. Then he went back to his original position and kissed her some more. She touched her tongue to his, and he took the kiss deeper. She closed her eyes. Somebody moaned. The intense desire she had to feel his hands on her breasts made her forget where she was. She moved her body into his, felt his growing erection, and rubbed herself against him in an effort to ease her own need and stimulate his.

She wasn't playing hard to get, so much as she was playing to get him hard.

There was a swift knock on the door, and she heard Ms. Jeffries call her name right before she stepped through with Gracie on her heels. Vance turned and put his hand out to introduce himself immediately, like he'd been standing there waiting for Jane to walk in. Luckily, Jane Jeffries was as dazzled by Vance as the rest of them were because she barely gave Piper's heaving chest, stiff nipples and flushed cheeks a glance.

Piper burst out laughing. She was handcuffed and turned on and had fallen off the charts of the ridiculous scale. Yeah, she was going to Henderson—even if she had to quit her job to do it.

Vance had already fallen for Piper.

Her sweet, gentle kindness. Her soothing touch. The way she kissed.

Goddamn, the way she kissed.

Her sexy bedroom curls sweeping across baby blue eyes that lit up whenever he looked her way. And the way his chest puffed out and he owned the world whenever he stood towering over her petite, little body with all those smokin' hot curves in just the right places.

He couldn't wait to lay her down, spread her out, and feast upon every inch of her flesh. He had to keep his hands tucked into the pockets of his pants more often than not, because all he wanted to do was touch her. And one touch of that soft, supple skin was enough to turn him to stone in the johnson department.

Yeah, he'd already fallen for Piper, so what he was learning about her today was simply icing on the cake.

The lunch with her coworkers, managing partner Jane Jeffries included, was as entertaining as any lunch with a group of females was likely to be. They were all sharp—Katie was especially quick-witted—and their easy banter had nothing to do with the practice of law. It was about recipes and restaurants, social trends, explicit TV series, friendships, pets, children, parents, and one rowdy night shared by the four of them. Piper beamed with pride as she misrepresented Vance's status as Henderson Country Club's latest golf champion, and then shared the story of the newly formed Super Hero in Training boy band in Henderson, suggesting to the rest of the women that the drive over would be worth their while whenever the band played again.

Vance found Piper to be a good listener, a talented story teller, and was able to laugh at herself more than he would have guessed. Especially when she confessed about the bribe she was offering King Kong and the rest of the Raleigh police force in order to get her overzealous defensive ass off their radar.

And now he stood in Piper's Piped-Out apartment, surprised at her exquisite taste. Yes, the fabrics were bright and Piper-like, but he felt comfortable among them. Her little boutique dining room was charming—a doll house come to life. Her artwork and knickknacks added whimsy, and the entire place reflected Perfect Piper, exactly as he'd imagined she'd grown up to be.

But her bedroom!

Now here was something interesting. It wasn't bright and Piper-like. It wasn't overtly feminine or masculine. It invited, coaxing you in with its soothing color pallet of green and ivory and with the lush tactile fabrics that covered the mahogany sleigh bed. The room was…sensuous. And after Vance looked his fill, he raised an eyebrow toward Miss Beaumont.

"A side of you I've yet to…uncover."

"You like it?" she asked quietly.

He nodded, being careful not to put words to the warring factions taking over his mind. No one with his sexual history had any right to wonder about, or feel jealous of, any lovers who may have come before him. Still, his emotions waged war between the dynamic desire to take Piper in this room, on this bed, forcing all other lovers from her mind, and his desire to simply burn the place down and let all her memories turn to ash. He searched her face, standing in her shoes the moment she found all that junk inside his bathroom cabinet. Thank God he had done what he had. He hoped it would be enough.

"I'll start loading the cinnamon rolls into the truck while you pack. Take your time," he said, kissing the top of her head and taking one last glance around before he left her bedroom.

There were ten sheet cake boxes full of Piper's enormous cinnamon rolls. On each box she had printed out instructions for heating one to three rolls in the microwave at a time. She also had hand-written the note "Thank you for your hard work and loyal service" on each box along with "Homemade by Piper Beaumont" in very legible script.

It was a blatant attempt to establish a better working relationship, and Vance felt pretty confident that it was going to work. Still, he felt a lot more anxious than Piper seemed to be as they wheeled all the boxes into the precinct on a borrowed dolly.

Kong was there, paving the way for her redemption by ushering Piper into the snack room and oohing and aahing over her benevolence. The cinnamon rolls were a smash hit, but they were not the star of the show. Piper herself made the rounds, talking individually with each of the officers, asking about their families, their beats, if there was anything Collins & Reese could do to make their jobs a little easier. She took a lot of ribbing from the cops, a couple snide remarks, and one ribald joke with good-natured grace.

She was perfect. Surprise, surprise.

It was six o'clock in the evening when they pulled into his father's garage. Vance pushed Piper toward the cocktail trio sitting on the pool deck while he took her suitcase and yellow tote inside. Piper was drinking something pink and slushy when Vance joined his family after changing into shorts and grabbing a beer. They sat for a while going over the highlights of the day before Vance pulled Piper to her feet and said he had something he wanted to show her.

They walked down the hill hand in hand, passed the garage, and headed over to a shed charmingly constructed to look like an old barn. Inside sat a gleaming green and black ATV four-wheeler. Piper squealed.

"Is this your dad's?" she asked stroking the handle bars and running her hand over the long, black leather seat. "It looks brand new."

"It's mine," Vance told her, "and it looks new because I take care of it."

"You gonna let me drive it?" she asked in her silky southern drawl, batting her pretty blue eyes at him.

"Good Lord, woman, you are going to be the death of me. No," he said, harshly and quickly before he gave in. "You may not drive it. This is a serious machine and it's way too heavy for the tiny likes of you. But," his voice soothed, "climb on up and I'll take you for a spin."

She squealed again, hopping up on the seat in her soft cotton sundress. He watched the white and yellow fabric bunch up around her thighs as she seated herself, taking hold of the handlebars like he hadn't just told her no. It made him grin. Piper lived out loud, and she had no idea she was only five feet tall.

He threw a leg over the seat and sat himself behind his new favorite toy—Piper. He batted her hands off the controls, guided her palms to the sides of his thighs, and told her to hang on to him.

He revved the engine, which caused Piper to start suddenly, so he pulled her back snug against him, reveling in the feel of her between his legs. "Hold on," he said into her ear, and off they went, out of the barn, around the back of the property, and down a long, gradual slope.

The grass was a mix of brown and green, the recent lack of rain having taken its toll. There was a long but narrow stand of trees off to their left, which Vance worked their way around. He shot back along their edge, putting the manor house on the hill out of sight. He drove on farther, pointing out a stream running along the property and the way the sun was drifting into the top of the trees so Piper could get her directional bearings. He brought them to a stop in a shady spot and turned off the engine.

"It's lovely here," Piper said before he had a chance to explain. "This would make a great spot for a campout. Feels like you are in the middle of nowhere but with all the comforts of home just a short distance away."

"You like to camp?" Vance questioned, frowning at the back of her head.

"Oh, God no. I was thinking about you and all your crotch-grabbing friends."

"Crotch-grabbing friends?" He laughed. "Who grabs their crotch? Around you," he added.

"Jesse James played his crotch on stage all night long last Sunday. And I distinctly remember a lot of crotch scratching by you and Brooks and the rest back in your baseball days."

Vance laughed as he pulled up the curls covering the back of her neck and ran his lips over her soft, pale skin. It must have tickled because Piper hitched at first but then settled back against him letting his lips have their way.

"Piper," he whispered, "not only do you taste good, you have good taste," he said in between kisses. "I'm thinking of building a house…right here," he said, taking a handful of curls and turning her face so he could kiss her jaw. "What do you think?" His other hand slid around her middle, sliding over her belly, back and forth. And just as he was getting lost in the feel of her, he could tell she was suddenly alert. Focused.

"It's a beautiful spot," she said. "And kinda cool that it's part of the Evans Estate. No zoning restrictions other than what your father mandates." His lips and tongue were making a slow study of the curve of her shoulder when she said, "You could put up something small and inexpensive, and I bet your father would just give you the land. Ooh, and when I come to visit, I bet I'd get kitchen privileges at the big house."

"Big house?" Vance's head snapped up.

"Sure," she said like it was the best idea ever. She began to squirm around, turning to face him in the seat as she went on. Her eyes were bright with excitement as she settled herself in front of him, her legs folded meditation style. "Something a little bigger than the pool house. Ooh and right down here behind the trees. It would be like a cozy, little honeymoon cabin," she said, snuggling in and kissing the bottom of his dumbfounded chin.

Vance looked down into all that joy and didn't know whether to laugh or cry. "Piper," he said, taking her by her upper arms and giving her a slight shake. "How is it you have no idea who I am?"

"What do you mean?"

"I can afford to build more than a little honeymoon cabin," he assured her.

"Vance," she mouthed, distress flowing over her face. "I didn't mean…I was just saying this is a really nice opportunity. I know that the cops in Raleigh don't make a ton of money, and I can't imagine Henderson pays their employees any better. Building something here is…is cost effective."

"I'm not just a cop, Piper. I thought I told you that."

"You have. You told me about your little start-up business with your father."

Vance barked out a laugh.

"What?" she said, becoming irritated. "Vance, I'm just trying to keep you out of debt. My parents suffered with it, and it's not a pleasant place to be. And as much as you claim to looove your truck, you do enjoy driving your father's cars and having toys like this one," she said, indicating the machine they sat on. "And sure, you'll probably inherit a little money someday, but hey—your dad has another kid coming and with the cost of college out of control—"

He kissed her then. Just pulled her to him and shut her up with the biggest, happiest kiss of his life. She was worried about his money. Of all the things Piper should be worried about in a relationship with him, money was not one of them.

"Sweetheart," he said against her lips. "Baby doll," he said, pulling away and brushing her hair back from her face, falling in love with those pink cheeks all over again. "I love that you are worried about my money, but there is no reason for it, I promise you. I've had more money than I know what to do with since I was sixteen and bought my truck. Making money is my hobby, and I do it quickly and easily, always have. Sometimes to the detriment of my own stupid self, like the night you were standing in front of me and asked me to dance. All I was thinking about was dollar signs, so I missed an opportunity with you. I'm doing my best not to ever make a mistake like that again, but I love money. So I'm going to be making a lot of it."

"Wha—?" Piper was stupefied. "But you live in the pool house. You drive a piece-of-crap truck."

Vance laughed. "I said I'm good at making it. I didn't say I was any good at spending it."

"Well, I can help you with that," she offered, as if that was now the problem she needed to solve.

"I'm certain you can," he said. "Starting with this house." He looked around the land surrounding them. "I want a big house, Piper. And I'm not building it here to rival my father. I'm building it here to honor him. To expand on his dream and his accomplishments. He's given me every physical thing I could ever want. He is generous beyond generous. I like him. I like Genevra. And I want to be close to my baby brother."

"Brody," she offered.

"Yes." He laughed. "My baby brother, Brody."

Piper's sweet smile lit up his insides. "Oh, but there is one thing I'm definitely going to outdo my father on," he said, gifting her with a big cheesy grin. "The kitchen I build? It's going to make his kitchen look small. It's going to fucking dwarf his," he growled, wrapping his arms around her.

Piper shrieked with laughter.

"I'm going to build a kitchen that Perfect Piper can get lost in for days," he said, nuzzling her neck. "One that she won't ever want to find her way out of," he went on as she untangled her legs and threw them up over his thighs. He put his hands underneath her ass and lifted her so that she straddled his lap. "And I want a hand-painted,"…kiss…"lava stone"…kiss…"countertop,"…kiss, kiss, kiss…"topping an island big enough that I can lay Naughty Piper down and have my way with her." He stroked his straining erection against her cotton-covered crotch, her dress bunched up around her waist.

"Mmm," she hummed. "And what about The Lawyer Beaumont?"

"What Lawyer Beaumont?" He moaned against her mouth, tilting her pelvis at just the right angle so he could rub his full, khaki-covered, length against her. If he had thought to bring a blanket, he would have laid it out and made love to Piper for the first time in the exact spot where their house was going to be. It would have been a good omen.

But he'd fantasized too much about having her in his bed. He was willing to wait. Wait just a little longer to make this sweet, sweet, precious, tiny bit of a girl his.

"So…wait. Wait," Piper said, pulling out of their kiss-induced stupor. "So, explain to me—about your job—your work. You keep saying you aren't much of a cop, and I gather from a couple things you've said that you coach some sort of a team, but truly, I don't have an idea of what you and Pinks are doing for your dad. So how 'bout enlightening me, before I get too wrapped up in all your sexy talk about lava stone countertops and being lost in your kitchen for days."

She started running her fingers through his hair, tickling his scalp, so he closed his eyes and agreed to tell her everything if she just kept doing that.

So she did, kissing his nose and his eyes along the way, as he explained first about his "destined for the State Championship" baseball team and then about his investment in Lewis' company and other businesses in town. He talked about what his father did and explained that he was not working for his dad, but working alongside his dad in their new joint venture of Evans & Evans Investments.

And then he told her about what really mattered to him. About getting Brooks elected mayor, and their ambitious dream of putting Henderson on the map through the power of a strong and viable economy. So that Henderson would draw in young professionals and families and become one of the premium places to live in all of North Carolina.

And then the East Coast.

And then the entire country.

Vance felt Piper's hands move through his hair and down the back of his head, coming around to cup his chin with both of her tiny hands. He opened his eyes.

"You love Henderson," she said with awe and warmth.

"No," he said quietly. "Brooks loves Henderson."

Her brow furrowed.

"Brooks is motivated by his love for this town and the people who live here. It breaks his heart that most of our generation has moved on, moved away. That's what he wants to change. He wants to bring Henderson back to life.

"My motivation is not at all noble," he said, wrapping his arms loosely around her back. "My motivation is revenge. At least, it was originally," he said, considering. "Things seem to have shifted a bit," he realized.

"Revenge?" she asked.

"Revenge." He nodded. "What better way to flip my mother the bird than by making sure the town she walked away from becomes one of the Top Ten Best Places to Live in America?"

Piper blinked. "Your sole purpose in life is to be able to send a big 'fuck you' to your mother?"

"I wouldn't say it is my sole purpose—and I can't believe that nasty word just came out of Perfect Piper's mouth."

She huffed.

"Don't huff. It probably started as a big 'fuck you' to you too, you know."

"To me?"

"Yes, you. You left. Just like my mother did."

"I was ten!"

"That didn't make it hurt any less. I'm *not* saying this is at all rational, but I'm telling the truth here."

Silence.

"I came back," Piper said. "I came back in eighth grade. I came back in twelfth grade. I would have come back the night I met you at The Charlie Horse if you had just stuck around a little longer."

He kissed her hard and fast, not wanting to think about that—about how the last five shitty years of his life were his own damn fault. She pressed her hands against his shoulders, so he eased off a bit, gentling his kiss. It wasn't her fault, after all, and here he was, acting like a bully.

"I'm sorry," he whispered, stroking her hair and licking her lips. "I know you came back. I know my crap life has been all my fault."

"Stop it, Vance. Your life hasn't been all crap. Not by a long shot."

"I know. But it would have been so much better so much sooner if I had just…known it was you."

"Known what was me?"

"That kiss, back at the Charlie Horse. Piper, the entire reason I ran off was because kissing you *reminded* me of you. It brought back every happy memory I had of you and of my mother. And for a while, I leaned into it. And it felt good—so damn good.

"But then, I got scared. Because it had taken me a lotta years to banish hope. Hoping my mother would come back. Hopin' I'd see you again. I couldn't risk going back to hope—hoping the girl in my arms wouldn't run out on me like my mother had—so, I ran out on her."

When Vance found the courage to look at her directly, he saw the tears shining up her pretty blue eyes and his gut clenched. "Piper, all that is just bullshit under the bridge. It's a part of our past and it's gonna make a great story someday. Trust me when I say I am not that guy anymore. I'm not leaving you in a bar or standing by the side of the road ever again. I swear it. Besides…" he said, leaning in to kiss her just as sweetly as he was able, "we have now come to the part in our story…where the small-town cop…with zero jurisdiction…has kidnapped the beautiful Lawyer Beaumont and handcuffed her to his bed for two…whole…weeks."

Piper sighed against his lips. "I swear, for all your talk, Officer Evans, you had better make this good."

Vance pulled back and laughed. "I swear to God, it's like dating three different women." He picked Piper up, turned her around, and situated her in front of him, before starting the engine. "And I'm not sure how I feel about Naughty Piper challenging my skills in the bedroom."

"Wait!" Piper stuck her hand out, stopping him. Vance throttled down so he could hear her. "Back to this house. Have you planned a budget?"

"About 3.5 million. And relax, Price Waterhouse. I have it in cash."

"Cash?" she said, swiveling around. "You have 3.5 million in cash?"

"Give or take."

"So? So…you're a millionaire?" She blinked in astonishment.

"Piper, have you not been listening? Yes, I'm a millionaire—many times over. A full-fledged millionaire who drives a beat-up pickup truck. Deal with it."

Piper squealed, turned herself around, and flung her arms around Vance's neck, laying kisses all over his face. Vance laughed, fighting to keep his hands on the handlebars. "I'm sensing millionaire trumps cop," he said.

"Oh, I was crushin' on the cop pretty hard," she said, "but the potential for hand-painted lava stone in your kitchen just hit one hundred percent."

"Is that right?" he said, trying to pull her off of him. "Well, if that's all it takes to get you to throw yourself at me, you're going to go crazy when you see what I've got to show you next."

CHAPTER THIRTY

The main house was conspicuously dark when Vance and Piper walked up the path to the pool house together. When Vance opened the door to usher Piper inside, the tiny chandelier hanging over the small dining table greeted them with quiet ambiance. Inside his bedroom, lamps on the bedside tables glowed softly. Everything looked in its place. Vance wanted Piper to be comfortable. In fact, he'd thought of little else since her first visit. He pointed out her suitcase just inside the bedroom door and then took her by the hand, walking her to the bathroom.

"Okay," he said, opening the cabinet under the sink. "Everything in here is new. New hair dryer, new curling thing, new combs, new brushes. New girlie shampoo, conditioner, soap, et cetera. New towels," he pointed out. "New spongy thing and new soapy net thing. I don't know what the hell most of it is. I had some saleswoman help me. But the point is it's all new. New for you."

He closed the cabinet and liked the way Piper was smiling at him.

"There's more," he said, leading her back into the bedroom and pointing at the bed. "Brand new sheets that have never been slept on by anyone, including me. I had help with those too. New pillows. New mattress pad. The mattress is not new. I find it very comfortable, but if you don't like it, we can take care of that tomorrow."

Piper squealed and did a swan dive onto the bed, rolling onto her back and reveling in delight. Vance crawled onto the bed and over her. "We can get a new comforter too. I'd like you to pick it out."

Piper reached up to wrap her arms around his neck, pulling him down to her. "Thank you," she said as she kissed him. "Thank you, thank you, thank you."

"There's one more thing," he said, rolling to the other side of the bed. He sat up and opened the drawer of the bedside table. He pulled out a piece of paper, looked at it, and turned to hand it to Piper.

"Oh, thank God," she said, laughing. "I was worried you were about to pull out a band new vibrator."

"As if. I barely touched you the other night and you detonated."

Piper pushed him flat on the bed and straddled his hips in her sundress, paper in hand. "That's because you are hot. How lucky was I to fall in love with a ten-year-old who grew up to look like you?"

"You think I'm hot, huh?" he said, licking his lips, moving his hands down to the hem of her dress. He tried to pull it up over her head, but Piper batted his hands away.

"Wait! Wait. I haven't read this." She brushed blond curls out of her face and straightened the now-wrinkled paper before starting to read.

"Notice the date," he said. "The day after you were here for dinner."

Piper's eyes scanned the page. "Why did you need a blood test?" She whipped the page away and stared down at him, wide-eyed. "Are you sick?"

"Piper." Vance sat up and tossed her onto her back, straddling her and pinning her wrists to the bed. "I needed a blood test for you. So you'd know I was healthy. Free of STDs."

"Oh. Is that what all those numbers meant?"

"Yes. I wanted you to have proof, so…you know…you don't have to worry."

The blue eyed smile she gave Vance had him melting from the inside out, especially when she reached up and caressed his cheek. "I'm glad you're healthy," she said quietly. "Thank you for that."

And there she was: Perfect Piper.

Vance's stomach seized. He moved himself up into a sitting position, blinking his eyes and trying to tamp back the fear. "Piper," he said through a long slow breath. "I really don't want to screw this up."

She pushed herself up, leaning back on her hands. She tilted her head and gave him a little smile. "You can't possibly screw this up."

"I really want us to work," he said.

"I do too."

"I'm talking long term."

Piper fell back tossing her arms over her head—giggling—squirming in delight beneath him. "Then you'd better put some of your legendary moves where your mouth is, because I'm not committing to anything until I see how well this notorious reputation of yours is gonna work out for me."

And…back to Naughty Piper.

Vance grinned. Naughty Piper was a handful, but the kind of handful he specialized in. The Bad Cop in him was ready, willing, and able to show Naughty Piper every last one of his moves. He leaned over and whispered, "You're on."

"Where are you going?" she said when he started backing away.

"I need a shower." He opened a drawer and pulled out a pair of basketball shorts. "I'll run next door and leave this bathroom for you." Then he threw out some Bad Cop orders. "Don't be drying your hair when I get back. No putting on makeup. No nothing. Just…you. I want to finally…see…." He looked her body up and down. "Christ Almighty. Ten minutes," he yelled as he strode for the door, slamming it shut behind him.

༄

When Piper came out of the bathroom, the bed was turned down, the lights were off, and Vance stood with his back to her, lighting a candle over on his highboy. The sight of his naked back in the candlelight created the same effect as a lot of good champagne bubbling through her system.

She stood still, peering across the room in great appreciation of the well-defined muscles of his back and sides. Her heart rate increased as her eyes traveled lower to the exercise shorts which barely clung to his hips. Giddy and nervous, she was licking her lips when Vance turned around. He folded his arms across his chest.

Her gaze shot to his face, finding his expression full of disbelief and mock outrage.

"Are you...ogling me?" he asked in his police-officer-interrogation voice.

"Who wouldn't ogle you? You're magnificent. I'm used to lawyers who do not—at all—look like this."

"Please do not bring your other lovers into this bedroom. I'm working on this Perfect Piper fantasy. One where she is still as innocent as she was in fourth grade."

"You can just keep that going, because when it comes to all this nonsense here," she said, twirling her finger at his chest, "I *am* innocent. And I'm feeling just a little woozy because of it."

"You are?" he asked, inching slowly in her direction. "Woozy is good. Woozy I can work with." He sidled up close, taking both her hands in his and interlocking their fingers. "I like this lacy, little tank top and tiny whatever-is-happening under there," he whispered, as he leaned down for a kiss. "We aren't going to rush this," he said, tickling her mouth with his. "We are going to take our time. We're going to—" He pulled back and looked at her sharply. "You seem a little jumpy."

"I am," she panted. "I'm definitely feeling jumpy. I'm feeling... you know, anxious."

"Then maybe you oughta lie down," he suggested with a mischievous grin. When she didn't do his bidding right away, he ordered, "Now."

"Oops. Sorry." Piper scuttled to the center of the bed, running her mouth as she went. "You're just a little bit mesmerizing. I'm starting to see how this whole man-whore thing got itself started. You can hardly be blamed for your promiscuity when you are this... spectacular. I mean, you just have to take off your shirt and women must come flocking."

"Piper." He shot her a serious warning. "I don't want your past in here, and I certainly don't want what will now only be referred to as my misspent youth in here either. Just us. Have I made myself clear? Now lie back. And if you must talk, the only thing I want to hear coming out of your mouth is a very detailed description of your favorite, unfulfilled fantasy."

Piper laid her head back, feeling the bed move as Vance knelt at her feet. "Sorry. I'm just…" she said, shaking out her hands, "revved up."

He sat back on his haunches, picking up her right foot. He leaned down and kissed the top of it and then stroked his hand over the kiss. "All right," he said in a soothing voice, starting to massage her foot. "Maybe this will relax you."

Piper stared up at the ceiling, her hands fidgeting. "Wouldn't it be better just to, you know, go ahead and get our first time over with?"

Vance looked up at her stunned. "Get it *over* with?"

Uh-oh.

Vance dropped her foot, crawled up her body, leaned his handsome face into hers and growled, "You want to get our first time *over with*?"

"I'm nervous."

"Tough shit. I did not spend the last five years practicing on women I didn't like just so you and I could get this over with."

Piper tried to stifle a grin. "Is that what we are calling it now? Practicing?"

"Damn right. Now take a deep breath, lie back, and start telling me about Naughty Piper's wildest fantasy."

"Mmm, that feels good," she said as he slid his hands down her legs and picked up her right foot again. He started tugging on the length of each of her toes. "Okay. All right. My fantasy." She took a deep cleansing breath and let it out slowly.

Vance went to work on her other toes and her jumpiness subsided by small degrees when he began using his thumbs to massage the underside of her feet.

"I'm wearing a yellow dress," she said.

"Of course you are," Vance whispered over her toes.

"A yellow dress and really high heels," she continued.

"No."

She lifted her head up. "What do you mean, no?"

"No shoes. You're in bare feet," he said, not even bothering to glance up at her.

Hmm. Bare feet.

"Okay, I'm in bare feet," she said, lying back and looking at his ceiling. She hadn't noticed that it pitched at an angle. "But the dress is short. Like a little too short, with a full skirt so when the wind blows it moves against my thighs. Ooooh, that feels really good."

His thumbs and fingers were massaging around her ankle bones. "You are clear that I was asking for a sexual fantasy, right? Not a *Project Runway* fantasy," he said to her ankles.

"Mmm. They have to start somewhere. This one starts on the steps of the courthouse as I leave work one afternoon. In my short, yellow dress and bare feet."

He kissed her ankles.

"So, I'm coming out of work and down at the bottom of the steps there is this gorgeous, dark, sharp-looking…Maserati."

"Humph." Vance moved her right leg into a bent position, her foot flat on the bed and began kneading her calf.

"Ah!"

"Your calf muscles are tight. Probably from wearing all those high heels. You need to stick with the bare feet."

"That feels really good and really hurts all at the same time," she squeaked out while holding her breath. "Oooh."

"I'll go a little easier." He bent his head and kissed her knee. "Go on," he said, his hands busy loosening muscles.

"Ah, okay…so, next to the Maserati is this guy. And he looks a whole lot like my first love, only he's taller now."

Vance used only the tips of his fingers to run butterfly sensations up and down the backs of her legs.

"So my bare feet and I wander down the steps and stop right in front of him. And he is tall and smoking hot in a bad-boy sort of way with his T-shirt and jeans, dark shades, and wind-blown hair. As soon as I get close enough, he grabs my wrist and pulls me in tight against his chest, trapping me up against him."

"The guy has moves," he said as he bent her second knee and started working her other calf.

"He says he's been looking for me for a long, long time. And then he kisses me with such commanding finesse that I'm rendered limp and willing."

"Commanding finesse?" he asked as he used the heel of his hand to ride up her calf.

"Mmm, yes, and the next thing I know, he swings me up into his arms and then drops me into the Maserati."

Vance's hands stilled. "The driver's side?"

"No. That fantasy already happened. In this fantasy, he's a complete control freak with only one thing on his mind. The type that would handcuff a girl at work in broad daylight and kidnap her in front of her boss."

Vance's open mouth slid over her bent knee, sucking gently—his hands exploring the back side of her legs. He scraped his teeth over her other knee cap.

"Before I know it, I'm naked in his pool. It's dark, but there's a full moon so we can see each other pretty well."

Piper felt the bed move and her legs being shifted. She lifted her head to find Vance sitting cross legged, each of her knees draped over one of his. She dropped her head back to the pillow when he started massaging her thighs and paid very close attention to the long, titillating strokes he was running from her knee to her hip. His thumbs would slide lazily along her inner leg… right…until—they veered up and over her thigh. His touch came so close to her panty line that it provoked a strong blossom of desire.

She bit her lip, feeling the internal tightening as Vance kept his strokes long and slow on the way up, lighter and ticklish on the way back. It was heaven. Sheer heaven.

"What happens next?" he whispered.

His words drew her focus from the longing between her legs and she had to backtrack to remember what he was talking about. "Oh. I'm *definitely* not jumpy anymore. Where was I?"

"In the control freak's pool. Naked."

She smiled with her eyes closed. "Hmm. So, the water feels really…really good on my bare body. Decadent. Sexy. Bad-Boy takes my hand and floats me out with him where the water is over my head. He pulls my naked chest to his and, for the first time, I feel his bare skin slide against mine. I like it. I wrap my arms around his neck and he pulls me farther out into the pool. My legs are drifting behind me." Piper sucked in a breath. "Oh, God, Vance. That feels really, really good."

His hands were twisting from her inner thigh out to her hip.

Then he dragged them under her derriere, kneading her glutes as he pulled his palms back down the backs of her legs. He did this over and over, just the shadow of his thumbs grazing the lace edge of her lingerie and titillating the tender flesh beneath.

She felt herself go damp. Felt her nipples tighten and her chest heave. Her hands longed to stroke him—anywhere. She started to worry about how he was going to get her underwear off when she felt the bed move and a shadow blocked the candlelight. She opened her eyes to find Vance's face directly over hers, flaunting another mischievous grin.

"You keep losing your train of thought just when things start to get interesting." He ducked his head and kissed her. His tongue delved just to the inside of her lips. His voice was husky when he said, "Roll over for me."

Piper liked the idea of his hands on her back. A lot. She just had to rein in her longing in order for his request to sink in.

"Is there a problem, Miss Beaumont?"

She shook her head no, bit her lip, and rolled underneath the cage he'd formed with his arms. She pulled her arms forward and laid her cheek on her hands.

"Good girl," he said, shifting around so he straddled the backs of her thighs. His hands slid under her tank top, bunching it up around her shoulders. "You're such a tiny thing," he said as his hands smoothed their way from her lace-covered bottom to her neck. "I think leaving Henderson stunted your growth."

"I stopped growing in seventh grade." She sucked in a breath, her head and shoulders springing up as Vance dragged his tickling fingers down both her sides.

"A little ticklish?"

"Yes."

"I'll be careful," he said as his hands worked over her back and her shoulder blades. "Now, back to the pool."

"Mmm," she said, relaxing into his care. "Let's see…back at the pool…my hands are locked around Bad-Boy's neck, and I'm weightless in his arms as we drift, slippery skin against slippery skin. His kisses become more aggressive, and in between them he's whispering endearments. He tells me how much he missed me. How lucky he is to have found me. And now that he has me in his arms, he doesn't think he'll ever be able to let me go."

"Sounds like a pussy."

"You did request a fantasy."

Piper felt her top being pulled over her head and off her arms, but she was so focused on her story it didn't fully register.

"And then his talk gets sexy," she said quietly, luxuriating in the feel of Vance's hands on her body. "Real sexy. He talks about how turned on he is by my body while his hands create goose bumps over my sides, my back…my rear end. He has a lot to say about my rear end. He takes a couple steps forward and my legs drift down and wrap around his waist, and now we are touching from shoulder to hip and everywhere in between."

Piper smiled when Vance mumbled a curse right before sinking his teeth into the tendon between her neck and shoulder. "How come I'm getting jealous?" he whispered as he nuzzled his head deeper into that space. His chin, his hair, tickled as he sought the softer skin of her neck. He sucked a healthy portion into his mouth. Lust sprang from the connection, firing off ready signals to every sensitive spot in her body. Her feet flexed at the bottom of the bed. Her arms slipped down underneath her chest, clasping her hands together. She turned her face into the sheets and moaned.

Vance kissed his way across her shoulders, tasted his way down her spine, and lingered with his tongue at the center of the small of her back. His hands ventured farther, kneading the roundness of her derrière. "Relax," he urged against her skin. "Relax, baby doll."

She hadn't noticed that her body was clenched up tight. Even her face was twisted. She turned her cheek to the side, loosening up her hands, her arms, her legs, and then her feet. She breathed deep and let the internal tension seep away.

"Better," Vance whispered against the indentations on her lower back—his hands investigating the contours of her hips, her thighs, and her buttocks. "So we're in the pool. And we're naked. Your legs are around my hips."

"And everything's slippery," she reminded him with her eyes closed.

"And everything's slippery," he repeated. "So what happens

next?"

"Your...I mean, Bad-Boy's hands are free to roam because I'm doing all the holding on. So they move between our bodies to my breasts. Which, by the way, he's not seemed all that interested in. Which is highly unusual. Even gay men like my breasts."

She felt Vance stop everything. And that caused her to smile.

He flipped her over without warning. Her eyes flew open to find Vance looking his fill. "Baby doll," he said, "you do have magnificent breasts. You're so tiny everywhere, and then...these," he let the word draw out like he couldn't believe what he was seeing. "There isn't a thing about you that doesn't make me ache." He leaned down and kissed the tender skin between her breasts while he nudged her legs apart, laying himself in between. His mouth tongued one nipple, his hand molding itself to the other. "If you had any idea the number of fantasies about your breasts alone...."

Piper ran her fingers through his hair how he liked, scraping her nails lightly across his scalp. "I'm looking forward to hearing about those," she claimed, smiling down at the top of his head. "Oh, and Vance?" she said softly. "Even though I don't travel with papers, I am perfectly healthy. And I have birth control taken care of."

His head popped up. "Are you saying I don't need to wear a condom?"

"I'm saying I'm comfortable either way. Whatever you're comfortable with."

"Whatever I'm—? Damn, you really are Perfect Piper," he said before kissing his way farther down her body. His hand skimmed over her waist. His mouth sucked in the soft flesh under her belly button. "Piper," he said, his breathing starting to get heavy. "I've never had sex without a condom." His hands slid to her hips, gripping the sides of her lingerie. "And I guess I've never, really, made love before," he confessed as he pulled the lace down her hips and legs. "This is going to be my very first time."

Piper's heart melted with gladness as she kicked off her undies. Vance slid his hands back up her legs and stopped. "Oh. Dear. God," he breathed, looking at her naked body. "You're blond everywhere." His hands and arms stretched up underneath her back, his head bending low to kiss her right in the center of those blond curls.

And then he opened his mouth and kissed her again. "I've literally dreamed about this," he whispered before kissing her deeper," and I woke up with a raging hard-on."

As his tongue worked his Vance Evans magic, Piper sucked in a breath and lifted her hips off the bed. "I guess that works for you," he said before trying it again and getting the same reaction. "Piper, I swear to God that is such a turn-on," he whispered. His mouth went to work, his tongue circling and then stroking again and again, varying the amount of pressure he applied.

She was in a state of semiconscious bliss when one of his hands eased from underneath her and laid itself possessively against her tummy. His palm tugged the skin of her belly up making it taut, which caused the magic he was wielding with his tongue to trigger some crazy gymnastics within her nerve centers. She'd never experienced feeling so on the edge—teetering on the brink—milking all of the pleasure of that just-before-orgasm moment. She bit her lip to avoid whimpering while solely focused on his incredible mouth. But when she felt the breadth of two fingers ease inside her she couldn't help but moan.

"Mmmm," he hummed against her, which made her gasp. His fingers did a slow stroke somewhere inside, and all she could do was tell him how good it felt before her body convulsed into waves and waves and waves of delicious orgasm.

"Oh…Vance," she panted, thinking she was done. Thinking she was never, ever going to experience anything like that again. She started running her hands over her face and her hair, telling him how glorious that was even while her lower body continued to convulse with mini-orgasms. She wanted Vance to know.

But all of a sudden, she felt herself climbing. Vance hadn't stopped his magic. He kept using his mouth, his hand, and his fingers as if he hadn't just brought her to the greatest climax in the history of the world. He kept her body climbing, reaching. Like a circular staircase straight into heaven, her body kept going up and around, reaching another level, another climax and then going around again, coming to an even stronger orgasm, and then again and again, each one farther, longer, more intense. She groaned for him to stop. Pleaded for him to stop. And then finally ordered, "Stop now!" with her arms collapsing over her head.

After a few moments, Vance lifted his head and moved his hands, starting at both of her ankles and sliding them all the way up her legs, over her hips, up her sides, over her shoulders, and all the way up the length of her arms. His body followed behind his hands and he laid his long, sinewy form down on hers inch by magnificent inch until they touched skin to skin everywhere—his legs against her legs, his hips against her hips, his stomach against her stomach, his chest against her chest, his arms against her arms, palms flat against each other. His mouth consumed hers. Stretched out beneath him, Piper's body rejoiced, opened, and submitted.

"Piper," he rasped against her cheek. "If I hurt you, you tell me. I'll be able to adjust, but you tell me, okay?" She nodded. "You're so little. I don't want to hurt you."

He drew his hands down her body, and she felt a hand draw her left knee up. He bent his head, and then she felt him push against her. One arm came forward to support his weight while his other arm kept her leg bent as he slowly pushed for entry. He felt thick and substantial—exactly what her body craved. With all the lubrication they'd created he slid in easily, and she felt sensation *everywhere*. He pulled out and slid in farther, giving her more. And after he pulled out again, she saw him look down and watch himself slide all the way in, filling her completely. He groaned with such unabashed pleasure that Piper rewarded him by squeezing her internal muscles.

"Christ." He grimaced as his breath caught. His eyes were closed and his jaw was drawn tight. "How the…? Piper," he breathed as he licked his lips. He had hardly moved, yet he'd broken into a sweat. "That feels so good. You feel so good, but just…let me…give me…." She relaxed around him and he exhaled.

"Baby doll," he said as he leaned over and kissed her thoroughly, their bodies intimately connected. "What the hell did I do to deserve you?" he asked against her lips. He kissed her some more. "Your body, it's like…." He started moving his hips then, pulling his full length out and moving back in, nice and slow.

"It's like what?" she prompted.

He shook his head and kissed her again. Moving nice…and… slow. "That feels good," he said, seeming well-satisfied by the rhythm.

"Mmm, and my body is like?"

"Is like—Oh God," he blurted out, holding himself still, stopping everything. "Baby doll," he said, panting, looking down into her eyes, blinking sweat from his own. "Your body is the hottest, sexiest wet dream ever," he whispered. "And I mean that," he said as he started moving again, "in the best—oh God," he whispered, "possible…" he said before he cursed again, "…way. You're just so tiny. So slippery, so agile." He started pumping, deliberately pulling less length out and then thrusting back in. "And this no-condom thing," he said tightly, thrusting harder, "is fucking brilliant."

Piper did her best, but in the position Vance had her, she could hardly move. So she concentrated on timing the tightening of her internal muscles with his withdrawals.

"Oh, hell, yes." He pushed himself up and watched her face as he pumped faster. Piper spread her knee up and out, giving him more room, more leverage. Her reward was a shift in his features—as if he couldn't believe it could feel any better. The muscles of his shoulders went taut as Piper slid her hands over them, reveling in his power, his masculine form. That's when her awareness of the constant friction came into play.

"Vance," she whispered, starting to concentrate on what was building. "Keep going if you can," she breathed, finding a way to move in opposition now that it seemed vitally important. "This is starting to feel better than good," she told him. "I think…I think I might be able to come like this," she said in awe, closing her eyes and concentrating on the sensations of their bodies coming together.

"Piper. Sweet Piper," he breathed. "You are so good at this," he praised, spurring her on as he continued to pitch deep and thorough. "I knew getting inside you was going to be amazing," he whispered in her ear. "You are perfect—perfect for me. So come on, take what you need, baby. We can do this, baby doll. So good. That's it. So… damn…good."

His body had brought her to the edge and now his talk was throwing her over.

Her body wrenched upward as all sensation pressed down, coiled and tightened. A series of convulsions gripped Piper, squeezing excruciating pleasure from her body. Squeezing the part of Vance that plunged and bore, driving toward his own release.

Vance roared at the sensation. His body shuddered, and he held himself deep inside her as his ejaculation pulsed over and over, finally causing him to gasp for breath and pant at the finish. He swayed, struggling to keep above her, to hold his sweat-drenched body at bay.

Making a last-ditch effort to save himself.

Piper reached up and ran her fingertips through his hair and watched him give in.

Piper welcomed his weight as he gently laid his body down and tightened his arms around her. "I love you," he breathed into her neck. "Please don't leave me."

CHAPTER THIRTY-ONE

Piper rested her head on Vance's chest and snuggled up against his naked body in her own bed. Which was sheer heaven. The hell of it was that the dawn of that dreaded Monday morning—after two weeks and three days of vacation—had arrived.

After so many glorious mornings of walking out into the hot summer air and enjoying the twinkling sunlight glistening off the Evans' family pool, stepping back into her Lawyer Beaumont persona seemed so…restrictive.

She'd have to wear shoes.

She sighed and rolled to her back, because that wasn't the worst of it.

Now that she was back in Raleigh, she wasn't going to be able to waltz into the Evans' gourmet kitchen where she had carte blanche to bake and cook as she pleased. Or hop in the Maserati and take a picnic lunch over to Vance at his office. And poor Jesse was bound to eat all of the Toll House cookies she'd left him before she could get back to Henderson next weekend with a fresh batch. Pinks wasn't going to be happy that Hale had finished off the last of her 10 Molar Chocolate Cake, and Emelina had become addicted to her French macaroons.

Oh! And Tansy. Once Piper figured out Tansy hoarded her Sea Salt Caramels, she became Vance's secret weapon on the Tansy Langford front. Whatever Vance needed done was completed without a big fat quarrel as long as the request was accompanied by Piper's caramels.

So maybe she wasn't keeping people out of jail through her guilty pleasure of baking. But it sure seemed her efforts were appreciated just the same.

And now she'd be coming home every night to…nothing. Nothing but an empty condo. None of Vance's family, none of their friends, no crazy stories about the mounting gossip in town over the upcoming wedding. No Pinks and Jesse tossing random girls in the pool or crashing through the house with lacrosse sticks.

And no Vance, she sighed, turning her head so she could get in a couple of last looks at his handsome face. She was startled to find his eyes open and staring at her.

"You okay, baby doll?" he asked, rolling over on top of her.

"I'm fine," she huffed, stroking his hair the way he liked. "Just suffering the beginnings of a vacation hangover."

"Mmm," Vance said, kissing her chin and moving lower. "Turn in your two-weeks' notice this morning and call a realtor. We'll have you back in Henderson before you know it."

"I can't move to Henderson."

"Why not," Vance said, his head popping up. "Don't you like Henderson?"

"I love Henderson," she said tenderly, touching his face. "I love everything about it. I love your family and the people I met. I love… well, there's nothing I don't love. But my work is here."

Vance scoffed. "I can start throwing kids in jail on all kinds of trumped up charges. I'll get Brooks to do it too. We can create plenty of work for you in Henderson."

"The law firm is here."

Vance started kissing his way down her body again. "Brooks is trying to persuade Duncan to open a law firm in Henderson. The business boom we're creating is going to need a guy like him, and it's also going to attract more families to the area. Plenty of kids who will need cop-hating lawyers defending them."

"Ah! I am no longer a cop-hating lawyer." Piper insisted, but her stomach twisted. Something, something…but she lost her train of thought as Vance rolled her over onto her stomach and bit her derrière.

"You are not a boob man are you? *You,* Vance Evans, are an ass man," she said into her pillow. Vance snickered. She yelped when he smacked her backside.

"And you, baby doll, have one fine ass."

Yup, Piper thought as she faced her little…tiny…bo-ring office, with no fancy French oven or pretty bowls filled with rising dough. "I've got a vacation hangover for sure," she said out loud as she felt her stomach pitch. She went in search of Tums.

She felt the same way when she arrived on Tuesday morning and then again on Wednesday morning. On Thursday morning, when the sight of her office made her sick to her stomach, she gave herself a stern talking-to about getting her head back into the game, about the clients who depended on her, and the firm she owed her best to. Then she soothed herself with the thought that in less than forty-eight hours she could pack a bag and scramble back to Henderson for Hale and Genevra's wedding.

The talking-to seemed to work. She managed to get everything done with ease. Even her emails, done, done, done. She'd lunched with her office gal pals and filled them in with the PG-rated version of her two-week fantasy vacation with Vance. She had to leave out the time Vance insisted he make love to her on Davis' desk at E&E, and the time she got a little aggressive in the Rolls Royce while it was still parked in the garage. Oh, and she neglected to embellish the sketchy details she gave about the romantic episode in the Jacuzzi at three in the morning—or the seven different ways Vance took her both under the stars and in broad daylight at the site of his future home.

So, when Friday morning rolled around and the sight of her boring office sent her running for the ladies' room to heave her breakfast, Piper realized this new aversion to practicing law was starting to become a real problem.

The weather on Saturday, August 21 enveloped Henderson in glorious sunshine, low humidity, heavenly breezes, and temperatures in the low eighties. Hale Evans wouldn't have it any other way, they all said. The man was so wealthy and so in love that he could command the weather these days. Of course his wedding day would be just as exquisite as the bride he was marrying, they all said.

And that was just the beginning of what *they all* were saying.

Piper put on her new turquoise dress. Yellow may be her signature color, but she was getting sick of it. It had a short full skirt and straps that crisscrossed over her bare back. There was a sweet little bow where the X marked the center, and Piper felt pretty and feminine in it. She hoped the dress would get a favorable response from Vance. If nothing else, it showed off her poolside vacation tan beautifully.

She left the pool house and, after showing the catering staff where her groom's cake, her pretty petit fours, and the last-minute addition of her colorful French macaroons were to be placed, Piper found her way to the end of the long white-chair-and-rose festooned seating area where Brooks Bennett was holding court. It was then that she had her first opportunity to meet Brooks' sister, Darcy, and Vance's good friend, Lewis Kampmueller.

Annabelle and Duncan joined the four of them as all of Henderson seemed to pour across the grounds to where the outdoor ceremony would take place. The largest white tent Piper had ever seen—looking like it could cover a football field—had been erected to cover a stage for the band, a wooden dance floor, and large round tables covered in the sheerest of pinks. More pale pink roses than Piper could imagine ever being gathered in one place were hung from the chandeliers and stuffed into enormous crystal rose bowls. Genevra's roses, Hale had told Piper. They reminded him of Genevra.

"Duncan, when I'm mayor, is there any way to institute an ordinance against gossip?"

Everyone around Brooks burst out laughing.

"I am dead serious," he said. "You cannot believe the spiteful bullshit that is being bandied about Henderson concerning this wedding and Genevra and Hale. I know small towns have their issues, and gossip is one of them. But to spread speculation and harsh opinions as if they were facts? I don't like it. And I am determined to do something about it."

"You're just upset because it's Lolly's mother. It's hitting close to home." Annabelle tried to soothe him. "People can't help but talk about the two of them. They are gorgeous for one thing and have money to burn for another."

Brooks started to protest.

"I know," Annabelle told him. "Hale's wealth shouldn't give cause to throw stones, but it does."

"I just don't get it," Brooks said. "Because I'm not talkin' about the town in general. I'm talkin' about a lot of these women I'm seeing comin' in now. They've actually been invited to this wedding and they are still chirping like jealous wet hens. It burns my ass what I'm hearing about Genevra."

"What are they saying about Genevra?" Darcy asked.

Yes, Piper thought, what *are* they saying about Genevra? How could anybody say anything bad about Genevra? Genevra, who had taken the place of Piper's mother and best friend in the short time she'd known her. Genevra, who had opened her arms, her heart, and her kitchen to Piper. Genevra, who always had sage advice on dealing with her insecurities about Vance. What in the world could anyone possibly ever say negatively about Genevra?

"Forget I said anything," Brooks said. "I'm not repeating any of it. It would make me as bad as the rest of them. I shouldn't even have brought it up. Goddammit, I need a beer," he said, stomping off to a bar behind them.

Piper looked to Darcy and Annabelle. Annabelle gathered the two of them close and explained that it was just human nature for the women of Henderson to be a little bit jealous of Genevra. After all, she'd snagged Henderson's most eligible bachelor.

The music started to play, and the growing crowd began to take their seats. Piper followed along behind Annabelle and Duncan, feeling awkward until Brooks caught up to them and put a gentle hand on her shoulder. "Lolly wants us all up front," he told the group, indicating the second row of seats marked with a tulle bow and long stemmed roses.

She filed in with the rest of them, sitting between Annabelle and Brooks, happy her view wasn't going to be hindered by a lot of tall guests. The only people they were seated behind were Emelina, Pinks and Jesse James. Brooks pointed out Genevra's in-law's, Major and Mrs. DuVal, to Piper. They were seated directly across the aisle with their three sons and daughters-in-law, Lolly's aunts and uncles. He pointed out the attractive couple in front of them as Genevra's parents.

Piper settled into her seat, appreciating the beautiful altar that had been constructed, and growing in anticipation of finally laying eyes on the gowns Lolly and Genevra had spent so much time creating in secret.

A hand fell on Annabelle's shoulder, and then a plump little face underneath salt-and-pepper hair poked its way between her and Piper. Piper couldn't help but overhear the conversation that ensued.

"Annabelle, dear. Could it be true that Genevra's pregnant? With this rush to the altar, it does sort of scream shotgun wedding."

Annabelle turned her head and flashed the old busybody her most brilliant smile. "Now, Miss Adams. Is that any way to talk about the bride?"

Miss Adams chuckled and tapped Annabelle's shoulder affectionately. "I guess it's not. Forgive me. I suppose we can hardly blame Hale for wanting to tie the knot quickly at his age. I mean Genevra *is* lovely. It's not as if she's some blond, out-of-town, gold digger who has trapped our Hale into marriage by gettin' herself pregnant, is it?"

"No, no it's not," Annabelle laughed quietly, tapping Miss Adams' hand with her own. She threw Piper a wide-eyed, can-you-believe-that look as Miss Adams sat back in her seat.

Wow, Piper thought. Brooks had not been wrong about the gossip in Henderson, for Lord's sake. She shuddered to think what was being said about her. Because she *was* blond and she *was* from out of town. It was just a darn good thing that she wasn't...."

Oh shit.

Piper promptly sat forward and threw up in her purse.

CHAPTER THIRTY-TWO

Two Weeks Later

"You summoned?" Vance said, sitting his tense and pissed-off body in the middle of Brooks' desk.

Brooks looked around them, apparently not wanting to be overheard. Of course, when he got into Vance's face and yelled, "What the fuck is wrong with you?" well…that theory went out the window. Still, rookies scattered like cockroaches in the light, giving the two of them space.

Vance thought about taking a swing at Brooks. Just a nice, quick upper cut to the jaw to knock his big ass down a few pegs. But he remembered what happened yesterday when he'd taken a swing at Pinks. The Ninja went into serious defense mode, and Vance had landed on his back, hard. Three maximum doses of Advil later, he was still a hurtin' cowboy.

"You can yell at Tansy all you want," Brooks said, starting to rant. "I don't care if you pick a fight with Pinks or try to knock around The Outlaw. I don't even care if you reduce your poor grandmother to tears. But I am tellin' you one time and one time only, you do *not* fuck with Lolly, ever."

"Oh, what? She ran home and told her big boyfriend I was being mean? Well, screw her and screw you too. I didn't ask her to come over and try to psychoanalyze me." Vance hopped off the desk and headed for the door. He didn't need this bullshit. He really didn't.

"What the hell is wrong with you?" Brooks said, following him out the door. "Your father heads to Europe on his honeymoon and you turn into a tyrant and an asshole."

"This has nothing to do with my father," Vance insisted, stalking over to the Corvette. He was going to get in that orange machine and put it through its paces like he'd never done before. He was finally going to see just how fast this damn car could go.

"Piper, then," Brooks said, dogging him. "If not your dad, it's got to be Piper. What stupid-ass thing did you pull this time?"

Vance whipped around and slammed his buddy up against Brooks' own truck. "Was sending her three dozen yellow roses a stupid-ass thing to do?" he asked, his fist twisted up in Brooks' uniform. "Or was going with her to have dinner at her father's the thing that has her backpedaling? Maybe it's the fact that I call her twelve times a day because she only answers every so often and never calls me back? Clearly, telling her I love her was a stupid-ass thing to pull, because that only worked to keep her in my life for three fucking weeks before shit started to hit the fan."

"What are you saying?" Brooks asked, taking a deep breath. "Piper's...?"

"Killing me. She's killing me, Brooks. I swear to God, I will not live through this. My mother walking out was crazy bad. But this? Piper?" He shook his head, unable to voice any more of his fears. He let go of Brooks and took a step back.

"Third Base, talk to me. You don't want Lolly involved, fine. But let me in. When you're in the trenches, I'm in the trenches. So...talk. Or I'm going to beat it out of you."

"It'd probably hurt less just to have you beat me." Vance meant it sincerely. Because the pain Piper was putting him through right now, he wouldn't wish it on his worst enemy. For a man who prided himself on his instincts with women, he had been stunned, shaken, and destroyed over the last three weeks. And Brooks was right. He'd been taking it out on everybody.

"Piper started pulling away right after the wedding."

"She was sick," Brooks reminded him.

Vance shrugged. She hadn't seemed that sick to him. "She insisted she needed to focus on her work, to get back into the rhythm of being a lawyer. Like I'm supposed to have any idea what the hell that means. So I backed off, tried to be understanding, gave her some space. But the weekend comes and she won't come back to Henderson."

"So, you go to Raleigh," Brooks said.

"Of course, I go to Raleigh. I'm addicted to Piper. What's keeping me in Henderson other than my home, my grandmother, and my four different jobs? I go to Raleigh and things seem a little off, but I seduce her into bed and boom, things are back to normal. Or so I thought until I call her at her office Monday morning as I'm heading back to Henderson, and she sounds like she's been crying. I ask what's going on and she swears everything's fine, so I let it go."

"You let it go? A sobbing woman on the phone and you let it go? Have you not read your own freaking instruction manual? You never let a sobbing woman go."

"She wasn't sobbing on the phone, idiot. She just sounded like she'd been crying earlier. Regardless, I sent the roses, and when she called to thank me, she sounded…unnatural."

"Unnatural how?"

Vance did his best to express his growing irritation with a look.

"Third Base. I'm only trying to help."

"I get it. Just work with me here."

"Fine."

"We had dinner with her father that Thursday evening. The man couldn't have been nicer to me. Piper cooked us a beautiful meal, but the whole time she was antsy and dropping things. I mean, she was not herself. And I wrote that off as anxiety over me trying to impress her dad or something."

"Makes sense."

"Right? But we aren't back at her place for ten minutes before she straps on bitchy Lawyer Beaumont and picks a fight."

"About what?"

"Hell if I know. I was halfway back to Henderson before I realized I didn't know how it started or even what it was about. All I know is she pushed a few of my buttons and I was slammin' out her door and into my truck, putting the pedal to the metal."

"Next time, just grab her and throw her into bed."

"And the next time, that's exactly what I did. Shut her up and

kept her mouth too busy to make me crazy. I have stopped askin'
what's wrong and started throwing my weight around. Only now
she's not picking up her cell or her office phone."

"Maybe she's just having a real busy day at work."

"Let me clarify. She hasn't picked up her cell or her office phone
for three whole days."

"Oh."

"Yeah."

"That's not good."

"Ya think? So forgive me for biting Lolly's head off last night,
but I am this close to hitting the bottle and going on a full-fledged
bender or doing something even worse."

"What could be worse?"

"I am literally toying with the idea of breakin' the law I've sworn
to uphold."

"Shooting Piper is not going to win her back."

"No, but kidnapping her and holding her against her will might
give me a fighting chance."

"I did not hear you just say that."

"No. No, you didn't. And if I go AWOL for a few days and
the Raleigh police contact you about my whereabouts and the
disappearance of one shapely, little lawyer they all love to hate, you
know nothing."

Goody Two Shoes Brooks sighed like the weight of the world
was on his shoulders. His face twisted up in such pain Vance almost
forgot how miserable he was and laughed. "Okay," Brooks agreed,
forcing the words out of his mouth. "But having a felon as my
campaign manager is going to raise eyebrows around here."

Vance kept trying to assure himself that he wasn't really planning
to kidnap Piper. He was just going to throw a few of his bad cop
moves around, handcuff her, gag her if he had to, and toss her into
the back seat of his truck and then drive to an undisclosed location.
Because unless Jane Jeffries, the managing partner at Collins & Reese,
had chained Piper to her desk for the last four days, with a phone just
out of her reach, there was no excuse the woman could give him that
would explain why she had not returned his calls.

He thought about wearing his uniform in case anyone saw him escorting a handcuffed woman to his truck, but pushing his way into the law firm had gone so well while wearing a suit that he pulled another out of his closet. Dressed to kill, Vance arrived at Piper's law firm at four o'clock Friday afternoon, after three fucking weeks of things drifting downhill and two last-minute unanswered phone calls to her cell and business line. One Ms. Beaumont had hell to pay, and the devil had finally arrived to be given his due.

"I'm here to see Ms. Beaumont," Vance told the receptionist. After a few blinks, the woman asked if he had a scheduled appointment. He lied. "I do."

"And no one called you to cancel?"

"Why would they call me to cancel?"

"Because Ms. Beaumont is out sick."

"Out sick?"

"Yes. I'm afraid she's taken ill and is in the hospital. Perhaps a colleague of hers would be available to help you."

"Hospital?" His face probably went white. It sure felt like it went white, because his head was starting to pound like a royal motherfucker. "What hospital?"

"Memorial. Just down the street. That's where the paramedics took her after she collapsed on Tuesday."

"She collapsed and no one bothered to call me?"

"I'm sorry, Mr. Evans. You weren't listed on her schedule or we would have called."

"I'm not her client. I'm—I'm...." What was he? He wasn't her next of kin. That would be her father. "Did you call her father?"

"Yes, we called her father right away."

Fuck. And her father wouldn't call him. It's not like Vance had bothered to declare his intentions to the man when he'd had the chance. Piper's father wouldn't call him unless Piper asked him to, which she hadn't, obviously. Maybe she couldn't—which would be the only excuse she had for not letting him know she was in the goddamn hospital.

He didn't know what to hope for. Piper conscious and intentionally not calling him or Piper unconscious and unable to call him. Suddenly his mind's eye saw Piper lying in a hospital bed hooked up to all kinds of machines. That mental picture shot fear through him comparable to the one and only time he'd stared down the barrel of a gun aimed at his head.

He was about to lose it. Fast.

"Thanks," he told the receptionist and headed out the door.

It took him all of ten minutes to locate the hospital, park, inquire, and find her room. And surprise, surprise...if there wasn't one big, blockheaded police officer sitting right there, guarding her door.

"I was wondering when you'd show up," King Kong said, standing as Vance approached.

"No thanks to you. Don't tell me one of your goons put her in here," he growled.

"No, not one of my goons. She's dehydrated. Too much throwing up for such a tiny little thing with no ability to keep enough liquids down."

"Why didn't she tell me she was that sick?" Vance wondered, so out of his comfort zone on this.

"She's not sick," Kong declared.

"You just told me she was throwing up," Vance said, searching for answers in Kong's eyes as if he were in the middle of a labyrinth and everyone was speaking Chinese.

He saw it then.

That twinkle in Kong's eye.

That little smirk.

And that's when Vance turned around, eyed the nearest trash can, and promptly threw up.

CHAPTER THIRTY-THREE

Piper wiped away a tear as she listened to Vance's voice messages one more time. The desperation in Vance's voice on Tuesday was palpable, the anger that replaced it on Wednesday clear. But his plea for her to call him back on Thursday nearly broke her heart and still she had no idea how to tell him that she was six weeks pregnant.

Because she was blond, and from out of town, and for all of Henderson—if not the world—it would appear that she was a gold digger who got herself pregnant in order to trap Vance Evans into marriage.

And as much as she hated that thought, she would gladly live with all those horrible assertions, if only Vance could really know and believe the truth without a shadow of a doubt.

But circumstantial evidence was gonna weigh heavy in this case. Piper estimated that less than sixty minutes had passed between the time she learned Vance Evans was a millionaire and when she told him that he needn't wear a condom. That she had birth control covered.

Case—freaking—closed.

For the last three weeks, she prepared her defense. Yes, she had taken antibiotics, but that was weeks ago and shouldn't have affected the effectiveness of the pill. No, she hadn't skipped a pill, forgotten a pill, or willingly stopped taking her pills. She could swear up and down that as much as she wanted children, she did not set out to trick Vance into getting her pregnant.

Piper rolled over and moaned into her pillow. It all just sounded so lame.

She had become that girl Miss Adams was talking about, and poor Vance, her best fantasy come to life, was now reduced to being her inadvertent victim.

She heard the door to her hospital room open and close softly. "Daddy?" she said, rolling to her back and pushing her hair out of her eyes.

"I guess that fits," Vance said, coming to stand at the end of her bed.

There he stood, sporting all his Hollywood good looks in another freaking Armani suit. And he wasn't ranting and raving about the terrible injustice done to him, but staring at her with the sweetest, saddest little smile she ever saw.

She promptly burst into tears.

"Piper, baby doll," he said, coming around to the side of the bed opposite her IV. He took a handkerchief out of his coat pocket, sat on the bed, and handed it to her. The thought that he actually carried a linen handkerchief made her cry even harder. Only millionaires did that.

She found herself pulled up into his arms but, with her running nose and drippy face, she was worried about messing him up. So she pushed him away and blotted her face with the cloth. He stroked the hair back from her face, picked up the Styrofoam cup of ice water from the bedside table, and held the straw to her lips, encouraging her to take a sip.

"How did you find out?" she asked, sniffling.

"Just the way I'd always imagined. A big ape of a dude threw me enough clues that the truth finally sank into my thick skull. After which I promptly threw up."

"You did?" She couldn't help but smile through her tears at that. "That's pretty much how I found out too and exactly how I reacted."

They laughed together until it faded into quiet.

"Vance," she said softly, rubbing her hand over his, staring at his knuckles, "don't ask me to marry you."

"Oh, baby doll, you don't ever have to worry about that," he said.

It wasn't just his words that shocked her, but how he said them with such conviction. She simply had to look up to see his face.

His voice softened. "Is having my baby such a repugnant idea?"

"Of course not."

"Then why do you keep trying to throw him up?"

She laughed and cried and laid herself back against her pillow, not letting his hand go. "Him?"

"Vance, Jr."

She smiled, liking the idea. He smiled back, and for a brief moment Piper felt happy.

"Are you runnin' out on me?" Vance asked quietly, teasing a curl with one of his fingers. His eyes didn't quite meet hers, and his voice dripped with vulnerability. It about broke her heart.

"No. No, Vance, I'm not. I just didn't know how to tell you I was pregnant."

"Because you didn't think I'd be happy?"

"Because I thought you'd think I'd done it on purpose."

Vance cocked his head and quirked a brow. "Why would I think that?"

"Because you told me you were a millionaire. And then I told you that you didn't have to wear a condom."

"Ahhh," Vance smiled, light bulbs going on behind his eyes. "So you thought I would believe you were trying to entrap me."

"Yes. But not just you. All of Henderson is going to believe I'm trying to entrap you."

"What the hell are we worried about Henderson for?"

"You live there. People talk."

"Baby doll, people have been talking about me for years. Women have been tellin' me I don't need to wear a condom for years. I am not the fool you apparently think I am."

"You know I don't think you're a fool."

"Then why didn't you tell me right away? Why didn't you just say 'Vance, we are going to need to speed this thing up because Vance, Jr. is planning to make an appearance sooner rather than later?'"

Piper responded with a choked chuckle. "I was scared."

"About what?"

"About losing you. About you not wanting this baby."

"How could I not—? Piper, you know I love you. I practically spelled out my plans for our future when I described my ideas for a big house with lots of rooms and a huge kitchen. Of course I want this baby. I want this one, two more boys, plus at least one tiny little Piperette."

Piper began to cry all over again.

"Go ahead and cry. Cry all you want, I don't care," Vance insisted. "Because you, Perfect Piper, have solved my biggest dilemma."

"Really?" she said, wiping her eyes. "And what was that?"

"How long was I gonna have to wait to slip this on your finger?" Vance reached into the interior pocket of his suit and pulled out a ring with an oval diamond the size of Piper's thumbnail. And if that wasn't enough to make her swallow her tongue, it was flanked by two other enormous triangular diamonds. "We aren't getting any younger you know."

"Vance. It's—it's."

"I know."

"It's…perfect."

"I know."

"No. I mean…."

"I know." He kissed her and slid it on her finger. "It's the one you wanted."

"It is," she said in amazement, holding her hand up and admiring the crazy big diamond. "Only bigger."

"I'm a millionaire. Figured this was a good time to start spending my money."

"But you said you weren't going to ask me to marry me you."

"Oh, baby doll, I'm not askin'. I'm insisting. Pinks!"

Davis Williams, dressed in a suit, opened the door to Piper's hospital room and stuck his brown head in. "Yes, sir?"

"What's the ETA?"

Pinks looked at his watch. "The Vance County official should be here shortly. Brooks, Lolly, Jesse, and The Big Em are an hour out but have everything you requested in tow. Duncan and Annabelle are here sitting next to me.

"Can I come in?" Annabelle hollered.

"No!" Vance barked. "Pinks, what about the magistrate?"

"Officer Stevenson is working on it."

Vance turned to Piper. "Baby doll, you got a judge in your back pocket?"

"Do I what?" Piper choked. "Of course I don't have a judge in my back pocket."

"But do you have one that would like to perform your wedding on short notice?"

"My…? Vance, you can't be serious."

"I assure you. I am completely serious. Oh, shit. Pinks!"

"Yeah?"

"We need Piper's father."

"Annabelle is already on it. He's on his way."

"*Now* can I come in?" Annabelle asked.

"Jesus Christ," Vance said quietly. Then more loudly, "Just give me another minute, and I'll hand her over to you."

Squealing ensued. Pinks closed the door.

Vance angled his head, looking at Piper, waiting for her reaction. She was dazed, still digesting what was happening. Vance certainly didn't appear to be unhappy about the pregnancy. She looked down at her beautiful engagement ring—so similar to the picture she'd posted on Pinterest—at the same time remembering having wondered how Vance Evans knew about lava stone countertops. She cleared her throat. "When did you buy this?" she asked.

"Best question ever," Vance said, reaching into his suit pocket again and pulling out a folded piece of paper. It was folded so that only the name and address of the jeweler and purchase date were visible. Piper read it. He'd bought it in New York. Had already purchased it before he'd shown up at Collins & Reese and handcuffed her. Vance Evans had bought her an engagement ring before he'd told her he was a millionaire and before they had made love the very first time.

"Mitchell Frederick Ford."

"Excuse me?"

"The judge who will perform our wedding on short notice. Judge Ford. He'll jump right into this craziness and enjoy himself doing it."

Vance smiled. "Pinks!"

"I'm on it," he yelled through the door.

"Damn eavesdroppers."

"I love you," Piper said.

"That's working out really well for me today," Vance said. "Now I'm gonna let Annabelle, The Debutante Maker in here to create a bride out of all this mess sitting in front of me," he said, leaning in to kiss her wet face. "When you're feelin' better, and Dad and Genevra are back from their honeymoon, we'll throw ourselves a fancy reception. We'll invite all your friends and the entire police force in Raleigh. But right now, we're going to take care of the important part. So we don't waste one more minute having to find our way back to each other ever again."

All Piper could do was smile. And cry.

Vance stood up from the bed and drew his hand lovingly over her curls one more time. Then he turned and walked purposefully toward the door barking a Bad Cop order over his shoulder. "Now stop trying to throw up Vance, Jr!"

CHAPTER THIRTY-FOUR

It's always good to know people in high places.

Between the ten friends and relatives who now stood in the presidential suite of Memorial Hospital, they collectively knew enough of them to have upgraded Piper's room, drummed up a marriage license, a magistrate, a House of DuVal bridal ensemble complete with bouquet, and buckets of yellow roses with which to decorate. Even Jesse James had lived up to his title of The Outlaw by stealing the top of Hale and Genevra's wedding cake out of their freezer. Now defrosting, it sat on a round table in the corner, waiting to be devoured.

Piper, who was getting dressed behind a large screen of drawn curtains, had been given a short reprieve from her IV. She insisted she was feeling far more giddy than she was nauseous. Vance figured that boded well for the short but important ceremony that would bind her to him legally.

Bind her to him...legally.

Only legally.

Legally was good, he assured himself. And since he had the good fortune to get her pregnant, she was now bound to him through "Vance, Jr." forever more.

Yeah, this is, you know, perfect, he told himself as his heart started to pound and blood rushed to his head.

So then, why the hell am I having a panic attack?

"Third Base? You okay?"

Good ol' Brooks. Sees all and knows all.

"Yeah. No. I mean, I'm good."

"You're not good. You look like you're the one with morning sickness. Let's take a walk."

"No. No. I'm…." Vance finally looked his buddy in the eye. He wasn't fine. He was far from fine. "Yeah, okay, let's take a walk."

"Ladies," Brooks said to the room at large, "we're gonna give you a few minutes to get things in order. Gentlemen," he called to Pinks, Jesse, and Duncan, "how 'bout it?" He motioned for them to follow.

When they gathered in the hallway, Duncan looked between Vance and Brooks and asked, "What's going on?"

"Nothing," Brooks said nonchalantly, trying his best to divert everyone's attention away from the sweat breaking out on Vance's brow. "But since this is the last time the three of us will be together as bachelors and since we didn't have a chance to throw a proper bachelor party, one round of shots seems appropriate."

Duncan nodded though he was clearly concerned by Vance's demeanor.

"Pinks, Jesse, I need you two to stay here in case Annabelle needs anything. We'll bring you both back a beer for your trouble," Brooks said, his big hand on Vance's shoulder.

"We're gonna need a groom," Pinks said, deliberately eyeing Vance. "Cold feet or no, you don't set all this up and then run out on the bride," he insisted.

As if!

"You don't know what the hell you're talking about." Vance pulled back to take a swing at Pinks.

Brooks caught Vance's arm and threw his weight against him as The Outlaw scrambled in between Vance and Pinks, separating the two of them. The two who had become so close in such a short time and who were normally so in sync. Vance and Pinks stood seething at one another.

"I know what I'm talking about," Pinks growled. "You still aren't able to separate the best thing that's happened to you from the worst."

Vance turned away unable to look Pinks in the eye.

"Are you?" The Ninja pressed, making Vance face all of his demons.

"Well, you know what? Piper deserves more than that. So, go get your shot," Pinks suggested as if he was writing Vance off for good. "And don't come back until you know with certainty that that sweet little blonde, who has forgiven you more times than you deserve and who has repeatedly walked *back* into your life, has absolutely nothing in common with the woman who gave you birth. You are doing Piper a disservice if you worry for one moment that she'd ever do that to you or your baby. That is not who she is, and you know it."

He did. He knew it. And hearing Pinks say it opened a safety valve somewhere inside him allowing all the fight and panic to rush out. Brooks must have felt it too, because he let him go.

"You're right," Vance told Pinks, looking at him directly. "You're right, and I'm sorry I exploded but here's the whole of it. I didn't give Piper a choice with this marriage business. I just marched in, laid down the law, and told her we were getting married."

"A very bad cop move," Brooks said with a grin.

"Bad Cop gets 'em every time," Pinks chimed in with a wink.

"Jesus," Vance said. "What the hell kind of alternative universe have I created?"

"The kind where everything is finally working out for you," Duncan said. "You still need that shot?"

Vance shook his head "no" and wiped at his brow. "Besides, what's a shot without Harry serving them up? And I'm sure somewhere in our alternative universe, a post-civil-ceremony bachelor party must exist. Hell," he said with a short laugh, "if I can find Piper Beaumont, knock her up, and get her to marry me, let's face it, anything is possible."

Vance had to admit that if he could bottle what Annabelle Devine could do for a hospital room and a woman—turning them both into extraordinary works of art—he would never have to work again. *Of course, where would the fun be in that?* he wondered as The Outlaw's iPod began to play Mendelssohn's Wedding March.

Really? he thought. *On his iPod?* This circle of masterminds he'd collected was a gift that just kept on giving.

And as he watched his bride walk to him on her father's arm, Vance vowed that if his mother ever did cross his path again he would simply say thank you. Because staring at the little girl who saved him all those years ago, and now loving the woman she'd grown up to be, he understood Piper was the precious gift his mother had inadvertently left in her wake.

He hadn't realized it at the time. Didn't grasp the importance when the thought had first occurred to him that night in his truck with his arm around Piper. But he realized it now as he took her hand and gazed into her baby blue eyes. He sure realized it now.

Everything had always been working out for him.

"I love you," he said as his fingertips sought the ends of her veil, lifting it to reveal the face of his dewy-eyed blonde with those sweet pink cheeks. Annabelle worked from behind to arrange the blusher over Piper's curls as Vance did the one thing he'd told Piper she'd never have to worry about.

"Will you marry me?" he asked. But before Piper could respond he cut her off and asked it another way. "Do you *want* to marry me?"

"I do!" She beamed. "I have since fourth grade."

"Then forgive me for keeping you waiting." He leaned over and kissed her on the nose. "Judge Ford," Vance said, turning to the man. "You're on."

Acknowledgments

With great appreciation I acknowledge:

Tammy Kearly and Holli Bertram,
my hardworking critique partners.

Erin Wolfe and Nan Reinhardt, my invaluable editors.

Lisa Cumberpatch and Colleen Gleason
for their moral support and brilliant opinions.

Liz Cumberpatch, point guard of the
Daughters-of-my-heart Research Team.

Joan Hurley, Spanish teacher extraordinare who
translated Vance's conversation with his grandmother.

John McNicholas, real life business tycoon
who guides me in all things E&E, Inc.

Ginnie Pitler and Skip Lewis, who grew up in the real Henderson
and have embraced my fictional sentiment.

Jody Ford and Christy Crain, first readers & ego boosters.

And last but not least,

To all the readers who signed up on my website to receive word
when this book became published. It was really fun writing
Bad Cop knowing I had you waiting to read it.

Thank you!

Now take a look at what's coming next…

The Heroes of Henderson Series continues with
Top Dog
Heroes of Henderson ~ Book 3

Coming in 2014

Crain Carraway, Dallas business tycoon and sports fanatic, is not from Henderson. But his wife is. Although no one knows that because she managed to get cold feet *after* their impromptu Vegas wedding. Hiding out in her hometown, she's sicced her daddy's lawyers on him, doing her best to buy his silence and a quickie divorce.

Like hell.

It's taken him way too long to find the perfect Mrs. Carraway, and now that he's had the fortuitous luck to stumble into Henderson and his bride, he's not about to let her go.

Read on for a sneak peek.

The trouble with trouble is it always starts out as fun.

Four Months Earlier

Crain Carraway slipped inside the luxurious bathroom of his Las Vegas suite and shut the door quietly. Even though he couldn't sleep, it seemed that his beautiful bride was out cold after a very lengthy, highly energetic, totally off-the-charts, roll-me-over-and-do-that-again consummation of their marriage. God, she was something. Something fine looking and brilliant and just as sweet as the cherry on top of his ABSOLUT Old Fashioned. He couldn't believe she was his. All his. And he couldn't sleep because he wanted the world to know it.

Starting with his parents.

He dialed their number, checking the time on his watch. Dallas was two hours ahead of Vegas and on a weekday morning his parents should be up and at 'em. No doubt this would get their day started with a bang.

"Honey Bear!" his momma said in greeting, as if he wasn't thirty-five-years old.

"Momma Bear," he said back, playing her game. "Put me on speaker and round up Poppa Bear. I have big news."

"Big news?"

"Texas-size news."

His mother laughed. "Bigger than when you started CC Dallas, Inc.? Lucius!" his mother shouted. "Your son has Texas-size news he wants us to hear together."

"May as well grab a bottle of champagne while you're at it, Ma. You're gonna need it." Crain said.

"I'll bet that luxury suite at Cowboys Stadium came through," his father's voice echoed over the phone.

"Even better than that," Crain said, grinning at himself in the bathroom mirror. "Dad, do you remember that statuesque blonde I pointed out when you stopped in the office a month ago? The one trying to hide all that beauty under those smart-girl glasses?"

"Do I? That pretty little gal had you drooling like a Bluetick Coonhound."

Crain chuckled. "Guilty as charged. Well, it took some doing, but I finally got that pretty little gal to agree to a dinner date. I took her to Nick & Sam's."

"Best steakhouse in Dallas," his dad said.

"And she loved it. In fact, the date went so well she agreed to meet me for drinks at the Ice House the next night. One thing led to another very good night and, although I will admit she was a little bit tipsy when I asked her to accompany me to Las Vegas, I assure you she was completely sober when I asked her to marry me."

"You're engaged?" his mother exclaimed.

"Better than that. We're married."

"Married?" Poppa Bear sounded astonished.

"We eloped. Just last night. It was just…right. Everything about it was perfect. And I'm sorry you weren't here, but I know you're gonna forgive me when you meet my bride."

"Wha…ah…well of course we'll forgive you," his mother stuttered. "But darlin' boy, this is all so quick. So sudden."

Crain smiled, softening his voice in an effort to soothe his momma. "I know it seems that way, I truly do. But you know I've dated a lot of wonderful women over the years. And every time I figured out what I didn't want, I knew better what I did want. And this one, this one is the complete package. Underneath her bright and engaging business persona, there's a bewitching temptress just as sweet as praline pie. She's the one I've been looking for all my life, Momma. She's the one I want."

"You sound so certain."

"Because I am. I was certain the first time we met, and after date number two all I could think was how fast can I get this girl to the altar?"

"Any faster and you'd catch up to yesterday," his father said.

"And now I'm burning daylight, so let me get back to my bride," Crain countered.

"Wait!" his mother cried. "What's her name? Who are her people?"

"Well, I don't exactly know who her people are, Momma, because I've been solely focused on sweeping her off her feet. But I'll tell you what. Anybody who can raise a woman like her can't be all bad. Now I've got to go and talk my bride into a nice long honeymoon in Hawaii, so if you two don't hear from me for a couple weeks, don't fret. And in the meantime, Momma, you can start planning whatever extravaganza you've got in mind to introduce my bride to *our* people."

"I can tell you one thing," his momma scolded. "It's gonna look a whole lot like a church wedding and a big fat reception. You tell my new daughter-in-law the first thing I plan to do is to take her shopping for a wedding dress. I love you, but I am not particularly happy about this."

"Oh come on," he goaded. "You know you're a little happy about this."

"I'm very happy you're happy, darlin' boy. But I sure don't like missing my own son's wedding. Now bring that girl home, so I can hug her neck."

"Will do, Momma. Will do. Poppa Bear, I am signing off."

"I'll take care of your momma. You go take care of your bride."

"Over and out."

Crain hung up. And then he did what turned out to be about the dumbest thing a man with a Texas A&M degree could do. He took the time to text everybody he knew, telling them he had married the cutest Ole Miss Hotty Toddy ever found in Dallas. Yep, he was one happy groom. Right up until he made his bride a cup of coffee just the way she liked it—with a whole lot of sugar—and carried it into the bedroom.

"Sweetheart," he whispered, until he realized the bed was empty. "Sugar?" he yelled, looking around the room, his eyes coming to rest on the note written with her preferred red Sharpie. "Honey?" he said, moving forward to pick up the note.

Four little words. Four little words Crain Carraway had no idea what to do with. Four little words that left him certain of absolutely nothing.

The note read:

I'm sorry – cold feet.

Visit **www.LizKellyBooks.com**
and sign up to be alerted when *Top Dog* is available.

About the Author

Growing up every summer in a place where *dancing and romancing* are literally part of its theme song, Liz Kelly can't help but be a romantic at heart. And since her favorite author, Kathleen E. Woodiwiss wrote some of the world's greatest romances, she's just trying to give the world a little more of that. (Okay, maybe a little sexier *that*, but we are now in a new millennium after all.)

A graduate of Wake Forest University, where she met her handsome golf-addicted husband, (who is now sporting dark glasses everywhere he goes) Liz is a mother of two grown sons (also sporting dark glasses) and a miniature Labradoodle named Isabelle. They live in the *Fountain of Youth*, a.k.a. Naples, FL where dancing and romancing continues on ad infinitum.